Hope's RIVER

NEW YORK TIMES BESTSELLER

MARGARET MCHEYZER

EVERYTHING DESERVES A SECOND CHANCE

Hope's RIVER

NEW YORK TIMES BESTSELLER

MARGARET MCHEYZER

Working with my hands has always been my passion, so now I flip houses for a living. I love what I do.

I was happy where my life was heading.

Although I knew he wasn't the one, I was even content with my long-term relationship… until suddenly I wasn't.

I needed a change. So I got in my truck and asked the universe to help a sister out. It was then that I stumbled upon a cute small town called Hope River. Ironic really…

Not only did the name of the town hold significance from my past, but it led me to find something I thought was once lost.

Little did I know how significant this town would be for my future…

*A stand alone, second chance, small town romance.

Sometimes the best place to start,

is to take a deep breath and say,

I've got this.

Prologue

I 'M SO GLAD I'm skipping school today. It's the last place I want to be. I hate going; it's totally lame and useless.

Standing in line at the local café, I look around. It's busy, most of the tables are filled with adults.

Turning, my gaze catches a guy standing with an older woman, two people behind me. He gives me a small smile when our eyes meet. He's cute, with short dark hair, and a dimpled chin. His mom swings her arm around his shoulder, leans in, and gives him a kiss.

"Mom!" he barks at her when he sees me smiling. His voice is all nasally, as if he's sick.

"What, is sixteen too old for a kiss from your mother?" she playfully scolds. He seems to be my age, I wonder why I haven't seen him around at school.

"Just, don't." He lowers his eyes, breaking contact with me.

Giggling, I turn to the front and shuffle forward as the line progresses.

"We need to get to the doctor for your appointment, I hope they hurry up here," I hear his mom say. Ah, he *is* sick.

The girl at the counter is busy taking orders, and a guy is at the coffee machine making orders. No wonder the line is moving so slowly. There are only two of them.

Yes! There are only three more people ahead of me before it's my turn. Hmmm, what should I have? Maybe a smoothie. Or a latte. What do I feel like? Do I want something to eat with it too? Nah, I had breakfast before I had 'left for school.' Shit, I hope my Mom doesn't come into town this morning. She didn't say she had any errands to run.

God, I hate school. I wish my parents would let me leave. All I want to do is work with my hands. I freaking love helping Dad with his car, or doing stuff around the house. Why can't they let me leave school and study a trade? They let Charlie become a plumber. And all I want to do is build stuff, or tear stuff down.

"Hey!" I hear the girl at the counter yell.

Just like a flash, I look up to see what she's yelling for. The guy two in front of me, reaches into the cash register, grabs a fistful of money, and turns to run.

Nope, not on my watch, buddy. As he turns, and using all my weight, I shoulder into him, causing him to face plant and slide a few feet on the tile floor. It's enough time for a couple of the people sitting in the café to jump up from their seats, run over to him, and haul him up by the back of his t-shirt.

"You fucking bitch," he yells at me.

I look at him and shrug my shoulders. One side of his face is quickly becoming a lovely, radiant shade of red from where he face planted. "Hey, shouldn't have put your sticky fingers into something that doesn't belong to you."

"Fuck you." He literally spits at me, but I step back to dodge it.

Stealing and spitting? Are you kidding me? Two of what I consider the most loathsome acts. Without a moment's hesitation, I walk over and slap the guy in the face. My hand instantly stings, and the guy now has a matching angry red mark on the other side of his face from where he slid across the floor.

"Nice one," the cute guy says from behind me.

"Thanks." I stand with my shoulders back and my chest out.

The commotion in the store is pretty hectic; there are people everywhere. And before I know it, the police have arrived.

"Oh my God, you're so brave. Thank you so much," an older woman says to me.

"It's okay."

"I'm Abigail, and I own the store. I'm so grateful."

"I don't like thieves. And spitters are right up there too," I say.

"Excuse me, Miss. Are you the one who stopped him?" one of the police officers asks. There's a lot of talking, and people discussing what happened between themselves.

Oh shit! I'm going to be in so much trouble when I get home. Skipping school, *and* getting into a fight. Let's be honest here — it's not like it's the first time, and it certainly won't be the last.

Looking around, I search for the cute guy, but he and his mother are already gone.

Double great. I can't even get cute guy's name and number. And, I have to face my parents.

"I'd like to give whatever you want free of charge for a month for what you did today. I can't thank you enough," Abigail says.

Aww, how sweet. Not that I'll be able to use it once my parents find out what I've done. Hell, I probably won't be allowed out of the house until I turn fifty!

Chapter ONE

"YOU LYING BITCH. You're cheating on me," Grady yells.

I startle from sleep and blink a few times, trying to wake myself. Huh? What's happening? What time is it?

Reaching for my phone, I tap on the screen and notice the ungodly hour.

"Wake up!" Grady screams as he comes into our room, and flicks the light on.

"What? What's going on?" I sit up in bed, and rub at my eyes.

"You're cheating on me." He tries to steady himself with the door frame. But judging from his slurred words and unsteady movements, he's blind drunk.

"Grady, I'm not cheating on you. Get into bed." I pull the covers back, knowing his words are only driven by alcohol. Normally, he barely drinks. His behavior tells me he can't handle his liquor.

"I'm not getting in bed with you, you slut," he slurs.

My eyebrows fly up and I tilt my head to the side. "Excuse me?" Pushing the cover back, I stand to my feet, ready for whatever this drunk ass is going to say. I walk toward him to help him cross the room.

"You heard me. You're a slut." He pokes his finger into my chest and tries to step forward, but he quickly grabs the door frame again.

"Get your ass in the shower and sober up, you idiot. Then you can sleep on the sofa." I turn to go back to bed, but he grabs my hair and hauls me back. I swerve around to confront him. He lifts his right hand, and slaps me across the face. "You whore!"

What the actual fuck? In the three years we've been together, Grady's never once hurt me. What has gotten into him? He lifts his hand again, but this time I catch it by his wrist, and push him back. Quickly, I grab his balls in my hand, and slightly twist. Grady's eyes widen, as his mouth opens while he winces in pain. "You got one shot in. Do it again, and I'll be mailing these to your mother. We're done. Over." I let go of his balls, and Grady falls to the floor, doubled over and nursing the hurt I laid on him.

I'm not sticking around for this shit. What happened to him tonight when he went out with his friends for drinks? I have no idea what he heard, or what he thinks I've done. But he can be damned sure of one thing — I'm out of here.

I head into the garage, grab a suitcase, and start packing a few days' worth of clothes. I have no idea where I'm going, or what's going to happen next, but I need to get away. Not for my safety, but because if I stay and Grady comes at me again, I'll definitely be mailing his balls back to his mother. And not even priority mail.

Grady's managed to stand and is now sitting on the edge of the bed. His head is in his hands, and he's sobbing. "I'm sorry, baby," he says, his words still slurring.

"You should be."

"Please, don't go," he begs. He lowers his hands, and pleads for me to stay.

I turn to look at him, and shake my head. "I'll be back, and when I do come back, you had better be gone." I grab the handle of my suitcase, and roll it out of the bedroom and down the hall, toward the garage. Heaving my suitcase into the back of my truck, I back out of the garage, and turn down the street.

Stopping on the side of the road, I look up to the dark, starless sky. "Okay, universe, I need to get away from here for a few days. I need to clear my head, so send me somewhere cool." Taking a deep breath, I close my eyes for a split second to just clear my mind.

As I start driving, what Grady did hits me. I burst into tears, as my cheek throbs in a blistering burn.

What the hell just happened? In our three years together Grady has never, not once, lifted his hand against me in anger. What would drive him to do this now? What did he hear?

I reach for tissues to wipe my eyes, but of course the box is empty. "Are you shitting me?" I throw the box to the floor of the passenger side, then lift my t-shirt to wipe at my eyes and nose. "Great. Now I'm covered in snot."

I have no idea where I'm headed, except that I want to get as far away from here as possible. I put in an offer on a house over on Woolriff Street, but I'm not going to buy it now. If the real estate calls me in the morning to tell me my offer's been accepted, I'll let it go.

I can't flip another house with Grady on my team. Not now. Never again.

Finally, my tears stop, and I reach up to my cheek. It hurts, and I flinch. Why would Grady hurt me? My mind is reeling with every fathomable possibility. But not one single logical explanation comes to mind. *Why?* I smash my hand against the steering wheel. "Why, God damn it, why?"

I reach over and turn on the radio, hoping the music can put me in a better headspace, maybe shift my thoughts away from Grady and his erratic, downright weird behavior.

Queen's "Fat Bottomed Girls" comes on the radio, and I crank it up. It was one of Dad's favorite songs. I smile at a memory of Dad singing it to my Mom whenever he blasted this song from his garage. Mom would roll her eyes, and tell him she'd spike his food with a ghost pepper and watch as he choked to death.

A medley of old songs plays on the radio. With each and every one of them, I'm reminded of my parents. I should go back home and see them, but not like this. If Dad saw me like this, he'd hunt Grady down and kill him. And that's the last thing I want. I'm not a fan of confrontation, but if it comes looking for me, I won't turn away from it.

And this would be unnecessary stress on my parents.

There's a sign up ahead indicating I'm only twenty miles from a beach. Looking at the time, I realize I've been stuck in my head, and driving for nearly three hours. "Huh, so I'm going to the beach, am I?" Hopefully I can find a cute little bed and breakfast overlooking the water. Somewhere I can clear my head, and put together a game plan for what I'm going to do moving forward.

Turning off the exit for the beach, I travel for a good ten miles until I see a sign with an arrow that reads Hope River with a number ten next to it.

"You've got to be shitting me," I say as I look at the sign.

Well, if that ain't a clear sign of where to go, then I have no idea what is. I turn down the road the sign indicates. "Hope River, huh?" I let out a small laugh. The universe has a weird sense of humor. But hey, I'm here now, so why not see where this leads?

I really hope this isn't some small hick town where the locals only have one full set of teeth between them. Shit, what if they shove me into a hole in the ground to be slowly eaten by a bunch of toothless cannibals? Wait, how could they eat me without teeth? Would they gum me to death? Can you even die from being gummed?

I come up to a rickety bridge, and slow right down. On this side of the bridge, there's another sign that reads: Welcome to Hope River. Population ~~1486~~, ~~1487~~, ~~1489~~, 1488.

Jesus, do they announce every single person who comes in and out of the town? Slowly, I drive my truck over the narrow, old bridge and I'm surprised the weight of my truck doesn't fall through. How do distribution trucks get through?

Okay, okay, I may be over exaggerating. It's not that unstable, but it is one car width narrow. Looking out the window, I notice that there's a lot of open land, which is probably pretty by the daylight. Rolling the window down, the salty aroma of the ocean hits me hard.

The open expanse of beautiful land dwindles down to ordinary blocks as I approach the town center.

I can't help but notice how quiet it is here. It's nearly five a.m., and there's absolutely no commotion on the streets. "Wow," I say as I slow to a roll when I hit the outskirts of the town.

"Holy shit," I say as I pull up outside an old, abandoned house. It's a huge two-story Victorian house. The wood siding has been severely weathered, with some of it falling off. The yard is overrun by weeds and grass tall enough to pass my knees. There's a "For Sale" sign out in front that's hanging by one hinge, eerily swinging back and forth.

Getting out of my truck, I stand looking at the house.

I have no idea what the price of this house is, or even about the comps in the area. Hell, I don't even know if this is a suburb where real estate turnover is high. All I know is I love this house. I could buy it and flip it.

I get back into my truck, and immediately get onto every real estate page I can find, looking at the prices for what sells here in Hope River.

I can't find this house listed. Is this no longer for sale? Judging by the abandoned appearance, I doubt anyone would be living here. Well, I can't call the relator now, it's too early in the morning. And I'm tired, so I may as well put my seat back, and go to sleep for a few hours.

There's a tapping on my window, and I open my eyes to find someone in a police uniform standing at my window. I uncurl myself and sit up in the truck. I wind down the window, and yawn. "Morning, officer," I say as I tap my phone to check the time. The sun is breaking over the horizon, and my phone tells me it's just after six-thirty. An hour and a half isn't ideal, but at least it's something.

"License and registration," he says, all business as he looks inside my truck.

"Okay." I reach over to the glove compartment, and take both out. I hand them to him. He checks them, and walks back to his car. *A man of many words.* He comes back, and returns them to me.

"Why are you sleeping in your truck like a homeless person on the side of the road?"

Huh, what a way to greet someone. "I was driving through, and I saw that house." I pointedly look over to the old, decrepit home. When I see it in the light of the morning, it looks worse than I expected. *Awesome.* The more derelict, the better.

"Where are you going?"

"Truthfully, I have no idea. But I like the house."

"Old Roger's house?" He looks at me, then over the top of the truck to the house. "That old thing?"

"Yeah. Hey, I'm wondering if there's a bed and breakfast in town, or somewhere I can stay?"

He stares at me with his cold eyes for a long moment before replying. "No. The town over has a place you can stay. It's a good twenty minutes from here." What a warm guy this sheriff is. "There's also Mulberry Point, which is the next largest city from here. That's a good half hour west."

"Ah, thank you." I smile, trying my hardest to impress him.

He ducks down, and studies my face. Shit, do I have a black eye? I quickly look in the mirror, and notice a darkening shade of a promised bruise erupting around my cheek bone. "What's happened here?" His eyes are drawn to Grady's anger.

My eyes well up with tears, and I feel myself retreating. "Nothing." I'm not overly keen to recap a story I'd rather stay in the past.

"Are you in trouble?" His voice is edged with worry.

"No, I don't think I am."

He nods while keeping his eyes on me. He takes his phone out of his pocket, scrolls through it, and brings it to his ear. "Hi." He pauses. "Yes, I know." His lips draw up into a small smile. "Can you make up the room in the stable?" He nods. "Thank you, Gran." Lowering his phone, he takes a notepad out of his back pocket along with a pen. "This is May's house, she has a room you can stay in her stables. It's nothing fancy, but it's safe, warm, clean and has its own bathroom and kitchen. " He thrusts the paper into my hands. "A fancy truck like this one has GPS, right?"

"Yeah, it does." Why would he help me? He doesn't even know me. "Thank you," I add, still unsure as to why he's giving me his grandmother's address. I mean, I could be a serial killer.

"She's expecting you."

"Thank you," I say again. "Is there somewhere I can get a coffee?"

Mr. Personality stares at me for another few seconds. There's no sense of urgency around here. It's like he's moving in his own time zone. "Down the road, first left, then second right. It's on the main street of the town. You'll find a café that serves good coffee and even better pancakes."

"Thank you."

He tips his head once in acknowledgement and heads back toward his car.

It's so early. I hope the realtor is awake. Looking on the sign for the number, it has a lady's name, Eleanor. Grabbing my phone, I dial the number. It rings once and a woman answers. "Hello."

Okay, this is weird. No introductions. "Hi, I'm calling about the house up on Clayton Street."

"Oh, yes. How can I help?"

"It's for sale. Can you give me a price?"

"That house has been on the market for quite a while." I figured that from the overgrown lawns, the falling wood siding, and the for sale sign that's barely hanging on. "The family wants that house gone, and have said they'll consider any offer."

Are you kidding? They'll consider any offer? "Great, can you let them know I'm offering fifty."

"Oh, I think that might be a bit low. I can put it forward to them, but I think one hundred might sound more appealing to them."

No way. Even if I do all the work, and get Charlie down here to help me, I doubt I can rehab this house for anything less than fifty thousand. "Please pass it along to them and let me know." Judging by the comps in neighboring areas, it's not sustainable to pay a hundred thousand for the house, then invest another fifty thousand on rehab. Based on my research, there aren't really many comparable properties in the Hope River area. Interesting.

"Okay. I've got your number, so I'll call you back in a few minutes."

"Great, thank you." I hang up, get out of the car, and walk the perimeter of the house. I'm careful of where I step. Between the overgrown grass, and debris. I'm not sure what I'll tread on. I want to go up the front porch and have a look inside, but the porch looks to be rotting all the way through.

My phone rings, and I automatically know it's the realtor. "Hello," I say.

"It's Eleanor, I got in contact with the owners and they'll be happy with seventy-five."

"Seventy-five?" I do the numbers quickly in my head, and although it's not favorable, I might be able to make it work. "Okay. Let's do this. Where do you want to meet?"

"I can be out at the house at eleven. Does that work for you?"

"It does. Thank you, I'll see you then."

"What's your name?"

"Hope. I'll be waiting at the house." I hang up, and make my way back to my truck.

I need a bathroom, and a coffee.

Following the sheriff's directions, I head into town and find the local café. It's still early, but thankfully it's open. Looking around, I'm quite surprised by how quiet it's here. There's a general store on the opposite side and a baker next door to the café. Down the street I can see a huge clock tower and a garden with pops of color from vibrant flowers.

I wonder what else there is here.

When I open the door to the café, a small bell chimes.

There's no one here other me, and the woman working the counter. "Morning," she says. Her hair is cut short, and it's a brilliant, flaming red color.

"Morning. Are you open for coffee?"

"We are."

"Great. Is there a bathroom I can use please?'

"Sure thing. Down the back, to the right." She points to a corridor.

I head to the bathroom, and pee. When I come out, I head straight to the counter, where one of the locals is now sitting on a stool. He swings around, looks at me and crinkles his brows.

"What can I get ya?" the chick asks. I can't believe I didn't see her two full sleeves of tattoos. It's not exactly something you could easily miss.

"Double pump caramel, skinny soy with extra whip cream and no sprinkles."

The chick looks at me, and tilts her head to the side. "Darlin,' you get filtered coffee, water or a milkshake. What do you want to drink?"

"I suppose I'll have a coffee."

"Sugar?"

"Four please."

She stares at me again, and says, "Right, so you want diabetes, do you?"

I like this chick. She's busting my ass and I think we can get along. "Okay, how about two sugars?"

"One black coffee with two sugars coming up." She pours me a coffee, and adds two sugars to it. She pushes the coffee cup over to me. "So, you're new in town."

Crap, is this town really so small that they know every face? "Yeah, I am."

"Passing through?"

"Not exactly. I'm waiting for the realtor."

"Wait, you're Hope? Of course, you are. I should've known." The woman scolds herself for not realizing earlier.

"Um, how do you know me?" Don't tell me the sheriff has already started telling everyone about me.

"I'm Eleanor," she says with a huge smile.

"Eleanor? The real estate agent?"

"Yeah. I'm pretty diverse. I'm the realtor, and own the café, and I help out down at the library when I'm needed."

"When do you have time?"

She smiles, and wipes down the counter. "Usual, Murray?" she asks the old man sitting at the counter. He replies with a grunt. She pours him a coffee, and gives him a slice of pie. "Not a lot of houses get sold here. Actually, last one I sold was maybe a year ago. Once people come here, they generally stay until they die."

"Wow. Well I don't plan on staying for that long. I'm looking to flip the house, and leave."

Eleanor smiles. "I'm glad you think you're going to do that. Anyway, I need to go to my office and get the paperwork for Old Roger's house."

"I'll write a bank check for the sale of the house. Who do I make it out to?"

"Seventy-five hundred to Wyatt County. The owners just wanted to clear the back taxes on the house."

"Seventy-five *hundred?*" I thought it was seventy-five thousand. Holy shit.

Eleanor lifts her brows as she slowly nods. "If you want to give us more, then I'll be happy to take it off your hands."

"Seventy-five hundred is fair." Very fair. "Who owns the house? How long has it been derelict?"

"I've had the listing for about four years, and it's been vacant for at least a year or so before that. Old Roger owned it, and he passed away. Left the house to his sister, but she doesn't want it, and none of her family want it either. It wasn't in a very good state when he died, and they've defaulted on the land tax. They came out to look at it, but it's in bad shape."

"Is that Old Roger's house?" the old guy at the counter asks.

"Yeah, Hope here has bought it," Eleanor tells him.

"Ha. You bought that old piece of shit? Good luck with it. You're gonna need it." He picks his coffee cup up, and sips it.

"Where are you staying in the meantime?" Eleanor asks.

"Um. Well the sheriff knocked on my window this morning."

"Jake?" Eleanor says, her voice cracking, and her cheeks reddening.

"Is that his name? Jake?" She nods, and ducks her head. Oh, are they a thing? "He called his grandmother, and said I can stay there."

"His grandmother?" Eleanor looks to the old guy. He shrugs. "Oh, you mean Gran. She's a nice woman. She'll look after you."

"Elle, another coffee?" She smiles at him and pours another coffee. "You eating too, Hope?"

"Yeah, can I get some pancakes?"

"The cook should be here soon, but considering you need to wait for me to get the paperwork for Old Roger's house, you may as well make yourself comfortable."

"You know, while I'm waiting I might take a walk and see what there is in town." Standing, I push the stool under the counter. "What do I owe you?" I take five dollars out of my back pocket, and push it on the counter.

"On the house today. Do you want me to meet you at the house at eleven?"

"I'll come back here. I'll go for my walk, then I'll head over to see Jake's grandmother." I catch another weird look between Eleanor and the guy at the counter.

Walking out, I head down the street. It's still really early, so not many stores are open yet. The convenience store is open, and there's a guy sweeping the pavement. "Morning," he says as he glances up to see me approaching.

"Morning." I offer him a smile, but keep walking toward the clock tower. Looking around, I see a small hardware store. I cross the quiet street, happy to see the open sign. Walking in, I check out what they have and see if it's going to be what I need to flip Old Roger's house. They have a semi-decent variety and supply of everything, but I'll need to source a few things for the interior.

I reach for my phone, and see a ton of messages from Grady. "Yeah, not gonna happen, buddy." I read the first message, and it's filled with "sorrys." I delete the rest without even bothering to read anymore. I scroll through my phone and find Charlie's number. Dialing it, I bring it up to my ear. "Jesus, Hope, where the hell are you?"

"What do you mean?"

"Grady called me last night, looking for you. Didn't you check your phone?"

"I just deleted all his messages and calls. Anyway, we're over."

"Shit, what happened? All he said was he came home drunk, and you left."

I stop looking through the hardware store, and lean against one of the tower racks. "Really? I left because he came home drunk?"

"Yeah. Where are you? Did you go back to Mom and Dad's?"

"He left out one major key element."

"What's that?"

"He hit me."

"He fucking did what?" Charlie's voice rises in anger. "Where the hell is he? I'm going to find him."

"No, don't bother. I took care of him."

"What happened, Hope? And where the hell are you?"

"He came home drunk and was accusing me of cheating on him. He slapped me once, and when he went to do it again, I grabbed his balls and told him I'd mail them back to his mother."

Charlie huffs into the phone. "Where are you?"

"I got on the road last night and headed north. I found a cute town, which is why I'm calling."

"You moving away, sis?"

"Nah, I found a house to flip."

"Want me to get the team together?"

"I'm actually thinking of bringing just you up. I want to get my hands dirty again, get in the thick of it. But I'll find an electrician up here."

"What's the supply situation like there?"

"I'm in the hardware store now; it's okay. I'll send you the address, let me know when you're here."

"I'm finishing up with Acacia Street today. Should be ready for sale early next week."

"Do you think you can get that ready for me? Call in the agent. I already told Grady he's out, but I just don't wanna deal with any more from him."

"Yeah, leave it to me. When do you want me to come up?"

"When you're done with Acacia. I'll run the figures and comps tonight, and I'll give you a call about it all. I want to leave all that down there, and just spend some time getting back to what I love best."

"Getting your hands dirty *is* what you do best." Charlie makes me smile. "Send the address. I'll get this project buttoned up, and let the team know we're taking some time but we may need them on this project."

There's a restless scratch in my stomach. I think it's the way Charlie said *project*. I already have a connection to Old Roger's house. The house itself speaks to my soul. And I have no idea why I feel so emotional toward it. "Okay."

"What did you pick it up for?"

"Get this, I offered fifty, and they came back at seventy-five."

"Seventy-five thousand? Have you run the comps? Will it make money? How bad is the house?"

"Here's the funny thing. They wanted seventy-five *hundred!* And I suspect we'll be taking it down to the studs."

"Seven-thousand five-hundred? Jesus, you sure it's not a tear down and rebuild?"

"I like the looks of it and I don't want to tear it down. I'll get a thorough look at it later when I get the keys."

"It has to go through closing, so it may be a week or so before you get keys. Tell me about it."

"Look, I have to go. But I'll let you know how it all goes when I sign for it at eleven. I'll send you some pictures too. Stack your truck with our tools. And whatever you do, don't tell our parents about Grady, or tell Grady where I am."

"No, I won't." He takes a breath. "Do you need anything? Other than your tools, do you want any clothes or anything?"

"I packed a bag last night, I have most of the things I need, and I suppose I can find somewhere to buy clothes." I walk out of the hardware store, and keep going down the street. "The town is cute, but so small. But if I need anything, hopefully I can it find here or at least close by."

"Alright, I'll see you soon."

"Bye." Hanging up, I keep looking at the stores that are beginning to open for the day. I get back to my truck, grab the paper the sheriff gave me from my back pocket and type the address into the GPS.

Chapter TWO

PULLING INTO THE driveway, I see the house is set on acreage. There's a massive wrap-around porch with a swinging loveseat, and an outdoor setting near the front door. There are cute blue shutters on the windows, and a gray gable roof and crisp white paint on the house itself. The land all around the house is perfectly manicured.

Parking my truck, I get out and walk up to the house.

An older lady opens the front door, and steps out. She's wearing an apron, and has her hair tied back in a loose bun. "You must be Hope," she calls out as I approach her.

"Hi." I smile. Walking up the wide steps, I extend my hand to her. "Hi, I'm Hope. Um, the sheriff said I could stay here for…"

"That's right. Jacob did call me," she says, cutting me off. "I've got a room you can use. Follow me." She walks down the steps, turns to the right and rounds the house. I follow. "How long are you here for?"

"I'm looking at buying a house."

"Here? There's no houses for sale. People don't leave here once they're here. It's a small community, and everyone knows everyone."

I'm gathering that. "It's the Old Roger's house."

She stops walking, and turns to look at me. "That old house?"

"Yeah, I saw it, and I bought it."

"You do know that's an *old* house?" she asks as if I haven't seen it. She's pretty sprightly for someone her age.

"Yes, ma'am, I do."

"Pffft. What's this ma'am business. My name's May." She starts walking again, reaches the stable, takes a key out of her apron and unlocks the door. "Well, girly, that house is a handful. But here's the room." She steps aside waiting for me to enter the room.

"Wow," I say. The stable room is quite large, with a completely self-contained kitchen to the left of it containing a small dining table with chairs, and a living area to the right. "This is nice."

"First door on the right is the bedroom, and the second door is the bathroom. The sofa folds out to a full-size bed."

"Thank you."

"Now." She turns to look at me. "I see you have a bruise on your face, is the giver of that going to be showing up here? If so, do you need my gun?"

I smile. "No, not at all. It's not like that."

"I want no parties here. No strange men."

"My brother will be arriving soon. Maybe by the end of the week, or early next week. Can he stay with me?"

There's a long pause before she smiles politely. "I want to meet him before I say yes."

Fair enough. I can't ask for any more than that. "Of course," I say.

"Rent is due on the first of the month. If I like your brother and want him here, then rent will be twenty percent more to accommodate for his use of utilities." Talk about shrewd.

"That's reasonable."

"If I don't like him, he'll need to find somewhere else to stay." She's blunt and to the point. At least I know where I stand with her. I give her a curt nod. "What is it you do?"

"I flip houses."

May screws her nose. "Why on earth would you do that?"

No one's ever asked me before. It takes me by surprise. "Because I love working with my hands. And I'm good at it."

May's mouth contorts. "So you're going to restore Old Roger's house?" I nod. "I hope you keep its character. I wouldn't want to see it replaced with one of those modern, fancy-pants buildings that won't belong here."

I like May. She's traditional, yet spunky. She's not afraid to speak her mind, and I respect that. "I'd like to see what I'm working with first. Did you know the owner?"

"Everyone knew Old Roger. He was here all his life. Died about eight years ago I think. He was very well respected in the town. We hold a celebration for him every year."

How sweet. "I promise, I'll do my best to honor his home."

May steps forward, gives me the key to the stable, and turns to leave. "I expect you'll be tired tonight. Dinner is served at six sharp tomorrow, I'll see you there."

"Oh, thank you, but you don't have to feed me."

"Here's the thing you need to know about Hope River, Hope." She stops and cracks a smile. "What a coincidence, your name being in the town's name. Anyway, the thing you need to know about Hope River, we're a small town, but we're more like a family. We're all here for one another. We don't take well to strangers who want to cause problems. If you think you can bring your big city ways here, you may as well get in that fancy truck of yours and leave." Can she be any more forthright?

"May, I have no intentions on disturbing anyone or causing friction. I just want to get my hands dirty and flip Old Roger's house," I honestly reply.

"Then welcome to Hope River." She starts to head toward the door. "The ocean is about a mile or two that way. And Hope River is about three or four miles that way." She points in completely opposite directions.

"Thank you."

She gives me a small wave over her head as she turns to leave, and closes the door behind her. Although it's a stable, there's a long narrow window running down the length, allowing a ton of natural light in. I go to the bedroom, and discover it's rather large, with a queen bed, a multicolored rug on the floor, and a small walk-in closet. This place is better than some apartments I've rented. It's not overly large, but it's cute, and extremely clean.

I sit on the edge of the bed, and let out a sigh. It's not yet eleven, which means I still have some time before I need to meet Eleanor in town.

I may as well bite the bullet and call Grady. I call his number and he answers immediately. "Hope," he says sounding relieved. "I'm so sorry, baby. I can't believe what I did."

"We're over, Grady."

"But I didn't mean it. I'm sorry. I'll never do it again."

This is hard. "Look, even if you hadn't done what you did last night, I think we both feel the same way about each other."

"No, I love you," he says, but his tone is almost robotic.

"Grady, we're better as friends."

"But I love you."

"We haven't had sex in months, and we don't spend any time

together unless we're on a job. I know you're not happy, and I haven't been either." I lean my elbows on my knees.

"This is because of last night, isn't it? I'm sorry. What can I do to prove it to you?" There's a level of desperation in his voice, but I can tell, he's just going through the motions.

"We've been drifting apart for a long time."

"No!" he protests. "We love each other."

"Grady, can you honestly tell me you're in love with me? Crazy, giddy, can't wait to see me, in love?" There's a long silence on the other end of the phone. The quiet speaks volumes. "I'm not in love with you either."

"We can learn to love one another."

"I do love you, but I'm not *in love* with you. And even though what you did last night was a fucking dog act, it's not the only reason why you and I are better off apart. We don't love each other the way either of us deserves to be loved."

"Hope," he whispers.

"You're normally a good guy, Grady. You're just not *my* good guy. But I will tell you this, if I ever hear you've raised your hand to anyone again, I'll make good on my promise."

Grady takes several deep breaths, then I hear him let out a small cry. "Hope, I have something to tell you."

If he tells me he's hit another woman, I will end him. "What?" I find my posture changes, becoming more rigid, with my shoulders pulled back.

"I know you've never cheated on me."

Where's this going? "No, I haven't."

There's a long moment of silence. "But I cheated on you last night," he whispers. I go quiet. What a damn asshole. "Hope," he says after a moment of me being quiet. "I'm sorry."

"I take it all back. You can go to fucking hell, Grady! And don't think for one moment, you're going to get any share of the business. I've worked damned hard to build my business from the ground up. I'll send you a check for what I owe you. Be out of my house by the end of the week." I hang up, stunned and hurt.

I sit staring at the colorful rug on the floor. Suddenly, I burst into tears. The bastard cheated on me, came home, and hit me because of his own guilt.

Curling up on the bed, I hug the pillow and cry into it.

I know Grady and I were over long before what happened last night, but for him to take his guilt out on me hurts. There's a heaviness in my body, one that grows and clouds my heart. How could he do what he did?

Closing my eyes, I try and not think about him. It's over.

Shit, what time is it? I grab my phone and see I have several missed calls from Eleanor. Shit, shit, shit, shit, it's after one. Shooting up out of bed, I grab my truck keys and run out the door. I can't believe I fell asleep for so long. I dial Eleanor's number as I sprint toward my truck. Shit, shoes. I turn back, unlock the door, and slide on my shoes.

"Hello?" she answers.

"I'm so sorry! I fell asleep. I can be there in a few minutes."

"Hope?" she questions.

"Yeah. I'm sorry. I'm still trying to wake up. Let me try this again. Hi, Eleanor, it's Hope. I'm sorry I'm late, but I fell asleep, I'll be there in a few minutes." Jumping in the truck, I speed down the long driveway.

"I can come to you if you like."

"Oh no, that's fine. I need to grab a few things from the convenience store. And I'm dying for a coffee."

"I'll have it ready for you when you arrive."

I feel myself smiling. Eleanor is pretty cool, and I think we're going to form a friendship. The drive to Main Street doesn't take more than ten minutes, and when I get there it's actually busy. For such a small town, I thought there'd be tumbleweeds blowing down the street regardless of the time of day. How wrong am I?

The moment I'm in the café, a few people turn to watch me walking in. I can tell by the perplexed look on their faces that they have no idea who I am. Or, word has spread like wildfire, and they all know *exactly* who I am.

"Hi Hope," one woman says as she passes me on the way out.

"Hi," I reply and give her a small smile. I walk up to the counter, where there's only one available seat.

Eleanor sees me, grabs a cup and places it on the counter. She pours me a coffee. "Good sleep?" she asks with a cheeky smile.

"Yeah. I needed it. I'm really sorry about sleeping through our meeting. I've never been this tardy before."

"I was going to drive out to Gran's after I finished here if you hadn't showed. I've got the paperwork out in the back. Give me a second." She turns to one of the young girls working the front counter. "I'll be back in a few minutes. Can you cover the front?" The young girl nods, and Eleanor disappears through what I assume are the swinging doors to the kitchen. When she returns, she's carrying a stack of papers. "Grab your coffee, Hope."

Standing, I get my coffee, and follow Eleanor over to an unoccupied table in the corner. "Eleanor…"

"Everyone calls me Elle," she corrects.

"How long have you lived in Hope River?"

She looks out the window as she taps a pen on the paperwork she brought out as her lips slowly draw up into a small smile. "Oh, I think I've been here about five or so years."

"What brought you out here?" I ask, genuinely interested in how this red-haired woman with two sleeves of tattoos came to a town where I don't see anyone else with tattoos and red hair.

She keeps looking out the window. Her smile disappears, and

she blinks a few times before taking a deep breath. "Some of us have pasts we're not keen to remember."

Ouch, that sounds painful. Shit. She's had a bad time, or a stressful event in her life. I've hit a nerve, and I hate making her remember something she doesn't want to recall. "So, when can we close on the house?"

"I can push it for a quick sale. Five days?" Her eyes brighten, and she pushes past whatever pain I forced her to think of.

"That works for me. Oh, give me a second. Let me get my checkbook. It's in the truck." I stand and run out to my truck. Opening the glove department, I take my checkbook out, and return inside. In the short few seconds I took going to the truck and back, the sheriff is in the café waiting at the counter to be served. Sitting down, I notice how Elle's attention isn't exactly focused on me. "Thanks for waiting." She nods her head at my words, but I doubt she's even heard them. She has one arm up, bent at the elbow leaning on the table, and her head slightly turned so she's checking out the sheriff. She's trying to make it look like she's not staring at him. But if he turns around, he'll catch her ogling him. "Elle?"

"Yeah?"

Her eyes are still fixated on him. "Elle?" She turns to look at me, and her eyes widen in horror. She clears her throat, and tucks some of her wayward hair behind her ear. She squirms in her seat. "So?" I throw a quick glance over to the sheriff.

"Where were we?" She lowers her chin and shuffles through the paperwork.

"Elle," the sheriff says as he walks out of the café with a paper coffee cup in his hands.

She barely even acknowledges him. She gives him a small nod, and keeps flicking through the paperwork. He leaves, and I see her let out a sigh. "So, you and the sheriff are a thing?"

"What?" she squeals. "No! That's ridiculous. No, what, why?"

Aha! They may not be a *thing*, but I sure as hell know, she'd love them to be more than a *thing*. It's obvious to me she's crushing on him hard. "Why don't you ask him out?" I ask.

"Who?" Elle's face reddens.

"The sheriff."

"Jake?" her voice breaks. "We're just friends. He and I aren't like that. I mean, I'm not... you know, he's not... we're..." She shakes her head.

Yeah, okay. The fact she's tripping over her words, her face matches her red hair, and she could barely make eye contact with him, screams out loud that she'd like to have more. I'd be surprised if he hasn't noticed. "Okay, if you say so. Anyway, Old Roger's house." I'm actually liking the nickname the townsfolk use. Opening my checkbook, I start writing out the amount as Elle slides the paperwork over to me. I sign the check, place it on top of the signed paperwork, and slide it back to her.

"You know you're causing a bit of a commotion with the locals."

Tilting my head to the side, I look around the café, and notice a few people quickly spin away. I can't help but smile. "Why?" My stomach clenches with anticipation.

"Because they all want to know what you're going to do with Old Roger's house. Word spreads quickly here."

I can't help but marvel at how fast news and purpose of my presence has spread. I've been here less than twelve hours, and already people are talking. "Well, if they ask you, you can tell them, Old Roger's house is safe in my hands."

I notice Elle look down at my hands, then back up. "Those hands have seen hard work."

I know what she's looking at. The cracked skin on the back of my hands, the short-clipped nails, and the callouses on my palms. "Yep, and I loved every minute of it."

"I have a feeling you're going to cause more tongues to wag."

"I'm an open book, if anyone wants to know anything, they're more than welcome to ask me questions. As far as Old Roger's house, I'll wait 'til I get the keys to see what I'm working with."

Elle smiles. "Have you eaten yet? I can get those pancakes you wanted."

"You know, I'd really appreciate that. I'm starving."

"Elle, I need your help," the girl working the counter calls.

"Good timing, I'll get those pancakes for you," Elle says. She stands, taking the paperwork and smiles. "As soon as it clears the closing, I'll give you a call, if I don't see you around town."

Chapter THREE

KNOCKING ON MAY'S door, I step back and wipe my hands down the front of my jeans. I can hear May in the kitchen, and I know she's heard me, but she's not coming to answer the door.

Yesterday she invited me to dinner. Has she changed her mind? Stepping forward, I knock again. Maybe I should leave. She could've forgotten and doesn't want me here now.

May pops her head out into the hall and sees me standing at the front door. Crap, should I have made a pie or something? *Not that I can cook.* Brought her a bottle of wine? I have no idea what these small towns are like. The smallest town I've lived in was where my parents live, and that has over a hundred thousand people.

"Hope," she says.

"Hi May." I smile through the front screen door waiting for her to let me in.

She stands a good ten feet away. "You waiting for a red carpet and rose petals?" She places her hands to her hips.

"I knocked," I say, still unsure what to do.

"I heard. My ears work well. I assume you know how to open a door." Grinning I reach for the door, and open it. "Hey, who said you can come in?" May yells. Her brows are drawn in, and she has a harsh look on her face.

I automatically close the door and step back. Is she bipolar or something? "I'm sorry," I immediately apologize.

"Ha, just kidding." She starts laughing. "Come in." She beckons for me to enter her house. "Should've seen the look on your face, girly. *Priceless.* You were probably thinking, man, this old bat is a nut case. Right?"

"Well, I wasn't sure what to do."

"Come on, come into the kitchen. Supper's nearly done. You can set the table."

She leads me into her kitchen, and I smile the moment I'm in there. It's old fashioned, but certainly not old. There's a huge white country sink, pale green Shaker doors on the fronts of the cupboards, butcher block counter tops, and barn doors leading to what I assume is a walk-in pantry. The most impressive thing in this kitchen is the massive island with a granite waterfall counter. Although the granite shouldn't work with the butcher block, the light gray marbling ties in with the kitchen beautifully. "Wow," I say as I look around her kitchen.

"You seem surprised."

"I kind of am."

"Why? Because I'm old?" she teases. May opens the oven and this amazing aroma wafts through the kitchen.

"That smells amazing," I say as I duck my head to look into the oven. But she closes it before I can see what she's making. "What are you making?"

"Ahh, my doctor told me to cut down on meat. Pffft, he thinks I eat too much of it, and I should only be having one to two servings of meat a week. That's a bunch of hogwash if you ask me."

"So we're having some type of meat dish?"

"God no!" She flicks her hand at me, dismissively. She chuckles to herself. "Are you trying to put me into an early grave?" She shakes her head, but still has a huge smirk on her face. "Didn't you hear what I said? You young kids…" she teases. "We're having a caramelized onion tart with a salad."

"Sounds delicious, and smells even better." Leaning against the counter, May goes to the fridge, and starts taking out things to prepare the salad. "What can I do?"

"Can you cook?"

I grimace. "I can warm things up, but I'm not really good in the kitchen." My eyes widen as I add, "I can build beautiful, functional kitchens, but I'm not someone who can create anything edible in them. Never really have been."

May lifts her head as she's chopping the salad, and squints at me. "Lord, help this child if she says she eats that pre-cooked trash from the supermarket."

"No, not much of that. But we…" I clear my throat as a vivid image of Grady and myself driving back late from a house we're flipping appears. I straighten my shoulders and smile at May. "I used to eat out a lot. There were a lot of take-out places where I used to live. I had the choice of any cuisine I wanted. From Chinese to Greek food, all on our doorstep." Did I say our? "*My* doorstep," I rapidly correct. "It was always easiest to get something delivered when we…" I clear my throat. "…*I* was so tired after a day on the tools."

"Have you had a look around the town yet?"

"Just the main street."

May smiles. "Then you've looked around the town. If you want a Target, or Walmart they're a good twenty minutes from here. We don't have a restaurant but we do have the Café, which I assume you've seen?"

"I met Eleanor there. So, yep."

"There are three restaurants in the town over, and more beyond. You won't find a fast-food chain restaurant for a good fifteen miles around here."

"That's unusual."

"It's almost like untouched God's Haven here, Hope. One of the big restaurants tried putting in one of those fast-food places. It didn't work, they closed their doors six months after opening. Hope River is about family, and community. We all know everyone's business."

"I'm a fairly private person, May."

She lifts her head and gives me a small nod. "No such thing as privacy here. Get used to that. Speaking of which, what are you going to do with Old Roger's house?"

"I like restoring houses back to their original glory. I do add my own touches and modernize the mechanicals. But in all honesty, there are ivy vines growing up the side of the house and probably inside, too. I won't have any idea what condition that house is in until I get the keys to go inside." May starts laughing. "What's funny?"

"Kick the door down and get yourself a look." Her face is deadpan serious. "I'll do it for ya." And I have no doubt, she would.

"It's okay, I only have to wait a few more days. Gives me time to try and source some hardware, tiles, kitchen appliances and bathroom fixtures, those kinds of things."

"So you do this for a living?" I nod. "And it's worth your time?" I nod again. "It's a man's job though."

I despise it when people say shit like this. It gets under my skin, and I want to start an argument with them. "Anything a man can do, I can do too." Keep your cool, Hope. "Probably better."

"Huh," she huffs. "Good for you, girly. Do you like it?"

"I love it. My brother's my plumber, and I'm good with the design, but also with the hard work. You know, demo, building, laying tiles if I have to, floors, framing, dry-wall. Virtually everything."

"Here." She thrusts a bowl of salad into my hand. "Make yourself useful. Go set the table. You'll find all the plates under here." She indicates with her head. The dining table is large, and can easily accommodate twelve people with room to add more. I set the bowl down, then head back into the kitchen to get two plates, and two sets of cutlery. "I assume you'll be staying in my stable for a while?"

"Until I can live in the house, yes."

"Like I said before, I'll meet your brother before I decide if I want to let him stay with you."

"Do you live here on your own?"

She nods. "I do. From time to time my niece Tabitha comes to stay."

"You don't have kids of your own?" I ask.

The moment the question leaves my lips, I automatically regret it. May stiffens, and I see a sorrow pass through her. "Marriage and children weren't in the cards for me," she softly says.

I feel terrible. "I'm sorry. I was rude for asking."

She flicks her hand at me. "Hush, girly. No need to apologize. Now, the tart should be ready. Grab some glasses from the top shelf, and there's a jug of freshly made lemon iced tea in the fridge." She takes the tart out, places it on the counter, and gets a wooden board to slide it onto.

I get the lemon iced tea and two glasses and set them on the dining room table. "Do you need any more help?"

"No. Sit. Eat." She pulls a chair out, sits and piles the food on her plate.

I sit diagonal to her, and when she's finished, I help myself. "Did you know Old Roger?"

"Of course. Everyone knows everyone else here."

"Can you tell me anything about him or his family?"

"Old Roger's family was one of the original ones to settle in Hope River. He came from a long line of McGraths, and they paved the way for future generations. However, as time went on, a lot left and only a small handful stayed, Roger being one of the last."

"The house sounds like it has a lot of history. Is there a town library where I can go to research it? Maybe I'll find some information on the house, or the family. Do you know anything that might help me? Was Old Roger married? Did he have kids?"

May eats her tart carefully, as she stares down at her salad. A small smile tugs at her lips, before quickly disappearing. "Roger was married but his wife passed from cancer. They had two sons." She looks to me, but I can see there's a touch of sadness. May turns her head, and stares at nothing. She blinks quite fast, then suddenly takes a deep breath, smiles widely, and keeps talking. "He had two boys, Henry and Carl."

"And where are they now?"

"Carl passed away when he was only a few months of age. Died of what they called cot death back then. And Henry died when he was twenty-one. Roger lost so much. But he went on to live in his house, and became a cranky old bastard. Everyone knew it was because he lost his wife, then two years later he lost Henry. After that, Roger became a recluse. Refused help from the townsfolk, didn't want anything to do with anyone."

"How sad," I say as I find myself engrossed with the story of Old Roger. "What did Henry die from?"

May hesitates for a second, before she continues eating. "It rocked the entire town. It was like Roger's family had a curse on them. Henry died from being struck by a train. He'd gone out with his friends, and they got to drinking. He stumbled on the train tracks and didn't see the train approaching." Something tells me there's more to the story then she says.

"How devastating."

"It was enough to cause Roger to shut down any emotional connection to anyone. Can't say I blame him really. The town rallied around him, but he was never the same after Henry died."

"How long ago did Old Roger pass away?"

"Many years now, girly. Many, many years. I'm sure you'll find all the information in the library."

"Thank you, May. I appreciate the information."

"Do you have a team of people you'll be bringing here to help with whatever you're going to do to the house?"

I straighten in my seat, and let out a huff. "I do have a team of people, but I doubt I'll be bringing them here. I need to clear my head, so I'm thinking of putting in a lot of the sweat equity myself. And my brother, Charlie, he's just finishing up on a house we've flipped, and he'll get it ready to sell."

"Tell me something, girly, do you make good money doing this flipping business?" She waves her hand around.

"It's always a gamble. Sometimes I buy houses sight unseen, and find they need more work than they're worth. Usually I do my due diligence on a property before I buy it. But for some reason, I didn't with Old Roger's house. And that's completely uncharacteristic for me. But something about that house spoke to me. Sometimes, I prefer to restore than demolish and start again. Charlie on the other hand, would much rather we level and start again."

"So you'll be putting in a lot of work yourself then?"

"Most of it. Of course, there are things I can't do."

"Like what?"

"I'm not a plumber, but Charlie can do that. I can't run the electricals, or do the rough-in for them. I'll be looking for an electrician, and maybe a small team to help."

"You'll be coming to the flower festival on Saturday, won't

you? You'll meet a lot of people there who could probably help you." I look at May and shrug. "Girly, no one told you about the flower festival?" I shake my head. "Saturday morning Main Street will be closed, and by lunchtime, there'll be a large table down the center, where we all come together and each bring a plate or a bowl of food."

"Where do the flowers come into this? Because it sounds more like a street party then a flower festival."

May laughs, then leans over and places her aging hand on my arm. "I'm not giving anything away. But you'll be there? Don't worry, we'll go together, and no one will say a word if you don't bring a dish."

Wait, now I have to cook something? "I can make some things. I'm really good at making…" I stop to think what I'm good at. "Um." I tap my finger to my chin, thinking. "I can make a mean grilled cheese."

May chuckles. "I'm sure you can. But it's okay, you don't need to bring anything to this one. But you may want to get some cooking lessons while you're here, because I can guarantee, the next one you'll have to bring a plate of something."

Where am I going to get cooking lessons? I don't have time for cooking lessons. "Oh, okay," I say with concern.

May chuckles again. "You are so easy to read. I can see the cogs turning in your head. I'll call you when I'm making something I think you can easily learn. Don't worry."

"Thank you." That takes the pressure off. At least this way, I know if I'm here long enough for another one of these flower festivals, I don't need to bust my ass learning how to cook because May's going to give me some lessons. "What do you love about the town, May?"

"Everything. It's my home. I was born here. But I'll tell you what, the moment I could walk, I was out there helping in the stables, growing the vegetables. You haven't seen around the side, have you?"

"No, what's there?"

"My little vegetable patch. I'll take you out there when you have time."

"I'd love to see it. Thank you."

"Now eat." She pointedly looks at my barely eaten food. "And I'll be offended if you don't go back for seconds. A girly like you needs her energy to work on houses all day."

"I'm not working on one now. If I eat for two, I'll end up looking like two people."

"Hush, girl. You'll be at that house before you know it." She cuts another piece of the tasty tart, and slides it on my plate.

"Thank you," I reply. Truth be told, it's damned delicious, so I'm okay with it. I like May. I have a feeling May and I are going to form a firm friendship. I like her. And I have a feeling she likes me too.

FOUR

"**I**'VE GOT THE keys a day early. When do you think you'll be done there?" I ask Charlie as I sit in my truck outside Old Roger's house.

"I can be there on Monday."

"Okay, that gives me time to have a look inside, get a plan together, and arrange for a dumpster. How's Acacia going? Is it done?"

"Yeah, it's finished. We got a full price offer before it was even shown."

"What? Who…how?" I'm so relieved that house is done. It means I can give Grady what's owed to him, and we can split cleanly. Even though he doesn't deserve my consideration.

"One of the neighbor's daughters came and asked if she could have a look just before we got the staging in. She asked what we wanted for it, and I told her. She walked away, and when the staging crew showed up, she did too. With her checkbook. Paid full price."

"Get out. Just like that?" I ask.

"Yeah, just like that. She said she loves the fact it'll accommodate her family, and she loves how close it is to her parents too. So, Acacia is officially in escrow."

"Okay, this is fantastic. Well, I'll text you the address. You have to meet May first. If she likes you, she'll let you stay with me. If not, then you'll have to sleep in your truck." I laugh.

"Fuck. It's one of *those* towns, is it?" He huffs. "Am I going to have to wear long sleeves to cover up my tattoos?"

"Nah, the town's real estate agent has two full sleeves. The tattoos are fine."

"Any tips to get on this May chick's good side?"

"She's a character, I'll give her that. She's straight up, and says what she thinks. You'll be fine. But you can't bring anyone random around here. No one-nighters." I hear Charlie groan.

"Fine, I'll behave myself. Anyway, give me a damage report at what we're looking at. When do you go in?"

"I'm sitting out in front of the house now. As soon as I get off the phone to you, I'll head inside, though the front porch is rotted." I look up the house. "And there's an ivy snaking its way up and into the house."

"Maybe it's best if you wait for me," he says, his voice etched with worry. "Yeah, wait 'til Monday. It's only three days and I'll be there."

"Nope, I'm going in today. I know what I'm doing, Charlie. You don't have to worry about me."

"I know you know what you're doing. And I *do* have to worry about you, because I love you. Mom and Dad will kill me if you go and break your neck on a house flip."

I laugh. "Yeah, yeah. Whatever. I'll be careful."

"Keep your phone on you, in case you need me."

"Alright. See you Monday. I sent you the address, yeah?"

"Uh-huh. See you then, sis."

He hangs up, and I turn to look at the house. "Let's see what we're working with," I say as I get out of my truck and carefully make my way across the front porch to the door of this old, derelict Victorian. The wooden porch is significantly rotted, and will need to be completely replaced. I tread carefully, making sure my leg doesn't go through the decayed timbers.

There's got to be close to twenty keys on this keychain, which means finding the front door key will be a process of elimination. I take the packet of colored Sharpies out of my back pocket. On the third key attempt, I manage to open the door. I color code it black.

Opening the front door, the first thing that hits me is the smell. Like something's died, and it probably has. A skunk, dog, cat, God knows what we'll find in here once demo begins. I let the initial smell leave, cover my nose with my hand, and walk through the open foyer.

There's no denying this house is in need of major repairs. There are holes in the walls, and the balustrade on the staircase is barely existent. But the moldings are intricate and beautiful. We'll have to be careful with those, because I want to keep them, or at the very least, replicate them. I take loads of pictures with my phone.

Moving into what I think is the formal dining room, I look around. This room is grand, and in its heyday, must have been very elegant. There ceiling height has to be at least fifteen feet. "Wow," I say as I walk through.

This house has an amazing feeling to it. There's something majestic, but mysterious too. Whenever I go into these old houses, my skin always breaks out in goosebumps. They're so exciting, and I become giddy wondering what secrets they hold.

I walk over and place my hand to the wall. "I bet you've witnessed some amazing things in your life, haven't you?" I gently stroke the wall. "Have you got some secrets you want to tell me?" I whisper. Smiling, I can only imagine what this breathtaking house has seen, and heard. "I'm going to rebuild you, old girl. But in order to get you back to your beauty, I have to tear you down first. It's going to hurt, and you may think I'm not doing the right thing, but please just trust me."

Moving my hand, I turn and walk through a narrow door. "This isn't up to code," I say as I walk into a completely non-functional kitchen with no windows and cabinet doors falling off their hinges, or non-existent. "Nope, this won't do. Good size, though. What do you think, old girl? Would you like a nice big kitchen? We'll remove this wall and open you up to that massive dining room. What's in this side?" There's another door, which leads to an awkward, tiny half-bathroom. "That's revolting. Nope, you can't stay." I place my hand to the wall in the kitchen. "It's okay, you're in good hands now. I promise I'll look after you."

Leaving the kitchen through the narrow door, I cross the entrance, and go to the left of the lower level. There's another large room identical to the dining room, and behind it what appears to may be a bedroom. "Alright, this is weird." And there's another door to the side of it. When I open, it leads me into another room. "It's a maze, right?" That room has another door, and when I walk through it, I see the back of the staircase. Some kind of weird maze? Right then, let's move on.

I'm careful as I make my way up the stairs, because I can see some of the treads have rotted. Upstairs there's a narrow, incredibly dark hallway that leads to three large bedrooms, one smaller bedroom, and one upstairs bathroom.

"Ugh, carpet." The carpet upstairs in horrendous. It's stained, and old, and doesn't fit in with any of the millions of ideas going through my mind. Kneeling down, I peel the edge of the carpet back and thankfully beneath is beautiful hardwood flooring, matching the downstairs.

"My head is going crazy right now, old girl. I'm going to make you just as beautiful as you were when you were first built. I'll get to drawing up plans tonight."

I've seen what I need to see on the inside, now I need to check the back garden out. Carefully, I go down the stairs, and I'm surprised to find there's no internal exit to the back yard. Wow, how bizarre.

Walking out the front, I'm careful not to fall through the holes in the porch or front steps, and navigate through the thigh-high weeds to the back.

"Well, the good news is, blank slate." I turn, trying to figure out why there's no door opening on the back yard. "Totally bizarre. But hey, don't worry, we'll get there."

I head back to the truck, and send Charlie all the photos I've been taking. Within moments he calls. "Alright, don't hold back," I say as I answer the phone.

"Am I bringing the gasoline and the lighter?"

"No, you're bringing our tools."

"Hope, it looks like the only decent thing are those floors."

"I'm fairly certain, they *are* the only decent thing."

"Let's tear it down, and start again. How large is the land?"

"Nearly an acre."

"Shit, that's massive. We can split it and put two houses on that, sell it for more." I'm shaking my head. Old Roger's house speaks to me. She's whispering her pleas not to tear her down. "Oh man," Charlie sighs. "I know by that silence, you're not going to tear this house down, are you?"

"Nope."

"We're going to restore it, aren't we?" I begin nodding. "You're nodding, aren't you?"

"Yep."

"How long do you think it'll be before we get the permits?"

"That's like asking how long is a piece of string. I'll work on the plans tonight, and hopefully I'll get them submitted early next week."

"Wait, you don't need me down at Hicksville yet?"

I smile. "It's actually quite nice here, Charlie. You may even like it?"

"Are there clubs and restaurants?"

"No and no."

"Then there's no chance I'll like it. I'm going, I'll head down on Monday. I'm going to get my fill of parties, alcohol, and sex, because I'm not going to get that again for at least four or five months while we're in No-Fun Hicksville."

"Honestly, you're an ass. But get it out of your system now, because none of that goes on here."

"Yay," Charlie says in a deadpan voice. "Great. Really looking forward to this one. Make me a promise."

"What?"

"Let's flip this damn house, and promise me you'll never stray so far again."

"We'll see." I shrug. Old Roger's house and I have got an intimate connection. One I can't quite explain to anyone. "See you soon."

"Ugh. Bye."

Hanging up, I head back to my truck, rustle through the paperwork to make sure I have all the specifications, and start the drive back to May's. I need to take a good look at this, and decide what I'm going to do with this old girl.

Shit, I didn't lock the house. I highly doubt squatters would break in now, but I better lock her up before I leave. Turning my truck around, I get up to the house and search for the keys in my pockets. "Shit, where are they?" I pat my pockets again, to no avail. I must've dropped them inside somewhere.

I retrace my steps, and thankfully find them upstairs when I leaned down to pull the carpet up. As I walk down the stairs, I hear someone calling, "Hello."

Who the hell can this be? "Hello?" Opening the door, my mouth falls open. What the fuck? "It's you!" *Again?*

His mouth falls open as he stares at me. He lifts his hand, pointing. "It's you," he echoes my words.

"What the…"

Chapter
FIVE

Past

SOMEONE TAPS ME on the shoulder, and I turn to see who it is. "Hey, aren't you the girl from the other day? The one who tripped that guy who was stealing at the coffee shop?"

Oh, the cute guy from the café. The one with the dimpled chin and the mom who hugged and kissed him. "Yeah, that's me. And you're the one with the kissy mom." My damn stomach flutters.

His cheeks instantly redden as he looks down at his feet. He clears his throat, and follows it with a slight nod. "Yep, that's me." He lifts his chin and smiles. "That was super brave. I thought you were uber cool for standing up to that guy."

"I wish my parents had thought the same thing. I got into so much shit for ditching school."

"Why did you do it? You could've let him to steal that money, and bolted before the police got involved."

"I hate thieves," I answer candidly. "Pet peeve of mine. Along with the spitting thing too. Did you see I slapped him?" I ask proudly.

"I saw. You're a definite badass," he says with a grin "Anyway, my name's River."

"Don't your parents like you? That's a strange name."

River's eyes widen, shocked. "Um, okay then." This has turned awkward. Damn my lack of a filter. "Do you have a name, or should I call you *bruiser?*"

"I'm Hope." My stupid heart flutters. "Are you new in school? I haven't seen you around." *He's so cute.*

"This school, yeah. I transferred over today. Hey, can you tell me where this classroom is?" He shows me his schedule.

"Sure. It's down this way." I start walking in the direction of his class. "Are you from around here?"

"Not really. It's more like I'm from all over. Dad's military."

"Oh right," I say. "You move around a lot then?"

"Nearly every two years. But we've been here for just over the usual two years, so, we're probably going to move soon."

"That must suck. Moving around all the time."

He slows the walking pace, almost to a complete stop. "Not totally. There have been times I wish we'd moved faster, and other times I wish we could stay in one place for longer."

"But what about girlfriends?"

"What about girlfriends?" he repeats. He adds in a shrug.

"Or a boyfriend. Hey, your business what you do and who you do it with." I hold up my hands in surrender.

"If you're asking me to go on a date with you, that's all you have to do."

"I'm not asking you to go on a date!" I nearly shout.

"Oh, now you're saying you're too good for me?" The mischievous glint in his eyes tells me he's teasing.

Slanting my head, I wink. "You need to work for something this hot." I teasingly pluck at my t-shirt.

"Then should I tell you…you've got something on your nose?" He flicks his nose discreetly.

"What? No way." Turning away, I quickly wipe my nose. I look at my hand, and there's nothing there. He's laughing as he's slowly walking away from me. "You're an ass," I say. The bell sounds and I take off in the opposite direction. "Just for that, you can find your own way to class."

"See you at lunch," he shouts.

What? Now we're having lunch together? "Not if you can't find me." Damn it, I like him.

Sitting with my friends, I spot River walking into the cafeteria. He looks around, and spots me. He heads straight over, pulls out the seat next to me and sits. My friends stop talking, and look at him. "What do you think you're doing?" Deanne asks.

"I'm sitting here with Hope," he replies.

Deanne turns to look at me. Her eyes widen in horror. "Did you invite him?" she whispers in a loud enough way to make River feel uncomfortable.

"Oh sorry, is this a 'We Wear Pink on Wednesdays' kind of clique?" He takes his lunch out of his bag and starts eating it casually.

"Did you just call us Mean Girls?" Deanne snaps.

I chuckle. He's funny. I really like that about him. "No, but if you're not, why can't I sit here?"

"I'm going to get food." Deanne stands in disgust. "You coming?" she asks me.

"Nah, I think I'll stay."

Deanne rolls her eyes, but Melissa and Simone stand and

follow Deanne to get food, leaving River and me at the table. "You said if I could find you. You weren't exactly hiding."

"I wasn't trying."

"You wanted me to find you?"

"I knew you weren't really looking," I snap.

"Like I knew you weren't really hiding," he quickly retorts.

"You know, you're a pain in the ass."

I can see he's thinking about something to say. But the beaming smile speaks loudly. "Want to go on a date tonight?"

"Nah."

"How about tomorrow night?"

I shrug. "Maybe, but I doubt it."

He takes a bite of his food, and grins. "Fine. Don't then. Your loss, not mine."

"Oh, I see how this is. Now, *I'm* not good enough for *you*."

He chuckles as he looks down and shakes his head. "I prefer my own company anyway."

I chew on the inside of my cheek, stopping myself from retorting with some smart-ass remark. Screw it. "Don't let me stop you from hanging out with yourself and your mirror. I bet you're in a boyband too."

He rolls his eyes, but chuckles. "I'd prefer to hang with you, but hey, don't do me any favors."

What an ass. "Where are we going tomorrow night?"

"Nah, I don't feel like it now. The offer has passed."

He baited me! I was played. I lift my finger, pointing at him. "Never again, Robert," I say knowing his name is River.

He arches a brow, and stares straight into my eyes with the sexiest smirk ever. Oh shit. I'm in trouble. Deep doo-doo. He's *so* damn cute. That dimpled chin. Those dark irresistible eyes. The near jet-black slightly tousled hair. I'm in so much trouble. My stomach flutters as I watch, and wait for his reply. Instead, he looks at me and keeps chewing until he's done.

Once he's finished, he places his lunch waste back in his bag, zips it up, then stands. He hasn't said anything. Not a single word. He takes a step away, then turns and comes back to me. Leaning down, with his mouth so close I can feel the heat of his breath on my neck, he whispers, "Lucky I like you."

Closing my eyes, I swallow the lump pulsating in my throat. I wait for him to say more. Or kiss my neck. Or do something, *anything.*

Heat rises quickly to my cheeks, and I want to grab him and kiss him. I wait.

And wait.

"What are you doing?" Deanne says startling me.

"What?" I look around, and find River gone. Damn him. He's already gotten under my skin.

I can't have a boy distract me now. Nope, no way.

No, sir. You're not gonna make me like ya. No, no, no.

Then why is my stomach tumbling around with my heart beating like I'm an infatuated school girl? Maybe I am.

Crap.

Chapter SIX

"HOW... WHAT...?" I keep pointing to River standing at my door.

"What are you doing here?" he asks. He takes a step back, and looks around. "Wait, you bought Old Roger's house?"

"Ah…yeah." We're standing, staring at each other and wanting to say more, but not able to. I want to throw myself into his arms and hug him hard. But not after what he did to me. I straighten my shoulders and tell my stomach to calm down, and my heart to shut the fuck up. He broke my heart once before, and I'm not prepared to let him do this again. "What are *you* doing here?" I ask, pulling every emotion back so he can't see how he hurt me all those years ago.

"I live here. Just on the other side of Hope River."

Ugh, great. "Really? That's fantastic. But what are you doing here?" I lean against the door, and hope to God it doesn't collapse beneath my weight. Not that I'm heavy, it's just this house is so old and unsteady.

"I saw your truck, and was coming to offer my services if you need it."

"I'm good," I say shutting him down before he even has a chance to tell me what he's doing now.

"But you don't even know what I do."

Break my fucking heart! That's what you do. "I'm good." I strain to offer him a genuine smile. I've never been backward about being forward, but some things are best left in the past.

"What are you going to be doing here? Tear this old girl down?"

"No!" I snap. Calm down, Hope. "You might be able to get rid of things once they're too hard to work on, but I believe everything deserves a second chance. Houses especially."

"Hope, can we talk, please? What happened…"

Holding my hand up, I shut him down. I don't need to relive that night. No thanks. "No need to explain. I don't want to hear it. Honestly, it's all good. It's over with."

"Hope," he begs.

"River, leave it. It's in the past, which is exactly where it needs to be." He gives me a small smile. But his eyes tell an entirely different story. I have to move on and not let his presence here hinder me or the work on this house. "What services were you going to offer?" This is a small town, and I don't want to be an ogre. I'm likely only going to be here for a few months. And who knows? Maybe River can help with suppliers.

"I was going to offer whoever the new owners were, my electrical services. What are the plans here?" He looks around the house from the front door. "I've always wondered what it looked like inside."

Yeah, that was a subtle; *can I come in?* "Would you like to have a look around?" I offer as I step aside.

"Only if that's okay with you."

Play nice, Hope. "Sure." Let it go. It's in the past.

He steps in, and looks up. "Wow, look at these ceilings. And these floors are just gorgeous."

"Nothing a good sanding won't fix. The same hardwood floors are upstairs, under a ratty carpet."

"Are you going to change the footprint?"

I inhale deeply. "To be honest, I'm not sure what I'm going to do yet. I want to restore her, because I think she's beautiful.

"So you did it. You did what you wanted to," River says as he moves away from me and leans against the wall.

He really is so attractive. And tall. And sexy. *My God, stop thinking about him like that.* I can't help but look to see there's no ring on his finger. "It wasn't easy. But since I last saw you, which is what... four years ago?"

"Yeah, on your twenty-first birthday. At the club," he says as he looks down at his feet.

I hated how that night turned out. "I told you, I don't want to talk about it" He nods his head, and purses his lips tightly together. "My life has taken a huge turn. I started my own business, and Charlie works for me."

"Are you married?" he asks without hesitation.

"Are you?" I answer his question with a question.

He lifts his hand to wiggles his fourth finger. I do the same. "I thought you would've been snapped up by now."

"Please," I scoff.

"Anyone serious?"

"It's none of your business," I snap. Pushing off from the wall, I head to the front door. "You're an electrician, eh?"

He follows me to the door. "I am. And if you need one, I'm the only one here. I'm busy as hell, but I'd like to work on Old Roger's beautiful house." He takes a final look at it, and smiles. "I hope you restore her. She's special." His eyes meet with mine, and he gives me a small nod. "Anyway, I'll give you my number, in case you need an electrician."

Maybe I'll do to him what he did to me. Never call him. It doesn't matter, that's in the past. If I keep it strictly professional, and not get involved with him, this can work. "Sure, I'll need an electrician."

He reaches into his back pocket, and takes out his wallet. I know I shouldn't, but I glance in to see if there are any pictures of anyone, but I don't manage to see anything. He pulls out a card and hands it to me. His fingers brush a lingering touch against mine, and all the sensations I once felt with him come flooding back. "I'd better go." I pull my hand away from his. He doesn't make any effort to leave. "I've got a job I'm late to."

"Better go then."

He hesitates, but finally makes his way to the front door. Before he leaves, he turns and smiles. "You look just as beautiful as you did the last time I saw you. Actually, probably even more." His lips turn up into a strained smile. "I better get to my customer's house." He walks out the door, and I hear his footsteps make their way down the front stairs.

I can't fall for him again. We've never worked in the past, I can't see how we'd work now. I have to focus to fight any feelings I have for him.

Locking up the house, I get to my truck, start it, and drive straight to May's.

Of all the towns in this country, and of all the people to show up at my door, why did it have to be River? "You're cruel, universe. Here I thought you were showing me the house, and instead you bring River to my doorstep," I say aloud to no one.

Pulling up outside the stable, I lay my head on the steering wheel, wondering why on earth the universe would play such a cruel prank on me.

River Lockwood is the perfect man. From the first moment, I saw him all those years ago in the café, to right now I've wanted him. My head and heart are still aching from seeing him today.

Tap, tap, tap.

Lifting my head, I see May's standing next to my truck. I open the door, and get out. "You okay, May?"

"I was about to ask you the same thing. I came out to see if you were alive. Now I see you're perfectly fine. You look like you've seen a ghost though," she says dramatically. "All flushed in the face, and a bit sweaty around the collar." She stops talking, and her eyes widen. "Unless you were pleasuring yourself in your truck."

"What? No!" I nearly screech.

"Not my business if you go flicking your bean, finger painting..." She moves away as she starts walking back to her house. "Auditioning the finger puppets." She brings two fingers up and wiggles them.

"You don't have to keep going, May. I get the idea of where you're going with this," I say as I follow her.

"Girl's night in," she says over her shoulder. "Buttering your muffin."

Holy shit, will she stop? "Alright, alright. I get it already."

"Well, you better come in and make me a coffee and we can talk about what's eating away at you. We know there was no man between your legs, so it's not that." I can't believe she said that. I think my face is bright red. I walk in behind May, and I'm glad she hasn't turned around to see my horrified expression. Of course, she turns around. "Oh hush, girly. You never had sex before?"

"Oh, I have. I just never talk about it with anyone."

"Make us a coffee. I'm too tired and too old to make my own." She sits on one of the stools at her island counter. "Black, and one sugar for me." I'm not even sure how I got roped into making her a coffee, but I set about making one for her, and one for me. "Tell me about why you looked so..." Please don't say any more masturbation slangs. "Flustered," she says after carefully thinking.

"No reason."

"My built-in bullshit-o-meter is in the red. Let's try this again. What's wrong?"

I may as well tell her. "Um, I saw someone I thought I'd never see again."

"Do I need my gun? Is it the guy you're running from?"

"I'm not running from anyone, May. I left a guy, but I'm not running from him."

"So I need my gun?" She pushes her stool away from the counter.

"No need for guns. Honestly, Grady is normally a good guy who did something completely stupid. Actually, he did two stupid things."

May readjusts her seat. "Once is stupid, twice is intentional. What happened?" she pushes.

I bring over her coffee, and stand leaning against the island. She takes a sip and makes a face. "Don't like it?" I look at the coffee.

"You're certainly not a barista. But it'll do." May is as straightforward as anyone can be. I like knowing where I stand with her. "Don't think you're going to get away with not telling me."

"What do you want to know?"

"Tell me all about this Grady character. He was the one who gave you the bruise?"

"Yeah. He was." I don't know what to say without breaking down and crying. "He came home drunk, accusing me of sleeping with someone else and hit me."

"And?"

"I packed my shit and left."

"Excellent. Some people can fall into the cycle of abuse. Now, tell me why he's a good guy who did some dumb shit? Good guys don't raise their hands to anyone, especially women. And if I recall, he raised his hand to you."

"You saw it." I point to my face, where the bruise has now faded to almost nothing. "He called me and said he was sorry, and that it was him who cheated on me."

"Ahhh, I see," May says. Her grimace says it all. "He tried to blame you for his guilt."

"Basically."

"And now he wants you back?"

I shrug. "I have no idea. I told him to get out of my house."

"You own the house?" May asks, surprised.

"I do. And I'll be selling it."

"Hmm." She raises her brows as she pauses to think. "And is that what you want to do? Sell?"

"I'm not attached to Grady. But I also don't want to live in that house any more, either. I'm happy to move on."

"You can let go, just like that?" May lifts her coffee to take a sip.

Shit, how do I answer this? "I…"

"If you have to think about how to answer, then it's obvious. You and this Grady person weren't destined for each other. Because I can tell you, if you truly loved him, and he truly loved you, neither of you would walk away so easily."

I see the hurt in her eyes, and the way her shoulders slightly slump forward. She has a story, and I hope she tells me. "You loved someone once?" I ask as I lean on the counter, moving forward.

"Not loved, still love." She takes a deep breath and smiles. "But that's a story for another time." She shifts in her seat awkwardly. "Tell me, what had you all flustered outside?"

"A ghost from my past. And not Grady."

"Oh, this is getting good." She rubs her hands together. "Who is he? Or she? I'm one of these new-aged women who believes love is love and as long as it's consensual, then love whoever you want. You can be a lesbian, or a bi-sexual person."

I lift a hand, stopping her from continuing. "Tried that once, not for me," I admit.

"Oh, good for you, girly. That's a story to tell over a few ports, not now. Continue though, who did you see?"

"Just a guy I knew. But it doesn't matter, I won't let myself get involved again."

"Oh, 'again.'" May is quite invested now.

"Actually, not again. Not exactly. It's a bit complicated."

"The more you go on, the better this gets. Well, come on, details! I'm not getting any younger."

I start laughing. "You know what? It doesn't matter. I'll hire him to work on the house, and when I'm done, I'll pay him, sell the house and move."

"What does he do?"

"He's an electrician." Shit. Why did I tell her? She probably knows him. Nah, she can't know *everyone* in the town. He said he's just on the other side of Hope River. I'm probably safe.

"Oh, River Lockwood. How long have you known him?" You have got to be kidding me.

I shake my head. "Nah, it's not him."

"No?" I keep shaking my head. "Then it must be One-eyed Billy Mason. He's got to be pushing eighty-five, he's deaf in one ear, and walks with a limp since he had his knee replaced near ten years ago." Great, only two electricians in town.

Closing my eyes, I let out a long sigh. "It's not Billy Mason."

"No, girly, I never thought it was. That River Lockwood, he's a good boy. Came out here to help me wire up some things in the stable. Actually, in the room you're in. Didn't charge me a single cent. Said he heard I make the best lemon iced tea, and said he'd take that as payment."

Yeah, that sounds like River. A genuinely nice guy. "Did you pay him in form of lemon iced tea?"

"I made some calls, got him work," she responds before lifting her coffee mug, and finishing it. "He'll be helping on Old Roger's house?"

"I'll probably contract with him to do the electrical work." I want to ask questions about River, but I also don't want to get involved and get my heart shattered again. "Anyway, thanks for the coffee May. I've got to look at what I'm going to do with the house. My brother thinks I should torch it."

"You'll do no such thing. That house has meaning, and belongs in this town," her voice cracks with passion.

"But it sat abandoned for how many years before I came along? And in the meantime, no one wanted it, but no one wants me to tear it down."

May stands and takes her mug over to the sink. "Yes, that's right. Because small towns want a say in everything."

I shouldn't take it out on May. "I'm sorry," I say.

"Huh, girly. No need to apologize. Now, get out." She points to the door. "You do have work to do, and that house needs you to make it perfect again." She leans against the counter. "We all need you to make it perfect again."

"Thanks for the coffee, May."

"You're welcome. Get out."

As I leave May's house, I have a feeling Old Roger's house means a lot to everyone in Hope River. That just opens up a whole new world of pressure and responsibility to make Old Roger and the town proud.

Walking back to the stable, I can't get two things out of my head.

One; Old Roger's house.

Two; River Lockwood.

Why did he have to show up looking all sexy? Ugh, this is going to be difficult. But I refuse to get involved with him again.

Nope, not gonna happen. I'm not going to remember the way he used to hold me in his arms. Or the way he used to kiss me. Or even the way he…

Stop it.

Chapter
SEVEN

"ARE YOU READY for the flower festival today?" May asks while I make us a coffee in her kitchen.

"Do I have to do anything special for it? Am I dressed okay?" I look down at my jeans and t-shirt.

"You're dressed fine. Is my coffee ready, girly?"

"Pushy much?" I bring her mug over to her. She lifts it to her mouth, and winces. "Oh come on. You can't say that was a bad coffee."

"Meh," she lifts one shoulder. "It's fine."

"Do you want to ride with me? Or…"

"Or what?" she near snaps.

"Is my truck too high for you? You are, you know." I gesture to her petite height.

"I may be sixty-nine years young, but I can still get around and do things."

Shit, she's sixty-nine? I thought maybe late fifties, but no way in her sixties. "I didn't mean to disparage your age; I meant your height. You're a midget," I say being as sassy to her as she is to me.

May looks at me, her face stoically cold. She nods, pushes off from the stool, picks her mug up and finishes it all in one go. "You'll keep," she says and adds a smile. "Rinse your mug out. I'm not your maid." She grabs her cup, takes it over to the sink, and rinses it.

"I take it I'm driving." I don't mind. It's stupid to take two cars when we're going to the same place. "I'll be in the truck when you're ready."

"I'll be there in a moment."

Taking my phone out of my pocket, I see Charlie's been trying to call me. As I head out, I call his number. "Hey," I say when he answers. "Everything okay?"

"Yeah, just checking in. Have you worked out what you're going to do with the house? I hear Hope River has a great fire department," he says while chuckling.

"I'm not burning it. You'll love the house."

"After I level it, I'm sure I'll adore it."

"Nope, not happening. I'm trying to work it so we can have a more functional space. You'll be here Monday, right?"

"Yeah, yeah. And I know. Bring our tools." Charlie huffs and there's an awkward silence between us. "Grady's been trying to call you."

"Good for him." Charlie knows what happened, but I don't want to recap it anymore.

"Although I already knew, he told me what happened. So, I smashed him."

"You did what? Jesus, Charlie." I run my hands through my

hair as my knee bounces. "I don't need you to fight my battles, I'm pretty good at taking care of myself. Anyway, it's over. I told him to get out because I'm listing the house."

"You moving to Hicksville?"

"No, I'm flipping it and moving on. Like I always do. I think Hope River is way too small for me. And it's not Hicksville, even though that's what I thought when I first got here."

"Small town living, huh?" I can hear the mirth in his voice. "My little sister loving Hope River."

"I'm not. Anyway, there's something else."

"Shit, what now, Hope?" his voice drops.

"You remember River Lockwood?"

"Um." He huffs. "Oh, I think so. You and he were friends in high school, right? His mom is military or something?"

"His dad, yeah."

"What about him?"

"He lives here. And he's an electrician. And I'm hiring him to work on the house." Charlie starts laughing. "What's so funny?" I ask.

"What are the chances of that. Hope and River in Hope River."

Yeah, I've been asking myself that since I arrived. "I know." This has got to be fate's way of telling me I have to do this house, and River has to be part of it too. "Anyway, I'll see you on Monday. May and I are going into town for the flower festival."

"Flower festival? Jesus, Hope, you're already turning into one of them."

"Whatever." I look to my right and see May approaching. "Talk to you later."

"See ya Monday."

May opens the truck door, and places an aluminum covered tray on her seat. I grab it so May can hoist herself up. She does okay for sixty-nine. She easily got up into the truck. I thought I might have needed a stepstool for her; obviously not. "My sister called, and told me my niece will be arriving on Monday."

"Tabitha, right?"

"Yes. She'll be staying with me until at least the end of summer, maybe even longer," May says, her tone quite flat.

"You don't want her to be here that long?"

"It's not that. I adore the girl, but my sister ships her off to me whenever she wants."

"How old is Tabitha?" I'm kind of fitting all the pieces together.

"She's about to have her twenty-third birthday."

"When?"

"Next weekend."

"Huh," I murmur. How bizarre. Shipping your daughter off to your sister's house for her birthday.

"Yes, I know what you're thinking. What type of mother sends their only child off out of their house when the child is about to celebrate a birthday?"

Nodding, she's pretty much hit the nail on the head. "It's not my business."

"Because my sister is the most self-centered person I've ever known, who doesn't give a rat's ass about that child," May angrily spouts. She huffs, as she holds the dish in her lap, making sure it doesn't slide off as I drive. "That poor, poor child."

"Well, look at it this way. Obviously, you want Tabitha here, so maybe we can give her a great party."

May turns to look at me. "Knowing Tabitha, she'll want it to be just her and me. She's very low-key, and doesn't really like being in the limelight."

I already feel for Tabitha, and I don't even know her. It just breaks my heart.

When I arrive in town, I can't help but notice the cars parked as far off as a mile from the town center. "Is it always like this?"

"Whenever we have a festival. It feels like the entire town comes together. Of course, some don't. Like Madge who lives over on Leyburn; she's a patronizing old bat. Or there's Arthur who lives on Delta, he's a flat-out ass. He refuses to have anything to do with Hope River. But when he needs help, he's always the first to put his hand out. There's a few others I don't have time for, but generally speaking, most people come together for the festivals."

"My parents used to take Charlie and me to the state fair once every two years. They used to be heaps of fun. I loved every moment of those fairs, just being with Mom and Dad and Charlie, and going on rides. And eating funnel cake, and cotton candy." My soul is smiling just from the memories.

I drive past all the cars parked on the side of the road. I'm trying to be mindful of May's age. "I can drop you off and double back to park."

"Well, that's a waste of gas, isn't it? Park wherever you find a spot. I can walk, I'm not useless, you know?"

Man, May has a sharp tongue about her. She's not scared to say what she thinks. "Yes, ma'am," I reply as I see a spot ahead. I pull into it, jump out, run around to May's side and take the dish she's made. I don't offer to help her down, because I honestly believe she'd smack my hand away.

"See, it's not too far to walk." She leads the way while I carry the dish and fall into place beside her. "There's going to be a lot of people here who don't know you, but know of you. If anyone is bothering you, point them out to me."

"I'm okay, May."

As May walks, she gives me a sideways glance. "Hmm," she mumbles as she smirks.

The walk takes us only a few minutes, and when we get to the town center, I'm in complete awe. Just as May said, there's one long table down the middle of Main Street, made up of smaller tables joined end-to-end-. There are dishes, platters, bowls with salads and dips all scattered in the middle. There are a few chairs, but mostly people are standing around. May places her dish on the table, looks around, finds a chair, and drags it over.

"Hi, Gran," someone says as they rush past. She gives them a brisk nod.

Then I see the flowers. There are half-barrels everywhere, and they're overflowing with so many different flowers. "Wow," I whisper as I look around, taking in the enormous number of hues.

"Impressive, isn't it?" May asks.

"I've never seen anything like this." Down at the bottom of Main Street, there's a stage set up where a band is playing. "This is crazy." The atmosphere is buzzing, there are people everywhere and kids running around. "Even at the fairs I went to as a kid, it was never like this. There's so much interaction. Everyone really does know everyone."

"You've got that right," May replies.

"Would the pretty lady like a balloon animal?" someone dressed as a clown asks. He holds up a balloon, waiting for me to say yes.

"I'm okay, thank you," I reply.

"Scoot along, Joe. Go entertain the kids," May says as she flicks her hand at him.

"Looking good, Gran," he replies as he traipses past.

"I know," she calls after him.

"Hope, you're here," Eleanor says as she comes out with a mug of coffee for May.

"Yeah, I wouldn't have missed this for anything. This looks like crazy good fun."

"Down at the bottom." Eleanor points toward where the band is playing. "There's a mini Ferris wheel, a bouncy castle, and a few other games for the kids."

"I'll take a walk down and have a look."

"I'll come with you. Gran, are you okay? Do you need anything else?" Eleanor asks May, placing her hand on the older woman's shoulder.

"Go and have fun. I'm perfectly capable of looking after myself." May clutches her bag to her chest as she sternly glares at Eleanor.

"Thanks, Gran." Eleanor leans down and gives May a kiss on the cheek. "You have to see the night festivals. They're something else."

"Hi Elle. Hi Hope," some random kid says to us.

"Hi," both Eleanor and I reply.

"I have to ask," I start saying.

"What?"

"Everyone seems to be calling May 'Gran.' Why?"

Eleanor smiles. "Everyone knows her as Gran. But she doesn't allow anyone to call her Gran until they've proven themselves to her."

"Proven themselves? Like how? Scaling an active volcano?" I joke.

"Nah, she'll let you call her Gran if she knows you're not just passing through. If she thinks you'll put roots down here, then she'll let you call her Gran. Took her near a year to tell me I was allowed to call her Gran."

"Hi Elle, Hi Hope," another random townsperson says.

"Hi," we both reply.

"Everyone calls you Elle."

"Because my name's Eleanor."

"What do you prefer?"

"Elle's fine." The sheriff approaches us, and Eleanor's eyes widen. "Hi, Sheriff," she says in a small voice with a slight break in tone.

"Elle. Hope." He tips his head as he walks past. He looks different in civilian clothes. He looks more buff, but he still walks like a cop.

I can't help but notice the goofy smile on Elle's face, or her flushed cheeks, or her stiffened shoulders. "Ask him out," I say.

"What? Who?" There's that squeaky voice again.

"Come on, you're into him. It's so obvious. Ask him out."

"What? No, I'm not."

"We're back to this, are we? Okay, you don't like him."

I turn, and catch the sheriff checking Elle out. Oh man, these two have to get together. "Come on, let's go in the bouncy castle." Elle grabs my hand and rushes toward the big, inflatable tower. She's already taking her shoes off, and about to jump on it. "Come on," she calls.

"I'm wearing tight jeans; it might not be the best idea."

"Don't be a party pooper. Come on." She turns to the guy manning the jumping castle. "She's with me, Jerry."

He flicks his hand at her, and gives me a 'hurry up' look. "Why not?" I say to myself. Toeing off my shoes, I put them to the side, and go toward the castle. "I haven't been in one of these in years."

Elle's bouncing but slows it down and holds her hands out to me. Her large smile highlights her laugh lines, but nothing compares to the joy in her eyes. "Hurry up," she urges as she thrusts her hands toward me.

Grabbing onto them, she pulls me up, and I go flying into the bouncy castle. I stumble but find my feet before I face plant. Man, falling on the hard-plastic-slash-rubber material of a jumping castle could probably cause some serious burns. "Jeez, lady. Were you a body builder in a previous life?"

Elle smiles. She narrows her eyes, and jokingly says, "I'm one now." Then flexes her arms to show me her non-existent muscles.

We're jumping around, having the time of our lives. There are some younger kids in here, giving us sideways glances. A little girl bouncing around us, says, "Hi Hope. You're really pretty."

I have no idea who this kid is. "Aww, thank you. I love your dress. It's so pretty," I reply.

She stops bouncing and looks down at her knee length, bright flowery dress and smiles. "Thank you. My name is Rose and I'm eight years old, how old are you?"

Oh, okay then. "I'm twenty-five. And I love your name; it's as pretty as your dress."

"My Mommy and Daddy were talking about you. They said you bought Old Roger's house. Mommy said Old Roger was nice to kids. He'd save the best candy for them on Halloween."

"Rose, come on," I hear a lady call from the side.

"Sorry, I have to go. Mommy's calling me."

"Okay, well nice meeting you, Rose."

"Bye." She gives me a wave as she bounces her way over to the side of the castle, then jumps into her mom's arms. Her mom gives me a smile, and a small wave.

"Everyone here is super friendly," I say to Elle. "I'm not sure I know how to take that. It's kind of overwhelming."

"When I first came here, I had all these people talking to me, asking if I needed anything, offering everything from a home-cooked meal, to a place to stay, even money to help me. This is really a small town, and if you think for one moment you can keep something you're doing a secret, then you have another thing coming."

"So I'm gathering."

Elle jokingly pushes me, and I topple backward, one leg going in one direction, the other in the complete opposite way. It's at that moment I hear my jeans rip.

"Shit," I say as I stand and look for where they've ripped. I can't see anything, so I try to see if the butt seam has torn open.

This is where Elle is doubling over because she's laughing hysterically. "No! Please tell me it hasn't split?" I instantly move my hands to find, that I have indeed split the seam. "Crap."

Elle can barely stand from all the laughter. I move along the wall, using it as a barrier so no one can see. "Your ass is hanging out." She points, before collapsing on the castle floor from laughter.

"Elle. I'm not wearing underwear!"

"I know! I saw your butt. It's as white as snow."

My face has its own heartbeat because of how red it's become. "I've got to go. Help me."

Elle's laughing so hard but she manages to come over to me. "I'll stand behind you as you walk. I live across the road from the café, and I'm sure I have a pair of shorts you can borrow." She tilts her head to the side. "You're going commando, so, you know what, keep them. I don't want them back."

"This is so embarrassing. I can't believe this happened."

"Why aren't you wearing underwear?" Elle asks as she slides her shoes on. Crap, I have to put mine on too. This is going to be fun. I try to wedge my foot in while I use the castle to hide my wardrobe malfunction.

"Because I haven't had a moment to do laundry, and I only brought enough clothes to last a few days."

Elle wipes at her cheeks, and bursts into laughter again.

"Hi Elle, Hi Hope," some woman says.

You have got to be kidding. Can y'all stop saying hello to me! "Hi," I say trying to remain as nice as possible. But the air my butt is getting makes it a bit hard to keep a smile on my face.

"Don't mind her, she split her pants," Elle says as she points to me.

"Elle!" I shriek. "Why would you say that?" I say through gritted teeth, while trying to hold my butt seam together.

"Trust me, by the time we get back to Gran, she'll be laughing so hard." She flicks her hand. "Now, walk ahead of me, and I'll stick to your rear." She bursts into laughter again. "This is priceless."

"Not for me," I grunt as I start walking toward where May's sitting, which is apparently close to where Elle lives. Oh no. No. No. No. Who do I see walking toward me but River. Why? "Shit," I say as I duck my face, hoping he hasn't seen me.

"Hope?" He stops walking to talk to me.

"Hey," I say as I look behind me at Elle giving her the *'please help me'* eyes. "How are you?" Shit, why did I ask? I need to get out of here, and quickly.

"I'm great. I didn't know you'd be coming to the festival." River looks to me, and his eyes dart behind me. "Elle," he says, acknowledging her.

"Hey, River."

Great, a reunion. This is not what I need right now. "So," River says, dragging out the "o."

Even better, an *awkward* reunion.

Clenching my butt cheeks together, I can feel the air nipping at the skin. I move my hand as discreetly as I can to cover the giant hole in my jeans showcasing my ass to the entire world. This is super uncomfortable, I have to get out of here.

"Are you okay?" he asks looking between Elle and me.

"Yeah, but I've got to go." I point behind him.

"Hope, remember we've got to do that thing?" Elle says trying to save me. But her words are so rigid, that I can't help and turn and give her a what-the-fuck, look. She narrows her eyes at me.

"Okay, then. Don't let me stop you two ladies from doing *that thing*," River says. He steps closer to me, and I stiffen. His warm breath touches my cheek before his lips do. He slowly kisses my cheek. "Bye."

"Bye," I say with a voice crack. River walks away, and I relax my shoulders and let out a long sigh. What a terribly uncomfortable encounter. I know he was being nice, but I was rigid as hell trying to hide my lily-white ass from the greater population of Hope River.

"Whoa, have you two got history or something?" Elle asks. "And my flat is up there." She points ahead on the left.

"Something," I say.

"Oh, tell me. What happened between you and River? I can't believe...oh my God!" she shrieks excitedly. "How cool. You're Hope, and he's River, and you're both in Hope River."

"May said the same thing."

"Stop here." Elle takes a set of keys from her pocket and opens the door, indicating for me to enter first. "I've already seen your ass once, one more time won't hurt. Top of the stairs, the apartment on the right." I get to the top of the stairs, and wait at the landing. Elle comes up behind me, unlocks the door, and steps in. "You have a cute butt, Hope. I was thinking of pinching your cheeks, but thought I'd better not."

"Can we pretend this never happened? Please?" I beg as I follow her into her apartment. Looking around, I notice how quaint and cozy it is. "This is cute."

"Come into the bedroom." We walk down a short corridor that opens up to a fairly spacious eat-in kitchen and a living room with a small balcony. I go to look outside, where Elle has a view of Main Street. I can see River walking up the street a fair distance away. But I'd recognize his stride anywhere. "Hey, ass girl. My bedroom is back here."

"Sorry." I come back in, and go to Elle's bedroom. "Wow, I love this." She has fairy lights hanging up in her room, and a dream catcher positioned over her headboard. "Not what I expected," I say honestly.

"You thought I was more conservative?" she laughs.

"You got me. I thought I'd see a room filled with religious artifacts."

She rummages around in her closet. "Dress? Pants? Skirt?" she calls.

"Whatever you can bear to part with," I say, chuckling at my own pun.

She walks out holding a flowery dress, or a pair of black cargo pants that I normally live in. "Which one?" She looks at the dress and shakes her head. "I'll put the dress back. You're not wearing underwear, and I'm not giving you any of mine. You really need to do laundry, Hope. Here." She throws the cargo pants at me. "Bathroom is over there." She signals to a door on the left.

"Thank you," I call as I enter the bathroom. I slide my jeans down, and pick them up once they're off. "Holy shit," I say as I smile to myself. I can see the humor. This hole is massive. I thought it was smaller. I slide on the cargos, and find they're a bit big for me. But hey, beggars can't be choosers. I fold the jeans, and come out of Elle's bathroom. "Thank you; you're a life saver. Here, let me pay you for these." I take some money out of the pocket of my jeans.

"Not necessary. Consider it a favor, and one day you can pay it back."

"But when? Once this house is flipped, I'll be leaving."

"Who knows when we'll cross paths again. Anyway, it's all good." She holds a hand up. "Should we head back down to the festival? Oh, and River. You were going to tell me about you two."

It's not exactly something I want to relive, so I try and redirect the conversation. "You know what I need?"

"What?"

"I need a drink."

We head down the stairs again. "Hope River doesn't really have much of a nightlife. But there's a few nice places about twenty minutes from here. I'm sure you can find something there."

When I'm through, we head back down to the festival. May's

still sitting at the table, and we join her. "Hi," we both say together.

"Do you want another coffee, Gran?" Elle asks.

"No." May looks at the jeans neatly folded on my lap. "Why did you change?" She then looks at the pants I'm wearing. "And why are you wearing Elle's pants?"

I look around me, checking no one is too close. Leaning in, I whisper, "I split my jeans in the bouncy castle."

I wait for May's reaction. She stares at me, her face emotionless. Until she bursts into laughter. "Please tell me no one saw your underwear?" she says between fits of laughter.

"Oh, no, this one gets better, Gran. She's not wearing any," Elle laughs.

May stops laughing, and swings her head around so quickly to look at me. "Why weren't you wearing undergarments, girly?" I'm so embarrassed. "Were you waiting to get lucky? That only works if you wear dresses with no panties under it."

"Gran!" Elle says loudly.

"Pants aren't easy access. Trust me, I know."

I lower my head, and bring my hand up to hide my blistering face. "I wasn't trying to get some action, May. I haven't had time to do laundry, that's all."

"Oh hush, you haven't had time. You haven't even started on Old Roger's house yet, you've got plenty of time," she scolds.

She's kinda right. I've had the time to do laundry, I just haven't wanted to. "Fine, I'll do laundry tomorrow."

"Why not tonight?" May is certainly a pushy old lady. But so damn cool.

"I'd like to go out for a drink tonight."

"Nowhere here to drink. There are a few places not far from here. You're not going to drink and drive, are you?" she asks.

"No, I'll catch a cab." Both Elle and May make a groaning sound. "What?" I ask looking between the two of them.

"You may have trouble finding a cab any time we have festivals," Elle answers.

"Why?"

"We don't have a lot of cabs here. No one really needs them."

I chuckle to myself. Charlie called Hope River, Hicksville. Now I see, it kinda is. "Aha."

"What time are you going?" May asks, looking at Elle first, then me.

"Oh, um. I'm not sure Hope wanted me to go with her," Elle says. I can tell she's embarrassed May has even suggested it.

"I was hoping you would," I say.

"Yes! I haven't been out in such a long time. Between everything I do, I never have time to let loose."

"So it's settled. I'll take you both, and come pick you up," May says.

"Wait, what just happened?" I ask looking between a smirking May, and a surprised Elle.

"Girly, you have to learn. In a small town, we all rely on each other. So, when we get home, you get ready, and I'll take you. Elle, it makes sense if you get your things and come back to my house to get ready. That way I'm not driving all over the place. When you've finished drinking, I'll come and collect you both. That way I know you're both safe."

"Thanks, Gran." Elle jumps up and gives May a quick kiss on the cheek.

"Um, thank you," I say. But I can't really expect May to wait until we're ready to come home to come and get us.

The next two hours is spent walking around, eating way too much food, and talking to people I've never met or seen before, but who all know my name.

"Another Long Island iced tea," Elle says as she signals the bartender.

"Elle, I think you need to slow down on these," I caution her.

"Huh." She slouches in her seat, before looking at me and blinking rapidly. "Oh!" she slurs. "You should marry Rivrrrr." She starts laughing.

I blink a few times trying to see one of Elle, not two. "What? Why?"

She starts laughing, and garbles some noises. She leans over, and places her hand on my leg. "Cause you can be married in Hope Rivrrrr, bwahahaha. Hope and Rivrrrr. Rivrrrr. You can swim in the Rivrrrr. Bwahahahaha."

"Bartender!" I call. "Another White Russian." I hold my empty glass up to him.

"Hello, ladies. How are you tonight?" some guy says to us.

Elle looks at me, and starts laughing again. "We're gay," she announces.

"We're gay," I echo.

"Can I watch?" the guy asks as he leans on the bar and gives us a sleazy smirk.

Elle looks at me, I look at Elle, and we burst into laughter again. "We're gay for each otha," I slur. "You're not gay." I waggle my finger in his face.

"But I'm okay to watch, if you are." He winks at us. He sends a creepy vibe through me.

"You two ladies have had enough. Last drinks," the bartender says to us as he places our Long Island iced tea and White Russian down in front of us.

"Here." I throw a twenty at him.

"No! Don't take hers, take mine!" Elle snatches my twenty back, chucking it at me, and shoves her twenty at him.

"Take mine, I was faster." I push mine to him.

He looks bored. He rings up our drinks, then comes back and places the change on the bar. "Last ones," he says again sternly.

"I'll get you both home," says the creepy guy who's still lurking.

"Nah, we don't like men," Elle says. "Shoo." She flicks her hand at him, and we both continue laughing.

I'm not even sure what happens to him, but when I look around I realize there aren't many people left in here. "Hey, Elle. What time is it?"

Elle's holding her drink in her hand, and tips it all over herself when she looks at her wrist. "My drink!" she yells. She grabs her shirt, and tries to suck the drink off of it.

I'm laughing so hard I nearly fall off my bar stool. I drink my White Russian fast, and look at the empty glass. "What happened to my drink?" I look around for the culprit who drank it.

"You just drank it."

"Did I?"

"Bartender!" I call. He walks over to us, and stands, staring at us with his arms crossed across his chest. "One Russian who's white." I hold up three fingers, laughing. "And she'll have an iced tea from short island." I'm absolutely losing it.

"I told you, you're both cut off. No more."

"Can I have a Russian who's pink then? And a leaf from the short island?"

"No more." He shakes his head, but smiles.

"A yellow Russian? Or even just a Russian? And a drop from the island?" I beg.

"Do you want me to call someone to come get you?" he asks with a smile.

"Hey, Hope. We should walk home. Can you walk?" Elle asks as she stumbles toward the doors. "It's not that far." She leans into me, and we both nearly topple.

"You two are too drunk to walk anywhere. I'm calling someone for you," the bartender says. "Who am I calling?"

"What time is it?" I squint, trying to focus on my phone. "Shit!"

"What?" Elle asks.

"It's three in the morning. Is it three?" I ask the bartender.

"It is."

I point to him. "I love you. You're looking after us." Elle staggers back to me, and drapes her arm over my shoulders. "I love you too."

"I love you, man," she responds.

"I love you." I hug her tight.

"I love you," she says, her head nestling into my shoulder.

"I love you."

"I love you."

"I love you both, but now it's time to go home and sleep it off," the bartender says to us. "Who am I calling?"

"Sheriff!" Elle screams way too loud and runs out the front door on unsteady legs.

"I love you," I say again to the bartender as I follow Elle. The moment the night air hits me, my head begins to spin. "Oh, I don't feel good," I say. Looking around, I see Elle double over in the bushes, vomiting. "Elle." I wobble over to hold her vibrant red hair back as she vomits in the bushes. "Elle."

"I feel sick." She looks up at me, smiles, then vomits again.

The sounds of her throwing up makes me dry retch.

Bluch.

Hold it together, Hope.

Bluch.

I try to focus on making the world to stop spinning, and see a car driving toward us. The red and blue lights twirling around make me wobblier than I was only a few seconds ago.

"Hope?" I hear the deep voice call.

I look around, trying to figure out where the voice is coming from.

"Elle?" the voice breaks.

"God?" I look up, trying to stare at the sky. "Is that you?"

"Hope!" The voice is beside me now. I look to see the sheriff, and startle back when I notice him standing beside me. "What are you two doing here?"

I start tapping on Elle, hitting her repeatedly. "What?" Elle says once she lifts her head from the bushes. "Oh." Her eyes light up, and she smiles. "Hi there, Sheriff."

"What are you two doing out this late?" he asks looking between us.

"She was doing White Russians. I was doing long tea…islands. I think?"

"Were you just throwing up in the bushes?" The Sheriff looks over Elle's shoulder, rolls his eyes then shakes his head.

"Why are you spinning?" I ask him.

Elle holds her hands out, joining at the wrists. "You can handcuff me if you want?" She bats her eyelashes at him. "I've been a very bad girl."

"Get in the car. The both of you." He walks over and opens the back door for us.

"You can arrest me for being runk and 'sordily. Will you frisk me?" Elle asks. "Please?"

"Get in the damned car."

"Shhh. You gotta be quiet, Elle. 'Member it's a secret." I hold my finger up to my lips.

"What's a secret?" the Sheriff asks.

"Shhh. Don't tell him," I say.

Elle leans over and whispers, "Don't tell him what?"

"You like him. Shhh." Elle and I begin laughing.

The sheriff starts driving, and before I know it, the car stops. I open my eyes and I'm home. The door opens, and I'm being moved out of the back seat. I feel weightless.

"Dear Lord, how much did those two drink?" I hear May asking.

"The bartender said they put away quite a lot. They'll be in pain tomorrow. Don't let this one off too easily." He chuckles.

"I have no intentions of that." May laughs too.

Opening my eyes, I find myself being carried to bed. "Thank you," I say.

"I'll leave her to you. I've got to get Elle home."

"You think it's a good idea you leave her on her own tonight?" May asks.

The Sheriff blows out a long sigh. "You're probably right. I'll take her home with me and keep an eye on her."

"You're a good man, Jacob. A good man. I'm glad I took a chance on you."

"Have a good rest of the night, Gran."

I turn over in my bed, drag the covers up over my shoulders, and wait for the room to stop spinning.

Chapter
EIGHT

WAKING, I INSTANTLY sit up in bed. My head pounds, and my stomach is gurgling. Looking around, I try and figure out how I got here. There's a large glass of water next to the bed, and a packet of Tylenol too.

I blink several times, and try to get the dry, furry feeling out of my mouth. Light is coming through the window, and I can't help but feel the nausea quickly rising through my stomach, to the back of my throat.

Crap, I'm going to be sick.

Pushing the covers back, I grab my phone and I run into the bathroom, only just making it to the toilet bowl.

"Oh my God, am I dying?" I slide down against the wall, its coolness instantly making me feel better.

I look at my phone and see I have a message from Elle. **What happened last night?**

Chuckling, I reply, *I think we drank too much. I don't remember how I got home.*

All I know is I'm in the Sheriff's guest room.

Oh my God, did you two have sex? Wait...how did you get there?

No idea how I got here. And no, I don't think we had sex. I'm still in my clothes, except for my shoes. I gotta go, Sheriff just knocked on the door. Fill you in when I know more.

My God, what a night!

From outside the bathroom window, I hear the tractor starting. My head responds with increased thumping. "Shit."

It takes me a good minute to lift myself off the tiled floor, and make my way out of the bathroom. I grab the huge glass on my nightstand and drink all the water. Heading outside, I blink several times, trying to adjust to the bright light and the roar of the tractor. The very tractor May is riding on. She sees me, and pulls up beside me without turning the noisy machine off. She's wearing a straw hat that shades her face from the sun. But I can still see her smile. "Morning, girly," she yells to be heard over the tractor's roar.

I hold up a hand, and offer a small wave.

"Had a good night, did ya?"

"I can't recall a lot of it. I have no idea how I got back here."

"You can thank Jake for that."

Jake? The sheriff? What does he have to do with getting me home? "The sheriff?" I ask.

"Yes, ma'am. You best call him and thank him. Oh, and I need help with some yard work. Breakfast is waiting for you, then you better get your ass out here to help." May doesn't wait for me to say anything. The tractor roars even louder, and she takes off down the back of the yard. I swear she's doing it on purpose.

Shit, I better get myself ready to help May. I don't remember agreeing to doing this, but I have no idea what happened last night. Considering May's kind enough to let me live here, the least I can do is help her do some yard work, even if I am hungover.

The entire day I've been feeling green. I've helped May with yard work. The suffering eased down, but only just. Thankfully, May's cooked dinner.

"Girly, set the table," she calls.

Getting up from the porch swing, I head in and set the dining table. I walk back into the kitchen, and watch as May effortlessly flows in the kitchen. "You've been in the yard most of the day, and you still have energy to cook?"

"Yes, but you're cleaning though. And I need help flipping the mattress in Tabitha's room."

"Of course."

She continues cutting ingredients into a bowl. "May," I say in a small voice.

"Yes."

"If I did or said anything last night that offended you, I'm genuinely sorry."

Her hand stills for a second, before she keeps chopping a cucumber. "The only thing I'm offended about is I told both you and Elle to call me when you were ready to come home. Instead, Jake shows up here, near four in the morning, with two very drunk young women. I know almost everyone in Hope River, and I know you'd be safe here. But in the neighboring towns, I don't know even half of the people."

Aww, how beautiful. She's concerned for us.

"And before you go telling me you're both old enough to look after yourselves, this is only about safety. Neither of you could even stand up last night." May is so lovely. I know she means well, and she did ask me to call her when we wanted to come home. "Anything could've happened to either or both of you."

I walk around to her, and give her a hug. "I'm sorry, May. I should've called. Next time, I promise to call you."

"Next time? Next time, I'm coming with you both. You guys looked like you had fun."

Oh yeah. May getting drunk with us. Now, that would be crazy fun. "Which is Tabitha's room? I can flip the mattress while you finish up in here. Oh, and where are the bed sheets?"

"Tabitha's room is last door on the right down the hallway, and there are clean sheets on the bed. Flip the mattress and turn it top to bottom," she commands.

I walk down the hallway, and stop to look at some of the framed photos on the pale green walls. "Who's this?" I ask as I point to a family photo. I smile, loving the old fashioned family photos. It's so different now, everything's instant and digital.

In this particular photo, the parents are standing a good foot apart with serious looks, no smiles, and squinted eyes. Then there's an older girl standing to one side, and a younger one standing in the front. No one is smiling. How bizarre that they don't look happy.

"Which one are you looking at?" May calls from the kitchen. She cranes her neck, and smiles when she sees me staring at the photo. "Oh, that one." She wipes her hands, and I hear her walking toward me. "Well, that's Mama and Papa." She points to the obvious parents. "That's me. I was about sixteen I think there. And that's my younger sister. She would've been six. There's ten years' difference between us. She's Tabitha's mother. And that house." She points to the tiny shack in the background. "Is this house."

"Really? Wow, this is so different." I tap on the photo.

"Yes ma'am, it is. My sister couldn't wait to get away, and she did. I couldn't have thought of anything worse. So, I stayed."

"I don't mean to sound horrible, but in those days, large families were fairly normal."

May smiles as she stands staring at the photo. "My mother

had a lot of problems carrying children." She lowers her head slightly, before turning and walking back to the kitchen.

"I'm sorry." I've unearthed some pain for May. "I'll get to the bed." Opening the last door on the right, I'm greeted with a bright room that has shutters on the windows, an unmade bed pushed up under the window, a large chest of drawers and a door leading to what I think is a walk-in. I get to flipping the mattress, and making the bed. And when I leave the freshly made bedroom, May's already sitting at the dining table, waiting for me so we can have our early dinner.

"How's the head?" May asks. I sit, and May starts serving herself. "That boy was asking about you," she says casually.

"Who? River?" I ask eagerly. Shit, calm it down. I can't go back there again. "I mean, River?" I ask with a more subdued tone.

"Huh." May huffs, and props up an eyebrow. "Yes, *that* boy." She places a generous helping of salad on her plate.

"Oh, really?" Damn my squeaky voice. "Not that I care or anything, but what were you talking about?" I push my food around on my plate, pretending I don't care. May doesn't reply. When I look up at May, she lifts her chin, takes a deep breath, then crosses her arms in front of her chest. "What?"

"Really?" is all she says.

"What?"

"You obviously still care for him, and judging by what he was saying and asking, he still cares for you. Go out there, and talk to him."

"You have to tell me what you both talked about."

"What is this, Hope? Are we back in school where we're passing notes to each other?" She waggles her finger at me. "I'm not interfering." She kinda already has. "If you two are meant to be, you'll figure it out."

Reality takes over, and I shake my head. "We've tried that, and it didn't work. Anyway, you're right, you'd better not tell me. I don't need to know, because it'll just complicate something that doesn't need complicating. He works for me, that's it. Nothing more." May smiles as her head slowly nods. "What?"

"Good luck to you, girly. You're gonna need it."

What's that supposed to mean? And why the hell are the butterflies going crazy at the mere mention of his name?

Chapter
NINE

RECOGNIZE THE sound of Charlie's truck the moment I hear it.

Jumping up from my bed, I run outside to see his truck pulling up next to mine. "Charlie!" I yell. The moment he's out of his truck, I hug him tight. I don't know why, but I burst into tears. I've never felt so happy to see Charlie.

"Hey, are you okay?" he asks as he cradles me tight to his body.

"I'm just so happy to see you." I step back and wipe at my eyes. "Oh my God."

"It's my devilish charm you missed, isn't it?" he asks sarcastically.

"You're an idiot." I smack him on the arm. "Come, you have to meet May. She's so much fun. Did you find it okay? Did you come straight here?"

"One question at a time." I hook my arm through his, as we

walk toward May's home. I'm so happy to see Charlie. I didn't think I'd have a reaction like this one. "I found Hope River okay, it's actually a really pretty drive out. And I found this place okay too, obviously."

We walk up the front steps of May's house and I knock on the door.

May appears, wiping her hands on a tea-towel. "May, this is my brother Charlie."

May opens the door and casts an eye over Charlie. "You two are related?"

"Yes, ma'am, we are," Charlie replies with a smile.

"Hmmm. Thankfully, your parents have good genes. Both of you are attractive."

"Thank you," Charlie says in a deeper, manlier voice. He's all cocky at being called attractive.

I roll my eyes at Charlie's bravado. "Yeah, yeah, Whatever." I pinch him on the arm. "I just wanted to introduce you to May."

"Come in, I've made a pitcher of lemon iced tea, and there's a glass for each of you." May leaves the door open, and starts walking toward the kitchen.

"Be good," I whisper to Charlie.

He winks at me, and instantly I know he's going to charm May. He's been loved by every older person we've ever encountered. "What a beautiful home you have," Charlie says to May as he looks around.

"Your sister said the same thing."

"May, do you mind if I show him the picture?"

"Not at all." May takes out three tall glasses from her cabinet, and then heads to the fridge to retrieve the pitcher.

"Have a look at this." Charlie and I walk down the hallway. I stop in front of the family photo I was admiring yesterday. "See this house?" I point to the background. Charlie nods. "That's this house."

"Wow, I love it." Charlie does what I do. When we enter a home, we look at how straight a wall is, if the ceiling is caving in anywhere, or if the floors are even. "This is beautiful."

"Wait 'til you see the house I bought."

Charlie's shoulders drop. "I brought gasoline, a rag and a lighter. It's not too late."

The butterflies are stirring in my stomach, I'm super excited about this house. "Nope, no way."

"Ugh," Charlie huffs. "Fine. Just so you know though, I'm going to love this demo."

"You haven't even seen it yet."

We walk back toward the dining room where May's waiting for us. "Have you drawn up plans yet?"

"I'm trying but I'm not sure what I want to do with it yet. Definitely add square footage."

"Up or out, or both?" Charlie asks.

"I'm thinking both. But wait 'til I take you out there. You may have some ideas."

"If I can interrupt. You know you'll need permits?" May asks.

"Yeah. I haven't researched what I need for them yet. I do know that it's never the same in any two towns or counties."

"I can help there. Just let me know when you submit them, and I'll come with you. I can get them through for you faster," May offers.

"Really? Thank you," I reply.

"Yes, thank you, May," Charlie echoes. He takes a sip, and licks his lips. "This is really good."

"Of course, it is," May scoffs. "I made it."

I smile from behind my glass. Finishing my drink, I stand and indicate to Charlie to hurry up. "I'm sorry, May, but we have to go. I'm going to take Charlie over to Old Roger's house so we can walk it."

Charlie quickly finishes his drink, and takes our glasses over to the sink. "Thank you for the tea."

May follows holding the half empty pitcher. "You can stay with your sister. The sofa folds out, and it's comfortable." She's always so direct when she speaks. I dig that about May.

"Thank you," I say.

She flicks her hand. "Thank you, May," Charlie says. We walk out, and go to my truck. "I like her."

"Yeah, she's awesome. She's quite direct though. If she didn't like you, she wouldn't have let you stay with me."

"Let's head over and look at this house. Once we get some water and electricity in there, I'll stay there. Don't want to cramp your style."

"Cramp my style? Really?" I start my truck, and head down the long dirt driveway. "This is a tiny town, Charlie. Keep it in your pants, okay."

"Pfft. I'll behave myself, don't worry. Anyway, it's Hicksville, and I ain't putting anything of mine in anyone here." *Sure.*

We head through the town, and Charlie chuckles. "What?"

"This is it? The main street?"

"Yeah, it's not huge. The hardware store is okay, they can order stuff if we need it. About twenty minutes that way, there's a lumber yard, and a really good tile store. There's also a place that does custom kitchens, and the marble they have is gorgeous. But I'll keep looking."

"So, there's no way I can convince you to torch it?" I smack Charlie on the leg. "That's a definite no, eh?"

"No." We get to the house in no time, and I pull the truck up along the curbside. "Here she is." Getting out of the truck, I'm super excited to get in there.

"Ugh." He screws his nose up, and his lips turn down.

"Wow," I say the moment Charlie groans.

"It's a jungle out here."

"I've bought worse, Charlie. Remember…the first one we did." I tap my finger to my mouth trying to remember the street name. "Stony Crescent."

The second I say the street name, Charlie moans. "Shit, yeah. That was so bad."

"You wanted to knock that one down too. And what happened?"

"We made a shit ton of cash on it."

"Yep. Trust me. This old girl, she's something special."

"You've only ever lost money on one flip we did. And that was because the market tanked just as we finished. You do have a knack." We walk toward the front door. "The roof is shit and needs replacing."

"Yep."

"And there's a damned ivy vine growing up the side of the house, and likely inside the walls."

"Yep."

"The yard is like one massive jungle." He keeps pointing out all the negatives.

"Yep. Careful of those; you'll fall through the porch." I point to the rotting deck. Unlocking the front door, I step through and smile.

"Oh man." Charlie looks straight up and sees the coffer ceiling. "Shit, look at that. I haven't seen something like that in years."

"Yep. And I want to maintain it."

"There are a few different styles going on in here."

"There are." I lean against the wall, taking in every moment of this beautiful old house. "I'm thinking."

Charlie interrupts, "Shit, here we go."

"Move the staircase to the side. And open this entire area up." I use my hands to describe to Charlie what I want.

"Moving the staircase? Alright. What's over there?"

"Go have a look. It's a weird ass layout. A room in a room that opens up here, and over there."

Charlie walks in one way, then out the other. "It's dark. But it's obvious it isn't an add-on. Whoever had this house did some minor renovations. See here?" He points to the ceiling. There's a gap between where the wall should end, and the ceiling.

"I didn't notice that before."

"They probably needed extra space, and added a temporary room. What's over here?"

"The dining room."

Charlie walks in, and looks around. "This is massive." I nod. "And back here is the kitchen?" I nod again. He walks through the small door, and walks out not even a moment later. "Dark, and dingy. And there's a crappy half bath in the kitchen."

"Yeah, I'm thinking of taking this all back to studs. Strip it down. Try to maintain these floors though, and the coffer ceiling."

"There's almost no way we can keep the floors. We'll try, but I doubt it. What's upstairs?"

"Four bedrooms and a tiny bathroom."

"Give me a minute." He goes to the staircase, grabs hold of the railing and rocks it. "Yeah, real safe," he sarcastically says before taking off up the stairs. I can hear him walking around, and it doesn't take long for him to come down again. "It's tight up there. If you want to make any real impact, you're going to have to go out." He looks to the back, then disappears into the kitchen again. When he returns, he's scratching his chin. "No back door?"

"No back door."

"Show me the back." I lock up, and we make our way down the porch and around to the back. "Where's the border of the land?"

"See that line of trees down there?" I point into the distance. "There. We have room. And once we get it cleaned up, we'll see exactly what we're dealing with. But I'm still thinking." I grit my teeth because I know what Charlie is going to say. "Let's push this wall out, giving us extra living area down stairs. Upstairs, we can have a master retreat, with four bedrooms."

"Five bedrooms? Why five bedrooms?"

"The one thing I've noticed is families usually stay here for several generations. May has her niece coming to stay with her, and I'm sure others are the same."

"How far do you want to push this out? Like what, ten feet?"

"Maybe fifteen."

"Hope, what are you going to do with all that space downstairs? Create a ballroom?"

"Maybe a second master bedroom suite, and an office."

Charlie stares at me for a few seconds, before rubbing at his temples. "Whatever you want to do, Hope. You're the boss. But remember, it's just a house."

"Yeah, I know."

"When do you think you can have the plans drawn up?"

"A week, maybe ten days."

Charlie huffs, and takes one final look around. "Well, I have my tools here. You've already called for a dumpster, so I can start ripping the kitchen and bathrooms out."

"Get it tested for lead and asbestos first."

Charlie pushes me as we're walking back to my truck. "This ain't my first rodeo, baby sis. I know."

Opening the door to jump into the truck, I take one final look at the house, and smile. It's okay, old girl, I'm going to bring you back to life.

Meow.

Charlie and I both look at each other, then around. "Did you hear that?" I ask.

"Yeah, I think so."

Meow.

"There's a cat somewhere close." I look in the truck, but there's no cat. *Meow.* "You've got to be kidding!"

"What?" Charlie looks to where I'm staring.

There's a gray and white cat sitting in the bed of my truck. "Shoo," I say as I tap on the window for it to disappear. The cat turns its head, looks at me, and lets out a *meow*. Then it continues ignoring me. "Hey, get out."

Charlie gets out of the truck's cab. The cat sees him and jumps out of the bed and struts away. When Charlie gets back in, I watch as the cat sits, looking around it. *Meow.*

"Does this shit house come with a cat?" Charlie asks.

"Hell no. I'm not a cat person. It's the first time I've seen it here. It'll probably be gone by tomorrow." I drive away, not thinking twice about the stupid cat. "When we get back, if you want to familiarize yourself with what the town has, and the town over. I'm going to try and figure out the plans of the house. Find someone to take care of those crazy weeds and bushes."

"Yeah, on it. Let's get that cleaned out, and I'll call to get the dumpster delivered. I wanna get a start on this as quickly as possible. What's the time frame?"

"I want to push this out in twelve to fourteen weeks."

"Man, that's tight. It's a huge job, Hope, and if there's asbestos or lead it'll take longer."

We pull up at May's and I see another car in the driveway. When Charlie and I get out of the truck and head toward the stable, I hear May calling out to me. "Hope, Charlie, come here and meet my niece."

"Ugh, does she do that a lot?" Charlie mumbles under his breath.

"Not really, she keeps to herself. Stop being an ass, and come say hi to her niece."

"Fine. Only because she's nice enough to let me stay with you."

"Honestly, she doesn't meddle."

We walk up the stairs to the front door. May is holding it open for us. "Come in, come in. I want you both to meet Tabitha. Tabitha, come meet Hope and her brother Charlie."

"Hang on a second," Tabitha calls from the back of the house. Probably the bedroom I made up for her. From the back I hear footsteps approaching, and when I turn to look at Tabitha, I know without one single iota of doubt, Charlie is in trouble. Tabitha is just the most stunning woman I've ever seen. She's wearing a sundress that goes to her knees with black cowboy boots. Her long blonde hair falls to just below her shoulders, and she has pale, flawless skin making her vibrant green eyes pop.

"Hello, I'm Tabitha," she introduces herself. "My aunt has told me all about you. Hope, and Charlie, right?"

"Hi. Such a pleasure to meet you too." I hold my hand out to her. I turn to Charlie who looks like he's swallowed his tongue. He's staring at Tabitha. "And this is my brother, Charlie."

"Hi." She smiles at him.

"Um. Hi." He shakes his head slightly and blinks rapidly a few times.

"It's really nice meeting you, Tabitha. Charlie and I have a lot of work to do, and I'm sure you want to catch up with your aunt. Have a good night."

"We'll talk in the morning. Will you and Charlie join us for breakfast?"

"Yes!" Charlie yells. I look at him, and smack his arm. "I mean, yes, thank you." Charlie better keep his hormones in check, because I don't want him screwing Tabitha around.

"Thank you." I start moving toward the door, and Charlie hasn't moved. "Charlie!"

"Yep, I'm coming. Nice meeting you," he says to Tabitha

before turning and jogging up to me. "Oh, shit," he whispers as we leave.

I stop walking, and grab his arm. "Don't try to chase that girl, Charlie. I know what you're like, she's exactly the type you go for."

"I know, I know. Okay, I promise, I won't do anything with her." He crosses his heart. "Just so you know, it's going to kill me. But I won't do anything."

"This is a tiny town, and everyone knows everything. Don't screw this up."

"I said I won't. Have some faith in me."

"I do," I sigh. "Right, let's get to work." We head to the stable, where I start thinking about a new floor plan for Old Roger's house.

Chapter
TEN

"HOPE, HOW ARE things?" Elle asks as she rushes around the café. "Coffee?"

"Yes, please. How are you? I haven't had a chance to talk to you since our night out."

Elle starts laughing. "Jake said I was throwing up in the bushes out in front of the bar, and you were holding my hair back."

"Oh God," I whisper as I feel my face burning. "I forgot about that. Did he say anything else?"

"No."

I look around the café, and the only person who can hear is that old guy at the counter. I lean over and motion for Elle to come closer. When she does, I whisper, "Did you and the Sheriff…?"

"Nope. No, it's not like that with him. We're friends." She winces without making eye contact with me.

"Are you?" I ask.

"Nothing happened. Nothing's going to happen. It's not like that for us, okay?"

Hmm, we'll see. "Okay," I say placating her. Even so, I'm sure she wants more from him. "Can I get two coffees, and two blueberry muffins please."

"Two?" Elle asks.

The old guy at the counter turns and says to Elle. "Yeah, her brother is in town. What's his name? Chase, or Chuck or something like that."

I stare at the old man, still having no idea of *his* name, or how he knows about Charlie already. "Charlie," I correct.

"Ah yes." He holds a finger up as if I've reminded him. "Apparently, he's a nice kid. Got a team together to get the yard tamed over at Old Roger's house."

"He has? Already?" I ask. How does he know this before I do? But then again, why am I even surprised in this town?

"Oh yes. A few of the townsfolk put their hand up to help. I'm going to finish my breakfast and head out there myself."

"Murray, that's sweet of you," Elle says as she tops up his coffee.

Huh, I look at him. He doesn't look like a Murray. More like a Frank, or Joe. "Yeah, that's really nice of you, Murray. Thank you," I say.

"Yeah, it's my pleasure, Hope. You know, everyone's real happy you're going to do something with Old Roger's house. It's been sitting like that for so many years, but it has a lot of history too, and no one wants to see it torn down. Wait, you're not tearing it down are ya?"

"No, not tearing it down. But we're likely taking it back to studs."

"You know there's an army of men around here who'd be happy to help with it. Myself included."

I smile at Murray, and gently place my hand on his back. "Thank you."

"Here you go, Hope. Two coffees, and two blueberry muffins. Bring that brother of yours around. I'd like to meet him."

"I will. I'll see you later." I pay Elle, then take the two coffees, balancing them on top of each other, and the paper bag with the two blueberry muffins. Getting in my truck, I drive over to the house, which takes only a matter of a few moments. "Holy shit," I say as I pull up in front of the house.

Already there's a huge dumpster placed to the side of the house, which is quickly being filled by the ensemble of people working on the yard. "Hope!" I hear from the top of the porch. Looking up, I see Charlie. He jumps off the steps, and jogs down toward me. I hand him his coffee, and the bag with the two muffins.

"What...how? I'm not even sure what to say." I'm stunned by the number of people working.

"Something else, eh? I made two phone calls this morning. First was for the dumpster."

"Which is already here? When has that ever happened before in all the years we've flipped houses?"

"The moment I said it was for this house, they said they could load it on the truck and bring it out right away. Then I made one other phone call to a place I found so they could come and quote us for clearing the yard. Next thing I know, four trucks showed up with people, and they've all been working ever since."

"I've never seen anything like this."

"I know."

Charlie sips on his coffee, and all I can do is look around at all the people here. The yard itself is taking shape. And I think by the end of the day we may even have a clean slate. "We can't afford this many people, Charlie."

"They don't want payment. All they want is to restore this eye-sore behind me. Apparently, this house means so much more to people than what you or I could ever imagine. Now I can't use my rags and gasoline."

"They don't want payment? Who works for free?" I look to Charlie who shrugs, then sips on his coffee. "We can't let them do all this yard work, and not do something for them."

"Hey, you're the boss. You can do whatever you want."

This town is something else. "You know, when I arrived everyone knew my name within the day. And now these people, who don't really know either you or me, are sacrificing their day to come here and help." I turn to Charlie and place my hand on his forearm. "Doesn't that just, like…I don't know." I huff in frustration that I can't articulate what I'm feeling. "Doesn't that speak to your soul, Charlie? Out of all the houses we've flipped, when have we ever had a turnout of people who just want to help with no strings attached?"

"I can't recall a time," he answers candidly.

"Okay. Well, I'll meet you inside. We have to do something for them." I gesture toward the people who are working hard. Pulling out my phone, I call Elle.

"Hey. Everything okay?" she asks.

"Yeah, why wouldn't it be?" I don't give her time to answer. "Anyway, I need you to do something for me."

"What is it?"

"I've got at least twenty people working in the yard trying to clear it. Apparently, no one wants to take payment for their work. Can you get some food ready and bring it over to Old Roger's house? Enough for say thirty people?"

"Shit, Hope. Um, I can try. What time do you want this for?"

I look at the time on my phone. "It's already just after nine, and the yard is looking amazing. It wouldn't surprise me if they've been here for at least the last two hours. Do you think you can get food over here for eleven?"

I hear Elle suck in a breath. "I don't think I can get it done for eleven, but maybe eleven-thirty. I'll call in some help. Do you have a budget?"

"Whatever it is, it's fine. I'll pay you tonight if that's alright?"

"No problems. Leave it with me."

"Thanks, Elle."

We hang up, and I look around. A part of me wants to thank everyone individually, but I know if I start doing that, it'll slow all of us down. It's best if I wait until Elle gets here and make a small speech at lunch. Heading up the stairs, I smile at whoever I come across. But most people are scattered and working all over the land. I head in, and Charlie's already pulling the kitchen out. "Okay, wow. It's already so different."

"It'll look even better when we take this wall down." He hits the sledgehammer into the back wall.

"I think I've got most of the new layout drawn up. I'm trying to figure out upstairs though."

"What?"

"I'm thinking we have a bathroom in each room."

"What? That's insane. Not every room needs a bathroom." Charlie protests. "And don't forget, there are costs involved if you want to put a bathroom in each room. There's already a master suite going in, right?" I nod. "And four bedrooms?" I nod again. "Five bedrooms with six bathrooms? Who would want six bathrooms?"

"I'm thinking of creating two master suites."

Charlie blows out a large breath. "Two master suites? Yeah, you've gone insane."

"Look. Bear with me." He rolls his eyes as I start talking. "Come." I walk out of the kitchen, and turn to look at Charlie, trying to coax him out of the kitchen. I stand at the entry way. "If we have a master suite downstairs, that could be for in-laws, parents, grandparents, anyone. If we leave the stairs where they are, we can create this side as a first master suite that opens up to an outdoor patio. This side we can have as open concept living, dining, and kitchen. We can have a butler's pantry to the side, and a separate mudroom behind it."

"Then you're going to have the stairs in the middle of the space, blocking the view of the kitchen. It won't be open concept. And you know, open concept is what sells."

"Kitchens and bathrooms sell houses. But you're right, the stairs will be blocking the kitchen." We both stand looking at the space. "I think I'll have to stick with moving the stairs to the side. The issue with the house is it's wide, but not long."

"With an extra fifteen feet on the back, then it'll be wide *and* long."

Nodding, I think I've got the plan for the downstairs working in my head. "Actually, you know what?" I look at Charlie who shakes his head. "I'm going to change it completely."

"How surprising." He rolls his eyes. "Look, you do what you do best, and I'm going to keep going with demo." He flashes me a cheeky smile. "My favorite thing about renovations."

"Demo day," we say together.

I run out to my truck and get a notepad and pen. When I come back in, all I can hear is a flurry of noises — Charlie bashing away in the kitchen, and everyone else weed-whacking outside. Sitting on the floor, I stare at the space, imagining so many different layouts. The stairs are what's throwing me, and the more I stare at the space, the more I like the idea of moving them completely.

"Hello?" I hear a knock on the door, and look up to find River entering the house.

Lord give me the strength not to stare at his lips, or his beautifully shapely arms. "River. What are you doing here?" I ask. Please, please, please, don't stare at him.

"There's word you may need help with the yard. I've come to help." He gives me a small smile just before lowering his eyes. "But it seems like a lot of people have come out to help. So, I can…" He hooks his thumb over his shoulder.

"No, you don't have to," I say way too eagerly. "I mean Charlie could probably use the help with demo. Or you can help out in the yard. Any extra pair of hands will be a great help." I draw my brows in together. "Hang on, aren't you working?"

"My customer cancelled, and my next one isn't until two. So you can use me until then, anything you want." He sticks his hand in his pockets and struggles to keep the small smile off his face.

Use him? Hell yes. I can *use* him. He can strip his clothes off and let me run my hands all over his taut chest. God, he does something to me. He's the quiet type, so understated. Those damned butterflies in my stomach spring to life, as my heart flutters at his mere presence. I've missed River, so much. And I had no idea until he showed up here. "Sure," my voice cracks. *Hold it together, Hope.* "Charlie!" I call. Charlie's bashing away, and I doubt he heard. I start walking in toward the kitchen, and when I get in there, I find Charlie has protection over his ears. "Charlie!"

He's about to swing the sledge hammer over his head when he stops. Turning, he sees River standing behind me. "Hey." Charlie looks to me, then River. "I know you, don't I?" Charlie pulls his ear protection down around his neck and slides his gloves off.

"Yeah, River." River holds his hand out to Charlie.

Charlie looks at River, staring at him. River slowly lowers his hand. "Oh, that's right." Charlie looks to me and lifts his brows. "You two knew each other from school."

River clicks his tongue to the roof of his mouth. "Yeah, that's me," he says slowly.

"If I remember correctly, you two..."

"It's in the past," I say interrupting him. "River lives around here, and has come to offer his help. He's also the electrician who'll be rewiring the house, and doing all the electrical work."

Charlie looks to me, then River. "Well then. Now we've been

introduced, welcome aboard. I need help taking these cabinets out. Whoever put them in, put them in so they'd never move."

"Sure, I can help." River takes a pair of gloves out of his back pockets and slides them on.

In the meantime, I grab Charlie's arm, and lead him away, out of earshot of River. "Be nice," I warn.

"You know what, Hope? None of my business. What happened with you two, it's got nothing to do with me. But if he thinks he can come in here and hurt you again, I won't let that happen."

"It doesn't matter, Charlie. The past stays exactly where it belongs. In the damned past. People change."

"You're talking like you're going to give him another chance."

"I *am* giving him another chance. But not for us to be together. If I can move on, then so can you. Leave it alone," I point at Charlie as I warn him.

"I suppose once the house is done, we'll be gone. Right?"

"Yeah, of course," I reply. But I don't actually feel the words I've said. I mean, I'm not lying, I'm just so drawn to this house. Something is keeping me here, and I think I'm going to cry when I finally do hand the keys over to whoever buys it. "I'm going upstairs to see what I can do up there."

"Be careful, eh. It's not solid up there."

"Look on the bright side," I say.

"What?"

"If I fall, you inherit this beautiful renovator's delight."

Charlie leans in and says with a sober-straight face. "Rag, gasoline, lighter." He holds one finger up, then two, then three. "I've got work to do. Stop bothering the help," he yells over his shoulder.

I head upstairs, and look through all the rooms. Two of the four rooms have got these charming bay windows with large benches below them. I can imagine in the house's heyday, someone would've been able to sit on them reading a book as the light streamed into the room. This is the biggest of the rooms, although it's still boxy and on the small side for a modern bedroom. Looking out of the filthy, cracked window, I see everyone outside working to make the yard navigable.

I look at the ratty, old cushioned bench under the window, and instantly want to get rid of it. I try tugging on it, but it's as firmly attached as what the kitchen cabinets appeared to be. No use in trying without Charlie's help.

Or River's.

Damn it, I'm not really a fan of being confined in a closed space with him. But Charlie needs to keep going with the kitchen renovation. I can do this. I don't need anyone's help. I love demo. Not as much as Charlie, but I do love it. I try to rip the cushioned seat again, but there's no way. I run downstairs to grab my tool belt from the truck. On the way in, River's coming out holding one of the old cabinets. "You got it out?" I ask.

He eyes my tool belt. "We have. Need a hand?"

No. "Yes." Shit.

"What are you doing?"

Nothing, you can stay downstairs, a safe distance away from me. "Trying to remove a bench seat under one of the bay windows. But I think Old Roger has made it as impossible to remove as the cabinets were." *Shut the hell up, Hope.*

"Ahh, I see. I'll get Charlie."

"No need. We can do it together." I look at him suddenly aware of the connotation of what I said. "I mean, we can pull it out." Holy shit. Shut up! "I mean, we can hammer," pause. "It," another pause. "Out." Shut the hell up *now!* And there goes my dignity.

River chuckles. "I get ya. We can…" River stops talking and squints. "Let's just get this done."

Can this get any worse? "Yeah, right." I decide I shouldn't say anything else, and head up the stairs. River is right behind me. "So it's this room. I want to get this horrible thing out. What do you think?"

"This?" River points to the manky old cushion. "This is easy. Here, step back." Oh, he's trying to show off, is he? Okay then. I step to the side, knowing full well this thing ain't moving without our combined strength. He looks over to me, puffs his chest out, semi-squats, gets what looks like a firm grip and tugs. His face strains, and he lets out a mighty huge fart. "Crap."

"I hope not!" I say as I laugh.

"You weren't supposed to hear that."

"So you were meant to fart?"

"No! God, no. I'm so sorry. Let me try this again."

He gets in the same position. "Wait!" I say through laughter. He looks at me sideways. "You're not going to follow through and shit yourself, are you?"

"Haha, very funny, Hope. Just back away. I don't want to hurt you."

"By stinking me out of the room?"

He playfully snarls. "Okay, here goes. One, two, three." He pulls at the cushion, falling flat on his ass as he farts again.

That's it for me. I can't hold back the gales of laughter. Tears well in my eyes, and I can barely stand straight. "You sure you didn't shit yourself, River?" I bend at the waist trying to calm myself, but I just can't.

"Okay, okay. Maybe this time you can help."

It takes me a good minute to calm enough to be able to harness my strength instead of my laughter. "You ready?" I ask when we both have a grip?

"Yep. One, two, three." I let go, and River takes another stumble back, this time ripping the material before falling to his ass.

I can't even. Nope, this is such a funny thing. "Thankfully you didn't fart this time."

"You let go!" Standing, he comes over to the bench. "Are you going to help this time?"

"Let's not try pulling it off. Let's try prying it up." Again, my mind is going where it shouldn't. Judging by River's reaction, his is too. "You know what I mean." He grabs his hammer, and I grab mine. We find the smallest lip, and start banging at it. "God, I'm an idiot. I need the sledge hammer."

"I'll go get it," River says as he's already disappearing out of the room. I chuckle with an instant replay of him falling on his butt. River's back within a minute carrying one of the sledge hammers. "Stand back."

I stand back, as he starts laying into the bench seat. The box beneath breaks on the fifth hit of the hammer, then he maneuvers and wiggles the seating, managing to lift it completely off.

River throws it to the side.

"Hey, what's this?" I ask as I see an old tin box. Leaning down, I lift it, and pop the lid open. Inside, there's a silver pocket watch, a man's white shirt neatly folded, and a handkerchief. I unfold the shirt, and from inside falls a green velvet jewelry box and a sealed envelope. Lifting the objects out of the box, I'm surprised by their pristine condition.

"What is it?" River asks.

"Looks like it's a gift of some kind." I look around the room, and sit with my back up against the wall. River sits beside me. I hand him the gift, and I open the envelope. "It's a love letter," I say as I look at him.

River opens the small box, and inside is a pair of diamond and emerald drop earrings. "Wow," River says.

"Oh! They're so pretty. I wonder who they were for?" I wet my lips before I start reading the letter. The cursive writing is beautiful, and fluid. My heart skips a beat when I read the first line. *"To my darling angel."* Looking at River, I smile before I continue with the letter.

> To my darling angel,
>
> I hate having to keep our love a secret, but for now it's the only thing we can do. Every time I see you, my heart leaps with joy, then sadness fills me because I cannot hold you in my arms the way I desperately want. You are the most beautiful woman my eyes have ever had the pleasure of seeing. When I lay in bed at night, I often imagine you lying beside me. I crave the taste of your sweet lips, the touch of your tender skin, the love of your pure heart.
>
> When the moon is in full view of my window, I wonder if you're looking up and watching it with me. Are you, my love? Soon we'll be able to scream our love from the highest of mountains, and we'll be able to be together. But until the moment I can make you mine, I give you a small token of the love in my heart for you.
>
> When I saw these earrings, I knew I had to buy them for you. The green reminds me of the time we snuck out and had a picnic under the oak tree. We were caught in the rain, and the rolling hills glistened, making the grass smell like summer and look like precious emeralds.
>
> I can't wait for us to be together.
>
> You are my love. You have my heart. Until we can be together.
>
> X

I sit staring at the letter. "Wow," I say.

"Yeah, wow," River echoes my words.

I look down at the letter, and re-read it silently. My left hand lifts and I place it over my heart. So beautiful. "I wonder who this was intended for?"

"I have no idea. But who'd hide this? And look, there's an inscription on the back of the watch. It reads, *my heart belongs to you.*"

"Old Roger built this house, so it has to have been him. Maybe this was for his wife who died? May told me she died from cancer. Maybe her death was so painful he hid this, hoping to forget."

"I don't know."

"This is a beautiful vibrant green. I think I'm going to use it as inspiration for the house." I take the earrings out of River's hands. "These belong to someone who doesn't even know they were supposed to get them."

"Or they got them, and rejected them," River says.

"Wow, yes. It's a heartbreaking possibility. But I have a gut feeling, they never received the earrings, or the letter." I take several deep breaths, letting the words sink into my heart.

"I can see the look in your eyes."

"What look?" I give River a sideways glance.

"The one that says, 'I'm going to find who these belong to.'"

"My mind's spinning so fast. Part of me wants to give these to the rightful owner. But another part of me is urging me to leave it in the past, because if these were hidden, perhaps there's a painful reason why they never made it out of this room." I fold the letter carefully, and close the case the earrings are in. Standing, I place them into the box and set the box to the side. "But for now, I have a house to renovate. I'll figure out what to do with those."

River stands, and goes over to the window seat where we found the letter and earrings. He looks in the cavity, double and triple checking. "Do you find a lot of things in the houses you flip?" he asks as he gets to work destroying what's left of the seat.

"Once I found two thousand dollars. And another time I found a small quantity of drugs. But mostly it's trash, dead animals, termites, and mice. And loads of clothes. But nothing as intimate as those earrings and the letter."

"Do you enjoy doing what you do?"

"Love it so much. Giving something old a new life. Most houses I've done aren't this old, but most have been neglected. Nothing makes me happier than seeing a family moving into a house I've renovated. I know the quality of work we put into them means the houses will last at least another hundred years." I look to River, who's stopped working and is smiling at me. "What?"

"When you talk about renovating houses, you glow. I mean, something about it sings to your heart. I can see exactly how much you love it." He smiles. For a brief second, not even that long, he and I connect. Maybe it's the letter, maybe it's the mutual love of working on houses. Whatever it is, it's dangerous. We can't go there again. "I'll go and see if Charlie needs any more help," he says, obviously feeling this awkwardness.

"Yeah, good idea."

I take my phone out, and dial Elle's number. "Hey, I'll be there shortly after eleven. Had to call in the cavalry," she says. She sounds short of breath, like she's rushing around.

"Great, thank you."

"Wait, what's wrong?"

"Oh, nothing. I'm good. Anyway, see you soon."

"Okay, I'll be there."

Heading downstairs, I find Charlie taking a wheelbarrow full of trash out to the dumpster. "Hey, can you give me a hand? We need to set up a makeshift table; I've got lunch coming for everyone."

"Yeah. Um, let me see what lumber we have lying around." Charlie goes and finds a few old planks of wood that were lying in the overgrown yard. "How do you want to do this?" he asks.

"Back your truck up to mine, and we'll put the tailgates down, and lay the planks out across them."

"Great idea." He looks down at my hands. "What's that?"

"Something River and I found upstairs. I'll show you tonight." I open my truck, and place the tin box in the glove compartment. Charlie turns his truck around, and reverses it so its tail end backs up to my truck. He gets out, flicks the tail gates down, then places the planks of wood between them, essentially making a table.

I can't get my mind to focus on anything else other than the letter and the earrings. They mean something to someone, and I think in time I'll find out who they should have gone to.

Being consumed by the tin box, but more specifically the letter, has stopped me from thinking straight. It's not until I get a tap on the shoulder, that I'm able to pull away from my thoughts. "Elle!" I say as I turn to see her standing behind me. I give her a quick hug. Although she's smiling, she looks frazzled. "Are you okay?"

"Next time give me more than two hours' notice. Where am I setting up?" She looks around, trying to find the table. I point to the two trucks with the old wood reaching between both. "Resourceful. I like it."

"Do you need help?" I ask.

"Ah, yes." As we walk back to her car, I see May's truck approaching. "Oh good. She made it."

"You asked May for help?"

"May's helping, but so is Tabitha. You know she's a chef, right?" Elle asks.

"What? No, I had no idea."

"Yeah, she's a chef. Good one, too."

May pulls up in front of Elle's vehicle, gets out and opens the back door. Tabitha is right beside her in seconds. "Wow," I say, still surprised by how altruistic the people in this town are.

"Food's ready, Hope. Want me to call them in?" May asks.

"No, it's okay. I'll do it." I help finish setting up all the meals Elle, May, and Tabitha have prepared. First, I need Charlie here so we can both thank everyone for helping. I run through the cleared front yard, up to the house and find both Charlie and River inside. "Do you both want to come out?"

"Food?" Charlie asks with enthusiasm.

"Yeah, food," I confirm. Charlie's out the door without a moment's hesitation, leaving River and me in the nearly bare kitchen. "There's food outside," I say again trying to break the awkward silence between us.

River takes his gloves off and places them on the skeleton of the old counter. He walks past me, stops, turns, and pushes me up against the wall. His mouth covers mine, greedily kissing me. I'm not even sure what's happening, but I like it. The heat between us is causing my head to spin. It feels like it used to. Easy, steamy, *right*.

My skin tingles as he runs his hand down my arm and he grips my wrist. My heart is beating erratically and I hook a leg over his hip. Wait, what am I doing?

"Stop," I say breathlessly. My breath quickens as I close my eyes. Jesus, what was that?

River pulls away slowly. He leans his forehead against mine, then places a kiss to my nose. "I had to know, Hope. I had to know if you still feel the way I do." Leaving me panting, he lowers his head, offers me a small smile, and walks out of the room.

My head is spinning. What just happened? I hate feeling so overwhelmed when I'm around River.

No, I can't fall for him again. I can't live through this, not again.

Chapter ELEVEN

Past

PACING OUTSIDE THE movies I keep looking around for River. If he stands me up on our first date, I'm going to be completely humiliated. But he won't get away with it so easily, either. If I'm humiliated, he will be too.

I check my phone, and see it's just after six. He's late by a few minutes, and I'm beginning to panic. I don't want to be made to look like a fool.

My shoulders slump forward, as my chest deflates. Damn it. I really liked River. Like, *really* like him. For weeks, we've had this back and forth between us, and I thought he liked me too, which is why I agreed to go on a date with him.

I look at my phone again, and there's a message from River. **Running late, I'll be there in 10.** It was sent two minutes ago.

He's got eight minutes, and if he's not here in eight minutes, I'm calling Charlie to come get me.

I can feel my eyes prickling with tears, but I'm not going to let him get the better of me. No way. Nope.

"Hey, I'm sorry I'm late," I hear from behind me.

I take a deep breath, and find myself smiling when I turn to see River. "You're lucky," I say, pretending his tardiness didn't hurt.

"You mad 'cause I'm late?"

"What? No! More like annoyed. I was thinking about my revenge on you. Like super gluing your hand to your ass."

River smiles. "You wouldn't do that to me; you like me too much."

"Like." I roll my eyes. "Pffft, whatever."

"Yeah, that's why you agreed to go on a date with me. But we both know you've been digging me for ages. I'm simply irresistible to you," he teases.

We walk into the cinema and stand looking up at the board. "What are we watching?" I ask.

"Whatever you want," he replies.

"Really? Okay. I want to see that." I point up at the latest Disney movie. River crinkles his nose. "You said whatever I want."

"Disney though? Isn't that for little kids?"

"Don't be hating on Disney."

"I'm not. It's just there's so many other movies out. Like that one." He points to a poster of a guy wielding a blood splattered knife. I turn and lift my brows at him, obviously unimpressed. "What about that movie?" He points to another poster, this one is clearly action, with an actor jumping out of a burning building.

"Or, how about that one?" I point to my choice of Disney.

River walks ahead to the line to get the tickets. "Fine. But I'm only seeing it under protest."

"Duly noted, and quickly forgotten," I say.

"Popcorn? Candy? Sodas?"

"Yes, yes, and yes," I reply.

I watch as River progresses through the short queue. I should go stand with him, and pay for my share, but nope, he made me wait, so I'm making him pay. Next time he'll think twice about being late. He looks over his shoulder, and motions for me to go to him. I stand beside him as he's paying for everything. "You owe me," he says.

"I owe you a kick in the butt because you made me wait."

He smirks as he gets his change. He leans over, and whispers, "Lucky I like you." Then gives me a small kiss on the cheek. He hands me the bucket of popcorn, and one of the large sodas. "Come on, let's go watch this movie you insisted on picking."

The kiss is stuck in my head. I can feel myself burning with anticipation. I want more.

"So, you've told me you want to do something working with your hands, but your parents want you to go to college," he says as we walk slowly toward the theatre.

"Ugh, don't remind me."

"What do you want to do?"

"They think I should do something other than what I want to do."

"What exactly do you want to do?" he asks as we walk up the stairs.

"Anything to do with building. I love it. Any construction stuff, I'm there, ready to help. My parents think I should do something else. Like interior design." I make a puking face. "But that's not what I want to do."

"Tell them."

"I have, many times. They keep saying I should have something to fall back on, because women in the construction industry aren't really accepted. And they said that because I'm female, people may not take me seriously. Charlie said he wanted to be a plumber, and they supported him. Me I want to build, and they're telling me to go into design as opposed to working with tools." I shake my head, frustrated with my parents for not supporting me.

"I suppose they're saying this because they care for you."

"Yeah, but why is it okay for Charlie to be a plumber, but not okay for me to do some kind of construction? It's not fair." I can feel myself becoming more and more irate.

"Hey, I think you should do whatever you want. Maybe they'll come around. I don't know.'

"What are you going to do after school? I bet you'll go to some college somewhere. Or maybe join the military like your dad, eh?"

"Nope. I want to be an electrician. I want a nice steady place to live so I don't have to move around."

"But I thought you liked it." We find seats at the back, and sit.

"I did. But not so much now."

"Why not?" I take a sip of my soda.

"Because of you," he says while staring at me.

"Me? Why me?"

"Because I like you, and I don't want to move away from you. I want to stay wherever you are."

I gulp, as I move my gaze to look at him. We haven't even kissed yet, or held hands, or anything. "I'd like that," I say.

He hesitantly reaches over, and places his hand on my leg. "Is this okay?" I nod, and smile. The lights dim, and I move my hand under his to link our fingers together. He leans over to me, and whispers, "I like you, Hope. A lot."

The butterflies in my stomach are rejoicing, fluttering around like they're having a party. I turn, and his face is right there. Looking into his eyes, I can see he means every word he's spoken. His gaze moves to my lips, then back up to my eyes. His fingers squeeze mine. He wants to kiss me. I want to be kissed by him, *so damn bad.*

I move my head closer to his.

"I want to kiss you," I say.

"Then kiss me," he whispers.

I move in even closer. I can feel his breath on my lips. His chest is rising and falling quickly, and he's staring at my lips. I don't hold back; I kiss his luscious lips. It's causing my head to spin, I just want more of him. I want him to hold me, and keep kissing me. Movie be damned.

He pulls away, and places a gentle kiss to my lips. "I'm glad you did that, because I wasn't sure how much longer I could've waited."

I'm glad I did it too. Smiling, I flick the armrest up, and snuggle into River. He places his arm around me, tightening his grip.

"Thank you for tonight," I say when we arrive at my home. Linking hands with him, I lean in and give him a kiss. But I can feel something's a bit off with River. "What's wrong? You've been acting kinda weird since we left the restaurant."

He drops my hands, and steps back. River licks his lips, and lets out a long sigh. "You know how I was late to the movies tonight?" I nod. "I nearly didn't come."

"Why?" I ask slowly, my smile fading quickly.

"I didn't know how to tell you."

"If you tell me you already have a girlfriend, I'm going to kick you in the nuts." I point at him. I take another step back, and place my hands on my head, afraid I'm going to hurt him if he *does* tell me that.

"No, nothing like that." He steps closer, but I back away. "I only found out this afternoon."

"Found out what?" My back stiffens as I prepare for the worst. Please, don't let it be what I think it is.

"We're moving." He steps closer, but I counter. He clears his throat. "I'm sorry," he says.

I don't know how to respond to him. Is there any use in saying anything? With his dad in the military, this is what happens. I blink rapidly, trying to hold in the tears. It feels like my heart's been ripped out of my chest and stomped on. "When?" I ask with an unsteady, wobbly voice.

"They've known for a while and told me just before I left."

"You didn't answer the question, River. When are you leaving?" I say, stepping forward and poking him on the chest.

"We leave in the morning."

I stand staring at him, completely emotionless. I turn away and wrap my arms around myself. This has all been for nothing.

"Hope." I sense him stepping toward me, but I shake my head. The creak of our wooden porch beneath his weight stops. "I'm sorry," he says in a tiny voice.

"Please leave."

"Hope."

I turn to face him. "Stop." I lift my hand, halting him. "It's okay, I understand." I do the only thing I can. I give him a kiss on his cheek and walk away. I don't look back, *I can't*. It would absolutely shatter my heart if I looked at him.

So, I don't.

"Goodbye, River."

TWELVE

STARING AT THE coffee Elle's made, I can't help but think of *that* kiss. The way he pushed me up against the wall. The weightlessness that surged through my body. My heart leapt and soaked up every single second of our connection. My fingertips brush along my lips, remembering, *wanting*.

"Hey, you okay?" Elle asks as she drags out a chair and sits opposite me.

I blink a few times, trying to dislodge River's warm lips on mine. "Yeah, I'm great. Why?" Shit, has she heard something? This is a small town, and everyone seems to know everything before I do.

She looks pointedly toward my coffee. "You've been cradling that cup of coffee for the last ten minutes and haven't taken a sip. It's probably cold by now. What's going on?"

"Nothing," I respond immediately, before lowering my gaze.

"Uh-huh. You know, I might not know you well yet, but what I do know, is something's eating you up." Elle reaches out, and places her hand over mine. "Is it the town? It can be too much for someone at the beginning."

"I'm not going to stay here," I say.

Elle smirks. "Okay, if you say so."

"What does that mean?"

There's a glint in Elle's eyes. "I've been there, and said the same thing. But something about this town gets under your skin. And before you know it, you don't want to leave."

"But I'm not like that." Elle nods, though she still appears unbelieving. "What?"

"Look at me, Hope."

"I am."

"No, really look at me. I have two full sleeves of tattoos. I have bright red hair. I shouldn't belong in a place like this, but I do. Not because I forced my way in. Because this town took me in, embraced me, didn't judge me, and slowly seeped into my veins. It'll do the same thing to you. You'll fall in love here, like I did."

"Fall in love?" I ask, my voice breaking. She knows, she has to know.

"With the town, the people. Everything. As the cliché goes, *the sky in small towns is always the prettiest.*"

"I've never heard that before," I say. "Nor have I looked at the sky."

"Well then, you have to. And when you do, your heart will know this is where you belong."

"Morning, Elle, Hope," I hear someone say as the small bell over the door dings.

Looking behind me, I see Jake walk in. "Morning, Sheriff," I say.

Elle giggles, and her face gives away how she feels about Jake.

"Morning. Coffee?" she asks as she stumbles over her own feet to serve him. What is she, a school girl?

"Thank you."

How can he not see it? Is he blind? She's crushing on him so bad. "I didn't get a chance to thank you for driving us home," I say to Jake.

"You're welcome." He leans his arm against the back of the chair Elle was sitting in. "How are you liking Hope River?"

"It's different from what I'm used to. Everyone's really supportive and very nice."

"But everyone knows your business." He smiles, and I can see why Elle is crushing on him as hard as she is. Jake's tousled dirty-blond hair, and tall frame could easily make a woman swoon. Well, not me, but Elle. He's a bit too buff for me.

"Yeah, that's a bit hard to take," I say through a tight jaw.

"You'll get used to it. This town is like one huge family. Everyone looks out for everyone. And because of that, everyone will know your business, regardless of whether you want them to or not."

"Comforting," I joke.

"How's your brother, Charlie?"

Shit, I hope he hasn't done anything stupid. Like, you know, sleep with Jake's sister...or mother. "He's good," my voice is strained. "Why, what has he done?" I brace myself, waiting for Jake to say something.

"Nothing, to my knowledge. Why? Should I be keeping an eye on him?" Jake straightens, suddenly becoming every bit the sheriff he is.

"No, no," I playfully joke. Phew, that was a close one. "I promise he's a good guy. You'll get no trouble from him." Jake narrows his eyes, and puffs his chest out further. I can tell he's incredibly suspicious now. Shit, I shouldn't have said anything. "Why don't you come around to the house and meet him?"

"How's the house going?" Jake doesn't answer my question, but I suspect this is because he's wary of Charlie thanks to my big mouth.

"You know what, if the town didn't come together yesterday, I think it would've taken me at least a week to clean out the yard. I'm so grateful to them."

"I heard about the lunch you put on. Awfully kind of you."

"It's the least I could do considering they spent their day helping me."

"Your coffee." Elle comes over and hands Jake his beverage. He takes out five dollars from his pocket and hands it to her. "It's okay." At least she's more composed now and not a sniveling school girl who's just seen her favorite boy band member.

"Thank you, Elle."

She smiles and quickly disappears. I can't help but notice Jake checking her out as she heads back behind the counter. Jake turns forward, and he has a large smile on his face. "You should ask her out," I blurt.

"Sorry?" he says in his harsh tone reserved for his hard-assed sheriff persona. The same tone he used on me the night I met him.

"I mean, Elle and you would make a good couple. Unless you're already a couple with someone else?"

Jake looks over his shoulder at Elle, then lifts his coffee to take a sip. He turns to me, and nods. "Have a good day, Miss Sawyer," he says before leaving.

The small bell above the door tinkles as he opens, and closes the door. Um, okay then. Elle rushes over, and sits in the seat she was sitting in. "What happened? What did he say?"

Finishing my coffee, I place the mug on the table. "I'm not passing notes. You have to ask him out."

"Hope!" she whines. "Please, help a sister out here."

I click my tongue to the roof of my mouth. "I told him he should ask you out. It's obvious to me how hot you both are for each other. Just ask him to dinner. Here, even. Close the diner early, make a nice dinner and invite him."

Elle half shrugs as she looks down at her wringing hands. "I don't know," she says.

"Look, just do it." Yeah great. *I'm* offering advice on love. Me, of all people. "What's the worst that can happen?"

The little bell chimes again, and we both look over to the door, half expecting Jake to come back in. Instead, I'm greeted by the very handsome, dimple-chinned River. He looks at us as he passes, then does a double-take and stops to talk to me. "Hi," he says to me, then quickly looks at Elle and says, "Oh, hi Elle."

Elle smiles, the glint in her eyes saying she knows there's something going on between River and me. "Hi, River. What do you need?" She stands and indicates the seat she's just vacated.

What are you doing? I mouth to her while River's back is turned.

"Thank you. I'm not interrupting, am I?" River asks, waiting for a response from either myself or Elle.

"Not at all. I've got things I have to do. Can I bring you a coffee?"

"Yes, thank you. And I'll have bacon and eggs. You know the way I like it." River sits and looks at my empty mug. "Have you eaten?"

"Um, not yet."

"Hey, Elle," he calls over his shoulder. And when Elle turns to look at him he holds up two fingers. "Make that two coffees and two bacon and eggs."

"I have to go," I say. "I've got to get to the house." I move to stand, but he places his hand over mine.

"Charlie's there. He can look after whatever's going on right now. You need to eat." I look down at our joined hands, and he immediately pulls away. I sit back in the seat, and look down at my empty coffee mug. "I shouldn't have kissed you," he says the very moment Elle brings over another cup and the coffee carafe to fill both up. She gasps, then smirks. But my heart feels like it's just been torn out of my chest.

Awesome. Elle heard what River just said. Which means, she's going to want to know every single detail. And I'm not willing to share them with anyone.

We're both quiet as Elle finishes pouring our coffees, and when she leaves I whisper, "Can you maybe not say stuff like that so loud?"

"Hey, I'm not ashamed I kissed you. I'm just sorry about the way I did it. I just sprung it on you. But I had to know if you still feel for me what I feel for you."

"Look, it's in the past."

"Well, that's the dumbest answer I've ever heard. It doesn't matter what we had in the past, or what happened. What matters is the fact we're both here now and we still have feelings for each other. I'm single, and you're single, and we can finally try to make this work." He points to himself, then me.

I can't even try to deny his claim that I have feelings for him.

"*Try* to make it work?" He nods. "I'm leaving the moment this house is done."

River chuckles. "No, you're not."

"What?"

"This town, it seeps into your bloodstream, makes your heart beat faster, it does something to you."

"Why is everyone so in love with this place? There are small towns all over America."

"Not like this one. Besides, I know you're not going to leave."

"Yeah, and why's that?"

"Because I'm not going to lose you again, Hope."

I take a sip of my second coffee of the day, trying to come up with some kind of reason why we don't belong together. "I don't think my heart will be able to cope with you walking out of my life. And I'm not prepared to risk it." I take a deep breath, and add, "…again."

River nods. "I know I screwed up the last time I saw you, on your birthday. I should've told you, but I was gutless."

I hold my hand up. "It's not my business."

"Hope, you have to know, she and I…"

"Stop. I don't want to know. You told me you're single, and I'm happy for you. But what happened…" I shake my head. "It's not my business."

"Go out with me. Just one date, that's it. If you don't want to go out with me again, I'll back off and promise to never kiss you again."

Never kiss me again? Why does that send a spear of panic through me?

And of course, Elle brings out our breakfast. "Right, then," she says as she places my plate down, then River's. "Breakfast." Elle has got the best or worst timing, ever. I haven't made my mind up yet which it is. "What's the worst that can happen?" she throws my own words back at me. I narrow my eyes, burning a huge imaginary hole in her head. She winks before walking away.

"You have a knack for saying stuff when others are around," I say to River.

"One date. One date isn't going to kill you." He picks his knife and fork up, and starts eating his breakfast.

No, one date *isn't* going to kill me, but falling for him again very well might.

Chapter
THIRTEEN

Past

Thursday

"HOPE, CAN YOU get the door?" Mom yells from wherever she is in the house.

No, I can't. I'm looking at a house plan and trying to figure out how to improve it. "Yeah." I push up off my bed, take a deep breath before padding down the hallway to answer the door.

"Hope!" Mom yells even louder.

"I'm here, I'm here. You don't have to scream," I say as I walk past the kitchen to the front door.

"You've forever got your head on real estate sites looking for your first fixer upper."

"And one day I'm going to get it too," I say over my shoulder to Mom. Opening the front door, my mouth falls open as I take a step back. "River?" I squeak.

He smiles as he steps forward and sweeps me up in a huge hug. "I've missed you so much."

"What… What? I… What are you doing here?" My God, he looks so good. He's taller, and sexier, and just…*yum.*

"I'm only back for a few days. And I wanted to come and find you."

"Who is it?" Mom asks.

"It's River," I answer in a small voice, still surprised he's on my doorstep. "What are you doing here?" I ask again, unsure if he answered me the first time. I close the door behind me, and walk toward the porch chairs.

River follows and sits beside me. "I'm only here for a few days. Four actually. My grandparents moved about twenty minutes away and it's my grandmothers sixty-fifth birthday. She's having a party, so we're back for that. We leave early Monday morning to go back."

He looks so beautiful. His body is bulkier, and his hair is a little longer, but he's still perfect. "I can't stop staring at you."

"You look amazing, Hope. Can we go somewhere? Anywhere?"

Hell yeah, we can. "Give me five." I jump up out of my seat, and run inside where Mom and Dad are both in the kitchen, working on dinner together. "I can't stay," I say as I rush past them.

"Ah, why not?' Dad questions as he follows me into my room. He stands at the door, and crosses his arms in front of his chest.

"River's back."

"River? Who the hell is this River?"

I go to Dad and give him a huge hug. Stepping back, I start thinking about something to wear. "River. You remember, when I was sixteen, he and I went on a date, and he told me he was moving away because his father is military?" I say in one breath.

"The boy you cried over for a week?"

"That's him." I rush around my room like a cyclone, trying to find something clean and awesome to wear. Should I wear a dress? Ugh, nope. Maybe just stay in jeans. Oh, what about short shorts. Nope, too desperate.

"Hope," Dad says as I'm throwing clothes on my bed.

"Yeah, Dad?" I don't stop the tsunami of excitement racing around trying to find the perfect outfit to wear.

"I know you're eighteen now, and God only knows how damn determined and mature you are, but are you sure you're ready to go back there again, with him?"

I slow down for a second, walk over and give Dad another hug. "He's only here for four days, I promise, I won't allow myself to fall for him."

Dad huffs, and tightens his grip on me. "Are you sure this is the right thing to do? Especially considering he's only here for a short time."

I kiss Dad on the cheek. "I promise you, Dad, I swear I won't do anything stupid. We're just going to hang out." I cross my heart.

Dad's lips press into a thin, strained line. "I just don't want to see you hurt again." He backs away. "I'll leave you to it."

Right, back to it. Jeans and a t-shirt? Dress? Ugh. I don't know. Maybe tights and a t-shirt. No, not tights, that's too casual. Um, no I think jeans is the way to go. I grab a pair of black jeans, and try to find something cute to wear on top. "Why do I have nothing?" I groan through a clenched jaw as I go through all my tops, and shirts. I end up grabbing one of my Nike t-shirts and throwing it on. God damn it, what am I going to do with my hair? Screw it. A high pony it is.

I run into the bathroom, brush my teeth, and make sure I'm presentable. It's the best I can do on such short notice. The moment I'm done, I head into the kitchen. "I'm going out for a while. I'll be home a bit later." I give Mom and Dad a quick kiss.

"Home by midnight, you have work tomorrow," Mom reminds me.

"Okay. Bye."

"Did you take your phone?" Dad calls as I rush to get out the front door.

Crap, in my haste, I forgot my phone. "I'm just getting it now."

"You're eighteen, you'd think that phone would be attached to your hands twenty-four, seven. Don't lose it again, Hope. We won't replace it this time if you do," Dad warns.

"Okay. Bye. Love you." I slip my phone into my back pocket and return to the porch, where River's waiting for me. "Hey," I say as I close the door behind me.

"Hey." He stands from the chair, comes over, and hugs me. Sweeping me clear off the porch, he twirls then gives me a kiss on the cheek. "I've wanted to do that from the moment I saw you." He places me on my feet, and entwines our fingers together. "Please tell me you don't have a boyfriend?"

"Nope, not anymore."

His fingers tighten around my hand as we walk toward his car. He opens the passenger door, and waits 'til I get in before running around to the driver's side. He starts the car, and pulls onto the road. "I have no right to feel jealous of you for having a boyfriend."

"Well, quit being an idiot, because I don't have one now." He gives me a sideways glance as he drives. "I'm assuming you don't have a girlfriend, right?"

"Not for nearly six months."

I proudly lift my chin, *good*. I'm glad he doesn't have a girlfriend, because I'm not that type of girl. I'd never go after someone who's taken. "So, what are you doing now? Are you going to college?"

"Nope. Trade school to become an electrician."

"Oh my God! That's what you wanted to do two years ago. And you're doing it. I'm so happy for you."

"What about you? Did you convince your parents to let you build stuff?"

I hold up my hands to show the callouses, cuts and bruises. "I've got an apprenticeship. One day though, I'm going to buy a house, and flip it."

"I have no doubt you're going to do exactly what you want to do."

"So, where are we going?"

"Mrs. Mac's diner. I'm craving her chicken and waffles."

I sit back and smile, yeah, I'm so happy River's back. Even if it's only for a few days.

Friday

"Hi, gotta get ready 'cause River will be here soon. Sorry, can't talk," I say to Mom as I pass her on the way to the shower.

"Wait!" she calls.

"Don't have time. He'll be here in about half an hour, and I have to have a shower and wash my hair."

"Wait!"

The urgency in her voice stops me from heading into the shower. "Are you okay?" I ask.

"Yes, but I want to know what's going on with you two."

I don't have time for this. "Dad and I went over this yesterday. River's leaving on Monday to return home. He lives on the other side of the country, Mom. So I probably won't see him again for ages. We're just spending time together while he's here."

"Hope." She tilts her head to the side. "Whatever you do, be safe."

"We're not having sex, if that's what you're thinking," I nearly yell.

"Look. I know what he meant to you two years ago, and I know you. You can fall hard and fast. But remember he's leaving on Monday."

"I know. And I won't do anything stupid." I probably will, and live to regret it.

"Okay. Well, home by one."

"Mom!" I whine. "It's Friday, and I'm not working 'til Monday. Can't I be back by two, please?"

Mom rolls her eyes, shakes her head then gives me a crooked smile. "Only because he's leaving on Monday." I scrunch my mouth, and am dreading to ask a little favor. "What?"

"Tomorrow it's his grandmother's sixty-fifth birthday, and I've been invited. It's at a function center somewhere. Can I please be home by three? Just tomorrow? I promise, I won't ask for a late curfew ever again."

Mom smirks. "I'm sure you will at some stage."

"Please?"

Mom huffs. "Fine. But Sunday, you'll have to be home by midnight because you have work on Monday."

"I know, I know." I give Mom a quick kiss, and rush to my bedroom, where I start getting my stuff ready. "Thanks, Mom," I yell.

"Yeah, yeah," I hear her say.

I strip off my clothes, and get in the shower at record speed.

River's lips are soft, yet strong. I love kissing them. Parked at the beach, we're making out in his car.

Both front seats have been moved as far forward as they go, and we're an entwined mess on the back seat. He's peppering kisses up my neck, softly licking my tingling skin as he makes his way to my ear, and sucks my earlobe into his mouth.

"Oh God," I whisper as I close my eyes and let the sensation take over.

"Hm, I love the way you react," he replies. His hand is on my breast, squeezing and playing with my nipple. I can feel how excited he is.

"River." I pull away from him, and the moment there's some space between us, I already miss him. "You live on the other side of the country. A good five-hour flight. What are we doing here?"

He lays his head back, and closes his eyes. "I don't know. But whatever it is, I don't want it to end. I know it's going to be hard, but we can make it work."

I sit further back. "What? You mean a long-distance relationship?"

"Yeah, we can make it work. It won't be that hard. I can fly out once every six to eight weeks and spend the weekend here. You can come visit me too. We can do this, Hope."

I shake my head. My heart wants to leap into this, but I'm fairly logical, and I know long-distance relationships usually don't work. But I want River. With every fiber of my being, I want River. Finally, after what feels like forever, I say, "We can try."

"Here, give me your phone." He holds his hand out. Searching for it, I find it under the front seat. Ugh, how did it get there? I unlock my phone, and give it to him. "Under my phone number, I've added my address. I have your address, so we can't lose touch." I take my phone, and toss it on the front seat. I'm so skeptical. I don't want him disappearing again, and us losing touch. It hurt me so much when he left two years ago. "Don't worry, we'll work."

I smile as I move and straddle his hips. "I know, we will." He pulls me down on top of him, and starts kissing me again. He drags his fingers through my hair, then down my back. Slowly he lifts my t-shirt, and draws lazy circles on my back before moving his hands up toward my bra. "I'm not ready for this, River," I say as I pull back.

"Okay. We don't have to do anything you don't want to do."

I lay down again, this time with my head on his chest. Although I feel like a pretzel in this uncomfortable position, it's nice. Because we're close together. "I have to tell you something," I say.

"What is it?"

I close my eyes, tensing for the worst. "I'm a virgin, and I don't want to have sex in the back of a car."

His chest rises higher as he sucks in a deep breath. "I'm a virgin too, Hope. And I don't want to have sex in the back of a car either."

I sit up, looking at him. "You're a virgin?" Wow, talk about being surprised.

He chuckles. "Yeah, I am."

"But you had a girlfriend!"

"And you had a boyfriend. Does that mean you had sex with him?"

"I suppose not."

"It works the same for me. I didn't want to have sex with her. She was pretty superficial, and it didn't last long."

"Superficial, how?"

"She was more into her phone than spending time with me."

"I keep losing mine. My Mom told me if I lose it again, they're not replacing it." River laughs. "What?"

"That's what I love about you, Hope." *Love?* "You don't care for things like how many likes can you get on social media. Or make-up, or having your hair done a certain way. I mean, that's fine for most girls, but I like how you care about those things. You're real."

"Just so you know." I take a deep breath. "I love those things about myself too." I crack a huge grin.

River laughs, grabs me, and kisses the hell out of me. "We're going to make this work."

"I know."

I keep kissing him, and I can feel exactly how excited he is to have me sitting on top of him.

Saturday

There's a slow song playing, and River and I are on the dance floor, swaying from side to side to the beat of the song. We're close together, with my cheek up against his chest. "Have I told you how beautiful you look tonight?" he asks.

"I thought you weren't into girls who do their hair and make-up and stuff." Smirking, I know he loves the figure hugging dress I'm wearing. He's already told me, about forty-five thousand times. Okay, maybe that's a slight exaggeration.

I feel his lips against my forehead. "I'm into you wearing this dress." His fingertips gently run over the thin straps and down my bare shoulders all the way to my lower waist. He rests his hands just above my butt. He leans down, and in a soft voice he whispers, "I really like you wearing this."

Pulling back, I look up at him. "I wish you didn't have to go back tomorrow." Shit, I can feel myself falling hard for him. The tears welling in my eyes the most obvious proof. But the ache in my heart and the strong desire to claim him will make it hard to let him go.

He cradles my face in his warm palms, leans down, and places his lips to mine. "I wish I didn't have to either," he mumbles against my mouth.

"Then stay, we can move in together. Make this work," I say. But even as the words leave my lips, I know that's not only impossible, but illogical too. Before River says anything, I lift my hand and place it to his mouth. "I know, we can't. We're both only eighteen, and you've got your trade school to finish. I've got an apprenticeship and neither of us would earn enough to do that until we complete our training. I'm being stupid, that's all."

"I wish I could be here with you. But I can't. Not yet." He kisses me softly again.

"I'm being stupid and emotional. It's okay. We'll make it work. I swear, with you coming back every second month, and me coming to see you too, we'll see each other as much as we can."

We keep moving to the song, and everything else falls away. Our hearts belong to one another; we're meant to be together. It was obvious two years ago, and it's even more apparent now.

Damn it, I made a promise to my heart to not fall for him. But I know I'm breaking that promise.

Sunday

"Are you sure you want to do this?" River asks.

There's a fluttering in my belly, and my heart is racing. River's rented a hotel room, and even though I know I need to be home by midnight, I want to make our last night together something special.

Reaching for his hand, I have a strong desire to touch him. Feel him. Taste him.

I swallow back the words I want to say, letting my actions speak to River instead. Maneuvering on the edge of the bed, I straddle his hips, and kiss his lips. "I want this," I whisper.

"I want this too. So much."

I push him down on the bed, and take my t-shirt off, throwing it to the floor. His eyes widen as he watches me in awe. This feels so awkward, but so right. Hesitantly, I lower the straps from my bra. I'm not sure if I'm doing this right.

"Hey," he says as he sits up in bed and hugs me close to his body. "If you're not ready, we don't have to do this."

"I want to, River. Really, I do. But I'm not sure what I'm doing."

He tries really hard to hide the smirk. "Remember, neither do I. And I don't think the porn I've watched is anything realistic to go on."

I move off him. "Eww. You watch porn?" I ask.

"Ah, yeah. I'm a guy. I watch porn. Like most other guys. Haven't you watched any?"

"No." I sit next to him. "What kind of porn do you watch?"

River's cheeks flush red. Oh my God, he's embarrassed. How cute. "You know," his voice cracks, and I laugh.

"Come on, tell me. What kind of porn do you watch?"

"I like, you know..." He stands from the bed, and starts pacing. River runs his hand through his hair. "It's just...you know," he splutters.

"No, I don't know, which is why I'm asking. Maybe there are some tips on what we can do. Come on, I'm sure you've watched enough to know a thing or two."

He stops pacing the room and turns to stare at me. "You want to watch some so we can recreate it?"

"Oh my God! Yes, that's a great idea. These people are professionals, they have sex for a living. They've got to be doing something right."

River starts laughing. "I suppose. But there's some out there that's not so legal."

"Wait, porn is legal? Hmm, I wonder what they put on their tax returns under 'Occupation.' Huh, interesting." River lifts his phone from the small side-table and starts scrolling through it. "Are you getting us some porn to watch?" I eagerly ask.

"Hope, this is awkward enough as it is. Can we just..." He makes a hand gesture to quell my questions. I'm curious, that's all. "Can we maybe not talk about porn, because it's doing the complete opposite of what it usually does to my body."

I can't help it. I burst into laughter. "I'm sorry," I say as I roll on my side, holding my stomach. "It's just, I haven't watched porn, and you have."

"Doesn't mean I can do what those guys do. Man, how weird is this. Talking to my girlfriend about porn. And my girlfriend wanting to watch it with me."

I sit up, suddenly deadly serious. "I'm your girlfriend?"

"Yeah, of course you are."

He stands in front of me, I jump up and into his arms. Kissing him is so natural. We just, *fit*. All my inhibitions disappear, and I tear at his clothing, not even caring that neither of us have had any experience at this. It doesn't matter. Not now. We'll learn together, *tonight*.

River lowers me, and steps back. "Oh man, come on," I say. "Don't tell me you want to wait for marriage or something." I back away from River, and sit on the edge of the bed.

He doesn't say a single word. Instead, he walks over to me, leans down and just when I think he's about to kiss me, he licks my neck while unfastening my bra. Shit, my heart pounds as my skin burns with desire.

He gently pulls my bra off, exposing my breasts. Kneeling in front of me, he unbuttons my jeans, and starts to slide them down. "Lift your butt," he says so he can get my jeans past my hips.

Holy shit, this is really happening. Like really, *really* happening.

My mouth dries as my pulse quickens. River stands, takes off his shirt, and slides his jeans down his legs.

We're both in this hotel room River's rented, stark naked. Neither of us know what we're doing. My eyes follow his chest, down to his cock. Jesus. "Are you okay?" he asks.

"I understand the fundamentals of how everything works. I'm just worried it might hurt."

"It probably will, but I'll go slow, okay?" I nod. "You know my eyes are up here, Hope." I lift my gaze to find River smiling. Was I gawking? *Oops.*

"Look, there's something else." I cringe having to bring this up.

"Jesus, Hope. You're gonna make me self-conscious. What is it?"

"Protection. I want you to wear a condom."

He sighs a relieved breath. "I had no idea where this was going, but wearing a condom wasn't what I was expecting, not from you."

"I bought some!" I eagerly say.

"You did?"

"Yeah, what do you think this is? I am eighteen, and pretty open about everything."

River lightly smacks his forehead. "You did want to watch porn."

"Speaking of which, should we watch some? Get some ideas on how to do this?"

"I've got ideas," River says.

I look up at River. This has turned really awkward. Neither of us are doing anything, and judging by River's deflation, I think he's finding this weird as well. Not a great first time for either of us. "Um." River uncomfortably looks around the room. "Look, I think we're both too stressed about this. Putting too much pressure on ourselves."

"Thank God." He sits beside me. "Why don't I find us some porn. And if anything happens, it happens, if it doesn't, then it doesn't."

I let out a breath and smile. "Yeah, okay." This really hasn't gone the way I thought it would. It's nothing like a romance movie or book. They make it all sweet and nice. *This* is super awkward. "I'm cold. Look my nipples are sticking out," I say to River, shoving my boob toward him.

River stops scrolling through his phone to look at my boob. A darkness overtakes him. He drops the phone, and launches himself toward my breast. Holy shit! He sucks on my nipple, teasing, and flicking it with his tongue.

That one small act has flipped a switch inside me. Suddenly, a shiver rips down my spine, causing me to shudder and moan. "Oh yeah," I say as I lay back on the bed.

River hovers over me, his body pushing up against mine. I drag my nails down his back. My eyes roll back, as a flood of pleasure tingles down my spine. His mouth peppers small kisses down to my naval, then kisses me softly across from one hip to another. Is he going to...hell yeah, he is!

"Holy shit," I murmur when his mouth and his tongue are doing things to my pussy.

"Are you okay?" His hot breath brushes up against my inner thigh.

"Yeah. Keep going," I say. I feel him smiling before he works his magic between my thighs. With my eyes closed, and my fingers entwined in River's hair, I relax into the sensation of River's magic mouth and tongue. The warmth is quickly rising in me as River's mouth increases in tempo. An overwhelming desire shudders between my legs.

"Do you like this?" he asks.

I nod furiously, not sure if he's looking. Grabbing his hair, I revel in the excitement of him between my legs. My hunger grows, desperate for him to continue as the heat nearly has me ready to combust. "Faster," I rasp. River brings me right to the brink of explosion, teasing, prying every morsel of ecstasy out of me. "Holy shit," I say as I clench my legs around his head. My body convulses, but nothing like I've ever managed to do on my own.

River looks up, his face glistening from me. "I have to do that again," he proudly claims.

Slowly, he kisses back up my highly sensitive body. I'm not sure if I want to push him away, or flip him and climb on top of him. To hell with it. "Lie on your back," I say.

"Gladly." He lays down, and places his hands behind his head. He thinks he's going to get a blow job. Nope, not right now. Getting off the bed, I go to my bag, open the box of condoms, and take one out. I've been practicing. I knew this was going to happen, and I didn't want to fumble as I roll one on him. Ripping the foil packet open with my teeth, I go back to the bed and straddle his legs. "I thought…"

"Nope, sorry. Later. I want to do this now." Grabbing his cock, I'm surprised by the feel of it. It's really warm, and hard, but the skin is soft, like velvet. I wonder what it would feel like if it wasn't hard. I wonder, if I was a guy if I'd spend all my time touching myself. I chuckle.

"Oh yeah, great! You've got my dick in your hand, and you laughed."

"I was just thinking that if I was a guy if I'd have my hand on my cock all the time. And I wondered what it feels like soft."

"Hope, can you maybe not think about things that make you laugh while my dick is in your hand?"

I let go of his cock. "I'm sorry," I say as I lower my head. "This is weird for me. And I think it would be awkward for you too."

"My head was between your legs, and no, it wasn't weird. Actually, I really enjoyed it. So, can you please shut up and finish what you were doing?" he says in an easier tone.

"Sorry. It's just, I'm nervous and my mind is going crazy."

He sits up in bed, and kisses me softly. Eww, I'm not sure I like how he tastes. However, the taste is me. I suppose, if he can go down on me, then I shouldn't think about it as "eww," and more like, wow, this guy went down on me and did it happily.

Stop thinking, Hope. Just feel.

I break away from the kiss, and push him back so he's lying down again. Smiling, I take his cock in my hand and instantly, I feel it flex. He likes this, and I like that I can do this for him.

Pinching the top of the condom, I roll it down his hard cock. Okay, we can do this. We may both be virgins, but after this, we won't be. We're learning together, and I really like that we're both fumbling through this experience.

Once the condom is on, I suddenly become nervous. "I'm going to go slow, okay?" Licking his lips, he nods. I position myself over River, lining him up with me. Slowly, I lower on him.

Ugh, this is slightly uncomfortable. It's kind of pinching, and stretching me but not terribly painful.

"You okay?" River asks as he places his hands on my hips.

"Yeah, I just want to go slow."

"Go as slow as you need. But my God," He presses his lips together. "You feel so good."

It takes me a few minutes, but I finally sink down on him. Yeah, this is good. Slowly, I move my hips, loving the feeling between us. River's eyes are wide open while he watches me moving on him.

Yep, I think I've got the hang of this. The feeling is unbelievable. It's intoxicating. I can do this again, and again, *and again*.

The fact we're both virgins, correction, *were* virgins, makes it even better. I can't wait until he comes back, so we can do this for the whole time he's here.

God, I love this, and I think, I love him too. Actually, I think I've loved him since we were sixteen.

Monday

Stretching in bed, I feel the delicious ache of everything River and I did yesterday. Touching my lips, I remember every taste, every pleasure, every *sensation* our entwined bodies felt.

The touch of his fingertips as he drew circles on my back.

The taste of his lips on mine.

The thrill of our heated skin as we explored each other's bodies.

Hmmm, yes. God, I already miss him, and it's only been a few hours.

And the one thing I despised was saying goodbye to him when I had to go home. I hated knowing that this morning, he and his family will be leaving to go back home.

Reaching for my phone, my hand feels for it on my night stand. Wait, where is it? Jumping out of bed, I search around my night stand. Shit, shit, shit. Getting on my knees, I look under my bed.

Fuck.

I pull the pillows off my bed, and move the mattress. It's nowhere.

"Mom!" I yell. It's early, and I know she'll still be in bed. "Mom!" I rush into my parents' room.

"What is it?" Mom asks as she blinks a few times.

"Have you seen my phone?" I ask, looking around frantically.

"What?" She pushes the covers back, and sits on the side of the bed.

"My phone. Have you seen it?" I run out to where my bag is and ruffle through it trying to find my God damned phone.

Shit.

It's not in here. Wait, is it on the kitchen counter? I search the kitchen. It's not here.

"Did you lose your phone again?" Dad asks as he enters the kitchen, grabs a glass, and fills it with water from the faucet.

"What? No. Please no, no, no, no," I say frantically trying to find my phone.

"What's going on?" Mom joins us in the kitchen as she ties her dressing gown belt around her waist.

"Can I borrow your phone? I can't find mine."

Mom lifts her brows as she tilts her head to the side. Slowly, her brows lower, and her mouth downturns. She walks back toward her room. "I told you, we're not replacing it again, Hope."

Please, please, please let it be somewhere in the house. "Mom?" She's taking too long, so I go in search of where she is.

"Here."

Mom reaches me before I'm in her room. She thrusts the phone in my hands. Dialing my number, I bring it to my ear, and when it starts ringing, I lower her phone, and try to hear where mine is. I can't hear it anywhere. With each ring, my heart sinks lower and lower. "Shit!" I yell.

"You've lost it again, haven't you?"

"No, I don't think I have. It's got to be here." I try again. This time, it goes straight through to voicemail. "No!" I say, closing my eyes, and lowering my head. Wait, they're not flying out for another hour. I can make it to the airport. "Can I borrow your car?" I ask Mom.

"Why? What's happening?"

"I have River's number and address in my phone, but I can't find it. I need to go to the airport, because they leave in an hour."

Dad looks the clock on the microwave. "You won't make it in an hour, Hope. Not with traffic. And not to mention, the airport is nearly an hour away. You know you have to be at the airport and ready to go at least an hour before you leave. Which means, you won't make it."

I turn to Mom, desperate for her to understand. "I have to try. Please," I plead. "Please."

Mom grabs onto my hands, and smiles. "You'll be late for work."

"Please, I have to make it. I don't have any other way to get hold of him."

"Look, it's futile, you're not going to make it on time, and all that'll happen will be you'll end up upset and disappointed. And that's if you don't get a speeding ticket trying." My shoulders drop forward. "But, if it'll bring some peace of mind to you to try, then take my car and go. But remember, you have work."

Ugh, shit. "Can you call Tony and let him know I'll be late please? I don't have a phone now I lost it."

"Nope, you have to do it. I'm sorry, Hope. You need to learn how to be responsible for your things, and your actions," Mom says. She walks over to the fridge and opens it, getting the juice out and pouring herself a glass.

Pulling the stool out from under the island counter, I plonk my ass on it. Running my hand through my bed head, I don't know what to do. If I call Tony and tell him I'll be late for work, he'll lose it on me. And logically, I know I won't make it to the airport on time. It's impossible to get there within an hour even if there's no traffic and I get every green light between here and there.

I just spent the best four days of my life with River. Someone I never thought I'd ever see again. And now, because of my own carelessness, I'll have to wait until he comes to find me, because I don't even know his address or phone number.

"Maybe he's listed," Mom says with a softness to her voice.

"Yeah, maybe he is." My gut is saying: *he's left again*. But this time, I'm pretty sure it's for the last time.

My skin prickles with tiny goosebumps of disappointment. I can't believe I've lost him, *again*.

Chapter
FOURTEEN

"HOW ARE THE permits coming? What do we still need?" I ask Charlie as I walk the now empty kitchen. "Looks so much bigger, doesn't it?"

"Yeah, it does. It's going to be massive once we add the square footage in the back. I checked with the town planner, and the permits should be ready by the end of the week."

"Okay. The front and back are looking good. I didn't know what to expect with all that trash that was everywhere, and it being so overgrown. But it looks great. I can see what we're working with now."

Charlie leans against the wall and crosses his arms over his chest. "Want a crew starting Saturday?"

I click my tongue to the roof of my mouth. "Start them Monday, in case there's any resistance for the permits. I don't expect it, but we both know anything can happen. Still, let's do what we can ourselves."

"Have you seen the size of this house? And you want to make it bigger. You think we can do this on our own?"

"Don't be an idiot. I don't think we can do this on our own, but let's do what we can."

Charlie pushes off from the wall, and comes over to me, hugging me. "What's wrong, sis? You seem flat."

"Yeah, I am. I've got a lot on my mind, that's all." Stepping back, I close my eyes, and let out a long sigh. "It's River," I say.

"River? Why what's happening with you?"

"He asked me out."

"Oh, cool. Are you going to go?" Opening my eyes, I find I'm already shaking my head. "Why?"

"We have history, Charlie. And I'm not sure I want to revisit it."

"Well, this is getting interesting. I remember you've known him since school," he pauses and lifts his brows. "And I know you fell for him hard. Is that all?" he drags the last word, like he's skeptical.

"Do you really want to know?"

"Do I have to kick his ass? Because I so will." He puffs his chest out, all masculine. "Not like you need me protecting you. Actually, I should be protecting him!" He smiles.

"We have history, okay? Like close history." Charlie screws his nose. "I'm not telling you anything, so calm your ass."

"Phew, dodged a bullet." He wipes at his forehead, then places his hand to his chest. "So, what's the problem?"

"I'm not sure I want to revisit what we kind of had."

"Is it bad? Did he cheat on you or something?"

"No, nothing like that. It's hard to talk about, and I'm not sure if I want to get into it with him. But it feels like fate's bringing us together again."

Charlie rolls his eyes. "Fate? Really. That's another word for mumbo-jumbo, bullshit."

"You don't believe in fate?"

"Oh my God. Here we go. The whole 'the universe has bigger plans for us' crap." He wiggles his fingers in the air and widens his eyes. "It's just a way for those new age freaks to make a buck or two."

Ugh, it's like talking to a brick wall. "River and I have a past, and he asked me out on a date. But, there's so much we haven't talked about, and I'm not even sure I want to."

"Then don't go."

"But he's working for me now. I can't avoid him when he's doing the electrical for the house."

"Look." Charlie places his hands on my shoulders. "The moment this house is flipped, we're out of here. Back to where we belong. This is a small town, with a bunch of small-minded people."

"Hey," I say, defending all the wonderful people I've met. "Who's spouting the bullshit now? These people came here and helped us without us asking for it. That's not a small-minded mentality. That's something we've never seen before, so don't go saying shit about this town, okay?"

Charlie smirks. "Seems you're liking it here."

"I am, but I also know what you're saying. We'll be out of here soon enough."

"Yeah, so avoid him 'til we sell and leave." I nod, but I'm not feeling it. I want to get to the bottom of what happened the last time we met. "Oh yeah. You're screwed!" Charlie chuckles, staring at my face.

"What? Why?"

"This history you both have. It's deeper than you're letting on. And not to mention you're loving the town too."

"No, I'm not," I say in an unusually high-pitched voice. I clear my throat. "Let me try that again. No, I'm not."

Charlie takes a deep breath. "Look, sis, I know you. Usually you come, you're all business, and you get things done. This place though." He looks around the house. "Maybe it's this old girl." He places his palm to the wall. "Maybe it's the town. Or maybe it's the people." He pointedly glares at me. "But whatever it is, it's crawled under your skin."

"Are you saying I should go on a date with River?"

"Funny, isn't it? I didn't say a thing about him, but that's the only thing you heard. Seems to me you've already made your mind up."

I glare at Charlie. He gives me his cheeky smile. "Get back to work," I say as I walk away from him. "I'm going to look at flooring, tile and cabinets." I slide my sunglasses on as I start walking away.

"Want me to come with you?" Tilting my head down, I look at him from above my glasses. "That's a no, then?"

"Get back to work," I order.

I hear Charlie laughing as I walk out of the house. Getting into my truck, I look in the rear-view mirror, and see the same gray and white cat sitting in the bed. "Hey." I knock on the window.

Meow.

"Don't give me attitude. Get out."

Meow.

The cat looks at me, and I swear to fucking God, he rolls his eyes, then turns his head, not acknowledging me. "Hey!" I yell through the car to the back. The cat looks at me, then yawns, and lays down.

Getting out of the car, I go to the rear of my truck, where the cat's still laying, watching me. "Go," I say to him.

Meow.

"Don't meow at me, buddy. I've got somewhere to be."

Meow.

"You can't stay there. It's dangerous."

Meow.

"Go!" I point, as if the cat knows what I'm talking about. "Go." This time I add a foot stomp.

Meow.

"Wait, are you hungry?" His coat is scruffy, and he appears to be under weight. Maybe he's a stray.

Meow.

I don't have anything I can feed him. I'll stop at the convenience store in town and get him some food. "You have to move; you can't stay there. But, I promise, I'll bring food back for you."

Meow.

Why am I talking to a damn cat? It's not like it understands what I'm saying. "Move!" I yell at it, but instantly I feel bad for being horrible to the cat. "Look, I've got somewhere I need to be, can you please get off my truck, and I'll bring you some food when I return."

"Are you trying to bribe the cat?"

I startle when I hear River behind me. "No, don't be stupid." River's brows fly up. His face lights up with a cheeky smirk. "Yeah, I'm trying to get him to move. I've seen him here before, and I think he might be a stray."

"He probably is. Do you want him gone?"

"No, don't hurt him," I say automatically thinking the worst.

"Why would I hurt him?" He approaches the cat, and gently reaches out to grab him.

Hiss – grrr. The cat's ears perk up, and he looks like he's about to pounce on River.

"He doesn't like you," I say.

"Feral cats don't like anyone."

I walk forward, and pat River on the arm. "Stand aside, let me show you how it's done."

River steps back, and raises his hands in surrender. "Go on, cat whisperer. Do your thing."

"Pss, pss, pss, pss." I step forward carefully, making sure I don't make any sudden movements. "Here you go." I slowly reach forward so the cat can smell me. He's looking at me skeptically, but the moment my hand is inches from him, he stands and rubs his head on me. "Hey there, buddy."

Meow.

"You have to move, okay? I've got to be somewhere. I'll come back with food, okay?"

Meow. He jumps down, and circles himself up around my leg, brushing against me as he continues to meow.

"You've got to be kidding me." River steps closer and reaches to pat the cat. The cat hisses again at River. "He doesn't like me."

I can't help but laugh. I lean down, and scratch under the cat's chin. "Okay, I have to go, but I'll bring you food."

Meow.

"Do you want company?" River asks.

"You don't have work?"

"I just finished a job, and my next job starts in two hours. So I have two hours to kill. I thought I could come by and help." He looks toward the house, then back to me.

"Charlie might need a hand."

River's smile drops slightly. "Sure." He nods, and walks up to the house.

Ugh. I can't believe I did that. There's a question that's been burning in my mind since the moment I saw him, but I feel so conflicted. I know I have no right to ask, but in a way I do, too. I owe it to myself to find out as much as I can about what happened. "River," I call before he disappears inside. He turns, and I walk toward him, meeting at the bottom of the stairs. "I'll go out with you for dinner, but," I hold up a finger before he gets too confident. "We're only going as friends. Nothing else. Because I deserve to know the truth."

He nods as he takes in a deep breath and lowers his gaze. "That's fair," he says. "I'll pick you up at six."

"Hey, didn't you hear what I said. This isn't a date. I'll drive myself to wherever we're going."

"The only reason I said I'll pick you up, is because you're still new here, and don't know the town or neighboring towns like I do. But okay, I respect you, and if you want to drive yourself, then I'll message the address to you. I assume it's okay if I make the reservations?"

What a brazen bastard. "Yes, that's fine."

"Okay. Until tonight." He goes into the house, where I hear him call, "Charlie. You need a hand, man?"

I head back to my truck, and I'm happy to find the cat is nowhere to be seen. I have to remember to stop in town on the way back from checking out flooring, to get supplies for the cat.

The convenience store is small, but packed with a lot of things. The range isn't overly large, but there's enough of everything to get through.

"You must be Hope," the man behind the counter calls as I peruse the tightly stocked aisles.

I pop my head out when I hear my name. "Sorry?"

The older man behind the counter, says something to the person he's working with, then comes to find me. "You're Hope, right?"

"I am." I smile as I look for pet food.

"You're fixing Old Roger's house. There's a huge buzz around here about what you're going to do with it. Some of the folks were scared you were going to rip it down, but I knew from the moment you and May came to the flower festival, that you're not into destruction, are you?"

I could say this is creepy, but it's kind of endearing. And weird. More weird than endearing, but whatever. "I like giving things a second chance at life." I smile as I continue looking for cat food.

"I must say, I'm extremely grateful you've decided to restore the house. It would've been such a shame if you tore it down."

"Did you know him well?" I ask.

"I did. I'd take him his groceries every Wednesday. He'd invite me in, and he'd pour me a beer. We'd talk for an hour or so, then I'd leave. Did that every Wednesday, for many years."

I notice the thinning, gray hair, and the lines of experience on his face. "I heard Old Roger's wife died of cancer. Did he ever re-marry?" I ask, wanting to really know about the earrings, letter, and shirt I found in the tin.

"Old Roger?" he asks, I nod. "He never loved anyone ever again after Jean passed away. It kind of broke him. Then when Henry died, it sent him over the edge. He became more of a recluse. He'd let me in though, every Wednesday, like clockwork. But the death of Henry really changed him."

"What's your fondest memory of Old Roger?" I ask.

"He loved his family with so much fierceness. One time." He starts chuckling. "That boy of his, Henry, took Old Roger's car and crashed it into Gran's parents' car. Old Roger was so mad with Henry, he made Henry go to Gran's parents' house every weekend for a year to do yard work to pay off the damage."

"Wow."

"Henry was only a child, maybe fourteen, or fifteen. But he went, every weekend. He'd be there as the sun rose, and he'd stay until the sun set. Old Roger had a firm way with Henry. But he was fair. Everyone respected Old Roger for being fair. One day, one of the young kids blew his mailbox up, all in fun. Old Roger didn't get mad. Instead, he went to the kid's parents, and told them what he did. Then told the parents the kid would have to clean his house for two months for payment."

"I bet that kid didn't do that again."

"Next time you're in Elle's café, ask Murray. He was the kid."

"Was he?" I squeal a little too loud.

The convenience store guy nods. He looks in my empty basket. "Can I help you with anything?"

"Oh, yes, please. A stray cat has shown up at the house, and I'm looking for something to feed him."

"Is that the black cat?"

"No, this one is gray and white."

"Ah, the black cat wasn't friendly toward anyone. He'd go to Old Roger's house, eat, then leave. He was almost like a community cat, but he disappeared once Old Roger died." He rakes his hand through his hair. "Ha."

"How bizarre. This cat likes sitting in the back of my truck. Weird cat."

"Do you know how old the cat is because you'll need to get him food for his age. Here." He walks down an aisle, and I follow. "Are you adopting him?"

"Not exactly. I thought I'd feed him because he shows up."

The guy laughs. "Looks like he's adopted you. Anyway, here. Wet food, and dry food. Do you need bowls?"

"I suppose so."

"Here you go." He hands me two metal bowls. "Anything else I can help with?"

"Um, no, thank you…" I wait for his name.

"George."

"Thank you, George." I hold my hand out to him to shake, and clutch the handle of the basket in my other hand.

"You're welcome, Hope. Now, if you need anything, I'm here to help. I'm glad I got to meet you. Maybe, I'll get to meet your brother, Charlie."

It still blows my mind that everyone knows who we are. "I'm sure you will."

I walk up to the cash register, where George rings up my purchases.

Chapter
FIFTEEN

Past

T HE MUSIC IS loud, and I've been drinking since we got to the club.

"That guy's checking you out," Lydia yells over the loud music.

"I don't care," I reply as I look at who she's pointing out.

"Come on. You can't celebrate your twenty-first without a guy. Pick someone, and have a one-night-stand," she says.

"Who's having a one-night-stand?" Annabella asks.

Lydia and Annabella are the girlfriends of a couple of guys I work with, and they're great fun to hang with. But sometimes I think they forget I'm not into one-night stands. Not since the one guy I picked up, and went back to his place. He failed miserably at everything sex-related. "I'm not having a one-night stand with anyone."

"Come on, it's not like you and Grady are serious."

"We're not anything. We're just friends."

"Then you can have a one-nighter with someone. Look around, and pick someone. Anyone. If Grady and you aren't bumping uglies, especially on your birthday, then you have to screw someone tonight."

"No, I'm not doing that anymore. I'm happy just being here with you two. And I think Charlie and his girlfriend will be here soon too." I check my phone, in case Charlie's messaged. He hasn't, of course. That's normal for him.

"What about him?" Annabella says as she picks her drink up to sip.

I don't even bother looking. I grab my drink, slam it back, and stand. "I'm going to dance. You coming?"

"After my drink." Lydia holds up her half-full glass.

"Me too." Annabella copies Lydia.

I walk out to the dance floor, close my eyes, and move to the music. This feels fantastic. Just me, and the seduction of rhythmic music. I feel a pair of hands on my hips. I open my eyes, and turn to see the guy who was staring at me, grinding up against me. "I'm gay, and not interested," I say to him.

"It's okay, baby." He grips me harder.

"Not interested," I say again, then smack his hands off me.

"Come on, baby. It's just a dance."

What is it with guys and *baby?* "I said no."

He leans in and says, "You're a bitch. I could've rocked your world."

"I've been disappointed enough today. I don't need to see your micro penis to add to my frustration."

"Fuck you," he says as he grabs his crotch and thrusts toward me.

Thankfully, he leaves. Closing my eyes, I get myself back into the rhythm the music playing. Swaying and moving to the side,

I give myself over to the bass. The DJ layers Rolling Stones songs, making the old tunes so interesting.

Another pair of hands grip my hips. I swear, I'm going to kick this guy so damn hard he'll be shitting out my shoe for a month. Opening my eyes, I clench my jaw, and turn to find myself staring into the beautiful dark eyes of someone I never thought I'd see again.

"River?" I yell as I stop dancing.

"Hey." He leans down, and gives me a small kiss on my cheek.

"What... how? I... what?"

He laughs. We're moving together to the music, but the music has now been long forgotten. "Drink?"

"Yeah." We entwine our fingers together and he leads us off the dance floor. Lydia and Annabella both stare as we walk past them, hand-in-hand. I smile, and give them a small nod. We approach the bar, and River turns to me. "White Russian," I say.

"White Russian, and scotch, neat."

Oh, scotch, neat. *Sexy.* River pays for our drinks, and we take them to an available booth, away from Lydia and Annabella. I look over to them, and both are staring. Annabella gives me two thumbs up and nods eagerly. She then brings her hand up to her ear, making a telephone gesture. *Call me tomorrow,* she mouths. She's presumptuous. But yeah, she's probably right. My twenty-first and River. *Thank you, God!*

I nod before taking a sip of my third White Russian so far tonight.

"What happened?" River asks, breaking the non-existent ice between us. I know exactly what he's referring to.

"You wouldn't believe me even if I told you."

"Try me. At first I thought you were ghosting me, then when I came back, I found out you moved. I even got on social media to try and find you."

I shake my head, trying to forget what happened. "After that night." I indicate with a flippant hand gesture. "You dropped me off home, and I went to bed so happy. When I woke in the morning, I quickly discovered that I'd lost my phone."

I watch as River's eyes widen, then close before he drops his chin. "Shit."

"Yeah. I went back to where your grandmother had her birthday party, begging for a phone number, but they refused to give it to me. So I pleaded for them to call whoever organized it, to get in contact with you."

"No one called, or Mom would've told me."

"Yep, and then we moved." Even saying all this aloud sounds ridiculous. "I joined social media, and couldn't find you." I can see the disappointment on River's face. "I searched for you," I said.

"I came back to find you, but there was nothing. No forwarding address. Nothing. It was like you disappeared."

It took me a long time to get over River. He was my first love, and the man who took my virginity. Just like I was his first too. It's almost like it's cosmic; the universe pushes us together, only to tear us apart.

"Tell me you're not seeing anyone?" River asks.

Grady immediately pops into my mind. I'm not feeling guilty because nothing has happened. I could probably grow to love Grady, but River... I don't know. I haven't seen him since the night we lost our virginity to each other, and it feels like not a single hour has passed. "I'm not with anyone." But I also feel like I owe River the truth. Not like I'm lying though, because nothing's happening with Grady. "But there is someone who I'm kind of seeing."

River picks his drink up, stills his hand before it reaches his mouth. "Oh." He lowers his hand without taking a sip. His shoulders slightly drop before he asks, "How serious is it?"

"We've gone out twice, and we haven't even kissed. We're still kinda getting to know each other."

River smiles, obviously feeling okay with what I just told him. "Good."

"What about you? Are you seeing anyone?"

River's face tenses. His eyes slightly widen, and his jaw stiffens. "I was," he pauses and takes a long breath. "But I'm not now." He drops his gaze for a split second, before lifting it to look into my eyes.

He's never been untruthful to me, so I shouldn't worry. But he seems unusually tense, like he's under pressure. Still, that could be anything. It doesn't have to be related to this woman he's no longer with. It could be work, home, anything.

"What are you doing here?" I ask, trying to change conversation.

"One of my friends has enlisted, and he leaves on Monday."

"Ah, I see. One last hurrah then?" I look around, trying to pick out the group he'd be with. I find a rowdy group of guys, and indicate toward them. "Them?"

"How did you guess?" River asks, *strained*.

"They're the loudest. But, won't they miss you?"

"Nah, all they want to do is get drunk and pick up. I didn't even want to come, and changed my mind at the last minute. You know, this stuff, isn't my scene. But, let me tell you." He smiles broadly, showing me that cute dimpled chin, and beautiful dark, soulful eyes. "I'm *so* glad I changed my mind."

"I'm glad you changed your mind too. So, tell me. What's been happening?"

He shrugs. "I really don't want to talk about me. All I want to do is kiss you." Whoa, hello there. Where has this confidence come from? He reaches across and waits for me to put my hand in his. He pulls me off the seat, and onto his lap. "I've missed you so much," he says.

"I've missed you like crazy." I lower my head, so my forehead rests against his.

He laces his hands through the back of my hair, and gently guides my lips to his. Slowly, and like there's no other person in the room, he darts his tongue out to caress my tingling lips. *Jesus, just kiss me, will you?!*

Yeah, I'm not liking this slow crap. I devour his mouth, kissing him like I've never kissed anyone before. Our mouths are sealed over each other's, completely connected. My heart beats quicker with every passing second. My pulse races. My skin tingles while his hands grip my hair. Shit, every part of me is throbbing with a desperate desire. I've never wanted anyone as much as I want River right now. I just need to touch his bare skin, have it against mine. God, if we keep kissing like this, we might end up screwing right here, in front of everyone.

Pulling away, I see River's dark eyes are hungry with need. Shit, I can only imagine this is how I'm looking to him. Leaning down, I take his earlobe in my mouth, and tease it with the tip of my tongue. His hands are on my hips. The rumble that vibrates through his chest, echoes deep inside of me. "I need a drink," I say.

"Fuck, Hope."

"After my drink." *Hopefully.*

His eyes snap open, and a slow smile stretches across his beautiful face. "I'll get us some drinks." He taps my thigh, wanting me to get up. I grind against him. "That's not fair. How am I supposed to get up now?"

"You're already up," I tease.

His hands move around to my butt, where he smacks me. He watches as my eyes widen. "Oh, I see," he says. He grabs my butt, and moves me off of him. "I'll be back in a second." As he gets up, I see his phone fall to the ground from his back pocket.

"Hey!" The music is too loud for River to hear me. Dumb ass. I thought only I lost phones. I stand, retrieve it and place it next to me on the bench seat.

I look over to Annabella and Lydia, both of them are in their own worlds, dancing together on the dance floor.

I'm so excited. I'm getting laid tonight, and it's with River. *Woohoo!* It feels so right. Him, me, *us.*

I look over to the bar, where River's giving the server our order. He turns, notices me staring, and he winks. Shit, I think my insides have melted. Fuck, he's so hot. His dark hair, cute dimpled chin, smoldering dark eyes.

River's phone vibrates next to my leg, and automatically look down to see a message has come through.

My heart drops into my stomach. A bolt of ice shoots through my veins.

Claire says: *Hey baby, when you get home we have to make a decision about what our baby's name will be.*

What the actual fuck?

He's not only got a girlfriend, he's going to be a father?

What a fucking asshole.

Blinking rapidly, I do everything I can to hold the tears in.

I take several deep breaths. I can't believe this. He had his tongue in my mouth, and all the while he knew he was going to be a father?

Suddenly, the anger takes over. My hands are trembling from the sheer fury peaking inside of me. Nope. Not gonna happen.

"Hey," River says as he places the drinks on the small table already overcrowded with empty glasses. He looks at me, then quickly looks down to his phone. "Oh."

"You're gonna be a fucking father?" I yell.

"It's…"

"No." I throw the phone at him. "Go home, to Claire. You lying bastard." I pick my drink up, and throw that at him too. "You're not the man I thought I knew." I run as fast as I can.

"Hope, wait."

I'm not waiting. This isn't something small. This is a huge deal. He and Claire are going to be a family. I keep running, until I'm outside. And just like fate, there's a taxi about to pull away from the curb. I jump in, and close the door. "Please, just drive," I say.

"Sorry, but…"

"Hope!" River bashes on the window.

"Please," I beg as I burst into tears. "Please."

The lady looks at me, then a frantic River trying to open the door. She pulls away from the curb. "You okay, sugar?" she asks.

"Thank you for not throwing me out."

"One more fare will help me." I see her smile through the mirror. I'm sobbing as she drives. She hands me a box of tissues. "Where to?"

I take a few tissues, and give her my home address.

The River Lockwood I loved no longer exists. Or maybe, he never did to start with.

SIXTEEN

S ITTING IN ELLE'S café, I keep bringing River's number up on the screen. I know we're supposed to go out to talk about things tonight, but I can't do it. I can't bring myself to actually go. It doesn't matter, I suppose.

I write out a text and every time, I delete it.

"You look like you need something stronger than a coffee," Elle says. She slides into the bench seat opposite me. "What's going on?"

"Nothing," I say as I stare down at my phone.

"Aha. That's why you've been staring at your phone for the past hour and haven't touched your now stone-cold coffee."

I look up, then gaze over to the coffee. "Sorry."

"What's going on?" I shrug. "Right then. It's got nothing to do with River, has it?"

"It's complicated," I say.

"It really isn't. And even if it was, you can *un*-complicate it."

"It's not that easy."

"Why?" she pushes.

Placing my phone face down, I now have nothing but the back of it to stare at. "It's just not that easy," I repeat as I look up at her.

She nods slowly. "I think you're afraid."

"Damn right I am."

"Huh."

"What?" I ask.

"If you don't want to know, why are you sitting here like you're about to have your last meal?" God, I hate how observant she is. I answer her the only way I can. I shrug. "You know, it really isn't so complicated."

"Says the chick who's been lusting after the cop and refuses to ask him out," I snap. The second I speak the words, I instantly regret them. Elle's eyes widen, as she lifts her head, then gives me a small nod. "Elle," I say, trying to take back my bitchiness.

"It's okay." She plasters a fake smile on her pretty, yet hurt face. "Would you like any more coffee?" She stands, and runs her hands down the front of her shirt.

"I'm so sorry."

She holds her hand up, while she continues to hold her head up with pride. "Is there anything else I can get you?"

Oh man. I've hurt her, and I didn't want to do that. Elle's been nothing but kind to me, and I've been so horrible. "Elle, please. I'm so sorry."

"Apology accepted. Let me know if I can get you anything else." She leaves, and disappears into the kitchen.

I feel like shit now that I've hurt Elle. *Ugh.* I hate myself for being such a jerk. I flip my phone around, write out a text, and press send. *Can't make it, sorry.*

I slide out of the chair, leave some money on the table, and exit the café. I'm so preoccupied, I don't even realize someone's walking toward me until I quite literally bump into him. Looking up, I see Jake. "I'm sorry, Jake," I say as I try to make a quick getaway before I say something offensive to him too.

"You okay, Hope?"

Damn it. Why does he have to ask? "Yeah, I'm good. You?"

"What's wrong?" he asks without responding to my question.

"I'm good." I offer him a fake smile.

He stares at me, puffs out his chest, and widens his stance. He's doing the whole sheriff thing. "What's wrong?" He crosses his arms in front of his chest.

"Sorry, Jake. I'm running late. But, I'm okay. Just got a lot on my mind." I tap my temple, hoping he'll believe me. "You know, permits, house, repairs. All that stuff."

"You're not in trouble?"

Well, let me see. The guy I was once in love with lives in the town I ran away to, and now he's working for me, and stirring up a cauldron full of emotions. Trouble? Hell yeah, I'm in trouble. "Nah, nothing I can't handle."

"You know this is a safe town, and I'll do everything I can to protect you. But you have to trust me and tell me what's happening."

Now I have to tell him something. Shit, what do I say? "Jake, it honestly isn't anything at all. If I do run into trouble, I promise, you'll be the first person I'll come to."

Jake's eyes narrow as he takes me in. "I'll accept that, for now."

Man, what is it with everyone here? "Thank you. I have to go. A lot of work to get done on the house."

"It'll be getting dark soon."

"I have a generator I use. I think I'll spend some time there tonight." I need to be alone and away from everyone. Especially River.

"Okay." He tips his head, and walks into Elle's café. It still baffles me how those two can't overcome whatever shyness they both have, and just go for it. Anyway, it's not my business, I guess.

I get into my truck, and drive to Old Roger's house.

It's well after ten and I should go back to May's so I can shower and go to bed. I'm so tired, and hungry. Grabbing my bottle of water, I unscrew the lid, and finish what's left in it. My eyes are stinging, and I can't help but continuously yawn.

It's so quiet at night. There aren't any cars driving past, or anyone tooting their horns. Nothing like what I'm used to.

I walk out to the front porch, and lean against one of the support beams.

Closing my eyes, I focus in on the native sounds of the night. In the distance, I can hear an owl hooting, and crickets chirping. I can even hear the sound of the waves of the ocean.

Meow.

My eyes quickly open, and I nearly jump back until I realize it's the cat rubbing up my leg.

"Hey, buddy."

Meow.

"You hungry?"

Meow.

"Yeah, me too." I head down to my truck and get a small can of cat food, and the cat bowl out. Crap, the faucet in the kitchen has been torn out, so I walk around to the side of the house, where the outdoor faucet is still attached. I fill one side of the dual-bowl feeder up with water and carry it back up to the porch.

Meow.

"Yeah, yeah, I know. Here you go." I tear the cat food tin top open, and empty it on the other side. The cat looks at me, then the food. "You've got to be kidding, right? This isn't the right kind of food for you?"

Meow.

Sitting on the top porch step, I look at the cat. "If you don't like it, don't eat it," I say to the cat.

He blinks at me, then looks at the food again. He walks over, sniffs the food, and settles in to eat.

"Thought you'd eat it." I look up to the darkened sky, and watch as a handful of stars twinkle in the sky. The crescent moon is barely visible, but at least I can see it's the slightest of slivers.

I hear the rumble of a truck approaching, and I look to see if it's Charlie. It pulls up behind my truck, and the moment I see it, I know it's River.

The interior light flicks on when he opens the door, confirming my suspicion. He closes the door, and when he rounds the truck, he sticks his hands in his jeans pockets. "So," he says as he slowly approaches.

"So," I reply, not really wanting to have a conversation with him.

"I'm hoping you lost your phone again, and some random person messaged me to call off our date."

"It wasn't a date."

He half-chuckles and focuses in on the cat, who's still eating. "Okay, it wasn't a date. You didn't lose your phone, did you?"

A few years ago, losing my phone was something I did often. Now, no way. "Nope." I purse my lips together, then sigh.

He clicks his tongue to the roof of his mouth. Looking down, he too sighs. "We need to talk, Hope."

"I've been holding my tongue since the day you showed up here. And I've wanted to ask, but you know what? It's not my business, not anymore."

He slowly strolls toward me, and sits on the step beside me. "You never gave me the opportunity to explain."

Why does this hurt so much? My heart can't take another blow like it did on my twenty-first. I hold my hands up, abandoning this conversation. "It's not my business, River." I stand, and start heading down toward my truck.

"She wasn't pregnant," he desperately blurts. I stop walking. I know what I saw. Turning, I'm seconds from smacking him and his lying mouth. "Claire was lying."

I struggle to move. "Don't fucking lie to me," my voice cracks, but I'm a damn warrior and I hold in the volcanic emotions rippling deep inside.

"I'm not." He hasn't moved from the step, but he's edging forward ready to jump up. "Claire and I had a thing. It lasted all of about three months. And when I broke it off with her, she became a bit of a stalker. Showing up at work, calling me all the time. Then she dropped the bombshell that she was pregnant. With *my* baby." River runs his hands through his dark hair.

"What happened?" I ask as I return to where I was sitting. The cat sees me sitting, and curls up next to me. His body firm against mine, between River and me.

"I wouldn't run from my responsibilities, Hope. But I knew something wasn't right, too. So, I told her, we'll go to the doctor together."

"And?"

"Well, I made the doctor's appointment, and as the day was approaching, she was acting really weird. But, I had a gut feeling something was wrong. I wasn't sure if it was her, or the baby. The day of the appointment, she said she'd made a different appointment she couldn't get out of. She was avoiding it, which screamed to me how she was lying. I confronted her, but she kept to her story of being pregnant." He shakes his head, then turns away. I see he moves his hand. Shit, is he crying?

"What happened?" I push. I deserve the truth.

"I drove to the drug store and got a pregnancy test. I watched as she peed on the stick. She didn't want me to watch, but I just had this feeling that she was manipulating me. I made her pee on that damn stick in front of me. And we both watched it, until it came up with one God-damned line. *Not pregnant.*"

"Oh."

He stands, and starts pacing in front of me. "But you know the worst thing about all this?"

"There's something worse than being duped into believing you're going to be a father?"

"The whole time I thought she was pregnant, all I could think of was how I wish it was you carrying my child, and not her."

My heart skips a beat, and for once I'm actually speechless. I don't know what to say, or even how to react. Having a baby hasn't ever really entered my mind. I never imagined myself as a mommy, I thought I'd be flipping houses until I was too old to do that.

"You don't have to say anything," River says. "But you had to know. What you saw that night, was nothing more than a horrible joke on me. But the worst thing is, not only am I *not* a father because she was never pregnant to start with, but I lost you, again."

"That night..." I shake my head. "Broke me," I finally say after the longest of seconds. "I was shattered."

"We hadn't even exchanged numbers, so I couldn't call you." He comes over and sits again. The cat stirs beside me, opens his eyes, and hisses at River. "This cat doesn't like me at all."

I chuckle. "Look, it's been a long time."

"I know, and all I want is the chance to make it up to you again."

"River, it's pointless. Once this house is done, I'm moving on. And I can't take the chance that I'll be hurt again. I'm just coming out of a relationship with a guy who..." I stop short of telling him what happened with Grady. He doesn't need to know. It's in the past.

"But what if we can make it work this time? There aren't any outside forces keeping us apart."

"Except, this *isn't* my home, and it's yours."

"You owe it to yourself to try."

I stand, walk up to the door, close and lock it. Then I head down the steps. The cat follows me. "I owe it to myself to protect my heart. And you owe it to yourself to protect yours. We're not a good fit, River. Maybe we never were."

"You're wrong," he says within a nanosecond. "You and I have something. I know it, I'll just have to make you see it too."

I walk backward to my truck shaking my head. The cat follows me. "Goodnight, River." I get into my truck, and the cat jumps up into the bed. I don't know what I'm going to do with this cat, or with River. I pull onto the quiet street, and head toward May's. The whole time, my damn head feels like it's going to explode with the overload of information.

It doesn't matter anyway. Once Old Roger's house is flipped, I'm out of here.

Chapter
SEVENTEEN

WAKING, I STARE up at the ceiling of the converted stables. Charlie is snoring so loudly he probably wouldn't hear a freight train passing. I grab my phone, and remember I turned it off yesterday, trying to avoid River. Which, incidentally was futile.

I turn my phone on, and immediately I'm inundated with so many texts, phone calls, and voice messages. Sometimes, I feel like I'm a slave to the damn phone. But I also know I need it if I ever want tradespeople to be able to get in touch with me.

It's no use looking at any of the messages, so I delete them before I read them.

The cat stirs, and I remember I brought him home last night. He rode in the bed of the truck, like harnessed dogs do. But now he's curled up on the bottom of my bed, purring as he sleeps. Wait, have I inherited a damn cat?

I hear someone outside, and I slink out of bed to go see what's happening. Opening the door, I pop my head out to find Tabitha dressed and ready to go. "Shit," she says when she sees me. "You scared the crap out of me."

"Sorry." I smile. "Are you leaving?"

"No." She shakes her head. "I'm going to the growers' market to get some fresh seafood. I want to see what they have to offer, because I'm cooking tonight."

"It's like four-thirty in the morning. It's not even light yet."

"I'm a chef, and we get up at weird times. Anyway, I have to go."

"Can I come with you? It'll take me like five minutes to get changed."

She looks at the time on her phone, and I can tell she's itching to get there. "You have four minutes," she says playfully.

Hell yeah, I can be ready in four minutes. I run inside, go to the bathroom, splash some water on my face and get changed. I come out, re-tying my hair so it's out of my face. "Done."

Tabitha does a double-take. "You're a woman after my own heart. None of my girlfriends could ever be ready in four minutes."

"If you check your phone, you'll see it's only three," I proudly say as I quietly close the door behind me.

She checks, and nods with a huge smirk. "You go, girl." We walk to her car, and I get in the passenger side. "Why are you awake so early?"

"Being in this business, sometimes I'll work through the night because time is money. The longer I keep a house, the more it'll cost me. It's a bit different for Old Roger's house though. I'm using my own money, and don't have any carrying costs. But I still need to get it done."

She starts the car, and reverses out of the spot, then continues down the long driveway. "Do you enjoy it, flipping houses?"

"Love it. I couldn't imagine doing anything else."

"It's predominantly a male-orientated business, isn't it?"

"Yeah, it is. But more women are doing it now. I like getting my hands dirty." I hold up my hands to her. "See, short nails. Calloused palms." I chuckle, and so does Tabitha. "But the same could be said about being a chef. I mean, stereotypically, the woman does the cooking at home, but in a commercial kitchen, it's primarily male chefs, right?"

"Yeah. There are a lot of female chefs coming up though, in comparison to what you do."

"Look at us, both being rebels and all."

There's a long pause in the car, and I yawn as the tired hits me. "Aunt May really likes you."

"Does she? I think she's an amazing lady."

"She is. I wish she was my mom. But she isn't."

I can tell by the sadness in her voice that Tabitha's relationship with her mother isn't exactly strong. "She's very much a no-nonsense type of woman, and I like that about her. Nothing worse than people telling you what you want to hear."

"Tell me about it. Aunt May says you and your brother flip houses together? How does that work? Doesn't it get messy with you being related?"

"He accepts that I'm the boss," I say way too quickly. She laughs. "I trust him with my life, and I know he's good at what he does. There have been times we butt heads, but considering I'm the one who bankrolls all the projects, Charlie just goes with the flow. Even though I own the company, we're both in it together. He's really good at project management too, and between the two of us, we've got a lot of connections in the industry."

"But you haven't restored a house here in Hope River before, have you?"

"No! This is way out of my comfort zone. I live about five

hours away, so the usual tradespeople and contractors I work with aren't anywhere near here. But it's all working out, so I'm happy about that."

"I was so impressed with everyone helping to clear the yard. But that's what Hope River is. It's a community that looks after each other."

"Yeah, I'm noticing. Tell me about you. Are you working anywhere?"

"I move around a bit. I'm not settled anywhere, except here. But Hope River doesn't need a restaurant, so unless I find work in the neighboring counties, I'll have to leave and come back whenever I need Aunt May." She breaks my heart. It's like May is her touchstone, the one person she can rely on. How sad that her parents aren't there for her. Reminds me, I need to call Mom and Dad.

"What about your father?"

She groans. "Yeah, his idea of being a father is 'let's give Tabitha money and hopefully she won't notice that I'm too busy for her and don't *want* to make time for her.'" *Ouch.*

"Oh, man. I'm sorry." I look out the window at the sun slowly rising in the horizon. "Wow, look at that."

"Yeah, there's something about Hope River. It really gets under your skin, and then you never want to leave. Or if you do leave, you can't wait to come back. I know that's how I feel. Everyone says the same thing."

Except me. I'm leaving. "I can see that." The moment Old Roger's house is done, I'm out of here. Probably with the addition of a cat.

"But you're still leaving, right?"

How does she know? Am I that transparent? "My life isn't here."

"It can be. It's not that difficult to move here. It's not like you don't own a house."

"That's way too big for me."

"What about a family? Boyfriend? Don't you want those things?"

I'm forced to examine what River said last night, and I'm not ready for that. I'm not sure I'll ever be ready. "To be honest, I don't know."

"You know, I've had a shit upbringing. Not in the way most people conjure in their heads. More like abandonment issues. And I never want to turn into my parents, so for me, kids and partners will never be in the cards for me." Just like May.

"I'm sorry you've had that in your life. I can't say I relate to it, because I don't. It must be hard."

She shrugs. "We're here," she says. I wish I'd taken more notice of where Tabitha was driving to. This place is amazing.

"Holy shit, I had no idea a place like this existed here."

"It does if you know where you're looking. Restaurants from up to an hour away come here to get their produce."

We get out of the car, and walk down along the boardwalk. On the right side is the ocean. You can smell the rich saltiness from the water, and the breeze has got quite an early morning bite to it too. There are all kinds of fresh produce lining the other side of the boardwalk. "Wow."

"You can get everything from seafood, to locally grown beef, to freshly killed chickens, to every herb and vegetable known to man."

"Makes me wish I'd taken up cooking instead of carpentry."

Tabitha laughs. "I love this. I'm in my element when I come down here." We make our way through the plethora of people, and she heads directly to a seafood merchant. "These guys have the nicest softshell crabs. They're always plump and taste the best."

"I'm salivating and don't even know what I'd do with them. But my God, they look so delicious."

She turns to me and smiles. "So it's settled; you and your brother are coming for dinner tonight."

"What? We are?"

"Of course. Any allergies I should know about?"

"Shouldn't you ask May first? She may only want it to be only the two of you."

"Aunt May will be fine. Allergies?" she asks again.

"No, we'll both eat virtually anything."

"Great." She picks up a fish, and looks at it. "See this?" She points to the eyes. I nod. "Nice clear eyes, beautiful skin that's not slimy. No fishy smell. That means this was caught within the last few hours."

"Came in about an hour ago," the fish monger replies.

"We'll take this." She hands him the big, red fish. He wraps it for her, and she hands over the money. "Here, you can be my apprentice." She chuckles.

"Does that mean you'll show me how to cook?"

"No way. As a first-year apprentice, it means you carry all the food, and peel all the onions."

"Great," I say sarcastically. "All the jobs I'm sure you love."

"I could make you scale and bone the fish. Take out the guts. You know, all the fun things."

My stomach roils with disagreement. "Funny that, suddenly I'm super happy to carry all the bags, and peel all the onions."

She beams over her shoulder at me. "I thought so."

I like Tabitha, I think we could be firm friends. Maybe once I leave Hope River, she'll be someone I can keep in contact with. Like Elle, I'm hoping we can remain friends too.

"I'm about to head over to May's, what time do you think you'll be back?"

"I'm wrapping up here at the house, and I should be back in about half an hour. But, I want to take a shower first, because I stink," Charlie says.

"You always stink," I tease.

"Whatever. I'm going." He hangs up, and I can't help but smile. I love poking fun at Charlie. He's such easy prey. He always bites back, which makes him even more fun to torment.

I grab the bottle of wine I bought at the liquor store earlier, and walk over to May's. "Hello?" I knock on her door.

"For God's sake, girly. I'm not getting any younger here. Why do you even bother knocking?" I hear May calling from inside.

May is such a wonderful lady. I open the door, and follow the aroma. "It smells so good in here," I say.

"Hey there, neighbor," Tabitha says. "Where's your brother?"

"He'll be here. He said he's sorry, but he'll be about half an hour late. Can I help?" I walk over to the range, and lean against the counter, watching. May's sitting at the bar stool, chopping what looks like a salad.

"Yes, you can take over here. I don't want to do this anymore," May says as she stands, and walks out of the kitchen.

"Okay then. What am I doing?" I wash my hands before I take May's place.

"It's a pear, walnut, feta and arugula salad. I need you to slice the pear. Thinly, please," Tabitha says.

"Yes, chef!" I smirk, and Tabitha does too, but adds in an eye roll. "So, have you thought of opening your own restaurant?"

"I had one, but it got too big, and it wasn't for me."

"Too hard?"

"Nah. Well, yeah. But it became a business, more than just the food. And I was under pressure, which I didn't enjoy."

"But isn't being in a kitchen full of pressure anyway?"

"Yeah, it is. But when it turns into a chore, and the love is gone,

I don't want to do it anymore. I want to cook because I love cooking, not because I'm chasing a Michelin star, or I want certain celebrities to endorse me." I get that. If I stopped enjoying flipping houses, my heart wouldn't be in it and I'd stop.

"What about a chef for the celebrities?"

"It's not something on my bucket list." She shrugs. "I'm a qualified chef who doesn't want anything too big. Maybe one day, I'll open a café, like Elle's. Obviously, not here in Hope River, because that wouldn't be fair to Elle."

"Why don't you look into catering with Elle? You both worked well together and made that amazing spread on such short notice for me."

"I didn't have to go to culinary school to learn how to make a sandwich. I did enjoy it, but it's not something I can see myself doing."

"You know what? You're a pain in the ass," I say.

"I tell her that all the time!" May calls from the dining room.

"Yes, she does," Tabitha agrees. "Maybe something small, and only for dinner. That way I'm not competing with Elle. I have no idea. But truth be told, I'm not settled, and I don't know when I'll be ready to make a decision about something like this."

"I told her she can move in here permanently," May calls.

She may be in the other room, but her ears work perfectly fine. "Maybe," Tabitha shrugs.

Reaching for another pear, I notice I'm done. "I'm finished. What else would you like me to do?"

"Grab a saucepan from over there. See that small one?" She pointedly looks at the pans on the counter. I grab hold of one of them. "Yep, that one. Here, put it on the heat, and bring it up to medium high. We want it very hot."

"Do we need oil or anything?" I ask.

"Nope, we're toasting the walnuts. It'll bring out the nutty flavor and release some of their natural oils. But it's got to be really hot, and don't take your eye off them, I've thrown away many a blackened walnut because I've forgotten about them."

I wait a moment or two, and look at Tabitha for guidance. "Should I scatter the walnuts yet?"

"I think so. Put them in, and keep shaking the pan."

There's a bowl of nuts beside me, and I toss them in. They immediately start making a sizzling noise, and it fascinates me how it can be so audible without any oils. I shake the pan, making sure they don't turn black. I see them changing color right before my eyes. "Look at that." I point to them.

"Keep shaking the pan, we don't want them to burn."

I shake it, then place it back on the flame, then shake them again. "Hey, look at me go. A regular chef."

"Let's go with a novice cook," Tabitha says.

"Novice is right," May yells out.

"Hey. No picking on the guest," I say as I defend myself. But I know they're joking.

"You're burning them," Tabitha says.

"Shit a brick," I say as I take them off the heat.

"That would hurt, so no thank you, I don't want to shit a brick," May says.

Tabitha and I laugh. "They look done. Let them cool a bit, then you can scatter them over the salad. There's feta cheese in the fridge, break that up, and scatter that too please."

"Knock-knock," I hear Charlie calling from the front door.

"What is it with you two? Are you trying to make an old lady exercise? Is that it?" May says to me as she walks past me to the front door. "Get in here. We're waiting for you, and we're hungry." Charlie offers May a cellophane-wrapped bunch of brightly colored flowers. "You're forgiven for being late."

"Suck-up," I say to Charlie.

He spies the bottle of wine sitting on the kitchen counter. "Says the chick who brought wine."

"Maybe it was already here," I say.

"Dear Lord, give me strength not to yell at these two," May says as she reaches to get a vase.

"Sorry, May," Charlie replies as he lowers his head, but has a mischievous grin.

Tabitha opens the oven, a puff of heat escapes, and the aroma intensifies. Charlie and I both turn to look at what's coming out of the oven. My mouth instantly salivates, and I can't wait to eat whatever that beautiful, intense garlic aroma is coming from. I feel my mouth pooling with hunger. "Jesus, that smells good," I say.

"Hell yeah. I'm starving," Charlie echoes.

"Charlie, could you take that salad out to the dining table, Hope, I'll get you to grab the citrus couscous from the fridge, and I'll bring the salmon," Tabitha issues the orders.

"Was that fish the salmon you bought this morning?" I ask.

"Sure was." She places the salmon on a wooden serving board, and slices up some lemons.

May's already sitting in her spot, waiting with a fork in one hand, and a knife in the other. She's wearing her napkin like a bib. I burst into laughter when I see her. May looks around, and cheekily smiles. She's so much fun.

I grab the pinot grigio I bought with me. The wine glasses are already on the table, so I open the bottle and pour into all our glasses. May looks at the conservative amount I've poured and stares up at me, "I'm not a cheap drunk, girly." She gestures with her finger for me to add more. I top her up. "That's better."

We all start placing food on our plates, and the chatter around the table is easy.

"Do you like being a plumber?" Tabitha asks Charlie.

"I don't mind being a plumber, but when we're restoring houses, it's demolition that's so much fun. I've been trying to convince this one, though, that the house she bought needs detonation, not restoration." He points to me.

"I'll wash your mouth out if I ever hear you say that again," May says, quite seriously. "That house is part of Hope River. It belongs here just like I do."

"Sorry," Charlie says again.

"Actually, maybe you can help me, May. Did Roger ever find love again after his wife passed? Maybe someone in secret?"

"There's no such thing as secrets in this town. Why do you ask?"

"I found something when River and I were upstairs." I take a mouthful of salmon, and it literally melts in my mouth. "Oh my God," I mumble. "This is heavenly."

"Thank you." Tabitha beams proudly.

"What did you find?" May asks.

"I found a small tin box, and it had a letter, and a pair of earrings, and shirt in it. It was enclosed, and hidden under a window bench seat. It's had me thinking maybe it was buried for a reason."

"What did the letter say?" May asks in a small voice. She's not looking at us. Instead, her gaze is firmly on the table, and her knife and fork are placed on the plate. Her face has gone pale.

"Aunt May? Are you okay?"

"I'm fine, dear." She smiles at Tabitha, then meets my eyes. "Please tell me what that letter said."

"I've got it next door. Would you like to read it?" May nods, unable to say anything. Shit, was this meant for May? Are the earrings and the contents of the tin container supposed to be hers? I pick my glass up, down what I've poured for myself, and run over to the stable to retrieve the tin.

Meow.

The cat lifts his head from where he's sleeping on my bed, meows at me, then lowers his head and falls fast asleep within seconds.

What a diva cat.

"Ah, here you are." I pick the tin up from where I left it, and take it back over to May's. I find Charlie sitting at the table, looking incredibly guilty about something. Tabitha appears angry and is giving Charlie death stares. May is quietly eating. "What happened?" I ask Charlie directly.

"Your brother is an idiot," Tabitha responds with a sobering, murderous coldness.

"What did you do?" I ask Charlie.

"I didn't mean it. I was just asking a question."

Instantly, I feel sick. Like me, Charlie doesn't have the gift of a filter either. He'll say whatever he thinks without actually thinking. "What did you do?"

"Tabitha offered some of that salad stuff." He jerks his chin toward the couscous salad. "And I asked her what kind of salad it is."

So far, that doesn't sound unreasonable or anything for Tabitha to be mad at. "Yeah, and when I told him it was couscous salad, he said, and I quote, 'What kind of foo-foo frilly crap is this? Where's the meat and three vegetables?'"

"You carried out the damn salad," I say to him.

"But it's fancy stuff. The fish, yeah, that looks great. But this salad is for rich, pretentious snobs."

"Are you kidding?" Tabitha screeches, clearly upset.

I smack Charlie on the back of the head. "Come on, man. Don't be an ass. It might not be what you're used to, but try it."

Tabitha snatches the plate out from under Charlie. "He doesn't get to try it now. He's being a dick."

"Charlie," I say through gritted teeth. "Don't be an ass."

"I'm sorry," he says, though it's a token apology. "I'll eat whatever you give me. I didn't mean anything by it."

"You know what? Go make yourself a sandwich. I'm not feeding you."

Holy shit, these two are going to tear each other apart. "I'm sorry," he says again.

"Apology not accepted. You're an ass. And, next time I cook, you're not invited."

"Oh come on, darlin'," don't be like that," he pleads.

Did he really call Tabitha "darlin'"? I look at Tabitha, and see the fury in her eyes. "Charlie, what kind of flowers do you want for your funeral?" I ask trying to diffuse the melting pot of bubbling emotions.

"I'm sorry, Tabitha. I really didn't mean anything by it. I mean the salmon tasted so good, please let me finish it. I swear, I'll never complain again about anything you feed me."

"Because I'll never feed you again."

"For the love of God. You two are behaving like horny teenagers. Will you just have sex and get it over and done with?" May snaps at them both.

My eyes widen, and I try to hold in my smile.

"I don't even like her."

"I certainly don't like him." They point at the other.

"You're both foo-foo. Either have sex, or shut up!" May says as she lifts a crooked finger, pointing at both. "Now, may I have a look through the tin, please?" May's voice calms as she turns to me.

"Of course, here you go. I was going to go to the library to try and find information about the house."

"Where did you find this?" May asks as she opens the tin.

"Upstairs, in one of the bedrooms."

May's hands shake as she opens the lid, her eyes widen, and I see a small smile stretch her lips. She touches the folded shirt, then carefully lifts it and places it on the table.

All our dinners are long forgotten as we watch May. She opens the box, and when the gleaming earrings sparkle under the dining room's recessed lighting she lets out a small sigh. She carefully brings her fingertips up, and gently strokes the earrings. Almost like she's caressing them. "These are perfect," she says.

"They are, aren't they?" Tabitha says as she leans over to get a better look.

"I'm going to use the color of the earrings to highlight the house."

"Are you?" May looks up to ask. Her happiness is there, for all of us to see. She takes the envelope and flips it around to look at the front. "May I?" she asks.

"Of course." She slides the letter out, and settles back in her chair. Her eyes become misty, and quickly she brings her free hand up to cover her mouth. Suspicion rapidly arises. Does she know who this letter was destined for? Could it be her? Did she and Old Roger have a thing? But that really doesn't make sense, she would've been very young, and he would've been too old for her.

"May, are you okay?"

She looks up from the letter, and a genuine smile spreads across her aging face. "I couldn't be better." She folds the letter, and places it back in the envelope. "Thank you for allowing me to read this." She places the lid back on the tin, and slides it over to me. She then turns to Tabitha. "This meal isn't foo-foo. It's simply perfect." She keeps eating her meal, and I look to Tabitha, then Charlie.

"Aunt May, are you okay?" Tabitha looks at the tin, then back at May.

"Oh darling, I couldn't be better." She places her palm to Tabitha's cheek. "Now, can we all eat this beautiful meal Tabitha has prepared for us without any arguing?" She looks at Charlie, then Tabitha.

"Sorry," Charlie says in a low voice as he drops his chin. He's saying a lot of that tonight.

"Sorry, Aunt May."

Sitting down, I keep eating. "May, do you know who wrote that letter? Or who those earrings are meant for?" Please tell me it has something to do with you. I'd love to hear the story behind it.

"I'm afraid not, girly. It was so beautiful though, it touched me. If I knew, I'd certainly tell you." She smiles while wetting her lips with her tongue. May glances down at her dinner plate, and squeezes her eyes shut for a brief second. "Now, tell me, how's the house coming along?" Her gaze darts between Charlie and me.

"Mmmm," Charlie mumbles as he shovels some of the couscous salad into his mouth. "It's good." He nods.

"So the foo-foo tastes okay?" Tabitha bites.

"All I said was…"

"Charlie," I scold. He looks at me, and I widen my eyes, then swiftly kick him under the table.

"Sorry. Yeah, it tastes really good. Thank you for giving me my plate back." Tabitha half grins, and Charlie turns to May. "The house is going to look so good."

"And the plans? Have they been approved?" May asks.

"Any day now. I'm waiting for them to say we can go ahead and do what we want."

"I know some people. I'll get it approved for you," May says as she delicately eats her dinner.

"Thank you. That would be helpful, wouldn't it, Charlie?" I look over to notice Charlie's eyes firmly watching Tabitha, whose own gaze is lowered as she stares at her food. Her mouth is moving slowly, chewing. Charlie's eyes are about to pop out of his head while he's watching her. Charlie's lips part slightly as he leans forward.

I kick him again under the table.

"What?" he snaps before looking at me and realizing I've caught him ogling Tabitha. "Sorry?" his voice cracks.

"It's generous of May to talk to the town about the plans for the house, right?"

"Yes, yes, yes." He places his knife and fork down, and stands. "Excuse me. Bathroom please?"

"Down the hall to the left," Tabitha directs.

"Thank you." He nearly runs out of the dining room toward the bathroom.

Did I miss something? First, they fight, and now Charlie can't take his eyes off Tabitha.

You know what? I have too much going on in my life to worry about Charlie too. He's old enough to make his own decisions and take care of himself. He'd better keep it in his pants though, because I really like May, and Tabitha.

Chapter
EIGHTEEN

"COME ON, DO you want some breakfast?" I ask the cat.
Meow.

"Of course, you do." I grab a tin and walk over to the cat's bowl. Emptying the tin, the cat begins eating. "I suppose I better name you something. What can I call you?"

The cat stops eating, looks at me with the most self-righteous glare, then meows.

"Right then, I suppose for now I'll keep you calling you *the cat*. It's not like you can protest, can you?"

"Are you talking to the cat?" Charlie asks once he's out of the shower.

"I'm thinking of naming him, but I don't know what."

"So, you're keeping it?"

"I don't know." I half shrug. "Anyway, what are you doing today?"

"I'm just waiting for the go-ahead so I can rip all those walls out. The plan looks really good. This house is going to be massive."

"Hopefully May can get us approval quickly. In the meantime, start on removing all the siding, and windows."

"I'll get a team together. Do you think May can get those permits fast-tracked."

"I'm actually amazed they've stalled us. I thought we'd get them faster. The entire town is behind this remodel, and I honestly expected the permits would have come through already."

Meow.

"Hello, buddy," Charlie says as he leans down to pat the cat.

Grrrr. The cat growls, baring his teeth at Charlie. He then turns, and rubs his body up against my leg, purring.

"Ugh, whatever. I don't like cats anyway," Charlie splutters at the cat.

"You love cats," I say.

"Not that one." He points to the little guy rubbing himself up against my leg.

"Don't take it personally, he didn't like River either."

"Yeah? What makes you so special?" Charlie grabs his keys, sits on the sofa and slips his sports shoes on. I look at them, because he knows how paranoid I am about safety. "Don't worry, I have my steel-toed boots in the truck. I know what you're like, Hope."

I lean down and pet the cat. "I won't be far behind. I'm stopping in town because I want to look at some paint colors for the house. I've got some ideas, but I want to see how they'll work. And, I'm going to search for some stone for the kitchen counters."

"Okay. As soon as you know about the permits, let me know, and I'll co-ordinate a team." Charlie leaves, and I'm right behind him.

Meow.

The cat is right behind me.

"What are you doing?" I ask the cat.

"You do know they can't talk back?" Charlie says slowly as if his revealing a big mystery to me.

"I know. But he's following me." I kneel by the front door, and the cat rubs himself up against me again. "You have to stay here."

Meow.

"You're a weirdo," Charlie calls as he walks to his truck.

The cat runs ahead of me, goes to my truck, and jumps in the bed. "I'm the weirdo?" I point to the cat. Charlie flicks his hand at me, waving as he drives off.

I get to my truck, and look at the cat curled up in the back. "I'm going to have to buy you a harness so you don't jump out while I'm driving."

Meow.

"Maybe you should get in the truck, that way I know you won't jump out." The cat curls up, and makes himself comfortable. "Just get in the truck." I watch as he looks around, completely ignoring me. "Fine, but if you get hurt, it's on you. I'm not rushing you to the vet."

Meow.

"Who am I kidding, of course, I'll rush you to the vet."

Meow.

"Shut up and stay in there. Don't move."

Meow.

Stupid cat.

I pull up at the place I found about twenty-five minutes from Old Roger's house that has a variety of stone. I'm still deciding if stone is what I want for the house's counters. Or butcher block, or maybe concrete.

Getting out of the truck, I look in the back to make sure the cat is still there.

Meow.

Before I can even turn away, the cat is beside me, circling around my feet.

"I'm not holding you, so you better get back in the truck so you don't get hurt."

Meow.

"Go." I tap the back, trying to get him to jump up. Nope, he won't move. "Fine, but if something happens…" I walk away, and I sneak a look behind me, to find the cat is actually following. "Alright. Well, keep up."

I head into the showroom, and the cat is right beside me. "Hello there," an older gentleman comes over to me. He looks down and sees the cat. "Now that's a first. A customer bringing their cat with them," he says with a chuckle.

"Trust me, this cat is a pain in the butt. He won't go back in the truck."

"So, he's a dog-cat?" He laughs.

"I suppose he is."

Meow.

"What can I do for you today?"

"I'm renovating a house, and I'd like to look at the selection of stone you have. I'm not entirely sure where I'm going with it yet, but if something catches my eyes, I might buy it. I'm nowhere near ready for installation though, so if I do buy something, can you keep it on premises?"

"Of course. What size do you need?"

I take a deep breath and take out my measurements from the

plans I've drawn up. "But, I'm also looking for the bathrooms too."

He looks down at the measurements, and grimaces. "This is massive."

"Yeah. It is."

"Let me take you out to the yard, and I'll show you what we have." He leads me down the back of the showroom, and out to a mammoth outdoor yard. All I can see is different variants and grades of stone. "What types aren't you after, so we can bypass those."

"Laminates and tiles are completely out. I'm looking for either marble or granite. But I'm not a hundred percent committed to either."

"I hear you. Let me show you what we have, and we can go from there." He stops and points to the right. "Here's all the marble we have. It goes down to where that exit door is." Then he starts moving again. "We have granite on this side. We've got a more extensive range in granite."

"Wow, this is nice."

"Is there a color you're after?'

"Something light. I'd like a small amount of veining, nothing too over the top, because I'm thinking of deep green lowers, and white uppers."

"Green?" he asks, surprised.

"I know, seems crazy. But I actually found a pair of diamond and emerald drop earrings in the house. So, I'm using their coloring for inspiration."

He's nodding. "Well, I've heard crazier. But it's your house, and if you want green lowers, get yourself green lowers."

"Actually, it's a house I'm renovating, then selling."

"You're a house flipper? There are so many houses out here that need some love. Where did you buy?"

"Over in Hope River."

"Oh, not that old, decrepit house that's falling apart? It's down on…let me think. Is it Clayton Street?"

"Yeah, that's the one I've bought."

"Wow. I'm totally impressed. That place…" He shakes his head. "Takes someone with a lot of patience and more importantly knowledge to renovate *that* house." He runs his hand through his thinning hair.

"My brother wanted to tear it down."

"He's a smart person. Should've listened to him."

I laugh. "I couldn't. There's something beautiful about bringing something so old back to life. Anyway, the townspeople would've crucified me."

"Funny thing about towns. They don't want to do the work, but they're there to tell you how to do it." He chuckles again. "Small towns, eh?"

I walk down the aisles, and a slab of marble catches my eye. "Oh, I love this. The gray marbling and veining through it is beautiful. I have to say, this is one of the prettiest pieces of marble I've ever seen."

"Thank you," the guy says proudly. "And that's one of our most expensive too. This one will run you near six thousand dollars."

I let out an audible breath. "Six thousand."

"Yes, ma'am. It's Calacatta Oro. Let me measure it up, make sure it's the size you're after. It might be too small." He unclips a tape measure from his belt, and measures the length and width. He looks at the plan I've drawn up. "This one will be enough for all the counter spaces in your kitchen. But not enough to do all the bathrooms."

"It's so pretty though."

"At six thousand, you'd want it to be beautiful. We do have cheaper options."

"Nah, I'm afraid now that I've seen this one, I simply love it. Alright. Put a sold sticker on it. I'll take it."

"Great, follow me, and we'll get the paperwork started. Are they your exact measurements?"

"I might change my mind. So, let's not cut it yet."

He chuckles. "I can do that." He looks over his shoulder to me, then drops his eye level to beside me. "This cat of yours, what's his name?"

"I have no idea. He's adopted me. I think he came with the house."

"Seems like this is more than just a house flip to you. Diamond and emerald earrings, a cat…what else will you find?"

There's another thing waiting for me, one thing I can't have. *River.*

Chapter
NINETEEN

THERE'S A BUZZ at the house today. Sure enough, May worked her magic and came through with approved plans. Charlie has rallied together a crowd of people, none of whom I know.

"Where did you find these guys?" I ask.

"I'm skilled in the art of people finding," he says as he stands beside me and crosses his arms in front of his chest.

"How long do you think it'll take to strip it right back?"

"With this number of people, demo should be done in a day, maybe two."

I look around, and there has to be easily twenty people working here. "This is amazing."

"See that guy over there?" He points to an older man wheeling debris from inside the house, down the makeshift ramp, and to the giant dumpster.

"Yeah."

"He said his daddy helped build this place with Old Roger. And he wanted to help, so he can say to his children and grandchildren that he helped rebuild it."

"Wow," I say. This town is forever surprising me. "The plans are all good. Once we've stripped her down, then we'll start putting her back together. The concrete trucks should be here Friday morning to pour the foundation for the extension."

"I'm already digging the footings out. They'll be done by tomorrow at the latest."

"Excuse me, Charlie?" one of the young guys interrupts us.

"What is it?" Charlie says, getting down to business.

"We've got a problem in the back." He looks nervous, like he's afraid to tell us.

"What's the problem?" I ask as the three of us head out back to see what's happening.

There are four guys standing around looking at something.

"Ah, that tree's roots are growing up under here." Charlie gets into the ditch, to see that the roots have destroyed the old clay pipes running under the ground. "Part of old houses, boys," Charlie says. The guys back away, and wait for further instruction.

"That tree is too pretty to get rid of," I say looking up at the beautiful overhanging branches.

"I'll get someone to come look at it, Hope. It's not healthy; you can see that. The branches look dry and dark, and the leaves aren't healthy and green. But, let me get someone in, and we'll see if it's worth keeping. If it is, you'll have to make this bump-out smaller. We won't be able to have the extra space come out so far."

I look up at the tree. I'd hate for it to go, but if it's not healthy, it'll destroy the house if it falls. There's still the beautiful tree out the front. "Get someone in, let's see what they say."

Charlie turns and gives further instructions to everyone,

before hoisting himself out of the hole, and retrieving his phone from his pocket. I head inside to look at what progress is being made.

The downstairs is about half ripped down, and I can hear a lot of commotion from upstairs, so I carefully avoid getting hit by fly away materials, as I take the rickety steps up to the second level.

"Jesus," I say. Demo upstairs is nearly done. There are still a few original walls, but most have been taken down. I assume the walls still standing are load bearing, which will mean we can't remove them without putting temporary support beams in first. And we can't do any of that until we know exactly what we're working with.

"Excuse me, Miss Hope," one of the guys says to me.

"Yes?" I smile.

"Is Mr. Charlie somewhere? I need to show him something."

"You can show me."

"Okay." He leads me to a far corner, and points. "I'm sorry," he says.

"Shit." Kneeling down, I run my hand over the wood and it crumbles in my hand. "Termites."

"Yes, sorry," he says again, as if it's his fault.

"Is this the only area you've seen them?"

"No, some more here." He points to another spot.

"Alright, thank you." Some of these planks have been completely destroyed. It looks like the termites have only just started feasting. He walks away and continues ripping things up, and throwing them out, leaving me to deal with the termite issues.

Charlie comes up to find me still kneeling, as I look around. "Termites?" he asks.

"Yeah."

"Tent or replace?"

"I'm not sure yet. We'll wait until everything is out, then we can make a decision."

Charlie walks around the massive area upstairs, closely inspecting every exposed piece of wood. "I'll call a specialist and let you know what they recommend," Charlie says as he looks down at his phone.

This house is a hive of activity. It's loud, and there are a ton of voices with the expected accompaniment of swearing. Building sites are always filled with testosterone, men who sweat, and loads of colorful language.

"What the hell?" I hear Charlie call.

"What is it?"

"The fucking cat," he says, looking beside me. I almost forgot about the cat.

"He helped me pick out a stone countertop." I pet the cat before heading back down the rickety, scary steps and going into the bathroom. This seems untouched, so I run out to my truck, grab my tool belt, and return to the bathroom. Yes, demo day! I love demo day *almost* as much as Charlie does.

All the workers have left, and it's just Charlie and me at the house. *And the cat.*

"This place is so big. I can't quite get over how large it is."

I look around, and totally agree with him. "What are you doing tomorrow?" I ask.

"Pest control will be here first thing, and then we'll know where we stand with the termites. I think we can replace some things, but it might be cheaper not to replace everything. We'll see what the pest guy says. Then, I have someone coming to look at the tree out back. If it's dead, I'll arrange to have it ripped out."

"Concrete's coming Friday for the footings."

"Okay, if we need to tent it, we can still do the stuff outside. The footings, pouring, all of that," Charlie says.

"What do you think? Eight weeks?"

"For here? Nope, I think closer to twelve."

"Okay, let's try and get it done in twelve."

"Hope, we're tearing nearly everything out, and restarting. Anyway, I'm tired, and hungry, and I'm going home. How long will you stay for?"

"I'm going to walk it, and see if I can come up with anything else."

Charlie runs his dirty hand through his hair. "You like your quiet time. I'll see you back at the house. If I'm snoring, don't wake me."

"I won't."

He goes to his truck and takes his work boots off. He throws them in the back, then walks around the driver's side. "Want me to pick you anything up for dinner?"

"Nah, I might head into town. Grab something there."

"See ya."

He closes the door to the truck, starts the engine, and pulls onto the road. I know Charlie's tired, but he loves this as much as I do. It's in our blood.

Meow.

"You should've gone with Charlie. He could've fed you."

Meow.

Note to self, grab another bowl so he can have food here too. "You'll have to wait until we get home."

Meow.

Once back inside, I take the plans out, and keep looking at them, trying to visualize how everything will turn out. This place will be so large. I think multiple generations will be able to live here comfortably.

"Have you been avoiding me?"

The deep voice makes me jump out of my skin. Turning, River's standing at the door holding a pizza box. "No, why?"

"I bought a pizza, and saw you were here, so thought I'd stop by and see if you're hungry." Pursing my lips together, I raise my brows in question. "More like I was hoping you'd be here, because I want us to talk."

"River, we've gone over this. There's nothing for us to talk about. In a few weeks, I'll be done here and gone."

"Come, sit with me. Have something to eat." He opens the lid, enticing me with the aroma of the pepperoni, and the sight of the molten cheese.

"Pizza is a sin." *But so damn good.*

"Yes, yes, it is. Now, come on."

He sits on the front porch, where we were less than a week ago. I sit to the side, making sure the pizza box is between us. "Thank you, I'm starving."

"I thought you would be."

He waits until I take a piece, before he takes one too. "You and I, River..."

He holds his hand up, stopping me from saying anything else. "Tonight, we're just two friends having dinner. That's it. There's no pressure, no explanations, no anythings. I heard Gran helped you with the permits."

Why am I even surprised that everyone knows what's happening? "Yeah, she did."

"And there's problems with the tree out the back?"

I blink, still not believing how much he knows. "Do you have a direct line to what's happening here?"

He smiles. His gorgeous chin dimple highlights his strong, square jawline. "Everyone's talking about the house. They're super excited about what you're doing here." He looks behind him.

Meow.

The cat tiptoes over and curls up next to me.

"So you'll sell it once it's done?"

"That's the plan."

"Plans can change. Anything can happen," he says. "See, you've got a cat. Maybe you and the cat can move in."

"Nope. Way too big for me."

"You might end up having your own family, Hope. You never know, you might grow into this place."

"I don't see that being in the cards for me, River."

River bites into his pizza and looks around. "I think you need to stop being so damn controlling and uptight," he says as he takes another bite.

Wait, what? "Sorry?" I say.

"You're being a stubborn ass. You're meant to be here, with me. And the sooner you get out of your own damned way, the better it'll be, for both of us." He takes yet another bite.

He's rendered me speechless. I find myself kinda turned on by him right now. But the logical part of my brain is jumping up and down, having a tantrum. "Problem is, River, whatever we could have won't last. I'm leaving once this house is finished."

"No, you won't. You're supposed to be here."

"Stop trying to get in my head. It's not going to work."

River offers me another slice, but I shake my head. He closes the box, then stands. "I don't have to do anything. You're already questioning if it's the right decision for you to leave. If I have anything to do with it, you'll be staying. Maybe this house is too big for you. You could move in with me."

The moment I'm on my feet, I've disturbed the sleeping cat. But the anger fueling me doesn't give a shit if I've disturbed the cat or not. River's walking back to his truck, completely oblivious to how wrong he is, or even how he's making me feel. "Hey," I say loudly, but making sure I'm not yelling because I don't want to wake the neighbors. He keeps walking. I run up and stand in front of him. He stops walking and looks down at me. "You have no right in telling me…no, you've…can't." I'm tongue tired and muddled. I want to yell and scream, but I won't. "You can't, you're…" I poke him in the chest, mad at him. He's standing there, looking amused. "Stop being so smug, you bastard."

"Now I'm a bastard, am I? Why, because I'm right? Because we belong together? Or because you're a pain in the ass who's standing in the way of her own happiness?"

"You don't think I'm happy? Why, because I'm not dating someone? I need to be dating to be happy? I'll have you know…"

He drops the pizza box, and pounces on me. He passionately weaves his hands through my hair, and demands my mouth with his. He untangles his left hand from my hair, and places it around my lower hip, pulling me closer to him. I fight him, wanting to get away, but my resolve is dwindling the longer we stay connected.

I find my strength and push back from him. "You…" I shake my finger at him, still unable to form a coherent sentence. "You…" I say again, stepping further away from him.

He stands tall, looking damned pleased with himself.

I want to scream and yell, and smack him. I want to do so many things. But the biggest emotion overriding every negative one, is lust. I want him to grab me and kiss me again. I want to taste him, feel his naked warm body up against mine. Jesus, I've missed him so much. My body is reacting in the craziest of ways.

And I do something I never thought I'd do. I fly into his arms, and jump up, wrapping my legs around his hips. Our mouths stay connected, grazing, kissing, *owning.*

Arching my back, River's hand slips under my shirt, touching my heated skin. Jesus, what am I doing? Why am I so crazy around him?

"Hope," he whispers.

His lips touch my neck, and trail softly up to my ear.

"God, yes," I say as I keep my eyes closed and tilt my head to the side.

"We should take this inside, unless you want everyone to watch."

"Watch…yes. What? No!" I push away again. "Put me down, please." River hesitantly, carefully places me to my feet. He looks just as confused as I feel. "We can't do this, River." His hands are still possessively clasping onto my hips, refusing to completely let me go.

"Why not?"

There's a lurching in my chest as I break away from him. "Because we've never worked before. I can't fall for you again." *Damn dust mites.* I wipe at my eyes. "I couldn't survive that happening again. It's easier if we don't start anything. That way, I can't get hurt."

He walks away from me, shaking his head. Turning, he stops and says, "You're not the only one who risks getting hurt, Hope." He turns again, walking away from me.

I have to tell myself, it's for the best.

So why does it hurt so much?

Chapter TWENTY

THE HOUSE HAS to be tented for two to three days. This morning, I'm taking myself back down to the ocean where Tabitha and I went to the growers' market.

I park close by, and walk down to all the stalls. Along with the seafood and all the different fresh produce, there's also an assortment of handmade crafts, jams, cookies, breads, everything a person could want. It's later in the morning than the last time I was here, and now it's bustling with so many people.

I walk around from stall to stall, having a look at all the local products available. But what's really drawing me in is the sound of the water crashing up against the shore.

One of the vendors is selling fresh homemade donuts. I can smell the cinnamon sugar drifting through the air, mingling with so many other tempting aromas. It's loud, and busy, but there's also a calmness to the area.

"Hi, Hope," someone says.

I have no idea who's calling me and when I turn, I see the little girl from the flower festival. Crap, what's her name? "Hello…" I stall for a second, trying to remember her name. "Rose! How are you?"

"I'm good, thank you. How are you?" Seriously, this kid is way too grown up.

"I'm very well, thank you. Are you waiting for some donuts too?" I ask. Her mom turns and gives me a small smile.

"Yeah, these are so yummy. Do you like donuts, or do you *love* donuts? Because I *love* donuts." She rubs her little belly.

"I love them so much. And I'm thinking I'm going to buy some for my brother Charlie, because he loves donuts even more than I do."

She smiles angelically at me. She's such a cute kid. Her soft brown curls fall halfway down her back, and her big brown eyes are full of expression. "Mommy and Daddy said Old Roger's house is going to look really good when you're finished." She motions for me to come close to her. When I do, she whispers, "I heard them talking about us moving into it."

This is news to me. "Oh. Maybe you'll have a new home soon."

She gives me a huge grin. "Rose, come on, it's our turn," her mom says. She looks at me again. "Hi, I'm Tania. And I'm sorry, but I already know everything about you." Sounds creepy, but it's not. It's small-town life.

"Hopefully not everything," I say, with sass.

"My husband and I are really eager to see what you're going to do with Old Roger's house. We've been thinking about moving into something bigger. When do you think you'll be finished with the house?"

"We're giving ourselves four, maybe five months to finish, hopefully sooner." I know Charlie and I have already said we want to push it out in twelve weeks, but I'd rather tell people longer and finish sooner than the other way around.

"Have you set a list price yet?"

"Not yet, sorry. But, if you'd like to give me your number, I can always call you when I do."

Her eyes light up. "Oh, my goodness, I'd love that! Thank you. I've driven past a few times. Yes, I know it sounds like I'm stalking, and I kind of am," she openly admits with a laugh.

I take my phone out, and type in her name and number. "It's okay. I became aware fairly quickly how important that house is to everyone."

"It used to be one of the finest houses in all of Hope River, but then…" Her enthusiasm dies down. "Anyway, thank you. If there's anything I can do to help around the house, I'd be happy to do anything. Painting, cleaning, anything."

"Thank you." How generous.

"Come on, Rose. Let's go. See you around, Hope." Tania smiles, and Rose waves as she eats her donut while they walk away.

"How can I help you?" the donut guy says.

"Can I get two dozen please."

He packs twenty-four in a box, and I pay him. Walking toward the ocean, I see a coffee cart, so I stop and grab myself a coffee. It's such a lovely day, that I head down to the beach to people watch. Nothing stalker-ish or bizarre than sitting on a bench, drinking a coffee, eating from a box of twenty-four donuts while watching people in their bathing suits. Nope, nothing weird about that.

"Hi, Hope," a woman says as she walks past.

No idea who that was. "Hi," I call, and offer her a small wave with my donut hand.

The sun is climbing, and although it's not overly hot, there are still people laying on beach towels, and swimming in the ocean. Funny because it's a weekday, but still kind of early. It's like they're on their own time schedule. Don't people work around here?

Sipping on my coffee, I'm enjoying the view, in a 'hunter' kind of way. I don't even feel bad that I'm checking out a few of the guys. I mean, if they're eye-candy, it would be a travesty not to ogle them…from a safe distance…and from behind my sunglasses so they can't see me checking them out.

I can't help but notice the number of obviously good-looking men, with smoking hot *wet* bodies emerging from the ocean, or embarking upon a quick swim before they head off to work.

"Hmm," I mutter as I watch one particular guy. He's swimming out, and although I can't see them, I can only imagine how muscled his arms are. The waves aren't very large, but enough to knock him back a few feet as he tries to swim further and further out. I bring my coffee up to my mouth, and find it hovering just in front of my lips. I'm invested in how far out the guy is going to swim before he decides to turn back. The further away he gets, the more I'm cheering him on. I want him to get in a great swim to burn off whatever is going through his head.

I wonder what he's thinking about, out there alone in the surf, where the only thing keeping him company is his thoughts. Is he wondering if he made the right decision about taking that job? Or maybe he's worried that he doesn't have enough for retirement. Or possibly his sixteen-year-old daughter has just told him she's pregnant. What does someone think about when facing the wrath of untamable and unpredictable water?

What would I be thinking about?

If I want to be honest with myself, I'd say I'd be thinking about River. But if I want to push my feelings for him so far down that I never feel anything again, then I'd say I'd be thinking about the damn cat.

Blinking, I keep watching the guy fighting against the waves, and not letting the water deter him from where he wants to go. I'll give him credit though, he's stubborn and persistent. Finally, he stops swimming, and stays bobbing in the water for a good minute or two. Is he thinking that he wants to go on, or that he's had enough and wants to come back because he's got to go to work soon?

Yeah, yeah, I know. I should leave and go find tiles, but, something about the way that guy is resolved to get his morning swim in, is somewhat intriguing. I want to know how his journey will end.

He looks around, and finally makes the decision to head back to the shore line. He swims a few strokes, then allows the water to bring him in before starting to swim a few more strokes. He nears the shoreline, and I find I still haven't taken a sip at all. My coffee is up near my mouth, and all I've been doing is staring at the guy and imagining how his story is going to play out.

I watch as he comes closer and closer to the shore line and slowly surfaces from the water. His black shorts cling to him and he rakes his hand through his dark hair.

Holy shit. My mouth waters, as I unapologetically stare at the beautiful man walking closer to me. Water drips off of him and I swear to God, my mouth is hanging open as I stare at how perfect he is.

Jesus, he's beautiful. Absolutely flawless, and so damn delicious. *Wait, if I lick him, he's mine, right?*

Shit. Is the universe playing with me right now? And of course, I realize that all this time, I've been ogling River.

I try to look away, to break this intense connection I have toward him, but I'm completely unsuccessful. I can't *not* look at Mr. Sex-on-Legs.

He bends to pick his towel up, and this is where I can slip away and he'll never know I was here.

Except, my stupid legs don't want to stand, and my even stupider eyes can't stop staring at him. Even worse, I can't run away. I'm stuck, fixated on the most divine man God has ever created.

Snap out of it, Hope.

I can't have him. We just don't work. We've tried in the past, and it's always ended in the worst of ways.

"Hope?"

Fan-fucking-tastic. While I've been sitting, stuck in my own head, River's seen me and is now standing in front of me with a towel hung low around his hips. I blink, trying to find the words, but my mind is going crazy, wanting to jump him right here and now.

"Hope?" he asks again.

"I can't have sex with you," I blurt in an awfully high voice. What the hell is wrong with me? Where did that come from? I clear my throat, sip my stupid, cold coffee and try that again. "Hi, River," I say this time with smoother delivery. But still, who am I kidding? I'd so go him right now, and I don't even care that sand would get in places it shouldn't.

"Well, you can't have sex with me? Or you *won't* have sex with me?" He smirks.

I have to stop looking at him. I lower my eyes, and of course, I take in that hand-sculptured V. "Yes." Shit. "I mean no."

"Am I underdressed? Is my body affecting you?" Now he's shamelessly flirting.

"Yes!" *Shut up!* "I mean no."

He laughs, and I *try* to tear my gaze away from him. "Should I cover up?"

"No!" Oh my God! Why can't I just zip my damn lips, and not say what I'm thinking? "I mean yes."

"So, I'm distracting? You like what you see?"

"Yes." I slap my forehead. "No, I don't. I'm not saying anything else. I'm leaving." I get up and swivel away from him. In my haste to escape from what could potentially be a dangerous situation for me, I end up tripping over the small step beside the bench seat and falling flat on my face.

Crisis averted…not.

The crack of my nose breaking, and the blood spurting out, mixed with my shrill, hysterical scream makes it all the more entertaining for anyone watching.

Great.

"Shit, Hope!" River helps me to my feet, and I can feel my nose throbbing. Actually, scratch that, I feel my entire face throbbing in extreme pain. I want to cry, and laugh. Definitely more cry than laugh. I think it would hurt too much if I laughed.

And just to add to it, I've managed to attract what seems like the entire town trying to help me. "Hope, are you okay?"

"Oh my God, did you see that? She fell flat on her face."

"Shit, I think she's broken her nose."

"Look at all the blood on the ground. I hope she's not HIV positive."

"Do you need help?"

The barrage of voices keep coming from all directions.

"I've got you," River says as he places his damp arm around me, and ushers me away from the crowd of people.

"I'm so embarrassed," I say as he walks us down the street.

"Don't be. You were consumed by my obvious handsome looks, and you misjudged the step," he says with a teasing voice. "It was bound to happen."

Even with the pain so bad I have tears streaming down my cheek, I want to laugh too. "I've never broken anything in my body." I look around, temporarily confused as to where we are. "My truck's back that way?" I point over my shoulder.

"I'm taking you to the hospital. Here, take my towel and place it on your lap." He unlocks his truck, and opens the door for me. While trying to juggle the towel and my phone, he scoops me up, and places me in the truck. "We need ice, and fast."

"Why?"

"Reduces the swelling. But I'd rather get you to the hospital. Hold the towel there, and place your head forward to let the blood drip out." He shuts the door, and runs to the driver's side. He gets in, and before I know it, we're on our way to the hospital. "Are you okay?"

"My pride is bruised as much as my face."

"Because you were checking me out? Or because you fell flat and damaged your beautiful face? Just so you know, it doesn't matter to me that your nose is the size of your head, I still think you're gorgeous."

"Shit!" I flip the sun visor down to see how bad I actually look. "Holy crap," I say as I notice the dark circles under my eyes, and how wide my nose now is. "Do you think I'll need an operation?"

"No idea."

I look at River, and panic has really set in. "I don't have time for an operation!" I say. "I've got a house I need to rebuild."

"Calm down." He places his hand on my thigh and gives me a reassuring squeeze. "Just wait to see what the doctors have to say."

When we get to the hospital, he parks and runs over to help me out of the truck. My face is throbbing, and it feels like my eyes are so puffy I can barely open them. "How bad do I look?" I ask.

"What's the scale? One being your normal gorgeous self and ten being you've run into the back of a parked truck?"

"If you tell me I'm a ten, I won't be liking you anymore."

"You're absolutely a one then."

We head inside and, luckily, I'm seen fairly quickly. Thankfully, River has somehow found a shirt.

"Thank you for bringing me home, and staying with me," I say to River.

"Doctor's orders, have a shower, something to eat and take those pain meds they prescribed you."

"It's really not that bad."

He looks at me with raised eyebrows. "I'm going to get you

something to eat." He starts looking through my cupboards, and discovers the serious lack of food. "What the hell have you been eating?"

"You know. Stuff," I reply. "Shit! The donuts."

"What donuts?"

"I bought some from a vendor this morning, and then this happened." I point to my nose. "I must've left them at the beach." I groan, upset with myself for leaving them behind. "Man."

River laughs and when I fling him an annoyed glare, he laughs some more. "You're damn lucky you don't need an operation, and all you're worried about is some donuts?"

"It's your fault anyway," I say.

"Why's it my fault? You were ogling me like I was part of a wet t-shirt competition. And you didn't want me to know you were drooling all over me, so you tried to run, and fell on your face. Literally." He looks in the fridge, then shakes his head again. "Tell me I'm wrong."

"You're wrong." Yeah, right. We both know I was shamelessly gawking at him.

"Aha. Anyway, I'm going into town to get you some real food." He opens the last cupboard and takes out a nearly empty box of Poptarts. "Really? Poptarts?"

"There's nothing wrong with Poptarts."

"Not at all, I loved them…when I was a kid."

"You're so damn judgey," I snap.

"Says the chick who was checking me out. Superficial much?" He grabs his truck keys off the counter where he left them when he brought me home. "I'm going home to grab some clothes, then I'll go to the store to get some real food. I'll be about an hour. Do you need anything?"

Him naked. *What? No.* It's the drugs talking. Well, it would be the drugs if I'd taken any. "You don't have to come back."

"I know."

I wait for him to say something else, but he doesn't. "So it's settled, you're not coming back."

"If you think so." He walks to the door. "I'll be back in about an hour," he calls. "Go for a shower."

Yes, sir, Mr. Grumble-Bum. "Fine."

I hear his truck start then leave. Suddenly, I find I'm really tired. I should close my eyes for a minute. But the doctor said I shouldn't go to sleep for at least another hour in case I have a concussion. Ugh, I may as well just have a shower. That way, by the time River returns. I'll be ready to eat something, and go to bed. What a complete waste of the day.

"What the hell happened to you?" Charlie asks as he walks into the stable.

"Long story. But my truck is at the beach. Do you think you can arrange for someone to go get it?" I search for my keys in my bag, and give them to Charlie.

"Tell me someone didn't touch you. Cause I'll fucking kill them. Is Grady…?" the question is serious, and I can tell Charlie will destroy anyone who'd lay their hands on me.

"No, I was an idiot."

"How?"

Shit, I'm going to have to tell him. "Long story short, I went to the growers market this morning, and was sitting on the beach watching everyone swimming. Saw a guy, was perving, hard. Turned out the guy was River. He saw me, I tried to run away and face-planted. The pavement won, I lost." I point to my nose.

Charlie's trying really hard not to laugh. But he sucks at holding in the hysterical, big belly laughs. "Shit, Hope." He wipes at his eyes. "That's so funny. Man, I bet you feel like an ass."

"Shut up and go get my truck."

Meow.

"Fine. But you know, I'm not going to let you live this down."

"Hope, I heard about what happened, are you okay?" Tabitha barrels in, completely unannounced. She looks at my face, and her eyes widen, as she covers her mouth with her hand, trying to hide the shock. "Whoa, you look terrible."

"I know. It looks worse than it feels. Lucky River was there to help."

"Because you were drooling all over him," Charlie adds.

"Shut up. We don't speak of these things," I say.

Tabitha looks to Charlie, then me. "Oh, did something happen?"

"She was drooling over River, then turned to run away when he saw her, and she kissed the pavement...with her nose."

Tabitha sucks in her cheeks, trying not to laugh. "Yeah, yeah," I say, feeling sorry for myself. "Can someone give me sympathy?"

"Nah, sorry," Charlie says.

"I could go and get Aunt May, she may give you some," Tabitha says.

"That's it, you're both off my Christmas card list. Charlie, get someone to take you and get my truck." I get up, and grab my pajamas out of the top drawer next to the bed.

"I can take you," Tabitha offers. "I'll come back and make you chicken soup if you like, Hope."

"Thank you, but River said he's going to the store. Thank you, though."

"Hmmm, I might make myself scarce tonight," Charlie says. "I don't want to hear you two going at it."

"Oh my God. Get out!" I yell at him. "River's just a friend. That's it. Nothing more."

"I'll check on you tomorrow," Tabitha says as she leaves first.

Charlie's walking backward, looking at me, while he's made an O with his left hand, and is using his pointer finger on his right hand to poke the O. "Out!" I say through a clenched jaw, which hurts.

Charlie then thrusts his hips, and pretends to pull the girls hair, and smack her butt. I don't say anything else, instead, I point to the door.

He's cracking up.

Truthfully, so am I. He's an ass. A protective big-brother…and an ass.

Meow.

"Damn it, you want food. At least I have that here. Hang on." I get the cat's bowl, and open a tin of food for him. "Should I name you something?"

The cat looks at me, crouches, and starts delicately eating.

"I don't know what to call you. I can't keep calling you *the cat,* although you seem to respond to it. Maybe that can be your name, *the cat."* He doesn't even acknowledge me.

Once the cat is settled, I grab my pajamas, and head into the shower. I look at myself in the mirror and nearly yell at what I look like. There's blood smeared in my hair, and down my shirt. There are heavy, black crescent-shaped bruises under my eyes. Actually, my entire face is puffy and swollen. "Wow, what a sexy babe you are," I say to myself.

I strip and turn the water to as hot as I can stand it, and get into the shower. It feels amazing as it pelts down on my back, almost giving me a massage. I lean my head back, and the water streams over my head, and my face. Looking down, I see the obvious tinge of blood as the water pools slightly before emptying down the drain.

Taking my time, I wash my hair, loving every single second of the pressure and the heat of the water.

I'm too scared to turn around and let the water touch my face, but I know I have to try and get as much of the dried blood off as I can. Turning, I wince as the water hits my nose. "Oh shit," I say. I can't tolerate too much of it, so I turn again, and choose to use the face cloth to clean that area instead.

I'd better get out of the shower. I could honestly stay in here all day and night. There's something soothing about hot water running over your body, especially if the day you've had has been challenging. You know, like perving on a guy you want to bump uglies with, but won't because you know you're leaving and don't want to suffer a broken heart again.

Turning off the water, I reach for my towel and wrap it around my body. Shit, I forgot one for my hair. I open the door to the bathroom, and take one step out to find River cooking in the kitchen. "Jesus!" I say when I see him.

He looks over his shoulder at me, looks back, then looks again. "Um," his voice is high. I watch as he visibly swallows, and takes in my towel-clad body. "You should change."

"I need a towel for my hair."

"But do you?" his voice is low and guttural. His eyes widen, and he shakes his head. Looking away, he continues cooking whatever he's stirring. "Don't mind me, I'm making you my Mom's chicken soup. Apparently, chicken soup is good for the soul."

I can't help but smile, because he sounds like he's babbling. "I'll just grab a towel. Be careful, I'm wet." What the actual fuck did I say? "I mean the floor is wet because I'm wet. From the shower. I'm not wet, *wet*, you know. I'm just wet." Shoot me now. Earth, open up and swallow me whole. Right this minute. God damn it, earth! "I'm just gonna shut up now." I point to the cupboard, although River's not looking at me. I can see his shoulders shaking as he silently laughs. Thankfully, he doesn't say anything.

Grabbing the towel, I'm sure not going to say a single word. I slip away into the bathroom, and close the door. Quickly, I wrap my hair in the towel, and get changed into my pajamas.

When I leave the bathroom, I find River sitting on the sofa, petting the damned cat. And the damned cat is letting him.

"He likes me," River proudly announces. "Finally."

"Traitor!" I say to the cat. "You didn't like him the other day. Why now?"

Meow. The cat purrs as River's petting him.

River looks up and says with a dead-straight face, "Your pussy just knows a good man is here."

My mouth falls open, and if my face didn't hurt so much, I'd screw my mouth up, and roll my eyes. "I can't believe you said that." I sit on the other side of the cat, and try to tempt him away from River.

"It's not my fault your pussy likes me."

"Stop," I say, trying to hold in the smile.

"What? You can see I'm stroking your pussy, and it's purring. Obviously, it has good taste."

This is a losing battle. "Fine, the cat likes you."

"Yes, the pussy does."

"Stop saying that."

"What?" He smirks.

I look over to the pot bubbling away on the range. "Chicken soup, eh?"

He gives me a nod. "Did you take your pain killers?"

"Not yet. I'll take it after I eat. I'm tired though, I could do with a nap."

River taps his phone to life to look at the time. "After you eat." He stands and walks over to the pot, lifts the lid, and is hit with a steam facial. "Man, I do that every time. You'd think I would've learned."

"So, you know how to cook?"

"A few things. Mom taught me. Said if I was going to move out, then I should know how to cook. She also said a man should learn how to take care of his love, so she doesn't feel like she's being taken advantage of."

I sit back on the sofa, and the cat moves to curl up beside me. "Remember the very first time we met? Or kind of met? In that coffee shop? I was ditching school, and you were sick."

"I wasn't sick," he says.

"Yeah, you were. Your mom gave you a kiss, and your face lit up like the flashing lights on a fire truck."

"That was when that guy tried to steal money, and you shoved him, or tripped him or something? I remember thinking to myself you had balls of steel. I thought you were the most awesome girl I'd ever laid eyes on." He smiles.

"I don't have balls of steel, I just hate it when people do something like steal. Or spit. Spitting is revolting."

"Why does stealing bother you so much? I mean, I hate it too, but I'd like to know why you hate it enough to bulldoze a guy who could've had a gun on him and shot you."

I keep petting the cat, who's now sound asleep beside me. "One Christmas, when I was like nine or ten, really young. Anyway, it was Christmas Eve, and we'd gone out to dinner. Dad had gotten a Christmas bonus at work, and he wanted to take us out to celebrate. We had the best night. Oh my God. Charlie ate so much he vomited, and we laughed so much, and just had the best time ever. It was honestly a Christmas I'll remember forever because of that. So, we came home about nine-thirty, and when we got inside, the entire house had been ransacked. They stole everything they could carry. Including our Christmas presents, and the rest of Dad's bonus, and the jewelry Mom wasn't wearing. They trashed all our bedrooms, even throwing eggnog all over the beds. They knocked the Christmas tree down, and smeared the Christmas pudding all over the walls. It totally destroyed Christmas for us." Shit, I can't believe I'm tearing up.

River comes to sit beside me, wraps his arms around me, and gives me a tight hug. "That's horrible."

"Stealing, to me, is one of the worst things a person can do. Mom cried for two days straight. They'd saved and bought us great presents they couldn't afford to replace. I hated seeing my parents so broken. I made a vow to myself to speak up when I see someone stealing something."

He kisses me on the side of my head. "That's horrible. I'm sorry you had to go through something so traumatic."

"Well, it wasn't you who broke into our house, was it?"

"No, of course not."

"Then you have nothing to be sorry for. But, thank you."

There are a few minutes of quiet, and my head is reeling with the remembered events and emotions of that Christmas. It still hurts. Not for me, but seeing the pain my parents experienced when we opened the door and saw the house trashed.

"I wanted to ask you something."

"Yeah, what?" I ask.

"This weekend is the candy festival in town, and I want to know if you're going."

I look at River. "The candy festival? What on earth is the candy festival?"

"A lot like the flower festival, but it's for different types of candy."

I blink rapidly a few times, trying to get my head around this all. "Candy, really? So, like Halloween?"

"No one dresses up, though if you'd like to, I won't say no," he cheekily adds. "Especially a hot maid outfit. With a feather duster," he mumbles.

"I'm not dressing up. I think my face will be enough to scare anyone away."

River flicks his hand. "We've all seen a broken nose before." He gives me another kiss on the head, then stands and heads toward the stove. He lifts the lid, but this time steps back so he doesn't get a face full of steam. He stirs the pot, then grabs a tablespoon, and tastes it. "Oh yum. Yeah, it's ready. Come on."

Getting up, I disturb the cat, who gives me a grumpy look before he repositions himself and goes back to sleep. I go to the cabinet to grab two bowls, but River beats me to it. "What are you doing?"

"I'm taking care of you." He reaches for the bowls, and ladles soup into one, and places it on the small table. "Sit, eat."

He's making it incredibly difficult for me to keep my distance from him. The more he does, the more I want. "Thank you." I look down and notice he's forgotten the spoons. I stand and take one step away from the table.

"What are you doing?"

"I need a spoon."

"Let me care for you, Hope."

"But you don't have to."

"You're the biggest pain in the ass known to man. I know I don't have to, but I *want* to. So please, stop fighting it, and let me care for you, *woman!*"

I can't help but smile with the way he called me *woman*. "Fine, it's only a damn spoon." I sip on the soup. "Why aren't you at work today?"

"You fell and broke your nose. You're more important. Anyway, I was able to move the jobs I had to tomorrow afternoon."

"Okay. Thankfully the house is tented for at least the next day or two, so I can't do much over there. But once the tent comes down, I'm back there."

"Good. You have to give yourself time to heal."

"I will over these next couple of days. Anyway, you heard what the doctor said. He wants to see me again in three days, to check on the swelling and how it's healing."

River takes a deep breath, then lets it out. "I'd prefer you to rest for at least three or four days."

"I'll make a compromise."

River lifts his brows. "Go on."

"I'll go back to work when I feel like I can."

"That's not a compromise, that's a *'I'm going to do what I want.'*"

"I promise, if I feel like crap, I won't go. Charlie can hold it together until I'm feeling better."

"Deal."

"But only if I think I need some extra time to heal." River grumbles. "Deal?" I hold out my hand.

River looks at my hand, then extends his. "I don't have much choice in the matter, do I?"

"Not really." I smile, pleased with myself that I can get away with it.

He takes a sip of his soup, then says, "And just so you know, you can come stay at my house so I can keep an eye on you, or I'll be staying here. And no, that's not negotiable."

"But…"

"No. If you're a stubborn ass about going back to work, then I'm going to be a stubborn ass about making sure you're okay to go back to work." He stares at me proudly.

"Fine," I grumble.

"Good. Eat up."

He's such a pain in the ass. But I'm so glad he's here.

Chapter
TWENTY ONE

W AKING UP, I'M temporarily confused about where I am. I can hear the sound of waves, and I can smell the ocean spray from here. Looking around the room, I remember that River brought me to his house last night.

Extending my arm, I reach for River. Nothing's happened between us. Nothing has happened, because I know I'm only here to restore Old Roger's house.

The sound of soft humming is coming from somewhere beyond the room. When I open the door, I find River in the kitchen, cooking. In sleep pants. *Shirtless. (Yes)*

God damn it, why does he have to look so good? I lean against the door frame, staring at him as he hums and makes breakfast.

Jesus, he's doing something to me. Every part of me is loving what I'm seeing. His dark bed-tousled hair, his broad shoulders, the perfect muscles slightly protruding on his back. My God. My lady parts are starting to tingle, and in this moment, I want to climb that boy like a damn koala scales up a tree. Holy shit.

"Stop staring at me," he says without turning.

I point at him, ready to argue how I wasn't staring, but my voice has decided to defy me and just squeak. What am I? A damn school girl?

"Omelet?"

"Depends, can I eat it off you?" My eyes widen, and I'm horrified that I actually spoke those words aloud. "I mean, yes, thanks." What the hell is wrong with me?

"Would you like me to lay on the table, or would the bed be a better place?"

I shake my head, completely mortified at myself. "I don't know what you heard, but I didn't say anything." I move closer to him, and really try not to look at him in the '*I'm so horny I want us to screw on every surface of your house*' way.

"Mushroom, spinach, tomato and cheese omelet for you, my love." He walks over to the table, places the plate down, and pulls out the chair, waiting for me to sit.

"Where's yours?"

He walks into his room, and comes back with a shirt on. Damn it, why? I liked my eye-candy. "I'm making it now. But you start eating, because it doesn't taste as good when it's cold."

"Then you have it, I'll wait for the next one."

I sit, and he pushes the chair in. He leans down, and gives me a kiss on the top of my head. "Nope. You eat. Mine will be ready in no time." He walks over to the range, flips his omelet, then brings over the coffee pot. He pours me a cup, and pours one for himself. He looks at my uneaten breakfast. "You're going to be a pain in the ass again, aren't you?"

I crack a smile. "I'll eat when you're ready."

"Okay."

Looking out the window, I can see the ocean maybe thirty

yards from where we are. "It's pretty here. How did you end up in Hope River?" I ask.

"I wanted to slow down. I um…" his voice sounds heavy, like he has a lot he wants to say, but he's scared if he tells me what I'll think. "I wanted to slow down," he says again.

"You don't have to tell me." But I'm itching to know.

"After that last night with you. The one where you saw the message…" I nod. "I didn't handle what Claire did to me well. It broke me actually. I started drinking, and drinking, and drinking."

"River, I didn't know."

"Of course, you didn't. It got bad, and I went off the rails for about a year. I refused to talk to anyone, until Mom found me covered in my own vomit, and she snapped me out of it, really fast. Made me go to AA, stuck by me. Although I was quickly turning into an alcoholic, it was just a coping mechanism for me. Claire did a real number on my mental health. Mom made me also realize, how much I…" he stops talking, and shakes his head. "It doesn't matter."

"No, tell me. What was it?"

He presses his lips together, and offers a weak smile. "How much I shouldn't have let it affect me." That's not what he was going to say, I know he's lying.

"And then you found Hope River?"

"Not really, it's like Hope River found me."

"That's weird, how does a place find you?"

"My Dad knows someone who lives about an hour that way." He points over his shoulder toward the right. "They were building a house, and Dad offered my electrical expertise. So I went to help, and I saw Hope River on the map, and thought, wow. It has your name and my name in the town's name, so I knew I had to move here."

"Because it has our names in it?"

He nods. "I also hoped that one day, Hope River would find you too. And, it has. Because you're here."

"You moved here for us?" My heart flutters with so much emotion.

"Yep. And I found this place. It wasn't in great shape, but now it is because of all the work I've put in it. I owe it to myself to be happy, and I'm happy here."

"Wow." Really, wow.

"And how did you come to Hope River? I know Old Roger's house hasn't been advertised for years, so how did you find it?"

This is going to be hard. I pick my fork up, and eat my omelet. "It's a bit of a story."

"I'm not going anywhere."

How much should I tell him? All of it? Part of it? "I was in a long-term relationship, and one night, he came home drunk as anything. He hit me."

"He did what?" River asks in a low voice.

I hold my hand up, as I lick my lips and take in a breath. "It's okay."

"No, it's not okay."

"I'm not condoning what he did I'm just saying, I had his balls in my hand and I told him I'd mail them back to his mother." River doesn't crack a smile. Instead, I can see he's ready to go find Grady, and kill him. I place my hand on his tense arm. "It's taken care of."

River's jaw is clenched, but he loosens it enough to say, "Go on."

"I packed a bag, got in my truck, and drove. Asked the universe to be kind to me. I happened on a sign that said Hope River, and I laughed, because I also recognized that it's our names combined. As I was driving through, in the middle of the night, I stumbled upon Old Roger's house, and the rest, is history."

"Let's go back to this guy."

"Let's not. He's in my past, not my future. I'm selling the house we were living in, and moving away from it. He worked for me, but obviously, he doesn't anymore." River's omelet is half-eaten, instead he's looking out at the water, thinking. "What's wrong?" I ask.

"Honestly?"

"Yeah."

"I don't know how to react."

"Um, okay. Why?"

"Part of me wants to find him, and kill him. Another part of me is angry at myself for messing up with you when I saw you at the club and letting you go. And another part of me wants you to stay with me forever, where I can protect you and look after you."

"I don't…"

He stares at me, and holds his hand up. "Before you tell me you don't need protecting and looking after, you have to know that's not what I meant. You're not a damsel in distress. You're feisty, and strong, and the biggest pain in the butt I've ever met. But I want you to stay because I…" He reaches for my hand, entwining our fingers.

Ring.

Ring. Ring.

River stops talking, being interrupted by his phone constantly ringing. "Ignore it," he says as he looks over at the counter top to where it hasn't shut up.

"Okay." I too look over. His phone stops, then starts not even a second later. "Answer it. It won't stop until you do."

He stares hard at me, brings his brows together and stands so abruptly the chair slides back across the floor. He picks his phone up, grimacing. "Mom, are you okay?" He runs his hand across the back of his neck. "Okay, calm down. Tell me what's happened." He walks over to the slider that frames the ocean so perfectly. He tilts his head to the side, then nods. "I'll be there by nightfall." Turning to face me, his expression changes from worried, to blank. "Okay. Okay. Yep." He hangs up, and leans against the glass slider. "I'm sorry, Hope. We're going to have to pick this up when I get back."

"What's wrong? Can I help? Can I do anything?"

"Yes, you can stay here until I get back." He strides into his bedroom, where I follow.

"What's going on?"

"It's Dad. He had a stroke."

His eyes fill with tears, and I can see he's doing everything to hold them in. Shit, I can see he's about to fall apart. "Hey," I say as I go straight to him. I step into him, and he envelops me in a huge hug. "What did your mom say?"

"He's in the hospital, I need to go."

"It's okay. He's in the best place he could be. It'll be okay." I don't know what else to say.

"I'll be gone for a day, maybe two."

"Take your time."

He kisses my forehead, then keeps packing his bag. "Where do your parents live now?" I ask.

"About five hours south." He looks at the time on his clock beside his bed. "If I leave now, I should be there around one. I'll call you when I get there."

"Okay."

He slides his sleep pants off, and I'm not sure I should be looking considering he's in a vulnerable state, but *damn*. Stop it!

He slides on a pair of jeans. *Damn it.*

Stop thinking with your vagina, Hope.

Anyway, it wouldn't be fair to start a relationship with someone whose roots are in Hope River. In a matter of weeks, I'll be gone. It's not a kind thing to do to him, or myself.

I have to break away from him. I've let this go on too long. It's not fair to either of us.

He packs his clothes, and is changed fast. He turns, comes to me, and laces his hands through my hair. Leaning his forehead to mine, he says, "Promise me you'll be here when I get back."

I can't promise that, because I won't be here. "Go, be with your family," I say in a quiet voice.

He kisses me again on the forehead, then picks his bag up and leaves. "Before I go, here's a set of keys. Can you please lock up if you go into town or anywhere?"

"Sure." I smile, but inside I'm dying. I know I've got to cut this off here or it's going to end with two hearts so shattered, neither one of us will be able to love anyone ever again.

It's got to end, now.

Chapter
TWENTY TWO

RIVER'S BEEN CALLING me, and I've been ignoring him. I spoke with him the day after he got to his parents to make sure his dad was okay, and since then, I've cut myself off from him.

It's the only way I can survive this. Whatever *this* is.

The moment he left, I knew I had to do the right thing for him, and for me. I called Charlie, and got him to come and pick me up.

Now, I'm driving home after seeing the doctor who examined me three days ago when I broke my nose. He's happy with the progress, and wants to see me again in four weeks to determine if I'll need an operation or not. He doesn't seem to think I will, but wants to make sure.

I head back to Old Roger's house, and now that the tent is gone, we are full steam ahead.

Charlie's assembled an amazing team of people he's pooled

from all over Hope River and the neighboring counties. They're truly amazing.

I pull up to the house, and the cat jumps out of the bed.

Meow. He rubs himself up against my leg.

I look down and smile. "I've made an appointment with the vet for this afternoon to make sure you're okay."

Meow.

Walking up to the house, I'm so impressed by what they've done. "Charlie!" I call when I don't see him.

"Hang on!" I hear from upstairs.

The number of workers here is mind-blowing. They're working quickly and efficiently. This old girl is nearly ready for us to start reassembling her again. Most walls have been opened up, the termites are gone, and the house has been nearly gutted, with only the few necessary structural support beams remaining.

A few of the workers do a double-take, but then go on about doing their job.

"Hey, aren't you supposed to be home resting?" Charlie asks when he comes down the stairs.

I ignore the question. "When do the stairs come out?"

"They're not coming out until we get the new staircase built. Now, will you go home and rest." He looks around, and watches as the workers representing all the trades work around each other. The only one missing is River, and that's because I'm timing my visit so he's not here when I am.

"How's the extension coming along?"

"Great. Go home." Wow, he's gone from asking nicely, to brusquely sending me away. He turns me and attempts to walk me out of the house.

"The footings?" I refuse to move.

"Don't you trust me? Because you're developing into an overbearing pain in the ass. You're gonna be one of those helicopter parents when you have kids. Standing over the kid, annoying them. My poor niece or nephew will wanna come and stay at Uncle Charlie's to get away from you."

I stick my hand on my hip. "First; You're not the only one who says that. I want to see. Second; I won't be a helicopter parent."

He rolls his eyes. "Pick your stupid cat up before it hurts itself."

Bending, I grab the cat, while Charlie is already ahead of me. "Jesus." I look at the huge hole in the wall. Standing on the edge, I can see the footings have been poured, and floor is going down. "Wow, it's going to be massive!"

"I know. I told you that. As you can see, we couldn't save the tree."

"I was going to ask. When is the rest going?" Most the tree has been chopped down, but there's still about a third left."

"Coming to finish the job tomorrow."

I sigh. "I didn't want to get rid of it. But it was dead, right?"

"One huge storm, and it would've come down on top of the house. Have you thought of landscaping?" I shake my head. "We've still got time."

"Time is money, Charlie. And I want this house done so we can get out of here." Charlie winces when I announce my eagerness to leave. "What?"

"Nothing."

"Charlie, what?"

"I'm liking it here. I was thinking maybe I could stick around a bit."

What? Charlie wants to stay? "You want to stay here?" He nods. "In Hope River?" He nods again. "The guy who called it a little hick town?"

"Yeah, that probably wasn't the nicest thing I said." He grimaces when I remind him of his words. "But I like it here, and I'd like to hang around for a while."

"And what about all of this?" I say as I extend my arms. "If I move back, you can't commute hours and hours to work for me, Charlie."

He looks down, and screws his mouth up. "What if you stay too?"

"What? No. This is just a job. I can't stay here. You know this; our life isn't here."

"What if it is?" he challenges.

"It's not!" I state.

"Why? What's so bad about moving here? Seeing how things go. Who knows, you may end up loving Hope River."

I shake my head, and walk away. I can't deal with him at the moment, and my face is hurting too. "Call me if there are any problems. I'm taking the cat to the vet."

"Hope…" he calls.

"Not now," I shoot over my shoulder to him with a wave. *Not now, not ever.*

The cat and I walk into the vet's office, and the cat twirls himself around my leg. "Hi, I have an appointment with the vet," I say.

"What's your name?"

What? Someone doesn't know who I am? That's quite refreshing. "Hope Sawyer," I say as I smile and lean against the counter. The receptionist can't take her eyes off my face. "I broke my nose," I say as I point to it.

"Oh, you're Hope." She smiles.

Scratch that. She knew who I was, but because my face is all busted up, she probably didn't recognize me. "Yes, I am," I say, frustration rearing its ugly head.

"Where's the cat?" She looks to see if I'm carrying him in a cat carrier.

"He's here." I point at my feet.

She stands, and looks down over the counter. "He's not in a carrier?" I shake my head. "He has to be in a carrier."

"Why?"

"Because all animals who come in must be restrained."

That's weird. But I guess, if a dog came in here, the dog might try to rip the cat apart. "Okay, I'll buy a cat carrier."

"What's the cat's name?" She starts typing, but stops and looks up. I don't know what to say. "The cat? What's his name?"

"I've been calling him the cat, so…his name is The Cat, I guess.?"

She chuckles. "How old is…" she pauses and furrows her brows. "…the cat?"

I shrug. "No idea. He showed up at the house I'm working on, and he's kind of adopted me. I'm hoping the vet can tell me."

The girl stops typing, and leans an elbow on the desk. "Oh yeah, I drove past Old Roger's house, and boy, it's going to be so beautiful. My husband and I have been talking about it. Have you got a price in mind yet?"

What? She's the second person who's shown interest in the house. "Not yet."

"Who's the real estate agent? It's Elle, right?"

Wow, she's eager. "I'm not entirely sure yet." Elle and I still haven't talked. I can't assume she's going to sell this house for me when the time comes.

"We're eagerly watching to see what you'll do with it. Anyway, take a seat, and the vet should be with you soon. You're in next."

"Thank you." The cat and I walk over to the red bench seat, and sit. The cat jumps up, and curls up next to me, and places his head on his little paws, and closes his eyes. He's got no idea of what's coming. The vet will probably be shoving a thermometer up his butt very soon. Poor cat.

"Hope?" a woman, probably in her late forties, calls.

"Come on," I say to the cat. He jumps down, and follows.

She leads us to a small sterile room, and closes the door. "Hello there," the vet says to the cat. "I'm Kate, and I'm the town's vet. Who have we got here?" She looks at the computer screen and smiles. "The Cat?"

"He showed up at the house, and has been following me around."

"Next time you bring him in, he'll need to be in a cat carrier."

"The lady at reception already told me. Sorry. This is the first time in my entire life I've ever had an animal."

The vet looks over at me. "Really? Animals are wonderful. They're so forgiving. People...meh." She scrunches her nose. "How can I help, Cat?"

Bending, I grab the cat, and stick him up on the examination table. He stretches, and flaps his tail in my face. *Meow.* "Yeah, yeah, I know, buddy," I answer. "I thought I'd get him checked out, and make sure he's good. If you can give me any tips about owning a cat, that would be helpful too."

She looks him over, running her hands down his back, his sides, and all around his torso to his hind legs. She opens his mouth and looks at his teeth. "Let's check you're not microchipped," she says and gives him a pat. I'm so surprised he's not barring his teeth at her.

Crap, I didn't even think to do that. What if I've kidnapped someone's cat?

She gets this small rectangle thingy, and runs it over the cat's back and head. Suddenly, I've found myself nervous. I chew on my nail as I watch her waving the small machine over him.

"Doesn't appear to have a microchip," Kate says. "Now, let's look, are you a boy, or a girl?" She grabs the cat, spins him around, and lifts his tail. Oh, great, a cat asshole. Literally. "See here?" She points to the cat's butt, then a relatively wider slit about an inch or so down from the butt.

"Yeah," I say with revulsion. I really wish I hadn't though.

"He's definitely a *he*. And judging by this, he hasn't been neutered."

Huh? She can't tell for sure? "What do you mean, judging by it?"

"Cats are a bit different from dogs. Their penises don't protrude. A female has a slit about here." She gives me a visual demonstration.

"Right." I'll stick to houses, they're much simpler. "And his age?"

"Judging by the slight discoloration of his teeth, and his adult fur, he's certainly over one year old, but I can't tell you how much older than that he is. He's got all his teeth, and none of them appear to need to be removed. It's hard to tell if there are no records for him."

"Right. Okay. Um, what do I do now?"

"The option is yours. You can keep him, we can try to adopt him out, or we can euthanize him."

"What? Put him down?" No damn way.

"The option is yours. But if you keep him, I have to tell you, it's a town regulation to have him neutered."

"I'm not getting rid of him. I'll have his manhood cut off. I'll keep him." I pet the cat.

"Okay, we can schedule a time to do that." She sits on a stool, and taps on her keys of the computer. "I can get to Cat on Monday. If you want to bring him in first thing in the morning, I'll do the surgery in the afternoon, keep him here overnight just to check his progress, and you can pick him up on Tuesday. How does that sound?"

"Yeah, I'm fine with that. Can you microchip him too?"

"I can. If you head out, Julie will be able to book you in for Monday. But first, let's get Cat up-to-date with his immunizations, because we don't know what he's had, I'll go ahead and give him everything. He'll need a booster in about a month or so. We'll send you a text message to remind you."

"Okay, great." I smile.

"I'll be back in a moment." Kate leaves the room, and suddenly I'm nervous for The Cat. I hate needles, which is the number one reason why I don't have tattoos. They freak me out. I've heard too many horror stories of people who go for simple blood tests and end up with terrible bruising from the nurses not getting the veins so they just keep jabbing away.

She comes back into the room, and I can feel myself about to be sick. Jesus, I have to distract myself. "How much food should I be feeding Cat?"

"He's a little underweight. So, I'd like to see him plumped up a bit more. With another three pounds he should be good. What are you feeding him?"

"I bought some food from the grocery store."

"Commercial food is fine, it has a little higher water content, which doesn't make it as nutritious. But it's not bad. I'd suggest a good quality dry food, which you can buy here if you want, or online. I'll write some brands down if you like."

"It's okay, I'll grab a bag from here."

"And give him no more than one cup of food a day. When he gains some weight, you may need to wean him down to around three-quarters of a cup. Is he an active cat?"

I look at Cat, curled up on the examination table. I chuckle. "He's a weirdo, is what he is. He jumps in the bed of my truck, and rides around everywhere I go." Kate screws her brows together, and slowly smiles. "When I went looking at stone for the counter tops, he came with me. He loves riding in the truck."

Kate chuckles. She scratches Cat under the chin, and surprisingly, Cat allows her. "Yep, you're a weirdo," she confirms. "Sorry, Cat, but you're not going to like the next part." I flinch away, my entire body shuddering when I see the needles. But Kate is fast, and Cat has no idea what just hit him. "Okay, we're done. I'll see you on Monday," she says to Cat. "You may find that he'll be tired tonight and off his food. That's completely normal."

"Thank you." I open the door, and a dazed and confused Cat jumps off the table, and follows me out to the reception area. Kate comes through and talks to Julie.

I walk out of the vet's office just over three hundred dollars poorer. Get a pet, they say. Pets are great, they say.

Three hundred for a vet visit, a small bag of kibble, and a date for him to become ball-less.

Poor Cat.

Chapter
TWENTY THREE

"HELLO?" I CALL as I knock on May's door.

"My God, girly. When will you learn that if the door is open, just walk in?"

I open the door, and start walking toward May. "I'm heading down to the candy festival, and was wondering if you or Tabitha need a ride in?"

"You can take me. I have no idea where Tabitha is though."

"Oh." I look outside for her car, but it's still here. "What time do you want to head in?"

"I'm making my famous potato salad. What did you...never mind, you can't cook." She flicks her hand at me.

"Yeah, thanks for the reminder," I jokingly say.

"Your face is looking better. You don't look so frightening anymore." God love May and her lack of filter.

."Thank you?"

"I said you look better, I didn't say you looked great." She looks down and sees Cat. "So, you're keeping him then?"

"Appears he's adopted me, not the other way around."

"How's the house coming along?" She places cling wrap over the large clear bowl she's made the potato salad in, then heads back to her fridge and continues taking out other vegetables.

"Really good. We're nearly ready to start putting her back together again. I'm excited to see how she turns out."

"I have no doubt she's going to be a beautiful, regal, old girl who's been given a new lease on life. Like when I got my knee replaced. Took a while before I was good, but now, I have no pain and I can keep going."

"I'm actually surprised because I've had two people asking if I've set a price on Old Roger's house yet."

"Only two? A lot of people are asking me what the sale price will be. I tell them to go to you. How many bedrooms will it be?"

"Five bedrooms, each with their own bathroom."

"Five bedrooms? Wow. I hope you'll allow me to look through it once it's done."

"You'll be my guest of honor." I smile, as I watch May quickly chopping up a huge salad. Lettuce, tomatoes, cucumbers, bell peppers, cheese, onion, and some fresh corn. She drizzles it with a dressing, tosses it together to coat everything, and wraps it in cling wrap too.

"I wanted to ask you, have you found out anything about those earrings and the letter?" her voice softens, while her eyes stay lowered.

"No, I haven't really had a moment to ask anyone. Do you know anything about them?"

"No. No, I don't. But I'd like to buy the entire tin from you."

Huh? Why is May so interested in the tin? She knows something, and it has something to do with her. "May, do you know who that letter and earrings were meant for?" I know I've asked and she's denied, but my gut is saying, not only does she know, she's likely supposed to have been the recipient.

Again, she doesn't lift her gaze, and she tries to shake her head. But her small voice defies her actions. "Yes, I do."

I want to know what beautiful tale of love belongs with that tin. "Were the letter and the earrings meant for you?"

May visibly swallows, then sucks in an audibly deep breath through her nose. She doesn't speak. The tears that fall on her counter top tell me everything I need to know.

There may be a love story behind that tin, but clearly there's been loss too. I can't keep it knowing the rightful person doesn't have it. I run out of the house and go to the stable, where I open the door, go straight to the cupboard, and retrieve the tin.

To me, the contents, although fascinating, don't hold much value. They belong to May. I head back into her house, where she's already straightened and seems to be back to her usual self. Except for the tiny quiver of her chin.

"May, I'd like for you to have this." I place the tin on the counter, and slide it over to her.

She looks at me, down at the tin, and back up again. "Oh no, darling, I can't take it. It's rightfully yours. You bought the house. I'll pay you for it."

Taking her hands in mine, I give them a small squeeze. "It's *rightfully* yours. And I want no payment for it. Perhaps one day, you'll be kind enough to share the history of how it came to be there and what the contents mean to you."

She sucks in another breath, and slightly nods. "It wasn't just love, it was soul-touching, epic." She picks the tin up, and hugs it to her chest. "Thank you, Hope. What you've given me means more than you could ever imagine."

"It's my pleasure to gift you with this. I only ask one favor."

"What's that?" She looks at me, and I can't help to see the amazing love in her eyes.

"I'd like to borrow the earrings at some point so that I can get the right green paint for the house. Would you mind?" She opens the tin, and takes the pouch out offering it to me. "No, you hold on to them. When I need them, I'll ask for them." She places the tin on the counter, and lays the earrings next to the tin. She throws her arms around me, hugging me with surprising ferociousness.

"Thank you."

"You're welcome. Now, are we ready to go to the candy festival?"

"Let me put this away, and then I'm good to go." She takes the tin, clasping it close to her heart, and walks down the hallway.

Meow.

Looking down, I see Cat's laying near the dishwasher. "What? You can't come. You have to stay home."

Meow.

"Come on, get your butt back home."

Meow.

I roll my eyes. "No, I'm not taking you with us. You'll get lost or trampled on. Come on, let's go."

Meow. He keeps sitting, refusing to move. *Meow.*

I walk to the front door, and hold it open. "Cat!" He slowly strolls toward me. This cat has serious attitude. "What are you, a teenager who doesn't listen?"

"Are you talking to the cat?" May asks when she enters the kitchen and grabs one of the bowls.

"He's stubborn. He wants to come with us, but I told him he has to stay here."

May easily cruises past me, holding one of the filled bowls. She gives me a sideways glance, and slightly tilts her head. "Is The Cat talking to you, Hope?" she asks in a slow deliberate voice.

"No, he's not. But I can tell he's being all judgey and shit with me."

"Aha, I see." She gets to the door and says under her breath but loud enough for me to hear, "And they say *I'm* a crazy old lady."

I chuckle. "Come on, I'm going. Get out." Cat stands, stretches, then yawns. He tiptoes like damn royalty past me. "You're a pain."

He glares at me, and saunters away.

"Hey, I own you, you don't own me." Yeah, right.

Shit, I feel so nervous being here today. I know I'm going to run into River, and I don't want to be forced to talk to him. I want to keep it as professional as possible.

"Can you see if Elle will bring me a coffee please?" May asks as she places the potato salad bowl on the table, then takes the one I'm carrying and lays it beside it.

"Sure. Do you want anything else?" I ask.

"No, thank you."

I walk up to Elle's café, and open the door. Elle's behind the counter, frantically trying to get things ready. She looks up, smiles, looks down, then back to me. Her smile drops.

So does my heart.

Murray turns and sees me standing at the entrance. "Hope, I haven't seen you in here for a few days."

"How are you, Murray?" I walk up, and stand beside him.

"Better than your face." He holds his mug up, and laughs.

"Yeah, yeah, I know. It's not as bad as it looks."

"Hope," Elle says with a coolness that sends shivers down my back.

"Elle." I try to offer her a smile.

"Right, I'm out of here. Thanks, Elle. On my tab, yeah?" Murray says.

"Sure thing, Murray."

Murray tips his head and exits the café, leaving Elle and me on our own.

I hate knowing I've hurt her. I have to fix this. "Do you need help?" I ask as I peer over the counter and see she's making platters of sandwiches.

She screws her mouth up, then nods. "Can you wash your hands, and there's gloves over there. Then I need you to cut those." She's giving me a lifeline, an opportunity to right my wrong.

I follow her gaze, and get to helping her. The tension is palpable. That's not how I want it to be. "I'm sorry," I say.

She gives me a quick look over her shoulder. "Thank you," she says.

"I was a wiener, and I shouldn't have been."

There are a few seconds of silence, before she laughs. "A wiener? You're calling yourself a dick?"

"Yeah, I am."

"It takes a strong woman to admit she's being a dick. And I appreciate it. Don't be a wiener again."

"I'll try not to. Anyway, did you hear I broke my nose?"

"I did. And I wanted to see if you were okay. River told me he was looking after you, so I left it alone. And now, he comes in here all moody and shit."

"What do you mean?"

"He's barely talking to any of us. He comes in, gets his coffee, and leaves. He's not his normal self. Don't get me wrong; he's never been a huge talker or anything, He's always been really pleasant. Now, he's like a grumpy old man."

Shit, I did that to him. My heart drops and my stomach clenches knowing I've hurt him so much it's affecting how he's acting in his own home town. The quicker I get this house done and sold, the better it'll be for him. When I'm gone, he can move on, and forget all about me. Elle says something, but I don't hear her because I'm caught in my own self-pity party. "Huh?"

"I said, how did you break your nose? I heard you were jogging and fell. Is that true?"

"Me? Jogging? No chance. But I was trying to run away."

"Sure, because that sentence isn't confusing at all," Elle teases.

Things seem easy with Elle and myself, we're back to the way we were. "I was ogling River while he was wet…"

"River was wet?" She stops what she's doing to look over to me.

"It's a long story. But basically, I was down at the growers' market, having just bought donuts and a coffee. So, I sat my butt on one of the benches, and was people watching. Wondering about what they could be thinking about."

"You do that?"

"Yeah, all the time. Don't you?"

"Hell, no. I already know nearly everything that goes on in Hope River. Anyway, tell me how you ended up with this lovely shade of black and blue around your nose and eyes."

"So, I was watching this guy who was swimming, and when the guy emerged from the ocean. I was ogling his nice, rippling, *wet* body. I had no idea who it was, until he came closer."

"River," both Elle and I say in unison.

"I may or may not have said something stupid like…Oh, keep in mind, I may have actually yelled it, not said it."

"Crap, what did you yell?"

"I may or may not have yelled, *I can't have sex with you,* because all I was thinking about was having sex with him."

Elle purses her lips together, and her mouth lifts on the sides. "I'm not laughing," she says.

Yeah, she is. "I may have turned and tried to run so I wouldn't screw him right there. And I may have tripped and face planted. And I may have embarrassed myself. Just a bit."

I look over to Elle, who's silently cackling to herself. "There are a lot of 'mays' going on in those sentences."

"I'd like to say the 'mays' are hypothetical. I'm going to pretend they are."

Her silent cackling morphs into full-on belly laughs. "What happened?"

"He took me back to his house to look after me and made me chicken soup."

"Did you two have sex?" Elle leans over to hear all the awesome details.

And this is where it all becomes awkward. I sigh, and finish cutting the sandwiches, then line them on the tray she's placed beside me. "It was heading that way, but no. He got a call about his dad."

"Ohh, this is when his dad had a stroke, and when River came back, he was so worried. But his dad is doing good. Thankfully."

"Yeah, thankfully." I try to end the conversation there. Not offering anything else. But I know Elle is itching for more details.

"Then what happened?"

I may as well tell her. "River and I have history. And it's never worked out in the past, so I can't go there again. It hurt too much, and I don't think I'm strong enough to go there again."

She clicks her tongue to the roof of her mouth, then huffs. "So, you're saying it won't work?"

"It won't work," I confirm.

"Why?"

"Because it never has in the past."

"Right. And why hasn't it worked in the past?"

"Circumstances. We're forever being pushed apart."

There's a long silence between us, which is totally uncomfortable. It's forcing me to remember the times we had together. "Do you want to elaborate?"

"It's like we're being pushed together, only for us to be ripped apart again. Three times, Elle. Three times we've found each other, and three times we've been pulled apart."

"How old were you both?"

"Sixteen, eighteen and twenty-one. And, now. But I can't do it again. When he first left, it hurt. But the second time, man…" My eyes well up with tears. "That one broke me. Absolutely tore my heart out and crushed it. Then the third time, I thought he betrayed me, and I ran without giving him a chance to explain. Now, we both lead different lives."

She smacks me on the upper arm. "Different lives?" she nearly yells. "What are you talking about? You flip houses for a living. He's an electrician who's working for you. How is that *different lives?* You're both here, in Hope River. Hope freakin' River. Get it? Both of your names are in the name of the freakin' town! Anyone can clearly see what you both mean to each other, and you're saying you lead *different lives?* Are you kidding, Hope?" Man, she's seriously hardcore passionate about trying to prove a point.

"Calm down before you explode," I say.

She closes her eyes, and breathes in deep. Opening her eyes, she gives me a small smile. "You have to give this thing you both have one last chance, because if you don't, you'll regret it for the rest of your life."

"Elle, once Old Roger's house is done, I'm leaving. And it's not fair to River or to me to start something that's already got an expiration date." I finish with what she wanted me to do.

"What a shame," she says.

Ugh, she's baiting me to ask her what she thinks is a shame. I won't do it. I refuse to. Nope, not going to ask. "What's a shame?" *Ugh, damn it, Hope.*

"It's a shame you can't see what's in front of you." She leans in and gives me a hug. "It's okay, we still have time. Now, can you help take these out? Oh, are Gran and Tabitha here too?"

"Shit! May wanted a coffee. I forgot."

"I'll grab her the coffee, can you bring these two out, then come back in and help?"

She rushes around grabbing a mug, and pouring coffee into it. She takes the mug out, and I follow while holding two platters.

Sitting beside May is River. They're talking.

Shit.

"Hope," he says as he stands and takes a step closer to me.

Shit, shit, double shit.

I shouldn't have come today.

I can't do this.

"Hope," he says again as he notices my hesitation. He takes the platters out of my hands, quickly places them on the table, then returns to me.

Elle notices how uncomfortable I am, glances between River and myself, and opens her mouth to say something. But I beat her to it. "Do you think you can take May home? I've got to go." I flick a look between her, then River.

Elle positions her body between me and River. She grabs my hand and squeezes it. "If you don't want him, tell him. But if you're scared, then I think you owe him the truth," she whispers.

I thought she was on my side. "Elle," I sigh, slightly frustrated.

"You owe it to yourself, and to him, to be honest." She steps back and smiles. "Sure, I can give Gran a ride home."

"What am I? Chopped liver? I can make my own damned way home. You don't have to treat me like a child!" May snaps at all of us.

"Sorry, May," I say as I lower my gaze in shame.

"Sorry," both River and Elle say.

"Elle, can you give me a ride home later, please?" May asks.

"Sure thing, Gran."

"See, I can arrange my own way home." She sits tall and proud, while reaching for a cracker.

I should've known better.

"Hope," River says reminding me we need to talk.

I'm resigned to the fact we both need to get this sorted once and for all. But is now the ideal time to settle this?

Ugh. I know if I don't get this done, then I'll keep avoiding him. Hell, isn't that what I've been doing? Dodging him at every possible opportunity?

Right, I have to pull my big girl panties on, and face this.

"Fine, let's talk," I say.

Elle's smile is wide. And I can't help but notice, May's is too.

Does everyone know?

What a stupid thought. Of course, everyone knows.

River catches up to me as I veer away from the listening ears, and watchful eyes. "My place or yours?" he asks.

I need to mentally prepare for this. I can't go in just like this, and have a discussion with him.

I stop walking, and River does the same thing. "Tonight. And at your place, not mine." That way I can leave when I'm ready.

"I'll make dinner for us."

"This isn't a date, River."

He narrows his eyes, then smiles. "But we both have to eat. Unless you want to watch me eat, and you can sit there hungry?"

Smart-ass. "Fine."

"A thank you would've been nicer."

Taking a deep breath, I look down, and nod. "Thank you."

"I'll see you tonight."

Yep, he will, I guess.

Chapter
TWENTY FOUR

M Y STOMACH HAS been going crazy. The butterflies have been on high alert since I got in my truck and headed for River's.

I'm parked in his driveway, and all I can do is look out the windshield toward the beautiful ocean. It's coming on dusk, and even though it's not full sunlight, I can still see the waves out at sea, that disappear to nothing more than rapid water as they get closer to the shore.

Opening the door to my truck, I'm hit with the sea salt aroma.

My stomach is knotting, and vomit is quickly bubbling up to the back of my throat. Why am I so nervous? This is what I want, right?

I walk the twenty-odd steps up to his front door slowly, dragging my feet, hoping to avoid the evitable. The, *final goodbye*. The, *we're best off as friends*.

Standing in front of his door, it takes every ounce of strength to knock instead of turning, running back to my truck, and hightailing it out of here. God, why is this so damn hard?

Lifting my hand, I make a fist to knock.

"Ugh, what the hell is wrong with you?" I scold myself as I step back, and turn in a pointless circle. "Get on with it."

I take a deep breath, look straight at the door, and face this head-on. Letting out the breath, I knock once, take a step back, and wait for him to open the door.

Get it together, Hope. Get. It. Together.

River opens the door, and he's dressed simply in jeans and a gray shirt, with bare feet. Jesus. Give me strength. Thank God I didn't shave my legs. He is one fine specimen of a man. His tousled dark hair is glistening, so he's likely come out of the shower. I want to shower with him.

What? No! No, I don't.

"Hope." He smiles then steps aside. Gesturing, he waits for me to come inside.

"River," I say in a rough voice. What the hell? Why does my body and brain keep fighting me on this? We're not suited. We don't belong together. He closes the door behind me and my eye goes straight to the picturesque sliding door framing the ocean. "That is perfect," I say as I walk over to it and look out.

"It's one of the reasons I love it here. Can I take your jacket?" I shrug out of my cardigan, giving it to River. He takes it, and places it on a coat stand. "I hope you're hungry, I've made clam chowder." Damn it, I hate how he can cook. Why does he have to be so great? "Wine?"

"No, thank you." I want a clear head. My hands sweat, and I run them down the front of my shirt.

The air between us isn't easy, or even pleasant. I feel like I should rip this band-aid off, once and for all. He must be feeling the tension too. It can't just be me. "Hope, why don't we take a seat outside while the chowder finishes cooking?"

I can't let myself be seduced by something I can't have. *This view, him, us.* I can't have it, because it's never ended well for us in the past; it won't this time either My heart is racing, and I feel myself on the brink of tears. "I can't do this, River," I say, blurting what I'm thinking.

"You can't do what?" he asks. "Sit outside and enjoy the sound of the ocean?"

I turn, looking him straight in the eyes. But I take a step back, because I know how he affects me. He makes me want to do extremely naughty things with him. I point to him. "You. I can't be with you."

"Because you don't feel anything for me?" He steps closer, I step back.

"Because every time we've tried, I've always ended up so broken, I didn't know if I'd be able to breathe again."

"And here you are, breathing," he challenges.

"Don't be an ass." I look away, annoyed. "I can't survive losing you again."

"What if this isn't *another* time, but the *last* time? What if everything's aligned for us *this* time and we're meant to be together?"

"And what if we're not?" I question. My shoulders sink down, and I walk over to the door. Turning my back to River, I try and gather my thoughts into words. "I thought what we had was perfect, but it only ever lead to heartache."

"You weren't the only one who was hurt, Hope."

"I never said I was," I snap at River without turning. "But I can't go through it again." Turning, I face him. "Aren't you tired of us being torn apart every time we think we've finally figured it out?"

"*Figured it out?*" He starts laughing. "All I know is that I've loved you from the moment you knocked that thief on his ass. *Figured it out?* We haven't figured out a God damned thing, Hope. Only that I love you, and I know you love me, even if you're self-sabotaging and refusing to acknowledge it."

My arms break out into goosebumps as my mouth falls open in shock. He loves me? I can't think about that right now, and nor will I be pressured into admitting to something I don't feel. Correction, I don't *think* I feel. Do I? I walk to the other side of the room, and lean against the wall, crossing my arms in front of me. "I'm not self-sabotaging; I never have. I'm happy!"

"Really? That's the only thing you heard, or the only thing you're willing to hear?" He heads straight over and hovers over me. I flatten against the wall. He moves closer, his body only a hair's breadth away from mine. River lowers his head, and leans his forehead on mine. "Our time is now, Hope." He brings his hand up, and gently strokes my cheek, down my neck, and all the way to my hip. I can't push him away. I don't want him to stop.

"River, I'm leaving soon, and I don't want to start something I know has a expiration date. It's not fair to you or to me."

"It doesn't have to end. Ever. You don't have to hold out for something more, because I'm here for you."

I can feel the tears wanting to break through. "And when it ends, then I'm done for, River. I won't be able to recover this time."

"This is what I'm telling you." He kisses my forehead. "I'm never going to *let* this end. Not now, not ever."

"How do you know something else won't come between us?"

He trails his nose down my cheek, and toward my throat. Jesus this feels good. "Have you stopped and asked yourself what you want?" With a feather light touch, he places small kisses against my heating skin. Pushing his body in, my leg automatically hooks around his hip. "Because all I've ever wanted was you." He grabs my leg, and thrusts into me.

I can't think straight. I'm powerless against him. "River, we can't."

"Why? Because you're hell-bent on trying to convince yourself you're happy without me, or because you know that with me we'll be perfect?"

"We're not perfect."

He moves his head so his lips are nearly on mine. I want him to kiss me. I want to kiss him so badly. "Good, I don't want us to be perfect. I want us to be perfect for each other." He brushes his lips against mine, causing an eruption of emotions to cascade through me. My heart is pounding, my breath is audibly loud, and my body is ravenous for him.

I stare into his eyes. "What are we doing?" I ask.

"For you, I'll do anything."

He lowers his mouth, taking my lips with his. Yes, I want this. I need this, I need this with him. I snake my hands around his back, then up into his hair. His lusciously thick hair is soft between my fingers. "River…"

He moves his hands below my butt, and scoops me up, forcing me to wrap both my legs around his hips. He pushes into me, and although we're both fully clothed, I can feel exactly what I'm doing to him. "I've missed you," his voice is rough with lust and desire.

Angling my body, I push into him, as I attack his mouth with a craving I've never felt before. My mouth is flooding with moisture, my body is so hungry for him, I can barely control the thoughts pulsating through me. "I've missed you, too."

My hands are all over his body, desperately trying to rip his shirt over his head. While balancing me against the wall with his hips, he lets me go for a second, as he tears his shirt off and lifts mine over my head.

Our bodies mold together, his heat and my heat mingling. "I want this," he says. "Tell me you want me too."

"I want you," I say, as I pull him toward me so we can keep kissing.

"Hold on," he mumbles against my mouth. I wrap myself tight around him, and he walks us to his bedroom. Placing me to my feet, he drops to his knees, and covers my stomach in light little kisses.

My body shudders, and my eyes roll to the back of my head. Oh my God. What are we doing? He unbuttons my jeans, and slides them down my legs. "Shit!" I yell.

"What's wrong?" He backs away, startled. "What? Are you okay? Did I hurt you? What did I do?" He appears panicked.

"No, nothing like that." I step away, which is quite difficult with my jeans around my ankles, so I bend and pull them up. River's eyes widen, and he sits back on his heels. "I haven't shaved my legs," I say.

"Um..." He tilts his head to the side. "Okay. And?"

"My legs are hairy."

His shoulders slump forward, and he glances around his bedroom like he's searching for answers. "Okay. And?"

"I'm hairy!" I spell out.

He blows his cheeks out, then releases the air. "And again, and?"

"You don't care?"

He shakes his head slowly. "Nope."

Now we've broken apart for a split second, it gives me time to get my thoughts back together. Sitting on the edge of the bed, I lower my head, and massage my forehead and temples. "River, I'm sorry, I don't think I can do this. I came here tonight to tell you we should just be friends. I got carried away, and I'm sorry."

He stands, leaves his bedroom and comes back in, this time with a shirt on and carrying mine. "I don't accept that you don't want it. But I'm going to be patient, and wait."

I take my shirt, and put it on. "We're not going to happen."

"Yeah, we are. Here's the thing; you're not saying no because you don't love me. You're saying no because you think you have to protect your heart. And I'm here, waiting until you decide to get out of your own way. You're your own worst enemy, Hope. But for now, that's fine." He lets out a frustrated, shaky breath.

"Dinner's ready." He walks over, gives me a small kiss on the lips, and walks out of the room.

I'm not my own worst enemy. I'm doing what I have to do to avoid another broken heart. That's not fair. He's wrong.

Pacing in his room, I'm becoming increasingly agitated with him. No, I can't let him get away with what he said. "Hey!" I nearly scream as I march out of the room into the kitchen. He's ladling some of the chowder into white bowls. "Hey!" I say again.

"Yes, love."

"I'm not my own worst enemy. And I'm not in my own way."

"If you say so. Do you want bread?" he asks casually.

I'm fired up, and he's so…relaxed. "No, I don't want bread." Shit, I think I do. "I mean yes," I say, still flustered. I move around the kitchen like I have the jitters.

"Bread it is. I bought this really beautiful bread from a lady who lives down the street. She makes her own. She's a lovely person."

"I'm not my own worst enemy!"

"Sarah."

"What? Who's Sarah?"

"The lady who bakes bread. So, so good. Here, come and have dinner." He places both bowls on the dining table, then returns to the kitchen to get the bread. "Here, try this." He cuts some off, and brings it up to my mouth. "Open."

I lower my gaze to the bread he's offering, and step away from him. "I'm not my own worst enemy."

He shrugs. "Your loss. It's beautiful." He pops it into his mouth, and while chewing makes obscenely delicious noises. Sounds that are throwing me off from what I'm thinking. "Ummm, so good."

My mouth dries, and I swallow hard trying to create moisture. I can't help but watch as River slowly chews. His eyes are closed, and he's obviously enjoying every bite of the bread.

My lady parts are quite excited, and desperately need

attention. Suddenly, I've forgotten what I was so mad at, and am invested in watching River eat. Pulling at the collar of my shirt, I clear my throat. River opens his eyes, and smiles at me. He's staring at me with dark eyes and his head is slightly lowered. He's just as hungry as I am, and not just for food.

Crap. I'm in trouble. Big, *big* trouble.

We stand, staring at each other for what feels like an hour. My entire body reacts to him. My skin flames with desire. I lunge for him, jumping in his arms, and knocking him back. He grabs onto me, and without asking, without thinking, we tear at each other's clothes.

And within nanoseconds, we're naked. I push him over to the sofa, and make him sit. This is going to happen, and I'm not even going to get in my own way and stop it. Kneeling beside him, I swing a leg over so I'm straddling him.

He grabs my hips, and tightens his grip. "You and I are meant to be together," he says.

I line myself up, ready to sink down on him. Looking into his eyes, I lean forward and kiss him, slightly moving down.

Knock…knock.

You have got to be kidding me! "What the fuck," I groan, as I move off him.

"They'll go away, don't worry about it."

Knock.

Knock…knock.

The knocking increases, like there's an urgency to it.

"You have to answer it," I say as I scramble to find my clothes. Lady boner is now gone. *Great — said no horny woman ever.*

"Get your ass over here," he growls through gritted teeth.

Jesus, I'm hot for him one moment, and then cold the next. What am I doing?

I quickly get my clothes on while the knocking becomes more furious. "Hope!"

What? Charlie? I look at River who's decided to get his clothes on, and I open the door. "What the hell, man?"

"We've gotta go."

"I should've put a damn towel on the door knob," River mumbles.

He looks at River, and crinkles his forehead. "Sorry, man," Charlie calls to River. He grabs me by my upper arm, and starts ushering me out.

"What's the damn rush? And how did you find me?"

"The house. There's been a fire."

"What the fuck?" I turn to River, confused, and fretting. "I have to go."

"I'm coming with you," River says.

I slide my shoes on, and run down the front steps just behind Charlie. When we're in Charlie's truck, I see River's right behind us, in his own truck. "What happened?" I ask as Charlie tears down the street.

"May got a call from the fire department, they couldn't get a hold of you, so they called her. She came and found me, and told me there's a fire over at the house." He's driving like a lunatic trying to get to the other side of town. Although, it's technically no more than ten minutes from River's house.

"How did you find me?"

"May told Tabitha, and Tabitha told me."

There are so many questions in that statement, but they'll have to wait. Charlie flies down the road toward Old Roger's house, and we see one fire truck out the front with its lights illuminating the entire street.

The neighbors are outside their houses, watching what's happening.

I'm completely confused. I don't see a fire. *Anywhere.* I could've been getting my freak on with Mr. Sexy.

Charlie pulls up alongside the fire truck and a firefighter walks over to us. "Hope, Charlie."

"What's happening?" I ask. Looking around, I see the sheriff talking to two young boys, maybe fifteen or sixteen years old.

"Those two came out here to set some fireworks alight," the fireman says. I look at his name tag and it reads MORGAN. "They were lighting them at the back of the house, but one of them thought they might get caught, so they moved things inside the house. It hit some debris, and caused it to catch on fire. They panicked, and one of them called it in." I can't help but give him a *'huh'* look.

"Why didn't they run?"

"Who knows?" Morgan shrugs. "Jake's having a talking with them now."

"Okay, thank you."

"There's a bit of damage inside, but considering what you're doing with the place, it's minimal." I got called away from a booty-call for *minimal damage*. Ugh.

"Right. Thank you for all your hard work."

"We didn't do much. But you're welcome." He walks away.

Turning to Charlie, I shake my head. "I know," Charlie says. "I would've run. I wouldn't have called it in."

I'm still shaking my head. Surprised. Confused. But mostly thankful that these two stupid kids weren't hurt, and there wasn't more damage done to the place. Jake sees me, points a finger to the two boys, then walks over to us.

The two boys refuse to make eye contact with me.

"Hope, Charlie," Jake greets. He looks over my shoulder and gives a curt small head nod. I feel an arm wrap around my waist, and I startle. Looking beside me, River stands and smiles at Jake. "River."

I step away from River. This isn't the time or the place.

"What happened?" I know Morgan gave us his story, but I want to hear it from Jake.

"Did Dean fill you in?" Jake looks over to Morgan. Oh, right, his name is Dean. He looks like a Dean. A very *sexy*, Dean.

"Yeah, he did," Charlie says.

"I've called the boys' parents. They should be here soon. It's up to you as to what you want to do." He turns to me. "You're the owner of the house."

"How old are they?" I ask.

"Thomas is fourteen, and Matt is nearly sixteen," Jake answers. "Matt has been in trouble with me before." Jake really is a man of little words.

"Matt's parents went through a messy, and very public divorce," River chimes in to add. "He's a good kid."

"He might be a good kid, but he's heading for big trouble if he keeps going on this path," Jake says. "I know he's been through a lot of crap, but this will only escalate unless someone shuts him down now."

River takes a breath and runs his hand through his hair. He's quite affected by this, and it piques my interest as to why. That kid is not River's problem, but he cares. And that makes me see him differently.

"Matthew!" I hear a car door slam shut, then a woman shriek. Crap, she must be his mom. Turning, I see a woman in scrubs charging up to him. She walks straight up to him, grabs him by the top of the ear, and drags him over to us. Holy shit, I thought only old school parents did stuff like that. I don't know how to react. A part of me wants to laugh, but I know she needs to be serious with her kid. I quickly glance at Jake, who's not even looking in this direction. He's turned his back, which means, he's turning a blind eye. "I'm so sorry," Matt's mom says to me. "He's been skipping school, and getting in trouble. I'm sorry, I know I shouldn't make excuses for him."

"Hope." I hold my hand out to her, hoping to calm her justifiably angry behavior. If he's doing this often, she may have had enough of it.

"Stacey," she says as she offers me her hand to shake. "You're going to be the death of me, Matthew. The absolute death of me!" she snaps at him. She's angry, but I can tell by the tears brimming in her eyes that she still loves him, even though she's having a hard time with him. "Please, let me know the damage and I'll find a way to pay it back."

The kid has yet to say anything.

I look at her, then him. "What have you got to say for yourself?" I ask.

He shrugs. "Answer her!" Stacey clips him on the back of head.

"Sorry," he says with no conviction.

"Jake, I want him arrested," I call loudly.

"What?" he yells. "I said I was sorry."

"You said you were sorry because your mom forced you to say it. You don't mean it, and you don't give a shit that you could've burned my house down, and maybe hurt or even killed people."

"Who cares, it's a heap of shit anyway," he grumbles.

His mom hits him across the back of the head again. I know she's trying, and you can see she cares. "Jake, handcuffs," I say.

"What? I'm sorry. I'm so sorry," the kid begs. "Really, Hope. I'm so sorry, I promise not to do it again." Tears well in his eyes, and his chin quivers as he holds in the sob.

"Are you? Because I don't think you care."

"I do, I promise I do."

"Prove it to me."

"How?" A tear leaks out of his eyes, and he wipes it away.

"Until this house is finished, you're going to come and work for me every weekend. You'll be paid five dollars an hour, but for the first four weekends, you'll work to repay the damage you've done."

"What?" he and his mother both say.

"If I repeat myself, the offer is off the table." This kid needs to know this is an opportunity to turn his life around.

"No, no! I'll do it!" he nearly yells.

"And once the house is finished, you'll come work for me," River says. Turning, I give him a questioning glare. "Excuse us a moment." River pulls me away.

"What are you doing?" I ask.

"This kid's father up and left, creating a new family with a younger woman. He doesn't want anything to do with the kid, and he doesn't give a rat's ass if they end up on the street or not. Stacey's doing the best she can, but she works crazy shifts at the hospital."

"The hospital I went to for this?" I point to my nose. He nods. "That's at least what twenty minutes from here?" He nods again. "And why are you doing this?"

"I'm getting busier. I can take on an apprentice, and if it keeps him out of trouble, then at least I know he won't end up a statistic, and it's helping both him and Stacey out."

My heart flutters. "You'd do that?"

"You're doing it, why can't I?"

"My offer was short term though."

"And mine's long term. I can keep an eye on him, and guide him. If he's working, he'll be too tired to do stupid things like this. He'll change. He just needs some guidance."

"It's not your job to guide him."

River laughs. "You still don't get it, do you?" I lightly shake my head, while half-shrugging. "We all look out for everyone in Hope River."

"I'm quickly learning this." What a beautiful, courageous thing River is doing. This forces me to see him differently.

River reaches down, takes my hand in his, and warmly squeezes. "He's a good kid, love."

Wow, River has taken me by complete surprise. I want to say something, but I'm not sure I know the right words. Dropping his hand, I walk back to the others, and look Matt in the eye. This kid needs to know we're on his side, but we won't tolerate bullshit from him either. "What you did in there will never happen again, understood?" He lowers his gaze, and gives me a small nod. "You're damn lucky I'm not pressing charges."

"Thank you," he says in a tiny voice. Then he looks to River, and shows him a hint of a smile. "I won't let you down," he says looking at River first, then me.

"You better not," I say with a hard, no-nonsense tone.

Stacey looks at me, then River and mouths the words *thank you*. This may be what he needs to make sure he doesn't end up being an adult asshole. God only knows, there's enough of them in the world.

Stacey and Matt walk toward her car, I hear her saying, "Don't think you're getting off that easily, Matthew. You'll be punished at home too."

The kid mumbles something, but whatever it is, between River and me, we may just have saved his life.

Thomas's turn. "Jake," I call. He comes over, and I jerk my head toward Thomas and his parents. "What's the story?"

"They haven't been in Hope River for long. The parents are furious with him. He was supposed to be staying at his friends' house, but snuck out to cause a bit of trouble. What do you want to do with him?"

"He's fourteen?" Jake nods. "I'll talk to the parents. But he's not getting away with it."

Jake leans in and says, "Maybe go a bit easier on this one then you did Matthew."

"I wouldn't want to be on her bad side," Charlie says under his breath.

"Nor would I," Jake agrees.

I walk over to the kid, and his parents. "We're so sorry," the father automatically says, though something's telling me he's not as furious as I thought he'd be. It's more like a token apology.

"He's really sorry too." Thomas's mother pushes him forward so he can apologize. I notice she's significantly younger than her husband.

What is it with kids? They do something wrong, and the parents have to prompt them to apologize. "What have you got to say for yourself?" his mother scolds.

"Joanne!" the father snaps at his wife. He turns to the kid, and looks at him. "Thomas!" He jerks his head toward me, then takes his phone out of his pocket and flicks through it.

You've got to be kidding me, right? He's got no interest in his kid, or this situation. Not to mention the way he talked to his wife. *Ugh.*

"I'm sorry, Hope," Thomas says as he looks over at his dad, who's completely indifferent now.

"I don't accept your apology."

I hear his mom suck in a breath. And his dad lifts his head from looking at his phone. Thomas hasn't lifted his chin. He bursts into tears, and brings his hands up to cover his face. "Am I going to go to jail?" he says between sobs.

"Don't be ridiculous," the father says in a condescending tone.

This father is not getting away with downplaying what his kid did. "The decision is yours. I'm going to give you a chance to right the wrong you did. You can come here every weekend for the next month and wash the trucks, and help around the house, or I can…"

"I'll do it. I'm so sorry." He drops his hands, and lunges at me, wrapping his arms around my waist while he cries into my chest. Right, then. I wasn't expecting that reaction. "I'm so stupid, I promise I'll never be so dumb again."

This kid is totally different to Matt. This has probably scared the shit out of him. And I honestly believe he'll never do anything like this again.

Lifting my right hand, I pat him on the back. Stepping back, he looks at me and gives me a small smile. "Don't screw this up."

"I promise, I won't. I'll be here six in the morning to start on my chores."

Jesus, six? "Seven is fine."

Both his parents stare at me, and I'm sensing by the pissed-off look on his father's face, that I'm in for tongue-lashing from him.

"Go to the car, son," his father instructs while scowling at me.

"Yes, Dad." He hangs his head, and walks toward his parents' car.

Here we go.

I pull my shoulders back, and lift my chin. I notice Charlie does the same thing. He stands a step back on one side, and River emulates his pose on the opposite side.

The father flings a vicious look to his wife. She too lowers her head, and walks to the car.

What the actual fuck?

The father takes a sly look around, seeing where everyone is positioned. "You have no right to make my son work for you."

"And your son had no right to trespass," I say with equal venom in my voice as he has.

"He's not coming here to work for free. What do you think this is?"

"I think it's an opportunity for him to not become an asshole like his father."

His eyes widen, and he steps closer to me with hands quickly balling into fists. Charlie is right beside me within a second, River pulls me back, and stands in front of the man.

"This has got nothing to do with you, River. Back away," the man threatens.

Charlie and River both stand in front of me, protecting me. I push through them both, and come toe-to-toe with this abusive piece of shit. "He's right, step back," I instruct Charlie and River. The tension is high among all of us. Any second, someone is going to end up on their ass, and it isn't going to be me, Charlie, or River. "You want to come at me, come at me. But I'll tell you right now, you'll find yourself knocked out, and it won't be because of them." My heart is pounding so hard inside my chest, and I feel like I'm going to be sick. "I don't back down from bullies. You may be able to intimidate your wife, but your son owes me for the damage he did to my property. He'll be here, or you and I will have problems. I'll have Jake arrest him."

This dick's jaw flinches, and he scowls at me. He quickly glances at Charlie, then River.

"It's agreed, Damian. Thomas will be here helping," Jake says as he appears beside me, creating a uniform front.

Asshole Damian plasters a fake smile on his face, and nods. "Yes, Thomas will be here." Asshole gives Jake another curt nod before shooting me a glare and returning to his car.

He pulls away with a chirp of the tires. I let out a breath, and feel my hands shaking. "Are you okay?" River asks as he gently rubs my back.

I smile, refusing to let River or Charlie see how terrified I am that I came so close to being involved in a confrontation. "Jake," I call.

"Yeah." He watches as the car disappears into the darkness of the night.

"Is he on your radar?" I jerk my chin toward the retreating car.

"He is now," Jake says sounding suspicious and angry.

"I'm amazed that in such a small town, no one has ever said anything about him," I challenge Jake.

"They moved here fairly recently, and have really kept to themselves. But, don't worry, Hope. I've got my eye on him now. And I'll be making sure I talk to his wife when he's not around."

"Thank you." My concern is for the wife and the kid. But it does ease my mind knowing Jake will keep an eye on them. I truly hope he was just angry in the moment, and he doesn't take it out on Thomas or his mother.

"I'll leave you to it," Jake says as he walks back to his sheriff's cruiser, turns the car around and heads back to the station.

River, Charlie, and I are left standing, looking at the house. The neighbors have lost interest, and have gone back inside. Charlie's holding a flashlight toward the house. "Let's have a look at what they did," I say.

"Hang on, I'll grab my flashlight too." River runs back to his truck, and returns with two. He hands me one, and turns his on. The three of us walk into the house, and have a look at what they've done.

"It's minimal." Looking around, I shake my head. "A grand at most."

"Maybe a bit more." Charlie points the light to some of the scorched lumber. "But it's okay, it's not that bad. Man, I don't remember us being little turds like this when we were their age."

"I was," I honestly reply.

"I can't imagine that," River says.

"Yeah, I was always skipping school. Then I was always losing my phone. Oh my God, remember that time we were blowing up everyone's mailboxes?" I ask Charlie.

Charlie looks at me with wide eyes, and an even wider grin. "We blew up our own to make it look like we were victims too." He laughs so hard. "Mom and Dad had no idea it was us."

"How old were we? Like twelve or something?"

"Jesus, Hope. Do you remember we stole that bottle of

bourbon from the store? And we drank the whole thing, and were so sick?"

"No, what? We never did that," I say trying to remember if we actually did in fact steal a bottle and drink it all.

"Yeah." He hits me softly on the arm. "It was just before Christmas one year. We went to get Mom and Dad a present and we stole a bottle of bourbon." Oh shit, the memory is returning.

"Nah." Hell no, I'm not admitting to that.

"Yes! Come on. We stole the bottle. And we saved it for New Year's Eve. Mom and Dad had some friends over, I think. And you and I snuck off to my room, and drank the entire bottle. You threw up all over the floor. I threw up all over my bed." He's laughing as he's recalling the story.

"Did you?" River asks, completely invested.

"No, I was a good kid."

"Like hell you were," Charlie shrieks. "Our parents were furious at us." He's laughing so hard he's nearly doubled over. "She got her ass handed to her by our parents. They were so angry with us."

"Nah!" I try to defend myself. "You got in shit, not me. They were angry you were such a bad influence on me."

Charlie keeps laughing. River's chuckling too. "Until I told them you stole the bottle."

"Traitor." I smack him in the arm.

"Why is it I'm not surprised at all that you were the one who stole the alcohol?" River says.

"Shut up!" I say with a smile.

"Come on, we'll look at this tomorrow. No use in trying to look at it in the dark." Charlie turns and starts walking out of the house. "Oh yeah, don't forget to tell River how when you threw up, you also peed yourself."

Slowly, I turn my head to glare at Charlie, but he's nearly gone now. If I could see what was on the ground, I'd chase him and beat his butt for saying that.

River snakes his arm around me, leans down and whispers, "We've got unfinished business."

My skin tightens, and suddenly my heart lurches, and not in a good way. This has been a wakeup call. Once this house is done, I'll be gone. I can't start something I can't finish.

"Good night, you two," Charlie calls.

"Night," River responds. I'm quiet the entire ride back to River's. I'm trying to think what I'm going to do. I like River, really, I do. But it's not fair to lead him on. It's going to end badly for both of us. He parks his truck when we get back to his place, and turns to me. "You haven't said a word since we left."

"I've been thinking."

He nods, and purses his lips together. "This isn't going to happen, is it?"

Letting out a sigh, I shake my head. "We're never going to work, River."

"You've convinced yourself, haven't you?"

"How can we, when I'll be gone soon?"

He looks forward for a few seconds. "Okay then."

That went much better than I thought it would. The best thing for me to do now, is to leave. Getting in my truck, I drive back to May's.

There's a terrible sinking feeling in the pit of my stomach. I knew it couldn't work between us. It never has in the past, so what makes me think it could now? Something would be waiting, ready to tear us apart.

It always does.

Chapter
TWENTY FIVE

T HE HOUSE HAS started coming together. The days River is there to do the electrical rough-in, I've been making myself scarce. I don't want to see him. That night two weeks ago doesn't need to be repeated. I was so close to having sex with him, but I'm glad I didn't. Because then, I'd be the asshole who'd leave and we'd both end up with a broken heart.

"Hey, wanna go out for dinner tonight?" Elle asks as I'm picking up a coffee for Charlie and myself before I head over to the house.

"Sure. I need a girls' night."

"You've been different, lately. What's going on?"

"Nothing," I reply in a monotone. "Nothing at all." I add in a click of my tongue.

"I'll pick you up? Say about six?"

"Make it seven. There are a few things happening over at the house. But I can't stay out for too long."

"It's a school night, is it?" Elle chuckles. She places the two coffees on the counter. The bell over the door chimes, and I see Elle's eyes widen, before she quickly lowers her head.

Must be Jake.

"Morning, Hope. The house is looking good," Jake says as he stands beside me.

"Yeah, it's coming together. We've got a lot happening today."

"I might stop by and have a look later, if that's okay?"

"Anytime. Anyway, I've gotta run. See you at seven?" I say to Elle.

"I'll be there."

"Where are you two off to at seven?" Jake asks.

"We're going for dinner. No idea where yet, Elle's organizing it."

"Will this be another drunken evening? Should I accompany you to be the designated driver?" Jake asks.

Yes! Finally, these two might get it on. "No, I won't be drinking," Elle says.

I shoot her a what the fuck look, clenching my jaw tight and widening my eyes. What the hell is wrong with her? He wants an invite. And he probably doesn't want me hanging around.

Jake smiles, but it looks like he's hurt more than anything. Here Elle is, lusting after Jake, and he's wanting to be included, and she can't read the obvious signs. "Make sure you both behave yourselves." Jake's police radio goes off, and he turns away to respond to it.

"I swear to God, Elle. I'm gonna smack you one."

"What? Why?"

She can't be so unaware. "He wanted an invite tonight."

"What?" she shrieks. She looks over toward Jake, then shakes her head. "Nah, he only said that because of what happened last time."

"Tell him he can come."

"What?" she shrills again. "Nah."

I grab the coffees, and the paper bag with the muffins, and walk backward toward the door. "Do it!" I say in a low breath.

No, she mouths as we both look over to Jake who's still got his back to us.

Do it! I try to point, but my hands are full.

No!

"Whatever. I'll see you at seven." I grab the handle of the door with my pinkie, and maneuver myself out of there while wrestling with the idea of returning and asking Jake to join us. It's not my place. She has to do it. *They* have to find their own groove without interference from me.

Me of all people.

A person who's always unlucky in love.

Getting in my truck, I place both coffees in the cup holders, and pull into the street toward Old Roger's house.

God, I hope River's not still there. He shouldn't be. He's done everything he needs to until Charlie lets him know we need the next stage of electrical done.

I pull into the street, and there's a swarm of workmen coming and going from the house. Looking at it from the outside, it's really coming together. I mean, it's still nowhere near ready, but considering the way it was it's looking amazing. At least we have outside walls now, and the roof should be finished today.

Closing my eyes, I take a second to just catch my breath. "Today is going to be an awesome day," I say to myself.

Yep, nothing is going to get me down. Not a damn thing.

I take the two coffees, and brown bag with the muffins, and head in to find Charlie. "Charlie!" I call.

"Hang on."

I have no idea where he even is, or where his voice is coming from. I look around, and can't believe the back. It's completely exposed.

Walking toward it, I love what I'm seeing. It makes it so much larger, even though the build-out will make it even bigger. I place Charlie's coffee on a workbench set up where the new kitchen will go.

"Hey, sis." Charlie comes over and grabs his coffee. His tool belt is around his waist, and he's looking all dusty and dirty. "Liking it?" I bring my thumb up to my mouth, and flick the short nail on my tooth. "Oh shit," Charlie says as he exhales loudly.

"What?" I look over at him.

"You've got the look. You're thinking, right? You're going to change something?"

He knows me so well. "Actually…"

"No!" he protests. "Nothing else." He takes a sip of his coffee, then says, "What are you thinking?"

"You have the plans on you?" He pulls a piece of paper out of his back pocket, and when I unfold it, it's a shrunken version of the plans I designed. "See here?" I walk the length of the back that's completely open because we haven't finished with the extension yet.

"Ugh, yeah."

"What if instead of having a sliding door to the back, we open it completely up, and have bi-fold glass doors from here." I walk to the opposite side. "To here?"

"So you want the entire back to be one huge glass sliding door?"

"Not a sliding door, but the bi-fold ones. So then, we can build a deck that takes it out say another ten feet, and it can easily transform the house, giving it more usable space."

"Right, because even with the extension, it's a tiny house," Charlie says in a sarcastic voice, and a deadpan face.

"Think about it, though. Once someone comes in through the front door, this is going to look impressive, and practical. The kitchen stays the same, but we change the island direction. It'll flow nicer, and be spectacular. Because we were going to have the sliding door here." I point where it was supposed to be. "And four windows here." I point to where they were supposed to go too. "This way, it's all open. What do you think?"

Charlie walks around, and looks at what I want. "There's no walk-in pantry on the plans."

"I didn't think we needed it, considering the size of the kitchen."

"You know what we can do?" he says, getting into the spirit of this.

"What?"

"We'll have the glass doors like you want, but instead of them folding out, we have them slide in on each other. I can build it out here, so they can slide back and are out of the way. And, instead of this part of the wall jutting out and looking odd, we can build it in, and create a walk-in pantry."

"I like that," I say. "I'll get the doors priced and ordered once you send me the exact measurements. I'll have a look at the kitchen and see what we can do to make it more functional. But I like that idea a lot."

"I'm not just a pretty face," Charlie says as he flexes his tattooed arm.

"I never said you were." I punch him playfully. "I'll finish my coffee, then put me on the tools, wherever you need."

"Upstairs. We need the man power to finish the build out before we can continue with the roof. It's nearly done, but we need ya."

"I'm on it." I finish my coffee, go out to my truck and grab my tool belt. I love this shit so much. This is what I consider fun.

"Oh, look at you," Elle says as I open the door.

"What, this ole' thing?" I playfully say as I twirl. "I went looking at doors today, and passed a goodwill store. I saw this in the window."

"No, way. You rock a mini dress so nicely. But I like how it's a bit flared at the hips. And I love this color on you, too."

"How's this? Ted Baker, and it still had the tags on it. And guess how much I paid for it?"

"Ted Baker? Those dresses are at least a couple of hundred. And it still had the tag?" I nod. "I don't know, maybe eighty dollars?"

"Twenty dollars."

"All I can say is, you look so damn good in it. I love the cute little heels too."

"You're looking quite cute too. I love the way you have your hair." She's flat ironed it, and it's quite severe, framing her beautiful face. "You know, I love how you have two full sleeves of tattoos, and you wear them so well."

"I love them. At first people were a bit skeptical, but once they got to know me, they didn't even notice the tattoos anymore."

Meow.

"I've got to feed the Cat. Hang on." I grab his kibble, and his bowl. "Here you go." I scoop out the kibble, and place it on the floor for The Cat.

He looks at the kibble, then me. *Meow.*

"I haven't let him come to the house, and he's being an asshole. More so than when I got him back from the vet after he was neutered."

"No man likes his family jewels taken away," Elle says with a laugh.

"Let's go. He's just going to be angry at me for leaving him. I think Charlie will be home soon, so he can pester Charlie."

"What did you end up naming him?" she asks as we walk out to her car.

I chuckle. "The Cat."

"Yeah, what did you call the cat?"

"The Cat."

"Yeah, the cat!" she says with more emphasis. "What did you call the cat?" she asks, slower.

I laugh and try again. "The Cat."

"Yes, the fucking cat. What did you call him?" she nearly shouts as she gets in the car and waits til I'm in before starting and leaving May's.

"I called the cat, The Cat. As in the cat's name is: The. Cat."

She drives out of the driveway, with a screwed-up nose, and an open mouth. "Wait, you called your cat, The Cat?"

"I did."

"The Cat?"

I bring my hand up to cover my smiling mouth, and laugh into my palm. "Yep."

"Poor fucking cat. You may as well had called him Dog."

"But he's a cat, I can't call him Dog. If it's any consolation, sometimes I just call him Cat, and not The Cat."

"Oh yes, we don't want to confuse anyone," she mockingly bites.

I laugh a little more. "So, where are we going for dinner?" I watch as she leaves Hope River and drives toward the town where I bought the counter top for the kitchen. She continues past, and enters another neighboring town. She drives through a very run-down area. "Man, look at some of these houses. Are they in the same county as Hope River?"

"Yeah, but this area is called Faith Haven. It's like the ugly step-sister out here. There's a lot of homelessness out this way. It's almost as if it's been forgotten, except we drive through here to get to some really nice restaurants and a great mall. It's slightly further inland but still only about a fifteen-minute drive from the ocean."

I wonder what the real estate is like here?

What? Nope, get that stupid idea out of your head Hope. Once Old Roger's house is done, I'm back to my normal life.

"Where are you taking us?"

"There's a cool place that opened about two months ago, it's a vegan restaurant."

I grumble loudly. "Vegan? Really? I need meat, Elle. I need the protein. I do a lot of physical work."

"Listen to you whine. All I ask is you give it a chance. If you don't like it, we'll leave. But I promise you, the food is so good. My favorite is the mac and cheese, and the mushroom with some stuff."

"Oh yeah, sounds appetizing. It's got *stuff* in it," I tease.

"Trust me, it's fantastic."

"Fine, I will. But if I don't like it, I'm saying so."

Elle smirks. "How are those kids working out for you at the house? Thomas and Matt?"

"They're both terrified I'm going to send them to jail." I chuckle. "They both needed someone to kick them in the ass, but mostly, someone to believe in them. They're doing really well. Thomas's father…" I shake my head and groan. "I'm not liking him."

"I don't know much about him. I've only ever seen his wife in town a handful of times. They never come to any of the festivals."

"Speaking of Jake." We weren't, but I have to bring him up somehow.

"Nice transition there, Hope. No, nothing happening. It's best nothing does happen."

"Why not? He's hot, you're hot. He's single, you're single, you should both just screw and get that tension over and done with." Elle shoots me a quick glance.

"What? It's not gonna happen."

She presses her lips together, and takes her right hand off the steering wheel to rub the back of her neck, before placing it on the wheel again. Elle's hiding something. Maybe she's not ready to share, but she can't go from hot and heavy for the sheriff to completely uninterested in such a short time frame. "Anyway, you and River…"

"Not gonna happen either."

"Oh, I know. He came by yesterday I think it was, and he had a woman with him."

A what? A woman? "As in a date?" My chest suddenly constricts as my mind races. I shouldn't feel like this, I should be happy for him. How can he move on so quickly? He told me he loved me.

"No idea. But I will say they looked fairly happy, I guess."

"What do you mean? Did they look happy or not?" I ask in rapid fire. Shit, why is this news making me angry? "Wait, stop. Don't tell me. It's not my business."

Elle smacks her lips together making a loud, audible pop. "Wow. Sounds like you're jealous."

"No!" my voice is tight. I take a second to gather my thoughts. River's dating. Great. He deserves to be happy, and I shouldn't stand in the way of that. "I'm sorry. I'm being stupid. Periods…you know? That time of the month makes me hormonal." I'm not really hormonal, but at least I can use it as an excuse.

"Huh, and here I thought you were acting a bit like a jealous ex-girlfriend.'

"We've never officially dated, so I can't be a crazy ex. Anyway, can we forget about River, please?"

"Sure." She finds a spot on the street and parks her car. "Come on." She gets out of the car all happy and shit. I get out, moody and seething. River has a girlfriend. I can't get that out of my mind. How can he move on so fast? Maybe I never meant anything to him to begin with. I can't believe it. "Hey," Elle snaps.

"Sorry, what were you saying?" I ask, as I stop my pity party and pay attention to Elle.

"Unless you're willing to do something about it, stop thinking about him."

"Harsh much?" But she's right. I can't let this consume me. "You know what?"

"What?" Elle leads me to a restaurant that looks way too fancy for it to be vegan. "I'm glad I didn't start anything with him, for this very reason. We'd never work."

Elle smiles, and nods. "You keep telling yourself that."

"Says the chick who doesn't want to try it on with the sheriff," I say with a snappy head wobble and a click of my fingers.

"Look, we're both fucked up. You and me. Let's forget boys even exist, and just have a nice night out, okay?" She holds her hand out so I can shake it. Like we're making a pact.

"Yes." I take her hand and shake it firmly.

"Hi, we have a reservation, under the name of Elle." Elle tells the guy at the counter with a smile.

"Your table's ready. Right this way."

Looking around, this isn't what I thought it was going to be. "I thought this was fancy from the outside, but it's more upscale hipster," I whisper to Elle as the guy shows us to our table.

We sit, and I wait for him to hand us menus. But he doesn't. "Your waiter will be with you shortly." He smiles and happily wanders off back to where he was.

A young girl comes over to our table, and places two glasses and a carafe of cold water on the table. "Hi, I'm Bethany, and I'll be your waitress tonight. Have you dined here before?"

"I have, but my friend here hasn't," Elle says as she points to me.

"Yay. A newbie." The girl claps. She is way too enthusiastic. But, hey, whatever gets her through her workday. "We don't have menus. What we do have are several light boards that rotate slowly with what we offer. We are fully vegan, and we also have nut free, lactose free and gluten free options."

"What, cardboard?"

"No, not cardboard. But it's amazing how many people think that until they try us." The chirpy girl smiles. "People have also said, 'you don't make friends with salad,' and 'what is this, rabbit food?'"

Holy shit! Did I say that out loud? I close my eyes, and can feel my cheeks burning. "I'm sorry. I have no filter," I say as I try to bury my face in my hands. Thank God I didn't say anything worse.

Elle's laughing. "Don't worry, you know what I said the first time I came here?" I shake my head. "I asked, 'is it like chewing on an old sock?'"

"Elle!" I shriek. Lowering my hands, I'm now more mortified at Elle's first reaction than mine. I look up at the girl, and offer her a pleading look. "I'm sorry," I say again.

"That's okay. But our menus are on the light boards; there's one on every wall. If you need anything, I'm here to help." She walks away, leaving us to look at the menu.

"Oh my God, Elle. I can't believe I said that. Why didn't you kick me or something?"

"Honestly, I said worse. And you know what? I try to come at least once every two or three weeks, the food is so good. Usually I get it to go, but I thought it would be nice to eat in today."

I look over at the light boxes, and notice there's not much to choose from. There's a total of eight main courses, and two desserts. "There's not much variety.'

"The menu is changing constantly." She looks at the menu too. "Do you like mushrooms?" I nod. "The pan roasted Portobello mushroom steaks with gravy. I kid you not, nearly the best thing I've ever eaten. I'm getting that."

"Have you tried the wild mushrooms, avocado and red

peppers?" Elle nods, her eyes light up. "I take it that's good too?"

"So good."

"Alright, I'll give it a go. What's the worst that can happen? We'll have to stop by your diner on the way home, right?"

"You won't have to. And let me tell you, I'm getting the pumpkin meringue pie for dessert. It's so good. If you want to get the dark chocolate mousse so we can share, I won't stop you."

"That dark chocolate mousse has my name all over it."

Elle calls the young girl over, and she types our order on a tablet before leaving us again. That girl is super chirpy and happy. I've gotta leave her a substantial tip. "You know what I was thinking about today?"

"What?" I ask.

"You've never really said anything about where you came from. Do you have lots of friends? Do you go out a lot?"

"Nah, not really. I'm more of a workhorse than a socialite. I'm not introverted or anything, but I like my own company. I've had girlfriends but no one really close. And I had Grady for a while, but..." I shrug. "You know. What about you?"

Elle's shoulders tense, and she sucks in a deep breath. "Same," she says, but I know that's a total lie. She doesn't want to tell me about her past. She must be ashamed of it. She looks over my shoulder, and closes her eyes. "I'm sorry, Hope. I had no idea."

"No idea about what?" I turn to see what she's looking at. *Great.* River walks in with his *date.* My mood drastically collapses, and I don't want to be here. I turn quickly before he sees me, but I know it's inevitable.

Of all the places for him to be. A vegan restaurant. With his date. *Ugh.* Shoot me now.

"We can leave," Elle offers as she begins to stand.

"What?" We really should, but no. I'm not going to leave just because River's here with his date. "No, nothing happened with us. It's fine. I want to try this food, so please, sit down and don't worry about it."

Elle slowly sits, but with a remorseful glimmer to her eyes. "We can go."

"Hey, he works for me. I have to see him. We're not fighting or anything, we're just...over." Although, my stomach is in knots, and my hands are trembling in my lap.

Elle sighs, then musters a smile. "Okay."

"Just give me a second. I've got to go to the bathroom," I say as I search for the sign to the bathroom. Standing, I head straight there without looking behind me, and find three doors, all with a unisex sign on them.

Even though none of them are occupied, I still knock before I open the door to one of the bathrooms. Someone pushes in behind me, taking me by complete surprise. "Why aren't you returning my calls, Hope?" River asks as he pushes me up against the wall.

His body hovers over mine, destroying every coherent thought. "We're over."

"We never started." He leans down, kissing me on my mouth. His kiss is filled with fever, need...*want.*

"Stop. You've brought a date." I try to push him away, but his size and strength are impossible to budge. *Thank God.*

"She's my mom's best friend's daughter. I don't want her, I want you." He trails his hand up my bare leg, snaking its way up my thigh, and teases me above my panties. The other hand is groping my boob, squeezing, and dominating me. *Hell yeah, I'm liking this.*

"Jesus, River," I squeal and look around in case anyone can see us. Stupid, because we're locked in a damn bathroom. "What are you trying to do?"

"I'm sick of you pushing me away. Get out of the way of our

happiness, Hope. We need each other." His fingers find their way inside of me, and I suck in a breath as he plays and brings me to the brink of having an orgasm. Right here in a fucking vegan restaurant.

Wait, is it really hot in here? Has someone turned the heat on?

His mouth takes mine, muffling my sighs and moans as I concentrate on increasing this ecstatic explosion quickly rising.

"Oh shit." I grab on to him, and try to grind against his hand. Shit, shit, shit. "I'm nearly there." I keep moving my hips, wanting him to bring me undone. Suddenly, he pulls away and slowly brings his fingers up to his mouth. "What are you doing?" I nearly leap on him to finish what he started.

He sucks on his fingers, and winks. "You want me to finish?" I'm nodding furiously. "Then come to my house tonight." He opens the door, and walks out.

What the actual fuckity fuck, fuck, just happened?

Straightening my dress, I try and not think about the agony in my pussy. I try to fix myself before I leave the restroom. Shit, I think my lady parts will explode if I just look at River as I walk back to the table.

Eyes down, don't look over at him.

I look around the restaurant, and no one seems to notice anything, but my trembling hands and quickened breath is a dead giveaway that I nearly came.

My mouth is completely parched, and I'm surprised to find our dinner sitting on the table waiting for me. "What took you so long?"

"River and I didn't nearly have sex!" I blurt.

Elle stills as she reaches for her fork. She looks up at me, confused. "What?"

I'm shaking my head. "I didn't say anything."

She leans over, her eyes widening, as a huge smile erupts on her pretty face. "Did you two have sex in the bathroom? First…

ewww. But second... hot. But ewww. More hot than ewww, I think."

"No, we didn't. He cornered me in there, and just kinda attacked me. His hands were like everywhere." I make a gesture around my breasts.

"But he's such a quiet guy. What did he do?" She bends in closer. "I want to know everything. Hell, if I'm not having sex, I want to live vicariously through you. Please be a dirty whore so I can hear all the sticky, awesome details."

I'm still shocked by what happened. I've never had sex in a bathroom anywhere before. Including my own. Ugh, how sad. I've never had shower sex. *Hmmm, shower sex.* "We didn't do much. He stopped just as I was about to," I stop talking and look around the restaurant. "Come," I whisper even quieter.

"Filthy bastard. I love it. Tell me more." She knits her hands together like she's praying, and I can't help but laugh.

"He told me if I want him to finish what he started I have to go to his house tonight."

Elle's eyes are so big. She picks her fork up and starts eating. "Eat girl.' She points to my food. "Because that filthy bastard is going to feast on you tonight. Umm, mmm." She snaps her fingers. "God, you're so lucky." She stops eating, and shakes her head. "I need to get me some sex. Or at least, a good vibrator." I cover my mouth to laugh at Elle. But my head is still scrambled. The reality is, I don't think I can just do a booty call. And I'm not entirely sure I can be with him. Elle's smile begins to fade. "Oh no. What is it?"

"Nothing. I'm all good." But I'm not, nowhere near it. But it's something I need to discuss with River.

A talk I'll have with my clothes firmly attached to my body, later tonight.

A conversation for later tonight.

Chapter
TWENTY SIX

D RIVING OUT TO River's house I have a million and one thoughts going through my mind.

The biggest one: I have to stick firm to my decision.

The next biggest one: I cannot remove one article of clothing.

My heart's pounding inside my chest, and my stomach is flipping and flopping like a damned fish out of water. I'm not sure how this is going to be received, but I have to protect myself.

Pulling into his driveway, I take a moment to get my head right. This is it for us. Only professional contact from here on in. I open the door to my truck, and everything is telling me to turn around and go home. I can't do this. But I have to do it. It's the only way we're going to find peace.

"Don't be a jackass," I mumble to myself.

Right. This is it.

Hesitantly I walk up the steps, hyper aware of the native sounds of the ocean crashing against the coast. The spray of the water lightly touches my face, and I look out to the ocean, and smile. It's so pretty here.

Lifting my hand, I ball it into a fist, and falter for a mere second before I knock once.

I'm such a wimp when it comes to River. I always crumble, unable to stay away from him.

He opens the door, and God damn it, he looks so good. His dark hair is lightly disheveled, and his dark eyes are looking at me like I'm his dessert. I swallow, and tear my eyes off his tall frame. Jesus, Lord help me. His jeans are riding low around his hips, and his white t-shirt clings to his upper arms.

Nope, not gonna ride him. Nope, no way.

He will *not* take his jeans off, we will *not* get naked, and I will *not* straddle that magnificent cock of his and go to town like my life depends on it. Nope, not gonna happen.

"I'm glad you came."

"But I didn't, you stopped before I did," I exclaim. Seriously, what the hell is wrong with me? I screw my face up, I should be shocked at my outburst, but I'm not. "Sorry."

"Come in." He steps aside, and waits for me to enter the house.

But, if I do, I know every single article of my clothing will be on his floor within four nanoseconds, and there I'll be, in all my glory, waiting for him to devour me. I step backward, away from him. "I'm not coming in."

"Public exhibition isn't something I'm really into, but hey, I'll give it a go if that's what you want." He smiles, but I don't. I've got too much happening in my head. "Huh." His smile quickly dissipates. "Right."

Where do I start? How do I tell him? "We can't do this."

"And here we go again."

I lean against the railing, and sigh. "We don't work."

"Okay." He crosses his arms in front of his chest, and looks at me, waiting for more.

Chewing on my bottom lip, I try to tell him what's in my head. I have to tell him the truth. "I fell in love with you all those years ago. And every time I'd get close to you, we were torn apart."

"Yep," he confirms with a head nod.

"I've never stopped loving you. But this time it's different."

"Why?"

"Because I know I'm leaving Hope River, and that's a circumstance that'll tear us apart...again. And I'm terrified it'll des..."

He holds his hand up. "Stop right there."

"What?" I crinkle my brows.

"You're terrified. You don't want to start something with me, because you're terrified."

"Well, I *am* leaving," I argue. "You've misinterpreted what I'm trying to say."

"Nope, I haven't. You're terrified that you and I *will* work, so you stay hidden in your own head, justifying throwing obstacles in the way because you can't deal with the hurt again. So, let's put all the bullshit aside, and admit to what's really going on. You're scared."

"Of course, I'm scared. Aren't you?" I yell as I step away from him.

"Nope."

Swinging around, I stare at him and don't see an ounce of doubt. "We get together, then something happens, and we're split apart. I don't know what it is, it could be kismet, or fate, or whatever. But we can't be together. It doesn't make sense."

"Because you're so happy with your life without me in it."

"No, that's not what I'm saying. Absolutely I prefer we were together, but…" I take a breath as I smack my hands together with each word I say, "We. Don't. Work."

"We *didn't* work, and now we *can't* work because you won't let it happen. Because again, you're scared," he's adamant, and won't relent.

Turning away, I walk around the porch to face the ocean. I hear the deck creak, knowing River is right behind me. "Okay, tell me what happens when I'm finished with the house?" I lean against the railing again. Placing my hand on my hip, I'm trying to make the most obvious point I can.

"Tell me what *you* think will happen."

"Your life is here, mine isn't. I'll sell Old Roger's house, and leave. You'll be here, and I'll be five hours away!" I tell him.

"And that right there is why we *won't* work, Hope."

"Finally, you're getting it. Long distance doesn't work."

He smirks as he looks out over the ocean. "It has nothing to do with long distance. It has to do with you."

"What? I don't want to move here." *I don't think I do.*

"But never did you ask me if I was willing to move for you."

Wait, what? He'd move to be with me? "What?"

"You've been so hung up in your own head, stuck with the idea that you won't move here, but never once did you ask me if I'd move to be with you. You've been blocking us all along, Hope." He steps into me, gently cupping my face in his warm palms, and leans down to kiss my forehead. "Ask me." My brows draw in together. "Ask me," he says again with a softer tone.

What if he says no? What if he says yes? I shake my head, unable to ask him to do something so drastic as uprooting his life, and moving. "I can't." I step away from him.

"So you're self-sabotaging again. You don't want us together even when I'm giving it to you on a silver platter."

"What? No, I'm not," I answer. I would never hinder my chances of true happiness.

"It wasn't a question. It was a statement."

"I've never self-sabotaged."

"Really? Let's look at your past. The first time, I couldn't help us moving, so neither you nor I could've stopped that. The second time you lost your phone."

"Yeah, but I told you I used to always lose my phone," I say trying to defend myself.

"Yeah, you did. But again, self-sabotage. You knew it had my number and my address, and you still lost it."

"That could've happened to anyone." I walk away from him, and place my hands on my head, frustrated and emotional. "How could you blame that on me?" I say through a tight jaw.

"Because you'll do everything you can *not* to be fully happy with your life. That way, you can say, '*See things don't work out, but at least I have my business.*'"

Does he honestly think I don't want to be happy? "How can you say that?"

"Because you can have it all, Hope. All you need to do is stand still."

"I don't run away."

"Yeah? What brought you to Hope River?" he rapidly replies.

My shoulders slump, and my chin slowly lowers. Shit. "I…" I swallow the lump in the back of my throat as I desperately try to moisten my dry mouth. "I can't do this, River. Not now." I head back to my car.

"So, because you're terrified, you're running. Again," he calls as I get more space between us.

"No, I'm not running."

"This isn't the way to move forward, Hope. The only way we can make this work is if you stay and we talk."

I turn on my heels, fury running through me. "Yeah, and what happens when you decide to leave? Or you decide to smack me because you're bored of me and you're out screwing someone else and you're trying to blame me for your infidelity? Or you decide I'm no longer enough for you? Then you leave, and I'm left with a massive hole in my heart, and you're out doing whatever with whoever else!"

River's mouth closes before he steps forward and rakes his hand through his hair. "You have to know, you may see yourself like that, but I don't."

"Like what?"

"Like you're not enough. To me, you're everything." He half shrugs. "When you're ready to be with me, Hope, I'll be here. But don't wait too long. I'm a damned good man who'll treat a woman well. Remember, I won't be on the market forever."

"Are you threatening me?" I get up in his face, mad at him for putting this on me.

He takes me in his arms, and kisses me softly on the lips. "Not threatening, just laying it out for you to understand, love. Eventually, I'm going to get really tired of waiting for you to get your shit together. Right now, right here, we can make this work, but you have to want it badly enough that you'll never even *think* about running again. I'm setting you free, and praying you come back to me. But until then, I'm done chasing." He places another kiss on my lips, then walks away from me. "Drive home safe." He leaves me outside, as he goes back into his home and shuts the front door.

What have I done?

Fuck!

It's probably for the best.

Chapter
TWENTY SEVEN

"YOU LOOK LIKE death," Elle says when I walk into her café.

"Thanks," I reply.

"What's happening? Why are you like that?" She makes a circular motion with her hand toward my face.

"Two coffees please, Elle, and a muffin for Charlie."

Her brows lift, and she adds in a slow nod. "Aha, that bad?"

I notice Murray's not in yet, and I carefully check no one else is listening. But no one is. "I haven't spoken with River for a week."

"Jesus. Here I thought he had you chained up in his room and was having his wicked way with you. That's why I hadn't messaged you. What happened? You were supposed to be a dirty whore, remember? I have to live through you."

Elle makes me smile, but really, I'm too caught up in my own head to offer her more than just a small grin. "Anyway, what's happening?"

"Nope." She waggles her finger at me. "What's happening with you two?" I rapidly blink, holding in my stupid tears. I look up at the light, and let out a deep breath. "Oh shit," she says.

"It's okay. It's better this way."

The bell chimes, and I turn my head, wiping at my tears. "Elle, Hope," Jake says.

I clear my throat, and paste on my fake smile. "Hey, Jake, how are you?"

"Jake." Elle curtly nods. "Usual?"

"Please." Jake knows he's come in the middle of something, and looks to me, then Elle, then back to me. "Is this something I should know about?"

"Nope," I answer before Elle gets in. "Nothing at all."

"The house is looking good. How long before you think it will be finished?"

"Soon." I might be short with my answer, but I'm in no mood to talk. Elle slides over my two coffees, and I pick mine up to sip.

"The townsfolk are excited to see it finished," Jake says.

"Yeah, I've had multiple people ask me for a price. But I'm not ready to give them one yet."

Jake nods, then looks at me, and Elle. The tension in Elle's café is fierce, and I know Jake's smart enough to tell that something isn't quite right. "What's happening?" he asks again, this time with more force.

I've got to say something, because I know he's going to be persistent. "Boy trouble," I finally reply.

"With the one who gave you that black eye when you first came to town?"

"No, not him. He's long gone."

"River?" Jake asks as he scrunches his nose.

"Actually, not even him. It doesn't matter, Jake. I'll be gone soon and everything will go back to normal."

Jake nods, picks up his coffee, silently nods, and leaves.

"Wow, aren't you a bright ray of sunshine," Elle snaps.

"Sorry that my life isn't as awesome as yours," I respond with equal irritation.

"Awesome? You think my life is awesome? Well done. You're so self-absorbed that you have no idea what anyone else is going through." She places the brown paper bag on the counter. "Charlie's muffin." She slides it over to me, and turns her back.

"Elle, I'm sorry," I say, trying to fix what I've done.

"Sure thing, Hope. You have a good day," she says. But it's obvious she's upset with me, because her smile doesn't reach her eyes.

Can this day get any worse?

I take the coffees and paper bag out to the truck. Opening the passenger door, I lean in and place the coffee cups in the cup holders, and swing the door out a bit too far. The door makes a loud banging sound, and I roll my eyes. "What fucking now?"

Moving out of the car, I slam the door shut, and notice how it's hit up against a pole, creating a small dent in the metal. "Are you kidding?" Jesus. Can't I catch a break? Angry at myself for not noticing the pole to begin with, I get in and put my seat belt on. Looking in the rearview mirror to check for oncoming cars, I see River in the distance.

I smile, but it quickly fades as I find myself dropping further into my seat. He's talking to someone, a woman. And not his Mom's best friend's daughter. Who's he talking to? Why is he talking to her? Are they dating? Are they screwing?

She places a hand on his upper arm, my eyes widen, and I feel like going over there and slapping her hand off him. What the hell? Who is she? Why has she got her hand on his arm?

Tearing my gaze away, I look forward, but quickly find myself staring at them in the mirror again. I've got to stop torturing myself. I've made my decision; we can never work. This thing we once had is certainly over now.

I sit forward, not giving them another look and pull onto the street to head toward Old Roger's house. At least I know the windows are going in today, and that large sliding door for the back should be delivered either today, or tomorrow morning.

My mind is completely consumed with River and that woman. How can he be with someone already? Why am I so bent out of shape because of it? He should be happy, and that's all I want for him.

POP!

What the hell was that? My truck swerves to the right, and the steering becomes quite rigid and hard. I pull over on the side of the road, and get out to see what I hit.

"You have got to be shitting me!" I yell as I kick the flat. "Really? I've had a shit morning already, and you're now throwing a flat tire in on the equation? Wanna throw any more crap my way?!" I yell up at the sky.

I could call roadside assistance to come and change the tire for me, but by the time they get here, I could just as easily do it myself. I walk to the back of the truck to lift the spare out.

Meow.

"I didn't see you come out this morning. I thought you were still asleep."

Meow.

"You're gonna have to move, because I've got a flat. I need to get to the jack and the spare. Get out of the way, Cat."

Meow.

He looks up at me, lowers his head, and closes his eyes. "Yeah, yeah, whatever. Move." I tap him, and he opens his eyes again. He stands, circles around, lays back down and wraps his tail around him. I slide him to the side, and lift my spare out.

"Do you need a hand there?" an older man asks as he comes out of his house to see what I'm doing.

"No, thank you. I've got a flat, but I can change it."

"If you need anything, I'll leave the front door open." He re-enters his house. Who leaves the front door open for a stranger?

"Thank you!" But I doubt he heard me.

I grab the jack and the lug wrench. I bend with the wrench to loosen the lug nuts on the tire.

Shit, how tight are these? Who the hell fastened them to begin with? A freakishly strong alien?

"Need a hand?"

Great, exactly who I didn't want to see again today. *River*.

"Nah, I'm good." *You better get back to the arm-toucher who was fawning all over you.*

I hear his truck go silent, then his door shuts. "You sure?"

Standing, I swing around angrily. "I don't need you to save me, River. I'm capable of doing it myself."

He holds his hands up and backs away. "I never said you needed saving. All I ever said was that you self-sabotage. Exhibit A." He points to the tire.

"You've gotta be kidding, right? You think I did this on purpose? I didn't."

"Nope. But I'm offering help, and because you're angry at me, you're refusing it. Like I said, self-sabotage." He smirks as he sits on the curb and watches me.

"So now you're just going to sit there and watch? Don't you have work? I know the house still has more electrical to do."

"I was on my way there now, but it can wait. I have it on good authority the boss won't even know I'm not there yet. She's temporarily preoccupied." He leans his elbow on his knee, balls his fist and places it under his resting chin.

"Get over here and help me then."

"Oh, nah, I better not. She's all about doing everything on her own, and I wouldn't want her to think I'm trying to change her or anything."

"Fine!" I half-yell. "I'll do it myself."

He leans back, extending his long legs in front of him. "Nice day today."

"Actually, no it isn't. I've had a shit day so far."

Meow. The Cat jumps out of the back, and goes to curl up with River.

I clear my throat and turn away from Cat, irritated he's getting along with River.

"Why are you having a shit day?" he asks as he tilts his head up toward the sky.

"Because it's shit," I snap. "Okay? It's just shit. And now, I have to change this damned tire." Standing, I kick it, frustrated with how today is unfolding. "UGH!" I yell at the stupid tire.

"Seems like you've got a lot going on," River says.

I swing around and look at him. "Aren't you the bright one?" I snap.

"Why thank you. That's awfully sweet of you to say." He chuckles, then pets my fucking cat.

"He's my cat, not yours." I want to scoop up Cat and shove him back in my truck. But instead, I end up loosening the bolts on the tire, then jack the truck up more. Thank God for hydraulic jacks or I might have needed to call Charlie, and I don't want to distract him from doing his job.

"I never said he was my cat. But seems the little fellow likes me." River's smugness is irritating me. "Oh, I forgot." River stands, disturbing Cat. "Sorry, buddy." Cat follows River to his truck.

Are you fucking kidding me? Cat is mine, not River's! What a traitor. River returns with a coffee cup and a paper bag which I know are from Elle's. He sits again on the curb, where Cat stretches out beside him. River rips the bag open and there's a perfectly grilled cheese sandwich cut in half. Ugh, the least he could do is offer me half. "Do I get some?"

"Nope, get your own." He bites into the grilled cheese, and

pulls it away from his mouth. The cheese stretches, making me hungry and pissed off all at once. Awesome, now I'm hangry.

I finally manage to get the lug nuts off, and then the flat tire. Getting the spare off the truck is challenging because it's heavy, but I still manage that too. Rolling the spare over, I squat in front of the wheel, and try to lift the tire high enough to slide it on the bolts.

"Need a hand?" River asks as he finishes his last mouthful of grilled cheese.

"Can you just lift the tire onto the thingies?"

"Thingies? Is that the technical term, or the Hope term?"

"I'm not a damn mechanic, River. I don't know what they're called." God, he's frustrating.

He lifts the tire onto the thingies, and steps back. "They are called bolts, Hope. There you go. I'll see you at the house."

"Wait, you're leaving?"

River let's out a deep sigh as he places his hands to his waist. He looks around, then turns to me. "Yep."

"Just like that? You're going? I've still got more to do here."

"You'll be fine. See ya."

River walks over to his truck, gets in and pulls away from the curb.

I'm left standing on the side of the road, with black soot from the tire on my hands, and Cat meowing next to me. "Ugh," I grumble.

I get the lug nuts back on, and get to the house as quickly as I can. I've got way too much work pending to be wasting time changing this stupid tire. And seriously, this day is already shit enough as it is. I don't need more to happen.

Taking the two coffees and muffin out of the truck, I walk up toward the house. At least it's looking fantastic. I can't wait to see what's been done inside.

As I walk up the makeshift garden path, my foot catches on something, and I stumble forward, making the coffee fly out of my left hand. "Shit! Why couldn't it be Charlie's coffee? Nope, it had to be mine," I mumble under my breath. I stop for a second, close my eyes, and take a really deep breath. *Please, let the rest of today go better than the morning has so far.*

I walk into the house, and see just how much of a transformation there's been since yesterday. The stairs have been framed up, the plumbing has been roughed in, the electrical is nearly completed, and the drywall has started going up. "Wow," I say, completely impressed with how it's all coming together.

"Problem with the counter," I hear Charlie call the moment he lays eyes on me. He walks over and sees I'm holding only one coffee. "No coffee?"

"I dropped mine outside," each word is filled with anger.

"Aha. So, you don't want to hear about the counter then?"

I thrust the bag and the coffee at him. "Talk to me."

"Drywall's going up, and will likely be completed by the end of the week."

I double look at him. "Are you kidding? The entire house will be drywalled by the end of the week?"

"Don't get too excited, because that's assuming we can be done with a few things upstairs."

"First, talk to me about the counter."

"The stone dealer called and said that when they were moving the stone you picked for the counters, the forklift tipped, the stone slid off and cracked. We can't use it. He asked for you to go down and pick another piece of stone."

"He's punking us, right?" Seriously, I don't need anything else thrown at me today.

"Afraid not. And..." His mouth twists as if he doesn't want to tell me something.

"What?" I shoot at him in a monotone.

"There are three windows that were delivered for upstairs, but they're the wrong measurements, and now we have to wait for the new windows to come."

"How long will that be?"

"They said around three to four weeks."

"Weeks? No. We need to move along faster than that. Show me." I take a deep breath and blow the air out.

Charlie takes a sip of the coffee, and screws his nose up. "It's cold."

"Drink the fucking thing, and don't even start. The morning I've had has been nothing short of shit."

"Then I won't tell you about the HVAC."

I stop short of the steps leading to the second level. I look up, and sigh. "Tell me."

"There's a national shortage of the unit we've ordered because of some manufacturing problem. So, I told them to change the unit and give us something with the same specs that isn't in short supply."

"That's no big deal, fine. Same price?"

"Eight hundred more."

Of course. "It's done, just move forward with it." Walking up to the second level, we go into one of the three bedrooms, where River's working. *Fantastic.* River looks up from where he's laying cable, and smiles. *Make this quick,* because I have to get out of here as quickly as I can. "What's the problem?"

Charlie points to the obviously large window leaning against the timber frame of the house. The window opening is too small for the replacement window. "That's the problem."

"That's a good three inches too wide."

"Four and a half," Charlie corrects.

"And we've already framed in. The exterior is done on this side of the house too."

"Yep."

"What's it going to cost to recut and reframe the window opening to fit these windows?"

"We have to get the engineer back out to make sure the bigger windows will work up here."

"And the cost?"

Charlie shrugs. "Maybe about a thousand."

"Is that with the discount for sending us the wrong windows? Which three windows are the wrong size?"

"Bedrooms one and two" He points toward them. "There's two in bedroom one, and one in bedroom two."

I stand back in the room, trying to picture how this is going to work. The dynamics of this bedroom won't change, but room two will have two differently sized windows. I walk out of this room, and go to bedroom two. Shit, it's going to look odd with two different size windows in here. "Can you call them and see if they can make one more this size?" I point to the larger one. "Then we can set both these rooms up with the bigger windows, and the other two rooms with the smaller windows. If they've got a bigger one, get them to deliver it. Then call the engineer and see what we can do with them."

"Sure. I'm hoping they have an extra one." He places his coffee cup on the ground, and takes his phone out of his pocket. I leave him so I can go see what's happening with the bathrooms on this level.

I don't want to see River, so I check he's not in the room before I go into the bathroom. Which is where River is. "Sorry," I say as I back away from him. He swings around to look at me, and I notice he's talking to someone on his phone.

"Yeah, okay. At six? Sure." There's pauses at the end of every one of his breaths. "Okay." He places his phone back in his pocket, and smiles. "Do you need me out of here?" River's so cold toward me, barely even making eye contact.

"I've come to check on what needs to be done."

He gives me a short nod, then continues roughing in the bathroom. The air is stifling, and I need to get out of here. Lowering my head, I blink back the tears and head into one of the other rooms. A room where River *isn't*.

Taking a moment, I compose myself while looking out at the barren yard.

"Okay, so I called the window place, they have another window the exact same size they're sending over to us. I called the engineer too. He'll be in this afternoon. Crisis averted. Well done, sis." Charlie pats me on the back. I don't say anything to him, I stand looking out to the backyard. "What are we looking at?" he asks as he stands beside me and mirrors my posture. Arms crossed in front of my chest, while gazing out where the window will be going.

"I'm just thinking."

"Is it gonna cost you money?"

No. I'm thinking about my life. "Maybe. Is it a stupid idea to put in a pool?" I blurt the first, and stupidest thing to come to mind so I don't have to tell him how I'm feeling sorry for myself.

Out of the corner of my eye, I see Charlie's double take. "First, why would you bother? The ocean is less than ten minutes by car. Maybe even five minutes. Second, do you have extra money you haven't told me about? Because if you do, you can throw some my way. I need a new truck."

Rolling my eyes, I tilt my head. "Your truck's fine. It's not even a year old."

He half shrugs. "I want a new one."

"You can have mine when I upgrade."

"Yours is two years older than mine!"

"Thank you for reminding me I need a new truck." Turning, I walk out of the room. I hear Charlie cursing that I'll be getting a new truck before he does.

"Wait, that's not fair!" he calls from behind me.

I look over my shoulder, and smirk. "Perks of being the boss. Unless of course you want the financial responsibility of doing all of this." I sweep my hand around.

"I can barely look after myself without your help. There's no way I'd be able to do this too."

"So, what you're saying is: I love my one-year-old truck and I'm grateful you're an awesome sister?"

"Whatever. Get out, I have work to do."

Charlie does cheer me up. Chuckling, I stop at the door and turn. "I'm going to go pick tile for the bathrooms and stop at the stone place. Also, I'm going to go find something to replace the front door that's here."

"What's wrong with the one we have?"

"Now that I see the space coming together, it doesn't suit the house."

"Whatever. You have the measurements, right?" I shoot him an *are you serious?* glare. "Good. Get out of here before I have you forcibly removed."

"Forcibly removed?"

He points out the door and I can't help but smile again. He's managed to slightly lift my spirits, which I needed today.

Chapter
TWENTY EIGHT

River

I HOLD MY beer bottle up, and wait for Jake to clink his against mine. "What are we celebrating?" he asks.

"Pain in the ass women."

"Shit, yeah, I'll drink to that." He clanks his beer bottle against mine, then takes a long swig. "What is it with them?"

I shake my head, and shrug. "They're irritating."

"Yep."

"They get under your skin," I say as I take another long drink.

"Yep," Jake responds.

"Then they're unsure of what they want so they give us the cold shoulder."

"Are you sure you're not describing Elle?" Jake chuckles, then takes another drink.

We both look up to the giant TV behind the bar, and watch the game that's on. Neither he nor I are really paying attention. "What are you going to do about Elle?" I look over to him, and catch him shaking his head.

"There's gotta be a reason she's so..." He shrugs as he furrows his brows. "It's like she's got all these walls up and refuses to let them down."

"Have you asked her?"

Jake turns his head, and lowers his chin at me. "Really? Elle's been in Hope River for what? Five years? And she's not close to anyone. I think Hope's her first friend. She knows everyone, but hasn't really formed any close friendships with anyone."

"Maybe she's a really private person who doesn't want to open up."

"Or, she doesn't want relationships so she can up and leave if she needs to."

Lifting my beer, I stop before it gets to my lips. I notice Jake does the same thing, like he's had an AHA moment. "You think she's hiding something?" I ask, totally intrigued.

Jake sighs. "Nah, I doubt it. Elle's just...I don't know, Elle. Truthfully, I'm not sure I'm ready for anything, not after..." He pauses and slightly shakes his head. "Anyway, talk to me about Hope."

After what?

I let out a low groan. "That woman is gonna be the death of me."

"Why? What's happening?"

"She needs time to figure out that she wants me."

Jake laughs. "Cocky much? What if she doesn't want you?"

"She wants me as much as I want her. But she's standing in the way of us being together. She's hell bent on leaving Hope River once she's done with the house. And not once has she asked me what *I* want, she's too caught up in what she *thinks* she wants."

"Or what she thinks she needs. But it's not a bad thing, at least she knows what she wants."

"Here's the thing, Jake, she doesn't. She says one thing, and the moment we're together, everything she says is gone and she wants to make us work. But she's not giving us a chance."

"You two have history, right?" Jake asks as he scoops up some nuts and shoves them all in his mouth.

"Yeah, we do. She's adamant on leaving here though, and going back to her old life."

"Don't be too hard on her, River. She walked out on a scumbag who hit her." He claps his hand to my back.

I know what's happened with Hope and the ex-asshole, but I'm sure she'd want me to let on about it. "What?" I ask, slamming my beer on the bar and turning to look at Jake. "He hit her?" Jake nods. "What do you mean? Who is he? Where can I find him?" Standing, I'm ready to go find this prick, and take care of him. He's made me angry, all over again.

"Calm down, Casanova. I don't know who he is, but I can tell you he's not from around here."

"It's her ex-boyfriend? Jake, if he shows his face around here…"

"You're not going to do anything. If he shows up, I'll take care of it. Now, sit your ass down and finish your beer." He pointedly looks to the bar stool. Sitting down, I straighten my shoulders and cautiously look around. "You've gotta calm down."

"She makes me crazy is what she does."

"I hear you, brother. Look, how long until the house is done?"

"Maybe another three or four weeks."

"Then you have three or four weeks to decide what you want, and go after it."

Scratching at the back of my neck, I feel my jaw tighten with frustration. "I know what I want. I want her. She has to figure out that she wants me too, but she keeps fighting it, and backing away more and more."

Jake chuckles, as he stands and places his hands in his pockets. "Come on, let's play a game of pool, so I can kick your butt and win back that money you stole from me last time we played."

"Stole? I won it, fair and square."

"You took advantage of me."

I make my hands into fists, and bring them up to my eyes. "Boo-hoo, little Jakey had his ass handed to him, and now he thinks he can beat me," I say in a condescending child-like tone.

"You're a dick," Jake spits, trying to goad me into a cheeky exchange. He smacks my back jokingly. "Let's up the ante."

I don't like this. "Yeah, how?"

"If I win, you have to take Hope out on a date."

"I'm done with her, Jake. She's screwed up and doesn't know what she wants. Until she makes her mind up that she wants me, I can't put myself through her hot and cold routine anymore."

Jake looks around as he puffs his chest out. "Fifty bucks then?"

I hold my hand out to him and he shakes it. I've gotta get Hope off my mind, and this is a good place to start. "Rack up." I grab a pool cue and roll it on the table making sure it's straight. Why the hell do I have to be in love with someone who's emotionally fucking challenged? I wish she'd get out of her own way so we can start our lives together.

"You know, you could always start a fire to keep her here longer," Jake says as he leans over the table, and breaks.

"First, I think the sheriff would arrest me, and second." I hold up two fingers. "Matthew and Thomas."

Jake laughs as he stands back and waits for me to take my turn. "How are those two working out?"

"They're good kids. Matthew's decent, and Thomas is too. But I don't like his father."

"I've been keeping an eye on him. The way he spoke to his wife that night, sends up red flags to me. I know scumbags when I see them."

"Why don't you step in then?" I lean over the table, and take my turn. The ball rolls toward the side pocket, and narrowly misses, rolling away.

"It's not the way the law works, River. I can't barge in there, tearing a family apart. Don't worry. I'm keeping an eye on them. But if you see something, you need to let me know."

"Only that the father is a jerk."

Jake takes his shot, sinking two balls in one go. "If I was to arrest everyone for being assholes, I'm sure you would've been on the list a few times." I stick my middle finger up at him, and he laughs. "How mature," he teases.

"I know the kid is working over at the house, so I'll keep an eye on him too."

"Thanks." Jake doesn't take his eyes off the table. He takes another shot, and sinks that ball too. He's going to kick my butt, damn it. "Got cash on you, or do I have to escort you to an ATM?"

I shrug one shoulder, take the last swig from my beer bottle and look over to the bar. "Don't know what you're talking about," I say, pretending we didn't make that fifty-dollar bet.

Jake straightens from the table, and walks over to me. "I can arrest you," he says with a smirk.

"For what?"

"Who cares. I'll find something."

Asshole. "I've got your money," I grumble as I take my wallet out of my back pocket.

"Good." He leans over the table, and cleans up.

"You know, now I know why you don't have any friends." I smack the fifty-dollar bill on the table. "No one actually likes you. Hell, I'm only here because you have a gun and a badge. Other than that, I don't think much of ya."

Jake picks the fifty up, tips his head and shoves it into his pocket. "I'm only here for your money."

"Again?"

"You want to lose another fifty? Sure thing. Fine by me."

"I'll make ya a deal."

"Aha." Jake looks at me from the other side of the table as he racks the balls up.

"If I win, you have to give me back my fifty dollars."

"And?"

"And what?" I question.

"That's if you win, what if I win...*again?*"

I scratch my chin, pretending to think. "You give me back my fifty-dollars."

"So? What you're saying is I give you back your fifty-dollars either way?"

"Great deal." I hold my hand out to him to shake on it.

Jake does the whole 'sheriff' face with me, which incidentally doesn't work. So I thrust my hand out further for him to shake. He takes the fifty out of his pocket, goes to hand it to me, then shoves it back. "Nope. But let's play again."

Damn it.

"Hi."

I'm momentarily confused as to where that *hi* came from. Turning, there's a cute blonde a good head shorter than me, sipping her cocktail through a straw. "Hi," I respond.

"I'm Lucy." She holds her hand out to me.

"River." I shake her hand, and go back to our game.

"Hi, I'm Lucy," she says to Jake, and holds her hand out to him. What is it with this chick?

"Jake," he replies in a curt, no-nonsense voice.

"My friend Michelle and I are passing through, and thought we'd stop for a drink and something to eat."

Wait, is she trying to pick me or Jake up?

Go away. "That's great." I look behind her, and don't see anyone else.

"She's in the bathroom." *Not interested.* "So..." She looks around awkwardly. This isn't going the way she wants it to.

"Where are you from?" I ask, instantly regretting the small talk.

"We're making our way over to LA." She smiles. She's cute and all, but not my type at all. I notice she didn't answer my question.

"You're a long way away from LA." I take my shot, and notice Jake's chuckling. *Save me, man.*

"Yeah, we don't really have anywhere to stay tonight," the chick says. Shit, what's her name again?

"There's a motel about fifteen minutes that way." Jake points to the north. "It's safe, clean, and reasonably priced."

I turn away so she doesn't notice me smiling. Jake has essentially shut her down.

"Oh, right. Well, thank you," she says as she backs away from us and walks back to wherever she came from.

Jake and I continue playing pool, when I look over my shoulder to see where the girl is. She's disappeared, nowhere to be seen. "You know she was hitting on me?" I say to Jake.

"And?"

"Just saying, she was hitting on me, and not you. Makes me better looking."

"I've still got your money, so makes me richer. Anyway, I probably did you a favor."

"Don't get me wrong, you definitely did. But I just want to rub it in... I'm much better looking."

"Whatever, Romeo. Play." He jerks his chin toward the pool table.

Chapter
TWENTY NINE

"WOW," I SAY as I stand at the entrance, taking in how amazing this house is looking.

"Tell me about it," Charlie says as he comes to stand beside me. "The drywall is all up. Today I'm installing all the wainscoting downstairs. The floors upstairs should be going in today, and once I've finished with the wainscoting, the floors will go in downstairs."

"It's a shame we had to rip those hardwood floors up, but there was no way we could've saved them with all these drastic changes."

"This place is going to look amazing once you've finished with it, Hope." Charlie folds his arms in front of his chest, looking as proud as I feel.

"You know what I'm absolutely loving?" I say as I walk toward the back. I push open the glass folding door. "These doors are nothing short of amazing."

"Maybe we can use them on some other houses when we get back home."

I turn to look at him. "Wait, you don't want to stay? A few weeks ago, you were ready to move here. What happened?"

Charlie looks down, then runs his hand through his hair and rubs the back of his neck. "Let's just say, *nothing.*"

"Did you hook up with someone?" I grab onto his arm, needing to know what's happening. "Who? What's going on?"

"Nothing." He walks back into where the kitchen is supposed to be. "What do you think if we frame this in so there's the butler's pantry here, and under the stairs we can frame it for extra storage?" He's gone back to being cold Charlie.

"What happened?" I persist.

Charlie shakes his head. "She, um," his voice cracks. Jesus, I've never seen Charlie like this before. He takes a moment to gather himself. Clearing his throat, he points to the space under the stairs. "What do you want to do here? I think it'll be a complete waste of an opportunity for extra storage if we don't do something. Frame it in, or shelves? What do you think?"

He doesn't want to talk about it. I have to respect him enough to leave it alone. "So the counter will be here, right?" I switch back to boss mode, and not sister mode.

"Yeah. It'll be from here, to here." He walks the length of the counter.

"Shit, that's massive. Okay, and the butler's pantry is going in here?" I point to where the frame is starting to come together. Charlie nods. "Range here, with a slide up induction hood. Huge barnyard sink here?" Charlie nods again. I stand back to think how this could all work. "And counter all along the back wall, right?"

"Right," Charlie confirms.

In my head, there's a clear picture of how this can work. If I move the butler's pantry and enclose the space, it'll look too boxy, and closed in. That's not going to sell as an open concept kitchen. If I bring the wall up on the butler's pantry, and stop it short of where the island counter is, it'll make getting around the island difficult.

"Yeah, whatever we do, it's going to close the kitchen off, and give it a pokey little room feel," Charlie says. "I've been trying to think of all scenarios to make it work without closing it off."

I gasp. Light bulb moment. "Why don't we leave the island as it is, and instead of creating the butler's pantry to go that way, we flip it and make it go this way? That will mean it's still open here, and we have a wall going here, but it looks like a continuous wall?" I turn to Charlie to get his feedback.

"We'll need to change the plumbing in the butler's pantry, but it'll definitely work."

"How much to change the plumbing?"

Charlie tilts his head down, and looks up at me with high brows and wide eyes. "A few hundred for the timber at most."

"Then let's get it done."

"Great, we should be able to start painting by mid to late next week."

"And the bathrooms upstairs? Have they been drywalled? Ready to go?" I ask.

"Not yet. I didn't order enough water-resistant drywall. Three of the bathrooms are done, and the fourth is nearly finished. It'll be done today when the rest of the drywall is delivered. All the bedrooms upstairs and downstairs have all been sound-proofed like what we talked about last week."

Looking around, I know there's more work to be done. If I stay and do things around here, maybe River will show because there's more electrical work that needs to be done. I want to impair something so Charlie has to call him, forcing River to come out. Ugh. I hate feeling like this. I should tell him how I feel.

But he said he was done with me. Maybe he means he's done with me for good. Jesus, have I screwed this up?

"What's wrong?" Charlie asks.

"Huh?" I look at him, then quickly turn away.

"You haven't been the same for the last few weeks. You're distracted, and you're irritable, and frankly, I'm not liking being around you." He leans against the wall, and crosses his arms in front of his chest. Charlie isn't going anywhere until I talk to him. One of the contractors walks in and stops at the door, staring between Charlie and myself. His eyes widen and I see him suck in a breath. "Give us a moment please," Charlie asks the contractor.

"Sure thing." The contractor takes a few steps backward and leaves.

"What is it? Is the house too much for you?" Lifting my chin, I narrow my eyes at him. "River?" My shoulders instantly slump. "You dancing around how you feel?" I let out a sigh and roll my eyes. "You can't live a life of not being happy."

"I am happy!" I snap way too harshly.

"Huh." Charlie's voice is thick with sarcasm. "Then why have you been so out-of-sorts lately? Actually, you haven't been all that awesome."

I shoot him a sideways glance. "Awesome? You think I'm awesome?"

"I think you're the best chick I know. But you've been walking around like your head is up your ass recently."

"Oh, nice, Charlie."

"If I don't tell you that you're being an asshole, who will? Maybe other people are too polite to tell you how you make them feel."

What the hell? "Now you're saying I make other people feel like shit? Thanks a lot." What a way to make me feel worse than I already do. I turn to walk out of the room.

"Hey. Stop being a raging cow."

My brows fly up, and I swing around to have it out with Charlie. "Oh, so you can't even call me a bitch."

"Because that's not a word I use. Anyway, you're the one who's being all high and mighty." He flips his hand up through the air. "Why can't you just get it together?"

"Says the guy whose longest relationship has been with his hand," I angrily spit.

"As opposed to the woman who every time she gets close to what she wants, she finds a way to screw it up."

"Have you and River both been talking? Because he said the same thing. You think I sabotage myself?"

"No, we haven't talked, because believe it or not, you're my sister and I have your fucking back. But I think you're hell bent on avoiding being happy. Why are you so damn scared to go for what you want? You're the ballsiest chick I know, but you're adamant about *not* giving this a real go with River."

"You have no idea what you're talking about!" I come up to him, and square off with him. He's pushed me and I'm ready for a damn fight.

"Really? Isn't it funny how you jumped into a relationship with Grady, but you never had a smile in your eyes for him the way you do for River. When you're around River, you're so much lighter, freer. I think you went to Grady because you knew you could never love him. It was a safe play."

I'm not even sure what comes over me, but I smack Charlie across the face. For a few seconds, with a wide mouth, and big eyes, I'm staring at Charlie. He tilts his head, Charlie is as shocked as I am by the slap. He immediately steps forward, and wraps his arms around me. "I'm so sorry," I say as I cover my face and cry. "I'm sorry."

"You've gotta get it together, Hope."

"I'm trying," I say between sobs.

"I love you, and I have a lot of respect for you. You've always been so damn strong. But it's okay to let your guard down, and tell River how you feel about him. It's okay to love so hard and so deeply that you don't ever want to come up for air," his voice is soft, and brittle.

Have I been so caught up in myself that I haven't even seen the pain Charlie's going through? Stepping back, I wipe my eyes, then give him a kiss on the cheek. My own self-absorption has prevented me from seeing how much Charlie is hurting. The silence in the room is deafening, it's killing me to know he's in pain, and I can't help him. I can't help him until I help myself. "Whoever broke your heart, Charlie, I hope they know the great guy they've walked away from."

He blinks rapidly a few times, before clearing his throat. He clicks his tongue to the roof of his mouth as he turns away. "It doesn't matter. I'm not cut out for any long-term commitments anyway." That very sentence breaks my heart. Because although Charlie has said the words, I can tell by the sheer pain echoing through them, that he's fallen deeply for someone who doesn't want him. I have my suspicions about who that is.

With his back to me, I head over, and hug him. Hard.

I need to fix this.

Hell, I need to fix me.

May's outside tending to her vegetable garden when I drive up the long, dusty driveway. She sees me, and waves when I get out of the truck. "You finished for the day already?" she calls.

I head over to her, and shoo a chicken away as it pecks around my feet. "I'm going to take a shower, and feed The Cat, and sit outside to listen to some music."

"Oh boy. It's like that, is it?" she asks as she takes in my appearance. "You look like someone's kicked your cat. I don't think music is going to cut it. And nor is a shower. Get your stuff, and go in and use my bathtub. I've got a bottle of whiskey that's open, and there's dinner in the oven."

She's so beautiful. "I don't want to impose on your and Tabitha's time."

"Stop your fussing, girly. Tabitha isn't here tonight. She's gone somewhere. I don't know where." She shrugs. "Now, get." She flicks her hand at me. "You know where the bathroom is. Go."

"Thank you, May."

"Aha." She keeps tending to her vegetables, and the chickens keep pecking around where she is.

Walking back to the stable, I grab a set of clothes.

Meow.

"Yes, I know, you're hungry. You decided to sleep all day, have you?" I pet Cat under the chin, as he lifts his head from my bed to watch me get my clothes ready for my bath. Cat jumps up, and circles around my legs while I prepare his dinner. I place his bowl on the floor and he sits down in front of it, and with delicate manners, he nibbles away at his food. I clean the litter box out before picking up my clothes and heading back over to May's.

"May?" I call when I get to her front door. I don't hear anything from inside, so I walk along the porch to see she's still outside in her vegetable garden. "May?"

She lifts her head, and waves. "Go in."

"Thank you." Heading inside, I walk into her beautiful bathroom, and run the water in her luxurious claw-foot tub. Stripping my clothes off, I climb in, and rest my head on the back as the water slowly fills the tub. Closing my eyes, I relax and enjoy the warmth of the water and the complete quiet.

Charlie's words are stuck in my mind. Did I start a relationship with Grady knowing I could never fully love him? Have I been waiting for River all my life? I can't get what Charlie said out of my mind. Am I not going to be fully committed to any future relationships because they're not River? Does that mean, the only man I'll ever truly love is River?

"Man," I say to myself as I open my eyes and look at my toes sticking out of the top of the water. Dunking my head under, I come up and look around the bathroom. "I'm fucked," I admit. "Truly screwed."

I don't know what to do.

Laying back, I try and clear my mind of everything, and just relax in the warm water.

Placing my arms on the edges of the tub, I tilt my head back, looking at the ceiling. Shit, is that mold up in the corner? I'll get Charlie to look at it. How have I not noticed it before? Maybe there's a bigger problem than the mold up on the ceiling.

The more I look at the mold, the more I want to get out and call Charlie to come have a look at what's happening here. I can't leave May with a bathroom that may require some renovation.

I keep staring at it as the water turns tepid, then cools to a point where I can't stay in here any longer. Getting out, I pull the plug draining the water before drying off and getting changed. I walk out of the bathroom with the towel around my head. "May?" I call.

"Yeah."

I follow her voice, and find her sitting on the porch. In her hand is a large glass of whiskey, and beside her on the small table, is a bottle, and another tumbler. She juts her head toward it. "Pour yourself one, girly."

"Do you know there's mold in the bathroom?"

"There is?" She places her tumbler on the table, and stands. Following her into the bathroom, I point it out. "Look at that. I've never noticed it before."

"I'll get Charlie to come have a look. There may be spores inside the wall. We'll take care of it."

"Just let me know what the cost is." She walks back out, sits, and picks her tumbler up. I won't charge her. May's shown Charlie and me nothing but kindness. I pour myself a drink, and hold it in my hand for a few moments, staring at the chickens running past the porch. "So," May says as she takes a sip of her drink.

"So," I repeat.

"What's happening?"

I take a deep breath before bringing the glass to my lips, and taking a small sip. "Nothing."

"Ha." She blows a raspberry. "Now there's some bullshit I've heard before."

"You don't sugar-coat anything, do you, May?"

"Ah." She flicks her free hand at me. "No time for sugar-coating at my age. Gotta tell people what I think before my time is up."

I chuckle. "I wish I was like you."

"You can be. Don't be a jerk."

I nearly spit my drink out when she calls me a jerk. "You can't say things like that when I have a mouth full of alcohol."

"Why not? It's the truth, right? You're feeling down because you're being a jerk toward someone. Is it River?" Jesus, does everyone know? "It's River, right?"

No use in hiding anything from May. She's old, perceptive, and isn't afraid to call me a jerk. "It's River," I confirm in defeat.

"Look, I can't tell you what to do or what to say. That's all completely up to you, Hope. But I can tell you this; don't live a life of regret."

"Regret? Why would I regret this?"

"Because you and that boy are meant to be together. Don't let these moments become fleeting memories that keep you up at night, and have you wondering, *what if*. Because, trust me, you'll live a life, and it'll be successful and maybe even happy, but you'll always regret the decision you made to walk away from someone who could've made your life so much richer than what it already is."

I look at her aged hands, and really see the wrinkles on her slim fingers. She's talking about the love she had for the man whose tin River and I found. "You loved him very much," I say as I look into her sad eyes.

"I still love him," she corrects. "And one day, we'll be together again. I hate how we parted, and I'll regret that until my very last breath. Don't be a fool, Hope. Don't let him go because you're frightened."

"I'm afraid it might be too late. He told me he's done with me."

May rolls her eyes, and tsks. "That boy looks at you like I look at fried chicken," she pauses and licks her lips. "Umm, hmmm. Fried chicken is so good." She cheekily smirks. "He adores you, probably as much if not more than you adore him. He probably said he's done with you because he's sick of you being a damn idiot."

May has managed to not only insult me, but make me laugh in the same breath. "What do you think I should do?"

"I think you need to show that boy that you want him more than you want fried chicken."

"That's hard to do, May."

"Why?" She shrugs. "Why is it hard to do? Are you from two different planets?" I shake my head. "Do you both speak the same language?" I nod. "Then the only thing stopping you, is you."

"But he's told me he doesn't want me."

"Pffft." She flicks her hand again. "He'll never look at anyone else the way he looks at you. You're his fried chicken, and he's yours, too."

Nursing my tumbler, I choose to remain quiet, thinking about my fried chicken.

"Ask yourself this, Hope. How would you feel if you saw River with a wife and children playing down by the ocean?"

I don't even want to try and picture that image. My heart is already breaking as I look out toward my truck. All I can see is River, a faceless woman and two children, building sand castles, and playing in the water. River draping his arms around the woman, and effortlessly picking her up and tossing her in the water as the two kids giggle and cheer him on. My eyes well with tears as I watch him in a future I was too afraid to grasp.

"And that right there is the reason you have to stop blocking all the good that can come to you, and embrace it with two hands. That boy is a good boy, and he needs a good girl by his side. Don't live your life regretting this choice. Live your life embracing him."

Turning my head away from May, I wipe at my eyes. "I've been an idiot."

"Yep," May agrees.

"Such an idiot."

"Huge idiot," she encourages.

"I can't lose him, May."

"No use telling this old lady." She points to herself. "Better figure this out before you end up like me." I swing my head around and narrow my eyes at her. "Not that there's anything wrong with me. Obviously, I'm a really cool ol' lady. But if I could, I would've told him how much I loved him before I lost him forever."

I place my tumbler down, and reach for her hand. "Will you tell me your love story?"

May smiles, and looks out over her land. "Some day."

Chapter
THIRTY

'VE TRIED CALLING River several times, but he's not responding. He's upset. I get it. I've been a *jerk* as May blatantly told me.

The house will be ready soon, and before I leave, I want to tell him how I feel.

It's only fair he's been ignoring me after all the hell I've put him through, I guess.

Parking the truck, I get out and walk into Elle's. Our relationship has been strained since I was an ass to her, too.

The little bell dings over the door, and when Elle looks up her smile quickly fades. "Usual, Hope?" she calls before I'm even near the counter.

"I've been an asshole," I announce loudly.

Murray turns his head to look at me from over his shoulder.

"Yep," Elle confirms. Gee, no one is letting me get away with anything. "Is that it, are you done?"

"I'm sorry, Elle. I'm..." I stop talking and look around, struggling with communication. "I'm not good with relationships and friendships. It's like I don't let people get close to me."

"Gee, what gave it away?" she sarcastically spits.

"I..." Again, I take a deep breath. "I don't want to lose our friendship. I'm an ass, and I'm trying really hard to not be one."

Elle stands behind her counter, nodding. "You're definitely an ass."

"I know."

"And you frustrate me when you get in your head, and refuse to listen to anyone."

I lower my chin, looking at my steel-toed boots. "I know."

"So, what are we going to do about your assiness?" I lift my head, and Elle's smiling. She's throwing me a lifeline, and I suspect, this is the last time she'll put up with me being such an idiot.

I walk around the counter, and hug her. "I'm sorry."

"I'm making this promise to you, Hope. Next time you decide to be a damn diva, I'm kicking your ass," she whispers.

Pulling away, I walk to the other side, and sit on a stool at the counter next to Murray. "When's that damn house going to be ready, Hope?" Murray asks.

"It shouldn't be too long now. It's nearly ready."

"Speaking of which, I've had a lot of interest in it. Am I going to sell it?" Elle asks.

"I've been thinking of something else, and I need to talk to Charlie about it first."

Elle places her hands on her hips. "You better not have anyone else sell it. I'm the best real estate agent in Hope River."

"You're the only real estate agent in Hope River," Murray corrects.

"Drink your damn coffee, Murray," Elle snaps.

"If anyone is going to sell the house, I promise it'll be you, Elle. But there's something I want to talk to Charlie about. Actually, can I have two coffees and two muffins please? I have to be quick, because we're nearly at the end, and I'm needed at the house more than ever." I push up from the seat, and wait for Elle to make the coffees. She places the brown paper bag on the counter, and I hear the bell chime as someone walks in.

The hair on my arms stands as I feel a warmth take over my body. I know it's River. I can feel the dynamic change as Elle looks up, smiles, then quickly darts her eyes to me before they widen.

"Elle, Murray." There's a slight pause. "Hope."

I have to get over myself and tell him how I feel. Turning, I smile as I drink him in. He's like the sun on the brightest of days, and the wind when it's howling the loudest, and the moon when it's shining the brightest, and the rain as it soaks the earth.

He's my universe, and I've been a fool for pushing him away.

I have to do something, tell him how much I want him before he finds someone else to look at like how he's looking at me right now.

His smouldering eyes lower and he forces a smile on his handsome face.

"River, can we talk?" I ask.

He lifts his gaze, and looks around. Suddenly, I'm painfully aware that Murray, and Elle are both staring at us. Shit, is everyone looking? I don't care. "No, now's not a good time," he says.

Oh. Shit, have I totally screwed this? My heart pounds inside my chest, and my body feels like it's made of glass and could shatter with the slightest breeze. But I can't let him walk away without me telling him how I feel. "Please?" I beg.

River steps backward, his hands high in surrender. "I can't," he says in a tight voice. His clenched jaw and rigid shoulders tell me he's hurt.

"Please," I beg again as I reach for his arm.

He shrugs me away. "I said, I can't." Turning, he hurriedly walks to the door.

"I love you and I'm an idiot!" I yell. All the chatter inside the café stops. As does River's quick escape. I step closer to him, although he hasn't turned to face me. I know every pair of eyes is on us, and frankly, I don't care. My cheeks are flushed with heat, my legs are wobbly, and my pulse is racing, but I have to tell him before I end up regretting my silence. "I've been a fool. So dumb. You've been the only man I've ever truly loved, and all I've done is push you away." My eyes sting as I blink away the threatening tears. I'm putting all of me on display for River to know how much I love him.

He hasn't turned to look at me yet, and although I've completely humiliated myself by professing my love for him so publicly, he needs to know before I lose him forever. I look around and Elle's smiling. "Go on," she mouths as she flicks her hand for me to continue.

"Everything inside of me is telling me to flee and not tell you how I feel. I…I…" I stammer, still trying to think of what I can say to make River see I truly love him. "I'm sorry, River. I'm sorry for how I've treated you, and pushed you away when all you ever wanted is to be with me. When I'm scared, every single one of my walls flies up. And what I feel for you, it terrifies me," I pause for what feels like hours. Placing my hand to my heart, I take a smaller step closer. But River still hasn't turned to look at me, or even said anything.

My chest tightens, and my throat squeezes together.

Crap, this can't be it.

I look to Elle again, hoping on some kind of encouragement. Her hand is on her chest over her heart, and her lips are downward turned, though still smiling.

I turn to River again. "I fell in love with you the moment I saw you in that café with your mom. It just took me until this very moment to realize it. All I can say is I want you, and I love you."

There's a heaviness in my belly that grows larger with every passing second of silence from River. Nausea bubbles in my gut as I wait for him to say something. *Anything.*

River's hand reaches for the door, he opens it, and leaves.

"Oh shit," I hear Elle whisper.

My shoulders slump, and my head lowers. My lips mash together as I keep from crying out with absolute pain. *What have I done?*

I don't have the guts to look at anyone, I do the only thing I'm capable of doing. I run.

I run out the door, to my truck, and take off down the street.

River doesn't want me. I've pushed him so much and so hard, that he doesn't want me anymore.

Sobbing, I keep driving, and driving, and driving.

The ringing of my phone startles me, and I look around to try and work out where I am. I find myself staring at unfamiliar landmarks. I know I'm not near Hope River, but at the same time, I don't even know where I am.

Pulling over, I reach for my phone, and see an unknown number. Clearing my throat, I pull myself together before I answer.

"Hello?" I answer, my voice slightly hoarse.

"Hello, is this Hope Sawyer?" a lady asks.

"It is." I wipe at my eyes, pushing the hurt away, even if only for a few moments.

"My name is Clarissa and I'm from the Wyatt County. I'm wondering if you have time to come in for a meeting."

I'm running everything this possibly could be about through my head. "What is this about? We obtained all the relevant permits and licenses we needed for the house," I say not even knowing why I'm blurting something like that out. I'm not usually nervous when talking to anyone from the government about the houses I flip. But wearing my heart on my sleeve for River has spooked me and left my emotions raw.

She has a small chuckle. "We know. You haven't done anything wrong, but we'd like to discuss something with you, and we're hoping you can help."

"You want me..." I say in a small, slow breath. "Okay. When would you like to see me?" I have no idea what's going on.

"We know you'd be busy with the house, so whenever you're available."

I look at the digital clock on the dashboard of the car. It's early, and I'm in no hurry to get back to the house. I was, but after my complete humiliation with River, I'm okay to stay away from the house, for now. "I can be there in an hour."

"Fantastic. Do you have the address or would you like me to text it to you?"

"I've been there, so I know where you are. And you said your name's Clarissa?"

"That's right. Just ask for me when you get there, and they'll let me know."

"Okay, thank you."

"Oh no, thank you, Hope," she says with cool confidence.

I hang up, and look down at the phone. What just happened? I suppose I'll find out soon enough. But my curiosity has been piqued.

Looking over my shoulder to check for cars, I catch a glimpse of a store front on the opposite side of the road. "Huh," I huff as I double look over it.

Suddenly, a few things I've been unsure of, start coming together. Now, to get back to the stable so I can get ready for this mysterious meeting with Clarissa. I have to take all the paperwork in with me, in case there's questions. And to ask May for a favor. I hope she agrees.

Chapter
THIRTY ONE

"SO, HAVE YOU decided what you're going to list the house for?" Charlie asks as we walk through the house to check what needs finishing.

Rolling the blue-spot tape out, I see one of the electrical outlets is half hanging out of the wall. I take a spot off the roll, and place it on the power point. "I've been thinking of something else."

"Huh. You've been very quiet lately. What's going on? Last week you didn't even come to the house for a few days. And when I asked you about it, you just shrugged and smiled. Did you find another house to flip?" He takes a blue spot and places it on the wall. "Whoever painted in here needs to be fired."

"You and I painted in here," I say.

"Then you and I need to fire ourselves." I smile. Cheeky bastard. "So, are you going to tell me what's happening? What are you listing this for? What did we spend?"

"We? You didn't spend a cent, I did," I answer with a laugh.

"Whatever. You know what I'm talking about. You've been coy and quiet, and I know you well enough to know, when you're like that, you're up to something. Have you and River finally found your groove?"

My stomach twitches, as I shake my head. "I don't think he wants me anymore."

"Yeah, well, that's bullshit. Every time I've had to talk to him, he always asks me about you."

"I've tried calling him, and seeing him, but he's completely ghosted me." My shoulders sink a bit further knowing I've lost my first love. I wish I hadn't screwed up with River.

"Maybe he's not ready to forgive you for being a dick. If you really love him, then don't ever stop because you never know what's on the horizon. Show him you want him, and don't stop showing him."

I stop what I'm doing, and look at Charlie. "Since when have you become so sentimental?"

He slowly turns his head. His brows are up, and his mouth is gaping. "Way to go, sis. Now, I'm hurt. I have feelings too, you know!"

I know he's kidding, but a part of me wonders if I did hurt his feelings. "I'm sorry, I didn't mean to be awful."

The side of his mouth quirks up and he nods. Turning, he goes back to looking for imperfections we'll have to fix. "I know. So, back to why we're here to begin with. The house is beautiful. It'll be perfect once you stage it for sale. Have you run the figures?"

I kind of cringe. I've made a business decision without talking to Charlie. Although this isn't Charlie's business, he is my right-hand man. He runs these flips for me and I trust him with not only my life, but with my money too. I walk over to Charlie, and hug him.

"Okay, what's going on?" He hesitantly returns the hug.

Stepping back, I lower my gaze before lifting it to look him in the eyes. "A few things are happening."

"Like?" Charlie's voice is tight, and skeptical. He steps back, and leans against the wall. "What have you done?"

"I'm not selling the house."

Charlie narrows his eyes while clenching his jaw together. "What are you holding onto it for? Wasn't the whole point for you to sell this, make some money and move on? Isn't that what we always do?"

"It is, and we're still going to make money."

"Is the market here down and you want to keep it until it picks up?"

I purse my lips together and tilt my head to the side. "Not exactly."

"Well, come on. Stop being a snot and tell me what your plans are." I look at Charlie. Did he really call me a snot? As if he's answering my unasked question, he nods and adds, "Yes, I called you a snot. What's going on? Are we moving in here? What?"

"Well, I've got an idea."

"For God's sake, spit it out will ya?"

For the next fifteen minutes Charlie's mouth goes from closed, to slightly open, to fully open. "So?" I ask.

As I explain my idea to Charlie, he pulls his shoulders back, as a proud, wide smile lights up his face. Yeah, he's on board. "I think I know someone who we can trust," he says.

"You do?"

"Yep, let me make a call." Walking away from me, he takes his phone out of his pocket. The house is large, and bare, making it easy to hear the low murmurs of his distorted conversation. I know he's speaking to someone, but not sure who. He returns within a few moments, with a sparkle in his eyes and his chest puffed out. "We've got a dinner date tonight."

"Yeah? Who with?"

Charlie's chin is high, and his shoulders are back. Cheeky bastard. He's holding out on me.

When Charlie told me what he was thinking, I couldn't agree more with his decision. We're not business partners, but this is a family business.

Sitting here, there's so much tension at the table. Tabitha keeps looking down at her plate, and Charlie seems distracted by something. Shit, was this a bad decision?

"May, this is beautiful," I say as I help myself to another helping of mashed potato and greens.

"Tabitha made the roast chicken," May says giving Tabitha credit.

"It was nothing," Tabitha says as she smiles at me, and gives Charlie a quick side glance. She flips her hair out of her way, and I hear a low grumble come from Charlie.

Hang on, has something happened between Tabitha and Charlie? Note to self: ask Charlie when we're alone. Side note to self: keep my nose out of it, it's not my business. Second side note to self: find out what I'm getting myself into. Triple side note to self: kill Charlie if he's been an ass toward Tabitha and makes me look like a fool.

"So, the reason Charlie and I invited ourselves over for dinner is because we have some news," I say.

"Oh really? How wonderful. Did you sell Old Roger's house?" May asks with genuine enthusiasm.

"No, not exactly. Actually, we're not going to sell it," Charlie says.

May looks at Tabitha, then to me. May scratches at her head, and Tabitha's head tilts to the side. They're both confused. "What are you doing with it?" May asks. "I thought you said you were going to fix it, then sell it. Did something change?"

Charlie and I exchange knowing glances. "Actually, a lot has happened," Charlie says, still smiling.

"Well hurry up, I'm not getting any younger here!" May snaps.

"I'm not selling Old Roger's house. Instead, I'm going to turn it into a bed and breakfast with a function area. And I need a chef, someone who can run the kitchen, and help out in front until we can find someone to run it full-time." I pointedly look over to Tabitha.

"Me? I'm just a chef though."

"A bed and breakfast? How wonderful." May claps her hands together.

"I only need you to help us get started with the bed and breakfast. In the meantime, I'll interview some people to run the it."

"Tabitha, this is wonderful news. I'm so happy. Please, please, please, consider this," May begs.

"I...I don't know." Tabitha's tight expression tells me she's skeptical. "I'm not sure if I'm the right person." Suddenly, she has no confidence in herself. This totally surprises me because she's always been so assertive in the past.

Shit, I don't want her to retreat. "I need the help, and your food is amazing. Please?"

Tabitha looks down at her plate with a tight expression, but she clears her throat before giving me a small nod. She licks her lips, before pursing her mouth tightly together.

Charlie exhales from beside me, and I can't help but really wonder what's going on with these two.

"Now, um. May, I hope it's okay, but can Charlie and I stay on in the stable please?"

"You pay your rent so I don't mind. Weren't you going to leave Hope River?"

"We were," Charlie says. "But both of us have changed our

minds." Tabitha looks up to Charlie, and her nose twitches before she offers both of us a smile.

Holy shit, something *is* happening between them.

"The county called me a couple of weeks ago, and wanted a meeting with me," I start saying. "You know over in Faith Haven where all those houses have been abandoned?"

May scrunches her nose, and makes an *eeeek,* sound. "Oh, Faith Haven? Where exactly in Faith Haven? You know, that's not a pleasant area. There's a lot of homelessness, and squatters. Gee, Hope, I'm hoping you haven't gone and bought a house there to flip. I think it'll be a waste of your money. No one will want to buy the house you'll work so hard to transform."

"Not exactly. I haven't bought a house there, no. The county and I have made an arrangement. They're giving me a row of houses on Oak Tree Parade, five houses on one side, so I can transform them and sell them. If the city is happy with what I do, then they'll give me the houses on the other side too."

May looks to Tabitha. Both narrow their eyes as if something doesn't add up. "They're *giving* you five houses?" Tabitha asks.

"They are."

"As in, the houses are just *given* to you?" she asks, still unsure.

"There is a catch, and we worked out some fine print."

"What's the catch?" May sets her fork down, and leans her elbows on the table, completely invested in what Charlie and I will be doing here.

"The catch is, the city receives fifteen percent of sale prices."

"What about the homeless people who use them to squat in?" Tabitha asks. "Although we rarely get snow in winter, it's still cold and they'll have nowhere else to seek shelter."

"Charlie and I aren't about to toss those people out anywhere. So, we compromised with the county, and over on Garnet Way in Faith Haven, there's an old, vacant gym that's been closed and boarded up for a while. The county is paying us to make that into a shelter for the homeless. Charlie and I will be starting the renovation of Garnet Way next week. It won't take us long, because it doesn't need to be stripped down. We're putting a deadline on it of six weeks."

"Six weeks? Is that enough?" May asks.

"The county has stepped up, and they're offering us help. So, yeah, it should be. It's quite straightforward. But, Tabitha, once it's done, I'd like you to spearhead a food program to help transition the homeless who do call those houses home, over to Garnet Way."

May stares at me. "I don't understand why the county is doing this." Shit, is May offended? "I mean, it's a great idea, but why now?"

"Because they've been keeping an eye on what Charlie and I have done with Old Roger's house, and they think this is exactly what's needed to advance Hope River, and the rest of the county. They told me they want more families coming here, and the only way they can do that is by making it appealing. The houses will be starter homes for younger families to settle in."

May sits back in her chair, with a wide smile. "I've lived in Hope River all my life. Matter of fact, I've never left." She looks around her beautiful dining room. "As you know, this home belonged to my mama and papa, and now it's mine, and one day, it'll be yours, Tabitha. And in all my life, I've never been prouder to be a resident of Hope River."

"Aunt May." Tabitha reaches across the table, and places her hand over May's.

"You're not a resident, May, you're a local treasure to the people here in Hope River. I think everyone is blessed to have you in their lives," I say.

May takes her hand from Tabitha's, and reaches for mine. "I think it's time you both called me Gran," May says.

Stupid dust mites. May wants Charlie and I to call her Gran. I'm so damn lucky. "Thank you," I croak as I unsuccessfully attempt to hold in the tears.

"Thank you," Charlie says in a strangled tone. Shit, even he's affected.

"Now, tell me, what's happening with that boy, girly." Gran moves her hand to pick her fork up and continue eating.

"I told her she's a jerk," Charlie responds going back to his smart-ass tone. He leans back in his chair, and crosses his arms in front of his chest, proudly.

"Yes, she is," May...I mean Gran says. "She needs to go after that boy, and tell him she ain't leaving and he's stuck with her."

"She needs a big gesture for him to know she's his. A huge romantic, sweet gesture," Tabitha chimes in while staring ahead whimsically.

"You know I'm sitting right here!"

"You better get your act together, girly. A boy as nice as him won't be around forever." Exact words River told me. "It don't look to me like you're fighting for him."

"I don't have to compete with anyone, because he told me he's done with me."

"Oh hogwash." Gran flicks her hand at me. "That boy loves you."

"That's what I said," Charlie echoes.

"He's waiting on you to pull that stubborn head out of your ass and tell him you love him!" Gran says.

"I said that too," Charlie says.

I flick an irritated look at him. "Brown-nose," I spit toward him. He cheekily smiles. Cocky bastard.

"You need a lesson in humility, girly."

"She just needs to be honest with him. In all the years I've been coming to Hope River, I've never seen or heard anything bad about him. Actually, he's a bit of an introvert. He's a good guy, and you're a damn fine woman, Hope. You're also smart, and really hot. You've got a brain, make it work for you," Tabitha says.

I pour myself a glass of wine and mull over everything the three are saying.

I'm truly blessed and eternally grateful. My career is in the best shape it's ever been. Now I have to figure out how to make River see that he and I belong together. And that I won't ever flake out on him again.

He's mine.

I'm his.

Chapter
THIRTY TWO

M Y HEART IS rapidly fluttering and my stomach rumbles with uncertainty. Excitement and nervousness both bubble through my veins. My skin tingles and I pick the folder up and try to fan myself as I drive.

This is ridiculous. I shouldn't be so terrified, but I am. What if he yells at me, then slams the door in my face? I can't make him love me. I can't make him want me.

Oh shit, I feel sick. I'm going to throw up.

I pull over on the side of the road, put the truck into park, open the door and jump out.

"What am I doing?" I say as I bend at the waist, grabbing hold of my knees while I take in deep breaths. Straightening, I look up at the moon, trying to find confidence to do what I have to.

I can hear the ocean waves from where I've pulled over on the side of the road. River's house is only a few minutes away, but I have to get this nervousness out of me. Placing my hand to my chest, I close my eyes. "I need strength. Please."

The sound of the ocean washes over me and starts to calm my frantic mind. "Live in the moment, Hope. Live in the moment," I say to myself.

I get back into my truck, and take one more deep mind-clearing breath. I start my truck, and head down to River's house. Pulling into his driveway, I turn the truck off and stare at his. Lifting my gaze, I notice he's standing out on the deck, looking out to the ocean. How has he not seen me? Or, has he seen me and he's ignoring me?

I lower my head to the steering wheel, and just breathe. My confidence is completely shot. Biting on the inside of my cheek, I notice the pain in my hands. Damn it, my fists are clenched so tight, I can barely straighten my fingers.

Ugh, just do it. *Get up there, and tell him.*

Lifting my head, I notice River's nowhere to be seen. Panicked, I look to my right in a frenzy in case he's left, but his truck is still here.

I look over to the passenger seat, and scoop the bright blue folder off of it. Staring forward, I tap my hand on my leg as it bounces up and down. The folder now laying on my leg jiggles with the tempo of my nerves.

"I can do this," I say as I take one final deep breath, pull my shoulders back, and find some God damned courage. "What's the worst that can happen?" I ask. My voice squeaks in defiance of my mind.

Yeah, well the worst that can happen is he slams the door on my face, and I'm stuck in a town where the only man I love refuses to have anything to do with me.

"Shit, Hope. Yeah, that sounds bad," I scold myself. And just like a light-bulb sparks my mind alive, another thought brightly appears. "The worst that can happen is I'll never know if I don't go up there and try."

I'd rather live a life knowing he no longer loves me, than a life of regret. Something May has been adamant about.

"Right." I'll never know if I don't get out of my truck. With the folder tucked under my arm, I leave the bubble of my truck, and walk up the steps to his front door. There's a tightness in my stomach as my blood pulsates through my veins. I hesitantly lift my hand, and knock on his door.

River answers the door nearly instantly. He locks eyes with me for a second, before lowering them then looking back up. "Hope," he says flatly. *Oh shit.* He brings his brows together, before relaxing his forehead. "Are you okay? What do you need?"

Jesus, he's so cold toward me. I deserve it though, after everything I've put him through. "I've come to make you an offer," I say as I clutch the blue folder tighter to my chest.

He leans against the door, still not inviting me in. The corners of his mouth slightly turn up. "An offer, eh?"

I look down to the folder, and nod. Shit, this is really hard. My body trembles as I wait for him to do something, *anything*. "Can I come in?" I finally ask after what seems like hours of standing at his front door.

River sighs loudly. "I suppose," he replies coldly.

Now, confronted with reality, I think this offer is stupid and immature, and he's going to laugh in my face. Oh my God, what the hell am I doing here? River steps aside, and waits for me to come in. I can't even look him in the eye as I walk past him. I walk over to the glass sliders, and look out to the beautiful, calming ocean. I hear the door close, and the latch click.

"So, what offer do you have?" he asks as I hear one of the chairs scrapes against the floor.

Turning, I'm confronted by River sitting tall at the table. He indicates I should join him. Sitting on the seat River's gestured to, I place the file on the table, and straighten my back. "This is an offer," I start with a trembling voice.

"Okay." He looks at the folder again, then me. Jesus, he's giving me nothing. Not a damn thing.

I begin fanning myself, suddenly overcome with a fireball of heat. "I should go," I say as I stand, scooping the stupid offer up from the table, and heading toward the door. I quickly unlatch the door, and slightly open it, before River reaches around, and slams the door shut. I can feel the heat rolling off him. He's so close to me.

"No, you shouldn't." My heart is crazily thundering inside my chest, as my breath hitches. He leaves his hand against the door, and brings his other arm up, trapping me between him and the door. His body is pushing up against my back. I can feel every part of him on me. "Talk to me," he whispers against my ear. Something wet touches my lobe, and I close my eyes and melt into him. "What do you want to say to me?" He thrusts his pelvis against me.

Run, run away before he hurts you.

No, never again. He won't hurt me. "I've got something for you," I say trying to keep my mind together, but my damn body is totally loving his hunger toward me.

He lowers his left hand, and runs it up from my upper thigh, to my hip where he possessively grips me. *Shit yeah.* "What do you want, Hope?"

"You," I blurt without even a second of hesitation.

"Bullshit. You run before it even has a moment to start," he says as he steps closer, pushing me up against the door. His hand moves up under my shirt to grip my breast.

I swallow hard, trying to keep my mind together. "I won't run," I say as I close my eyes, and lean my head back against his chest.

"You always run." He slips his hand inside my bra, and pinches my nipple making me cry out in pain and pleasure. "Do you just want a fuck?" He quickly removes his hand, and forces it down inside my jeans.

"Yes. No. I mean, *shit.*" He plunges a finger inside me, and I grind against his hand, desperate for a release. I thrust my hips against his fingers, and River keeps the tempo smooth and slow. "Faster," I plead. He kisses my neck, stopping only for him to lick and bite. Fuck, when did he learn to do that with his mouth? And his hand, oh my God, this feels amazing. Suddenly, River stops and moves away from me. "What? No. What are you doing?" I plead as I turn to see him stepping backward away from me. "Don't stop there."

I move, but he waggles his finger at me. "Nope. Not until I know what you came here for." He heads into his kitchen, takes a bottle of water out of the fridge and opens it. Bringing the bottle up to his lips, I'm mesmerized by how his mouth forms into a perfect O as his lips seal around the opening. Tilting his head back, he drinks about a third of the bottle in one go. Lowering the bottle, he brings his finger up to his mouth, and licks it slowly. Holy shit, has he got any idea of how damn sexy he is? "Hmm, I miss this taste."

Quickly, it dawns on me he's licking me off his fingers. Did someone turn the heat up? I fan myself with the folder, totally turned on by River. "Um," I squeak, unable to form any type of coherent sentence.

He places the bottle on the counter, he holds his hand out. I reach for his hand, but he retracts his and shakes his head. "The folder."

Am I still holding that damn thing? Stepping back gives me a few seconds to stand down from the lust-filled wanton ho I am, to being a damned smart business woman who knows a good investment when she sees one.

I pull my shoulders back, and walk over to the table. "Mr. Lockwood, if you'd care to take a seat," I say in my professional *this is a negotiation though really more like a hostile takeover* voice.

"Oh, it's like that is it, Miss Sawyer?" He pushes off from where he was leaning against the counter, and saunters over to where I'm sitting.

"Yes, it is."

He grabs onto my chair, and slides it over toward him. He grabs my knees, and pushes them open. "Talk." Moving his hand, he places it on my leg.

How the hell am I supposed to concentrate when he's so close to me? I can't do this. I look down to where his fingers are drawing lazy circles on my leg. Slowly, he's inching his hand up. This feels so damned good. He notices me staring, and stops, laying his hand flat against my leg. "Why'd you stop?"

"Because you're not talking."

Shit. Okay. Talk, Hope, fucking talk! Opening the folder, I hand him the first document. His hand moves up my leg and grabs the hem of my shirt. "I'm proposing a merger," I say. In one fluid movement, he lifts the hem and slowly peels the rest of my shirt over my head, and tosses it to the floor.

"Go on."

I'm sitting here in my pants and bra, and he wants me to keep talking? I can do this. "The merger is a business partnership." He leans around me, and unclips my bra, sliding the straps down, until it's completely off and my upper half is totally exposed.

"What kind of business merger?" He kneels in front of me, and takes one of my breasts in his mouth.

"Um!" I squeak, as I close my eyes, and push my chest into his mouth while lacing my hands through his thick, luxurious hair. Fuck.

He pulls away, and sits back on his heels. "I'll stop if you stop."

"No way, we can't have that happening," I blurt. River laughs, but waits. "Fine. So, I've been thinking that maybe you and I should merge together." Leaning forward, he takes my breast in his mouth again. Okay, keep a clear head, Hope. If you stop talking, he stops...sucking. "It would entail you and I become business *partners*," I shriek on the last word as he bites on my nipple. *Shit, shit, shit. Keep it together.* "We'd join...um." Closing my eyes, I thrust my breast into him while opening my legs further. "Us...um." Please keep doing that. "We'll tie stuff and um, I think we'll..." What the fuck am I thinking? He kisses his way across to the other breast, and takes it in his mouth, teasing and playing, while his hand expertly rubs and pinches. "We'll...um, together join, and I think build stuff and shit like that."

"Are you distracted?" he asks. I nod, then shake my head. I'm on cloud fucking nine is what I am. He undoes the button of my jeans, then unzips the zipper. "Are you stopping?" He leans back again.

"Hell fucking no, I'm not stopping, and you shouldn't either. But here, let me help you." I stand and he helps me shimmy out of my jeans so I'm left in just my underwear. Thank God they're a pretty yellow pair.

"If you don't want me to stop, then you know what you have to do."

I'm such a shameless hussy. "This merger will be a business partnership between River Lockwood and Hope and Charlie Sawyer." He grabs my hips, pulls me toward him, and opens my legs. River pulls my panties to the side, and he lowers his mouth down to my pussy. "We'll have an equal partnership," my voice is incredibly high pitched as I struggle to keep my head out of the clouds. God, he's gotten really good at this. "We'll rebuild houses, starting with five houses the county is giving me in Faith Haven." His tongue expertly flicks, and licks. Jesus, if he keeps doing this, I'm going to come on his face. "We'll um, split everything three-ways. And we'll um, call the business Vision Construction." Shit, I think I'm about to have a vision right now. He opens my legs further, as he absolutely feasts on me. Oh shit. I relax back into the seat, unable to keep talking.

River's mouth is a godsend. River himself is a damn godsend.

"And there's also another merger, where you'll be my wife, and I'll be your husband," I say as I grind my hips further on his face. What did I just say?

River pulls away, his mouth glistening from…well, me. "What?" he asks.

"What? Can you not stop, like not now? Maybe, when I've come."

"Did you ask me to marry you?"

"What? Who? Me?" He nods. "Yeah, I want us to be together."

"But you asked me to marry you." He points to himself, then to me. "You said you want me to be your wife and for you to be my husband."

Did I say that? "It's quite possible I was distracted. Your tongue was doing something pretty damn awesome to my lady parts. What I meant to say is I want you to be my husband, and me to be your wife. But if you can go back to finishing what you started, I'm happy to discuss this further after I've come…on your face…and on your cock." He tilts his head. "Please, can you come back and finish fucking me with your mouth?" River laughs. He stands, leans down and throws me over his shoulder like I'm a ragdoll. "Hey, what are you doing?"

"I'm doing what I should've done a long time ago."

As he carries me into his bedroom, my boobs jiggle, hitting him on his back. "My boobs are hitting you in the back."

"Shut up." He moves his head to the side, and he bites my butt cheek.

"Hey!" I protest. But in reality, I like it. "Do it again," I say.

"Kinky." He bites again, this time harder. He chucks me on his bed, and my boobs wobble in the most unflattering way, as does my stomach. He strips completely, and like a horny demon, tears off my cute yellow panties.

"Hey, I really liked those."

"I prefer them off anyway." He climbs up on the bed, positioning himself between my legs. "Yes," he says.

"Yes, what?" I ask.

"Yes, I'll be your business partner." He pushes into me, and I gasp with the sudden, welcoming stretch. "But no to the marriage proposal." He thrusts into me, slow at first, then his tempo increases.

"Why not?" I ask as he keeps pushing into me.

He stops, slings my leg up over his arm, and keeps going. "Shut up for a minute."

"Tell me why you won't marry me." God, how deep is he? I twirl my hips in counterpoint to the motion of his plunging, causing a delicious friction.

"Just shut up." He closes his eyes, and keeps thrusting.

"No, I want to know why!" I demand. He brings my leg up higher, making him go deeper. This feels so good. He stops again, and in one fluid movement, he rolls us over so I'm positioned over him. I move my hips, increasing the feeling I'm craving. "Why won't you marry me?"

He snakes his hands under the pillow behind his head, closing his eyes and biting on his lower lip. *Sexy.* "Hmm," he moans as I keep swiveling my hips on him. "Hmm." He licks his lips, then purses his mouth together.

Oh my God, what is he doing to me? I can't think if he keeps doing that thing with his lips. My concentration is quickly slipping, because I'm completely consumed by his mouth, and those sexy as fuck moans. I lower my top half so I can kiss him. The moment my mouth meets his, everything is different. *Better.*

I reach under the pillow where his hands are to entwine our fingers. He fumbles for a second before I feel it. "What's happening?" I mumble against his lips before pulling away. I tug my hands away from his, and find a square diamond ring on my fourth finger on my left hand. "What?"

"I bought this ring for you the day I found you were in Hope River. You're the only woman I've ever loved, Hope. I knew when I saw you in that café all those years ago, that one day you'll be my wife. Marry me."

Lifting my hand, I look at the beautiful ring. "Why was this under your pillow?" I ask.

"Seriously? Instead of saying yes or no, you're asking me why it's been under my pillow? To answer your question, because one day I knew it was going to be on your finger." *Oh, right.* "Is that a yes?" he asks after a moment.

I smash my lips against his. "Yes," I say.

"About time," he mumbles.

Epilogue

"THIS IS A good thing you're doing, Hope," Gran says as I drive her to the house. "To turn it into a bed and breakfast is wonderful. Hopefully that'll bring more visitors to Hope River and some will want to stay. I'd love to see more families move here."

Driving toward the house, I'm so pumped to show Gran what we've done. I just hope she loves the room I'm busting to show her. "Thank you. It really was an honor working on the house."

Gran clutches her bag on her lap as I near the home. I notice her hands tighten around the handle when I turn on the street. Jake and his team have closed off the road, but the moment he sees my truck approach, he motions for me to enter. "Wow," Gran says as she looks around.

There's a flurry of people, and the street has been set up the way it usually is when there's a festival on Main Street in town. I'm careful to park the truck in one of the neighbor's driveways three houses away from Old Roger's house.

Parking, I jump out, and run around to the passenger side to help Gran out of the car. "Shoo! Away, girly. What do you take me for? Old?" With normal May spirit, she slaps my hand away when I try to help her.

"My apologies," I offer as I step back and let her get out of my truck.

Gran is headstrong, because I can see she's slightly struggling, and I'm careful to be right there in case she loses her balance, and falls. But, she's also the most stubborn woman I've ever met.

"Hi Gran," Jake says as he walks to the truck, and tries to help her out.

"I'm capable of doing this myself, Jake. I've been walking way before you were an itch in your daddy's crotch."

Jake smirks, and I turn my head so she and Jake don't see me grinning. She gets out of my truck, and Jake closes the door behind her. "I can't wait to see what you think about what Hope's done with the house."

"When do you open for business?" Gran asks.

"The house is finished, but now that I'm turning it into a bed and breakfast, I need to get a few small things done. So, we'll be open for business by next weekend."

"Hope, the home is wonderful," a random man says to me.

"Thank you." I kindly smile, having no idea who he is.

"Gran, glad you could come," Murray says as he approaches us.

"I wouldn't miss it for the world, Murray. I want to see what this girl's been doing all these months."

"Hi Hope," I hear come from a soft, little voice.

Turning behind me, I see Rose walking with her parents, holding their hands, and she has the biggest smile. "Rose. Your dress is super pretty," I say as her parents slow their pace to keep up with us.

"I'm really looking forward to seeing what you did with the house," her mom says.

"Thank you."

"Mommy said she wanted to buy it, but now she can't," Rose blurts honestly.

"Rose!" her dad scold.

"Maybe one of the next houses I flip." I look at her mom.

Her mom narrows her eyes with a questioning gaze. "Is there another house like this in Hope River?" she asks. Judging by her vacant expression, she's trying to recall where the house would be.

"I've got five houses on Oak Tree Parade, over in Faith Haven."

Her mom grimaces, and sucks in a breath. "Those abandoned houses?" I nod confirmation. "Eww, I don't think so." She shakes her head.

"Challenge accepted," I say with a smile.

"You think you can make those houses into homes?" her father asks.

I smile cheekily. "Oh, I don't think I can, I *know* I can."

Rose's dad's face gleams as he keeps walking forward. "I can tell you, we're both looking forward to seeing your next project."

"Daddy, can I get cotton candy?" Rose asks when she spots the machine in front of the house.

"Sure can. Come on. Nice talking to you, Hope. Bye Gran, Jake." He tips his head graciously as the three of them walk ahead of us.

"I'll leave both you ladies here, because I have work to do," Jake says. "But I'll be in to take a look at the house when I get back."

"Sure thing, Jake. Thank you." Jake walks back toward the barriers blocking the street off. I turn to look at Gran, who's staring up at the house in awe. Her hand comes up to her chest, and she takes a small backward step. "Are you okay, Gran?"

Her eyes widen as she sucks in a sharp breath. "My goodness, Hope." Her lips part slightly as her smile grows bigger. "This is amazing."

"Would you like to see inside?"

"I love the door. The green is just beautiful."

"It's the perfect match to the earrings."

"Oh." She covers her mouth with her free hand while she keeps her bag tightly clutched against her chest. We slowly walk up to the house, and I move my arm out so she can use me for balance on the steps. She stops at the door, and looks at the sign I've had made. "McGrath's Bed and Breakfast," she reads. She turns to me, and grabs my arm. "Perfect."

"Thank you. I wanted you to see what you helped create." We enter the house where Elle and Tabitha are cooking together in the kitchen.

"Oh, my goodness. This is massive. I had no idea it was so large. And oh my. Look at that view," Gran says when she sees the massive sliding doors open to the back. "I never thought this house could be salvageable, Hope. But I suppose it just took the right person to have a vision."

I find myself standing taller, and prouder. What a wonderful thing for Gran to say. And ironic really, because Charlie's, River's and my business is called Vision Construction. "Thank you. But I do have something I want to show you. It's upstairs, do you think you'll be okay getting up there?" Gran turns and scowls at me. "So that's a yes."

"Hi Gran." River appears from the back, dressed smartly in tailored pants, and a white shirt. He approaches us, gives Gran a quick kiss on the cheek, then he kisses me softly on the mouth. "Do you like the house?"

"It's perfect," Gran replies.

"Have you shown her upstairs?" he asks as he places his arm around my waist and squeezes.

"We just got here. Everything okay out back?"

"Yeah, I just finished the lights. Rookie mistake, I didn't have enough. Anyway, it's all good."

"Are you two going to stand there making googly eyes at each other, or can I go upstairs and see what this big surprise is?"

"Sorry." Both River and I lower our chins.

Gran walks ahead to the staircase. "If I remember correctly, the stairs were over there."

"We moved them," I say.

Gran begins her ascent, and River leans down and whispers, "Meet me in the bathroom upstairs in one hour. We need to christen it."

Before I can even ask which bathroom, he kisses my neck, and takes off out the front door. Bastard. Now I'm going to be thinking about the fun we'll have in an hour.

"Hurry up!" Gran snaps. Man, she's great value. I love her short, direct sassiness.

"Sorry," I call as I trudge up the stairs to find her standing in front of the closed door to the room I'm eager to show her.

"This says *May's Room*." She points to the plaque beside the door. She then looks over to me, and widely smiles. "And the door is the same green as the one downstairs."

"It is. Each of the rooms are named after someone. There's Roger and Jean's Room." I point to the open yellow door. "There's Carl's Room." I point to the open orange door. "There's Henry's Room." I point behind me to the open blue door. "And there's May's Room." I pointedly look at the closed green door. "And downstairs, there's the McGrath's room. But, when you're ready, Gran. I'd like to show you the room I created for you."

Gran stands in front of the door, her hand nowhere near the

door knob. She sees the black square above the door handle. "Do I need a card to get in? One of those fancy ones?"

"It's unlocked."

She hesitantly reaches for the handle, and slightly pulls away. Skeptically, she turns to me. With tears in her eyes, I give her an encouraging nod. A small smile tugs at her lips, before she turns, and pushes on the door. She steps in, and I hear her gasp. "Oh my," she says as she stands in the room, looking around. Gran walks over and places her bag on the bed, before taking a slow step forward. She sees the massive frame ahead of her. *When the moon is in full view of my window, I wonder if you're looking up and watching it with me. Are you, my love?* Gran reads the writing aloud. She reaches out and touches the frame. "That was written in the letter from..." she stops, and bursts into tears.

Shit, what have I done? She hates it. Oh my God, I feel like I've disappointed May and hurt her. "I'm sorry," I say as I place my arms around her.

"Don't be sorry, my girl. Please! This is the best gift I've ever been given." She sees the other picture I've had framed. I scanned the one of her family, and had the photo restored and blown-up. "Is that the picture in my home?"

"It is. I had two created. One for here, and one for you."

Tears stream down May's face. "In this one room, there are so many beautifully perfect memories. You've not only restored this house; you've restored the love in my heart. Thank you, Hope. You've given me so much." She hugs me, and gives me a kiss on the cheek. "Would you mind if I spend a moment in here alone?"

"Of course not. Would you like me to wait for you outside?"

"Please no. I'll come find you downstairs when I'm ready. Go, make sure everyone sees the beauty of this house."

"Take your time." I head out of the room. There's a steady stream of people walking through the rooms. I can hear Charlie's voice bellowing from Roger and Jean's room. As people walk past, they offer their praises for what we've done with the house. I duck my head in, and tap Charlie on the shoulder. "May's in her room, can you make sure she's okay in about ten minutes? I'll go downstairs and see if Elle and Tabitha need anything."

"Sure thing." Charlie leans into me. "Everyone's loving the house, I've even had a few people ask me what our next project will be. One guy gave me his number and told me to call him when we're ready to sell one of the houses on Oak Tree Parade." He's nearly jumping out of his skin with enthusiasm.

"That's so cool." I clap my hand on his back, excited how awesome today is turning out to be. "Watch out for May, okay."

"Sure thing, *partner*." Charlie turns and starts talking to someone as I leave. Charlie was so happy I offered to make him a third partner in the new business. He deserves it; he works hard.

Heading down the stairs, I walk into the kitchen where Elle and Tabitha are frantically buzzing around. "How's it going? Do you need a hand?"

"Yes. Can you chop these lettuces up, while I go out the back and check the barbecue grills?" Tabitha asks.

"I've got it." Tabitha runs out the back to check on whatever she's cooking out there. "Thank you for helping, Elle," I say as I start chopping the first head of lettuce.

"Oh yeah, of course. Anything I can do to help."

"Hey, I wanted to ask. The houses over on Oak Tree Parade, can you sell them for us when they're done?"

Elle raises her eyebrow at me. "Was there another option?" she asks with a straight face.

"I just wanted to check you'll be okay with selling them." I keep chopping the lettuces.

"Hope, the house is amazing," I hear Jake say. I catch Elle smiling, and her cheeks turn pink when she hears his voice. But she doesn't look up at him. I think she's too embarrassed by the flush in her cheeks.

Turning, I see him standing on the other side of the counter, leaning against it. "Thank you, Jake. Hey, can you do me a favor? Charlie's upstairs showing the house, and May's in May's Room. Can you go check on her, see if she's okay please? I've asked Charlie, but there are so many people, he may get distracted."

"Oh, yeah. No problems. Before I go, Elle, a totally weird thing happened."

"What?" Elle asks, finally turning to look at him.

My God, when are these two going to get together. Her eyes light up like she's looking at the bright sun. And Jake winks at her. How damn cute. "One of the deputies came across a missing person report of a girl by the name of Layla, someone who looks virtually identical to you. Talk about doppelgangers." He shakes his head.

"Yeah," Elle says. "Weird, huh?" She turns forward again and continues preparing the food.

"I'll go check on May," Jake says.

I look over at Elle. Her hands are shaking, her face is totally devoid of color, and she's actually not preparing anything. She's holding the knife so tightly her knuckles are going white. "Hey, are you okay?" I ask. Elle's eyes are wide. "Elle!" I say, louder.

"Yep." She turns to look at me, as the knife swings to point at me with her death grip. My eyes glimpse down at the knife. Elle looks like she's holding her breath.

"What's going on?"

It takes her a few seconds, but she slightly shakes her head, and loosens her grip on the knife. Her shoulders relax, and color floods her face again. "What? Nothing." Quickly, she turns forward, and continues her food prep.

What was that about?

"One of the briskets is ready, and by the time I cut this one up, the other two should be done too," Tabitha announces as she carries in a huge slab of meat. She places it on the kitchen counter, picks up a knife and slices two pieces off. "Here, try it. Let me know what you think."

"Brisket equals heaven in my mouth," I say as I take the slice and pop it in my mouth. "Oh my God! It melts like butter. Elle, you have to try this." Elle's totally distracted. I need to talk to her about what's going on. But I can't now, not with Tabitha in here. "Elle!"

"Yeah?" She turns, not even hearing me say anything. "Oh, you're back already. That's looks succulent. Can I have some?" she asks Tabitha. She's pretending she's fine, but I can tell, something's way off.

"Yeah, of course. Here." Tabitha offers her a slice, which Elle takes, pops in her mouth and moans with satisfaction. "Good, huh?" Tabitha waits for Elle's approval.

"It's *so* good." Elle continues prepping the food, but her hands are trembling.

"Hi, Hope?" I turn to find Clarissa standing on the other side of the kitchen counter.

"Clarissa, I'm so glad you could come out today. Have you had a chance to look around?" Wiping my hands on a tea towel, I walk over to her.

"Oh yes. This is just wonderful. As I said in our meeting, there's been such a buzz of excitement around this house. Thank you for inviting me today."

"Did you bring your family? If so, please, stay for the festival. There's food constantly going out, face painting if you have kids, a balloon sculptor, all kinds of things happening."

"Thank you. Sorry, but I have to get home. But I will say this: you're exactly what Faith Haven needs. I'm so pleased we're in business together. Now, let me know when you start over on Oak Tree Parade and what we can do to help."

"Charlie and I have the team ready to start on the gym at Garnet Way within the week. We'll have that done quickly."

"I have no doubt. Take care." Her heels make a clicking sound against the hardwood as she walks out of the house.

"Everyone's loving you. You've brought life back to a sleepy, small town," Tabitha says. "Okay, this is done. I'll take it out front, then go and get the others from the barbecue."

I look at my watch, and notice I have ten minutes before I'm meeting River upstairs. *Dirty bastard.* Yes!

"I'll take it out so you can get the others," Elle offers.

"Thanks, Elle," Tabitha responds. "You're awesome."

Elle takes the platter of meat out of Tabitha's hands, and walks outside while Tabitha makes a dash out back to the barbecue. "Can I help?" Joanne offers. Shit, I haven't seen her since the night her son Thomas, and his friend Matthew were lighting firecrackers inside my house. Joanne stands maybe five foot two, and is quite petite in statue. She's also really timid and quiet.

"Joanne, it's good to see you. We'd love the help please." She looks around the isolated kitchen. "Elle's just gone out front with some food and Tabitha's around the back getting the meat off the grills. Both of them will be back soon, and I'm sure they will have something you can do." And I'm about to get my freak on with River. Hell yeah. Bathroom sex, in a house brimming with people. I'd better be quiet.

"What would you like me to do?"

"Um, I don't know. I can barely boil water! I thought Tabitha would have more people here, helping."

"They're coming," Tabitha replies as she walks in with her hands full of the two remaining briskets. "I've hired a couple of girls, twins actually, but they called me and told me they're running late and will be here before midday. So, it left just Elle and myself." Tabitha looks around the kitchen, then toward the front door. "Isn't Elle back yet?"

"I'll go check on her," I say, feeling something's just not right. "Oh, Tabitha, this is Joanne. Joanne, this is Tabitha, who will be our chef. Joanne can help until the twins show up."

"Yeah, I can do whatever you need me to," Joanne offers.

"Great, can you keep going with…"

I leave Tabitha and Joanne in the kitchen, and head out front. The street is quickly filling with people, and many say hello to me as I walk down the path, searching for Elle. "Hey, you okay?" River asks when he sees me. "And aren't you supposed to be heading upstairs in." He pulls his phone out of his pocket to check the time. "Like three minutes?"

"Have you seen Elle?" I ask. Distracted, I look up and down the street.

"Yeah, I saw her a few minutes ago. She said she forgot something, but she'll be back in about twenty minutes or so."

"What could she have forgotten?" Something's going on, and it started when Jake told her about the doppelganger. Shit, what was the name again?

One of the neighbors stops us and talks to us about how beautiful the house is. Every time River and I try to break away, they keep asking us question. A cheeky look passes between River and myself. The minutes drag on, until finally, after a good twenty minutes River politely excuses us both.

River and I head inside, ready for our risqué bathroom sex in a house filled with people. The girls who were supposed to help Tabitha have arrived, and there's food on every counter in various stages of preparation.

River sneaks a piece of brisket and Tabitha half-heartedly slaps his hand. "What?" he asks. "I'm a hungry man."

"Do you want me to take some of this out?" I ask.

"Yeah, whatever's ready. I don't know what happened to Elle," Tabitha says.

"No problem," I say, but Elle should definitely be back by now. River and I grab some plates and take them out to the tables. The uneasy feeling I noticed before is back and has intensified.

River's eyes are dancing with the devil. He grabs my hand and starts pulling me inside. "You and I have a date." He grabs me around the waist, and lifts me clear off the ground.

I'll talk to Elle later. Right now, I'm going to get my lady boner on with the sexiest man alive. He carries me up the stairs, then places me on my feet, and smacks my butt *hard,* when I turn around. "Get upstairs, and lock the door," he commands.

I fly up those stairs like I've magically sprouted wings. I check the Roger and Jean Room, and Charlie's standing just on the outside talking to people. He glances over at me, and scrunches his forehead.

I check the Carl Room, and I'm pleased there are only a few people dawdling in here. I head out to Charlie again. "Excuse me," I say to the man he's talking to.

"You both should be so proud, you've done an amazing job," he says.

"Thank you," Charlie and I say together. The moment the man's back is turned, I grab Charlie's upper arm and reach up to whisper in his ear. "River and I need to fix something in the Carl Room. It's off limits for a bit."

"What do you have to fix? I can help you with it."

"Eww, no you can't," I blurt.

Charlie's face morphs from confusion to understanding. "Thank God the rooms are sound proof." He screws his mouth up. "Just...lock the damn door."

River appears, and says, "Hope, I need you to look at something in this room. Tell me what you want me to do with it."

"If you don't know what to do with it, you shouldn't be using it," Charlie mutters under his breath so only River and I hear him. River shoots a smirk at Charlie. "I would say get a room, but it looks like that's exactly what you're about to do."

I turn to Charlie, and give him a shut-up look. "I'll fire your ass," I say through clenched teeth, though still playfully.

"I'm your partner now, so you can't. Go, get your freak on." He flicks his hand at me. "At least one of us is."

Shit, what's going on with him? Whatever. I'll deal with him later.

River and I close and lock the door, and within a second, River's tearing my clothes off. His lips are on mine, and we break away only long enough for him to tear his shirt off and unzip his pants. "God, I've wanted to do this from the moment you got here."

My heart is racing knowing there are people on the other side of the door. Thankfully, I can't hear them, which means they can't hear us either. River grabs me around my bare ass, and I jump up wrapping my legs around his hips. He balances me up against the wall, moves his right hand and positions his cock at my pussy. "Fuck, I love you," he says as he thrusts into me.

Draping my arms around his neck, I close my eyes and enjoy these few moments we have together. In this very breath it dawns on me, I'm so happy I finally got out of my own head, and told River how I feel. "I love you too."

Stay tuned for a sneak peek into
Our Chance.

Our CHANCE

Prologue

Someone drops something, and I startle awake. *Shit, have they found me?*

Pulling my hoodie over my head, I keep my gaze down as I dart out of the truck stop. How can I be so stupid as to fall asleep now? Anything could've happened. Thankfully, nothing did.

It's drizzly and cold as the sun begins to rise.

Looking around, I'm sure to keep my head down, and not look like I'm running. God only knows there's a ton of CCTV around here.

Just blend in.

I've been waiting and looking for a truck driver who doesn't appear too scary and see one walking out to his rig. I catch up to him, and smile.

He turns his head, and checks me out skeptically. I have to make this look like we know each other, so no one asks questions. "Hi," I say as I smile.

He crinkles his forehead, and gives me a small nod. "Hi," he responds cautiously.

"I'm wondering if I could hitch a ride please?" I ask as I discreetly try to look around me. I make sure I keep with his pace, nothing to cause alarm.

He inspects my appearance. Shit, do I give off the impression that I'm running? Is my oversized hoodie, and baggy track pants a giveaway? Crap, please don't call the police. "Are you running from somethin'?"

"I need to get to my grandmother," I say with my rehearsed answer. Jittery, I look around again in case they found me.

"Where's your grandmother?"

"She's down south." I swallow, waiting for his reply.

He pauses, and lifts his hand to scratch at his chin. "Show me what's inside your bag," he says after a drawn-out moment.

"Huh?"

"If you want me to take you, show me what's in your backpack. I ain't taking you nowhere if you've got drugs or a gun on ya."

"I don't want any trouble. I just need a ride. Please." I open the back-pack and show him what's in there. I cleaned out my bank account, and bought a couple of new articles of clothing. Everything else, I dumped. I couldn't even go back home. "Please," I say again once he looks in my bag and nods.

"Get in." He juts his chin toward his truck. "But I can only take you as far as Alabama."

I let out a relieved breath. "Thank you so much," I say. I hoist myself up in the huge truck, and when he merges onto the quiet street, I take my hoodie off, shaking out my hair. "I'm so grateful, thank you."

He gives me a sideways glance as he gathers speed. "What's your name?"

"L…" I stop before giving him my name. Crap, I can't do that. I might endanger him if he knows. "Elle," I say.

"Lelle?" he questions.

"Elle. Eleanor actually, but everyone calls me Elle," I say covering my near slip.

"Elle, huh? So, why are you hitchhiking in the middle of the night?"

Chewing on my nails, I can't tell him because if I do, he'll call the police. I can't have that happen. I'd end up like... Suddenly, I burst into tears. Every time I close my eyes I see the look on her face. I hear the sound. "Um," a strangled noise struggles to be loud enough for him to hear.

"Hey, it's okay, darlin.' It's okay." He sits straight up in his seat, and takes a breath. "My name's Earl and I've been driving trucks for nearly forty years," he says. "What do you do for a living?"

I can't tell him anything about me, or it might lead him in so much trouble. "I work in a diner," I say. The lies keep growing, but I need to protect Earl, and myself. I couldn't live with myself if Earl was hurt because of me.

"Yeah?" I say as I look out the window. "Do you like it?"

"Yeah, I do. Bouncing around from state to state." The more Earl talks, the more his voice is soothing which makes my eyes heavy. He tells me about his wife, and his daughter, who's married and is expecting her first child.

The more I listen, the more his voice eases the tsunami in my head. But Earl's voice can't stop me reliving that moment, and the look of sheer fear and panic on her face. Turning, I try to hide my face away from Earl so he can't see the silent tears clinging to my cheeks.

The sun rises, and I find my eyes are stinging from the hard night I had. My God, my entire world has turned on its axis in a matter of hours. What started as a fun night out with my best friend, has ended with me running as far and fast as I can.

Before I know it, my eyes close.

"Elle?" Someone pokes me, and I jump awake. "Sorry to startle you, Elle, but we've arrived in Alabama. I've got a buddy of mine who's coming through and heading down south, so he'll take you the rest of the way."

I'm battling to keep my eyes open because I'm so tired. "Thank you," I say with a croaky voice. I open the door, and turn to Earl. "I'm…" Crap, what do I say to him? "Thank you."

"Here he comes now." Earl points to a truck pulling into the station. Both Earl and I hop out of his truck, and we walk toward where his friend is parked. I'm careful to have the hoodie pulled up over my head, and my chin tilted down. I didn't even hear Earl talking to anyone when I was asleep. I must've been completely out of it. I'm surprised I slept so deeply, especially after what happened. "Jackson." Earl holds his hand out. "This is Elle."

I hesitate as my brain registers the name Earl's given. "Hi." I smile, but try to keep my eyes down. Jackson is a bit younger than Earl, and beefy, with short legs and a long face.

"Hiya, little lady," he says with the slightest Southern accent.

"Give us a minute, Jackson," Earl says. Jackson tips his head, and strolls into the roadhouse. Earl turns to me. "Look, I know you're in some kind of trouble." My arms tense, as I hold my breath, waiting for whatever he's going to say. "Here." He pulls out a wad of cash from his pocket, and offers it to me.

"Oh no, I'm fine," I say. Who has that kind of money on them? There's got to be easily a thousand dollars there.

"You're running and you're scared. And the only reason a girl runs in the middle of night is because she's in trouble. Take it, and one day, when you can, you'll pay it forward."

I try to swallow, but there's a huge lump in the base of my throat. "I'm…" I look at the money and shake my head. I can't take that from him.

"Jackson's a good man, he'll take you as far as you need, no questions asked. But for now, you will need this, and like I said, pay it forward when the time is right. Keep your head down, and don't go looking for trouble."

I blink away the tears. "Trouble found me," I say as my breath hitches. He thrusts the money into my hand. "Thank you."

"You're welcome. Now, be safe."

I'm choking back the overwhelming emotions rushing through me. Earl is a kind and gentle man. "Thank you," I repeat. "I want you to know you saved me."

He nods and smiles as he backs away from me. "It's not the first time, darlin,' and it won't be the last. Take care." He swings around, and heads to his truck, where I stand as he hoists himself up, gets in, and leaves.

Huh. He's done this before? Wow. What a man.

"You ready, little lady?" Jackson asks. I watch as Earl's truck becomes smaller and smaller. My head's hurting from crying, and what happened. "Here you go." He throws me a bottle of water, and a muesli bar. "Figured you'd need to eat."

I wonder if this is what Earl and Jackson do. Save people. It's like the universe has aligned and provided me with two guardian angels. Are people really that honorable? "Thank you, Jackson."

"Now, let's git going."

He easily gets in the truck, as I heave myself up too. Truck drivers make it look easy, but truthfully, I find it super awkward. Jackson talks as he drives along, mostly about how long he's been driving trucks, and about his sons and their jobs and how proud he is of his wife who's a self-published author.

Morning turns to afternoon, which turns to night. "I need to refuel the truck, and myself," Jackson says as he laughs. "S'pose you ready for something to eat?"

"Yeah, I'm really hungry. Thank you."

"There's a diner I like, 'bout forty or so minutes. We'll be there soon."

"Thank you."

True to his word, we're at the diner in under an hour. Jackson refuels his truck, and within half an hour we've eaten and are already on the road again.

The night is on us before I even know it, and I look out to the darkened sky. The stars are bright in the sky tonight, and as I stare at them, I can't help but replay the last thirty-odd hours.

I take in a deep breath, and can smell the salt in the air. "Are we near the water?" I ask.

"Close enough. We'll be passing alongside the water soon."

Closing my eyes, I inhale deeply. The ocean has always calmed me. Even when I was little, my grandmother would take me to the beach, and I found I was always more grounded when I'd get home.

Opening my eyes, I see a sign.

Welcome to Hope River. Population ~~1301~~, ~~1302~~, ~~1300~~, 1304.

Hope River. Jesus, is this my sign.

I take a deep breath as I stare into the dark. I think I know where I need to be.

Hope River.

Right now, *hope* is the only thing I have.

Chapter
ONE

Jake

"Thank you for the ride, Jake," Gran says as I pull up in front of her house.

"Do you need help getting inside?" I ask. But really, my mind is on Elle. She disappeared from Hope and River's showing of the new bed and breakfast.

"If you ask me again, I'll be forced to slap you with my handbag. Go." She shoos me away once she closes the door of my sheriff's car.

I watch as Gran climbs the several steps to her front porch, unlocks her door and walks inside. She turns and gives me a small wave. I flick my hand up and drive down her long, dusty driveway.

I quickly glance down at my phone. Elle hasn't returned any of my messages. When I told her about the woman who looked like her, I noticed how the color drained out of her face, and her breath hitched. I thought that was strange, but I've known Elle for years, and never known her to be deceitful. I thought I could catch her alone and talk to her, but Tabitha told me she hadn't returned and when I went out to search for her, she was gone.

Driving toward Elle's flat, I'm worried. My gut is telling me she knows exactly who Layla Dixon is, I have a feeling it's her twin sister. Maybe something's happened and Elle can't cope. I don't know, but whatever it is, I need to make sure she's okay.

Getting out of the cruiser, I walk up to the apartment, and

press the doorbell. I wait for her to answer. But she doesn't. I press the buzzer again. Nothing.

I hit the other buzzer, hoping Elle's neighbor is home.

"Hello," a man says.

"It's Jake."

"Sheriff?"

"Yeah. I need you to buzz me in." The second the door buzzes, I fling the door open and rush up the stairs. Elle's door is closed. I knock loudly. "Elle!"

The neighbor, I think he's name is Tony opens his front door and looks at me. "Everything okay?"

"Yeah, fine. I'm looking for Elle."

"I heard her come home about half an hour ago. Haven't heard her since."

Shit. Panic quickly floods me, and I'm about to break down her door if she doesn't answer it. "Thank you." Tony — or whatever his name is — retreats back inside. I bash on her door, louder. "Elle." I hear something from the other side, and I give her to the count of five. I step back, so I can break her door down, but she opens it. She's been crying, and she has a disheveled, frightened look in her eyes. "Elle."

She purses her lips together, then brings a shaky hand up to chew on her nail. "What are you doing here?" She looks downstairs toward the door as if she's waiting for something.

"Are you waiting for someone?" I ask as I quickly glance down the stairs, then back to her. She shakes her head. "What's happening, Elle?"

"Nothing," she says way too fast. She steps in front of the door, and shuts it so it's barely open behind her.

She's certainly hiding something. "Can I come in?"

"Um, no, now's not a good time," she replies with a shaky voice. She looks down the stairs again. "I've got to go. I've got some stuff to do." She steps back inside, but is careful in the way she closes the door so I can't see in.

I know there's only one way in, and one way out of Elle's apartment. So, I give her the space she's desperately seeking, and go back downstairs. I know Elle will be up in her apartment, watching for my departure so she can do whatever it is she's doing.

But that's not going to work on me.

I stand by the door, waiting.

Whatever is going on, I have to make sure Elle's safe. I wouldn't be able to live with myself if something happened to her. I couldn't let that happen again, not that the first time I failed was my fault, but it took me a long time to deal with the pain.

After nearly an hour and the front door opens as Elle steps through with a suitcase. She's wearing a hoodie pulled over her head. She looks to the right, then the left and startles when she sees me. "Jake!" She makes a fist and brings it to her chest. "Shit, you scared me."

"Where are you going, Elle?"

She slowly looks down at the suitcase, then back up at me. "Um, I'm going to do laundry," she says in a deliberate and obvious lie.

"No, you're not."

She lets out a deep breath, and starts shuffling from foot to foot. "Look, Jake, I'm sorry, I have to go." She lowers her gaze for a split second, before lifting her chin and pulling her shoulders back. She quickly darts a look behind me, before pressing her lips together. "I'll see ya later?"

I step forward and place my hand over her hand clutching the suitcase. "You don't have to run."

Her eyes widen, as she sucks in a deep breath. "Yeah, I do," Elle finally says in a tiny breath.

"Are you in trouble?" Elle backs away from me, but I move forward again, this time taking the suitcase from her firm hold. "I can help you." I reach for her hand, and gently take it in mine.

"No, you can't. I have to go."

"Tell me what's happening, I want to help."

She blinks several times as she looks up to the sky. Tears streak her face as they roll down her cheeks and cling to sun-kissed, flawless skin. "I can't," she finally says as she lowers her gaze. "I wish I could, but I can't."

I know this has something to do with Layla Dixon. I just have to figure out what. "It's about Layla, right?"

She stretches for the bag, but I move it back so she can't reach it. "It doesn't matter who it has to deal with. All that matters is I have to get out of here. And I have to go, soon. And by soon, I mean right now. I'm sorry, Jake."

"No, I'm not letting you go." I move her suitcase further back so it's completely out of reach for her. "I'll protect you from whoever you think you're in trouble with. I'll protect you."

"You can't," she whispers. Elle wipes at her eyes. "No one can." She bows her head, and cries into her hands, completely breaking down.

Jesus, what the hell is going on? "Elle." I step forward, and wrap my arms around her. She cries into my chest for the long time. "It's okay Elle, I'll protect you. But I need you to tell me what you're running from." Elle steps back, and wipes her eyes with the sleeve of her hoodie. Even with her now blotchy skin, and red, puffy eyes, she's still beautiful. "Come on, you're coming home with me," I tell her.

"What?"

"You're coming home with me. We can fix this, whatever this is."

"Jake, I can't involve you. It's not fair."

"And I won't let you run, so you have no other option."

"You think you can keep me here?" she argues.

"Don't test me, Elle. I'll keep you in the watch house if I have to. I don't want to, but I will. I'd rather you stay with me until we figure out what to do."

She lowers her hoodie, and runs her hand through her bright red hair. "I can't ask you to…"

"You're not asking me to do anything I don't want to do. We can work this out, Elle. Please, trust me. I've never given you a reason to distrust me in the past, so don't start now."

She looks down at the pavement, her eyes darting back and forth as she carefully considers what to do. But truth be told, I'm not letting her go. I'll throw her over my shoulder and carry her to the cruiser if she fights this. I'm not losing her.

"Okay," Elle finally says. "I won't run." She steps forward to take her bag.

"What are you doing?" I ask as I hold onto it tighter.

"I'm taking it back upstairs."

"You're not going back to your apartment, Elle. You're coming home with me. I've come here to see how you are, and something's terrified you enough to pack your bag and take off. That to me says you're frightened, and whatever it is that's scaring you, must be big. So, you're coming back to my house, where we can figure out what has to happen to keep you safe."

"Jake, I'm not your responsibility."

How do I respond to her? I want to tell her I care for her, and I haven't cared for anyone since, well since a long time ago. But that might scare her even more than she already is. "Because everyone in Hope River is my responsibility, including you." Especially you.

She looks over to my cruiser, then back to me. "Okay, I'll stay with you, for now."

I'll take that, but I'll keep an eye on her. Whatever has got Elle spooked must be fairly horrific if she's ready to pack and leave a place I know she loves.

I'll work hard at breaking her barriers down, and making sure she's safe. No matter what it takes.

ECHOES

OF YOU

PROLOGUE

The palms of my hands are sweating.

Standing in front of an unassuming building, I look up to see its sheer size. Still, it's inconspicuous because it looks exactly like all the other buildings surrounding it.

The sun breaks out just behind the brick building, casting the entrance into shadow.

Funny, that. Because I've been living in the shadows all my life. Now is the time for me to come out of the shadows, and speak my truth.

Speak our truth.

There's a line of cars in front of the building, all marked with the same lettering.

My heart beats quickly as a shock of finality runs through my veins.

This is where part of me will die and another part of me will live.

All my life I've been worried about what people think of me. But I can't continue on in a life where I'm only breathing. I need to learn to live.

I take several deep breaths, ready to cross the street and take the leap I've been longing for.

"You can do this," I say to myself. The sun is moving higher, the shadow becoming smaller.

Yes, you can.

I look to my left, and to my right, checking for oncoming cars.

I keep walking, crossing the street. I know if I stop for even a second, I'll talk myself out of going.

You can do it.

I walk until I come to the automated doors that slowly slide open.

Hopefully, they'll believe you.

I head to the counter, where a woman with dark hair pulled back in a severe ponytail and wearing a uniform is working on a computer. She looks up, but remains seated. "Can I help you?" she says in a flat voice.

My hands tremble, so I knit them together to stop the emotion bursting to come forward.

"I, um," my voice quivers with uncertainty.

"Are you okay?" She stands and comes closer to the counter. She looks behind me, searching for a hint as to why I'm so edgy.

"I, um, need to talk to the police unit that deals with sexual abuse."

Also by
MARGARET MCHEYZER

Perfectly Thin

When I'm thinner, no one will make fun of me.
When I'm thinner, I'll be accepted.
When I'm thinner, I'll be beautiful.
When I'm thinner, I'll be happy.
When I'm thinner, I'll be loved, and adored.
When I'm thinner, I'll like myself.
I can't wait until I'm perfectly thin.

Echoes of You

At seven I was adopted by the most loving parents in the world. In this perfect family, I also found my best friend, and sister Tina.
Throw into the mix my boyfriend Dylan, and my dog Zhen, life was good... until it wasn't.
A catastrophic incident unearthed echoes of my past.
It left me no choice but to confront my inner demons.
Will I be able to live through this again?

A Bump in the Road

Pregnant at 15.

These are the words I didn't think I would ever have to live with.

Alex and I thought we were careful.

Becoming accidentally pregnant was obviously written in the stars for me.

I can't know what the future holds, or if Alex will even stick around.

But the one thing I know for sure; I'll turn this hardship into a blessing.

With or without anyone else.

Luna Caged

I often stare at the walls and wonder what's beyond them.

The Elders tell me that nothing but sin, sadness, and disease lie beyond the wall.

Sometimes I hear things, noises that are strange to me. They're often faint, and when I ask the Elders what those sounds are, they tell me they are the tortured souls of thousands of people behind the gates of hell. I don't know what they mean.

I dream of leaving these walls, but the Elders insist this is the only place we're safe. They talk about danger, hatred, and the devil himself waiting just beyond. They tell us the walls were built to keep us safe.

Although I believe the Elders, I want to see the outside world for myself.

But there's no way out.

Or so I thought…

Luna Freed

I often stared at the walls and wondered what was beyond them. After my first escape, I realized that everything I'd believed, everything the Elders told us, and everything I thought I knew were all calculated lies.

Now I know the truth will set me free.

Addiction

Drugs ruin people's lives.

I should know, they destroyed mine.

I'm Hannah and I got hooked on ice. What started as a trickle, ended with a tsunami washing everything away; my family, my life.

I'm not sure you're ready to read my story; it's real and confronting.

Open the book, read the pages and see how easy it is for anyone to get addicted.

Ice affects all types of people. It doesn't discriminate.

It will SCREW. YOU. UP.

Drowning

I'm a cutter.

I cut because I find solace in it.

I cut because it helps calm my frantic mind.

I cut because the voice inside my head tells me to.

I cut because this is the only way I know how to handle life.

The Gift

I have something people want. I have something they cannot take or steal. I have something they'd kill for.

The something I have, isn't a possession, it's more.

Much, much more.

It's a gift.

It's part of me.

The Curse

It's been the butterfly effect.

I changed the course of my life because I warned a man.

I thought what I had was a gift, but it's quickly turning into my curse.

Now I realize I'm much more than a girl with an ability.

Because now... I'm becoming a weapon.

Dying Wish

I have three major loves in my life: my family, my best friend Becky, and ballet. Elijah Turner is quickly becoming the fourth.

He's been around as long as I can remember. But now he's much more than just the annoying guy at school.

My life was working out perfectly...until it got turned upside down.

Mistrust

I'm the popular girl at school.

The one everyone wants to be friends with.

I have the best boyfriend in the world, who's on the basketball team.

My parents adore me, and I absolutely love them. My sister and I have a great relationship too.

I'm a cheerleader, I have a high GPA and I'm liked even by the teachers.

It was a night which promised to be filled with love and fun until... something happened which changed everything.

Ugly

This is a dark YA/NA standalone, full-length novel. Contains violence and some explicit language

If I were dead, I wouldn't be able to see.

If I were dead, I wouldn't be able to feel.

If I were dead, he'd never raise his hand to me again.

If I were dead, his words wouldn't cut as deep as they do.

If I were dead, I'd be beautiful and I wouldn't be so...ugly.

I'm not dead...but I wish I was.

Chef Pierre

Holly Walker had everything she'd ever dreamed about – a happy marriage and being mum to beautiful brown-eyed Emma – until an accident nineteen months ago tore her world apart. Now she's a widow and single mother to a boisterous little 7-year-old girl, looking for a new start. Ready to take the next step, Holly has found herself a job as a maître d' at Table One, a once-acclaimed restaurant in the heart of Sydney. But one extremely arrogant Frenchman isn't going to be easy to work with...

Twenty years ago, Pierre LeRoux came to Australia, following the stunning Aussie girl he'd fallen in love with and married. He and his wife put their personal lives on hold, determined for Pierre to take Sydney's culinary society by storm. Just as his bright star was on the upswing, tragedy claimed the woman he was hopelessly in love with. He had been known as a Master Chef, but since his wife's death he has become known as a monster chef.

Can two broken people rebuild their lives and find happiness once more?

Smoke and Mirrors

Words can trick us.

Smoke obscures objects on the edge of our vision.

A mirror may reflect, but the eye sees what it wants.

A delicate scent can evoke another time and place, a memory from the past.

And a sentence can deceive you, even as you read it.

Grit

Recommended for 18 years and over

Alpha MC Prez Jaeger Dalton wants the land that was promised to him.

Sassy Phoenix Ward isn't about to let anyone take Freedom Run away from her.

He'll protect what's his.

She'll protect what's hers.

Jaeger is an arrogant ass, but he wants nothing more than Phoenix.

Phoenix is stubborn and headstrong, and she wants Jaeger out of her life.

Her father lost the family farm to gambling debts, but Jaeger isn't the only one who has a claim to the property.

Sometimes it's best to let things go.

But sometimes it's better to fight until the very end.

Yes, Master

***** THIS PROLOGUE CONTAINS DISTRESSING CONTENT.
IT IS ONLY SUITED FOR READERS OVER 18. *****

ALSO CONTAINS M/M, M/M/F, M/F AND F/F SCENES.

My uncle abused me.

I was 10 years old when it started.

At 13 he told me I was no longer wanted because I had started to develop.

At 16 I was ready to kill him.

Today, I'm broken.

Today, I only breathe to survive.

My name's Sergeant Major Ryan Jenkins and today, I'm ready to tell you my story.

A Life Less Broken

CONTAINS DISTRESSING CONTENT. 18+

On a day like any other, Allyn Sommers went off to work, not knowing that her life was about to be irrevocably and horrifically altered.

Three years later, Allyn is still a prisoner in her own home, held captive by harrowing fear. Broken and damaged, Allyn seeks help from someone that fate put in her path.

Dr. Dominic Shriver is a psychiatrist who's drawn to difficult cases. He must push past his own personal battles to help Allyn fight her monsters and nightmares.

Is Dr. Shriver the answer to her healing?

Can Allyn overcome being broken?

My Life for Yours

He's lived a life of high society and privilege; he chose to follow in his father's footsteps and become a Senator.

She's lived a life surrounded with underworld activity; she had no choice but to follow in her father's footsteps and take on the role of Mob Boss.

He wants to stamp out organized crime and can't be bought off.

She's the ruthless and tough Mob Boss where in her world all lines are blurred.

Their lives are completely different, two walks of life on the opposite ends of the law.

Being together doesn't make sense.

But being apart isn't an option

HiT Series Box Set

HiT 149

Anna Brookes is not your typical teenager. Her walls are not adorned with posters of boy bands or movie stars. Instead posters from Glock, Ruger, and Smith & Wesson grace her bedroom. Anna's mother abandoned her at birth, and her father, St. Cloud Police Chief Henry Brookes, taught her how to shoot and coached her to excellence. On Anna's fifteenth birthday, unwelcome guests join the celebration, and Anna's world is never the same. You'll meet the world's top assassin, 15, and follow her as she discovers the one hit she's not sure she can complete – Ben Pearson, the current St. Cloud Police Chief and a man with whom Anna has explosive sexual chemistry. Enter a world of intrigue, power, and treachery as Anna takes on old and new enemies, while falling in love with the one man with whom she can't have a relationship.

Anna Brookes in Training

Find out what happened to transform the fifteen-year-old Anna Brookes, the Girl with the Golden Aim, into the deadly assassin 15. After her father is killed and her home destroyed, orphan Anna Brookes finds herself homeless in Gulf Breeze, Florida. After she saves Lukas from a deadly attack, he takes her in and begins to train her in the assassin's craft. Learn how Lukas's unconventional training hones Anna's innate skills until she is as deadly as her mentor.

HiT for Freedom

Anna has decided to break off her steamy affair with Ben Pearson and leave St. Cloud, when she suspects a new threat to him. Katsu Vang is rich, powerful, and very interested in Anna. He's also evil to his core. Join Anna as she plays a dangerous game, getting closer to Katsu to discover his real purpose, while trying to keep Ben safe. Secrets are exposed and the future Anna hoped for is snatched from her grasp. Will Ben be able to save her?

HiT to Live

In the conclusion to the Anna Brookes saga, Ben and his sister Emily, with the help of Agent rescue Anna. For Anna and Ben, it's time to settle scores…and a time for the truth between them. From Sydney to the Philippines and back to the States, they take care of business. But a helpful stranger enters Anna's life, revealing more secrets…and a plan that Anna wants no part of. Can Anna and Ben shed their old lives and start a new one together, or will Anna's new-found family ruin their chances at a happily-ever-after?

Binary Law (co-authored)

Ellie Andrews has been receiving tutoring from Blake McCarthy for three years to help her improve her grades so she can get into one of the top universities to study law. And she's had a huge crush on him since she can remember.

Blake McCarthy is the geek at school that's had a crush on Ellie since the day he met her.

In their final tutoring session, Blake and Ellie finally become brave enough to take the leap of faith.

But, life has other plans and rips them apart. Six years later Blake and his best friends Ben and Billy have built a successful internet platform company 3BCubed, while Ellie is a successful and hardworking lawyer specializing in Corporate Law.

3BCubed is being threatened with a devastatingly large plagiarism case and when it lands on their lawyers desk, it's handed to the new Corporate Lawyer to handle and win.

Coincidence or perhaps fate will see Blake and Ellie pushed back together.

Binary Law will have Blake and Ellie propelled into a life that's a whirl wind of catastrophic events and situations where every emotion will be touched. Hurt will be experienced, happiness will be presented and love will be evident. But is that enough for Blake and Ellie be able to live out their own happily ever after?

Made in the USA
Monee, IL
30 May 2021

69852458R00213